USA TODAY BESTSELLING AUTHOR

DALE MAYER

A Psychic Visions Novel

SHATTERED

SHATTERED
Beverly Dale Mayer
Valley Publishing Ltd.

Copyright © 2016, updated © 2022

All rights reserved. Except for use in any review, the reproduction or utilization of this work in whole or in part by any electronic, mechanical or other means, now known or hereafter invented, including xerography, photocopying and recording, or in any information storage or retrieval system, is forbidden without the written permission of the publisher.

This is a work of fiction. Names, characters, places, brands, media, and incidents are either the product of the author's imagination or are used fictitiously. Any resemblance to actual events, locales, or persons, living or dead, is entirely coincidental.

ISBN-13: 978-1-988315-71-3
Print Edition

Books in This Series:

Tuesday's Child
Hide 'n Go Seek
Maddy's Floor
Garden of Sorrow
Knock Knock…
Rare Find
Eyes to the Soul
Now You See Her
Shattered
Into the Abyss
Seeds of Malice
Eye of the Falcon
Itsy-Bitsy Spider
Unmasked
Deep Beneath
From the Ashes
Stroke of Death
Ice Maiden
Snap, Crackle…
What If…
Talking Bones
String of Tears
Inked Forever
Insanity
Soul Legacy
Coveted

Boxed Sets and Bundles
https://geni.us/Bundlepage

About This Book

When something happens that shatters a life beyond recognition, what becomes of the soul?

Trapped in a gilded cage for as long as she can remember, Hannah has tried to escape numerous times, in countless ways. She's been told all along that something's wrong with her, something that her doctors can't diagnose. But what is life without freedom? Hannah would rather die than stay imprisoned forever.

Another escape and, once more, the door slams shut, with her locked behind it.

Then Trevor offers her a way out, one that might mean permanent liberation for her. But at what cost? Trevor doesn't know the truth about her. Despite her fear that he'll be like all the others and turn away from her in horror, she longs to share her secret with him.

Trevor has worked hard to make up for all the mistakes he's made in his life. Helping Hannah feels like the right thing to do—more than anything else he's ever done. But, to free her, the risks he takes ask more of him than he thought possible.

After all, enemies aren't only outside in the world. Some are inside us. We just don't know it …

Sign up to be notified of all Dale's releases here!
https://geni.us/DaleNews

CHAPTER 1

THE BLOOD …

It wouldn't slow.

It wouldn't stop.

It dripped down her arm, her hands. Droplets falling from her fingertips.

Only she felt no pain …

Except when she moved.

Hannah managed to take one step, then another. Her weight came down hard, her legs wooden. Her ankles stiff, unbending lumber blocks.

The motion jarring.

More blood flowed.

It dripped in a slow and steady stream onto the gravel beneath her feet. She was taking a big risk of being hit by a car, stumbling unseen in the dark on this narrow road, with no real shoulders, but she felt it was the only way.

Hannah watched the drips in macabre fascination. Where was it coming from?

Her head pounded. Her body throbbed. And her legs? Well, they'd been screaming for miles.

She had no idea where she was, how she got here, or why she would be walking along this lonely stretch of highway. Yet she knew she had to continue. It was important. She just didn't know why. And, of course, it was dark—black. The moon argued with the clouds above, giving her brief moments of luminescence. A heavy dampness clung to her nose.

A couple vehicles had passed her. But no one had stopped to help.

Why?

Surely she was visible? She carefully took another step and then one more. Someone would help her eventually. Right? She had to keep moving forward. She knew there was no going back. There was no other choice.

Keep walking. You're almost there, a soft male voice inside her head directed her.

"Where am I going?" She sobbed to the empty night.

Somewhere safe. I can help you.

Who spoke to her?

What if it was *him*? The man she'd been running from. At least she thought it had been a man. Or what if another person found her and didn't help her? She could become a victim again.

Those horrible images. Fights. Fire. Screams. All intermixed with sex scenes. Like that made any sense.

She gave a short, harsh laugh. She had no idea whether she'd been a victim or a victimizer. But it felt like she'd been beaten to shit and left to die. Her body injured. Her mind vulnerable. Weak. She frowned, trying to figure out the disjointed thoughts in her head. Her memories were fragmented, refusing to flow as they should. Was she okay? Had she been in an accident? Attacked?

Nothing felt normal or right. Nothing felt familiar, as if she was in someone else's nightmare.

A strange set of thoughts ran through her mind, telling her she was supposed to do something. Were they her thoughts? How could they be?

Two separate people were arguing inside her head. Someone pushing her to do something. Someone calling her away. Someone who could foretell the future?

Or was Hannah just arguing with herself, considering all angles, no matter how weird?

And then she was trying to stop other thoughts. *He* wanted to remove her. *He* wanted to hurt someone she loved. *He*'d tried to hurt him earlier today.

No, someone else had tried.

And failed, she thought.

But everything was mixed up. The thoughts were coated in fear and spiked with anger. And the words? Foreign, as if they weren't hers. Flashes of a young girl. Then an older one. A knife. Screams. All disjointed. Nothing made any sense. Confused and worried, she turned to stare at the trail of blood behind her, as she walked forward.

Of course she wasn't okay. She hadn't been okay for a long time.

More disconnected memories came to her mind. More foggy thoughts. Why hadn't she been okay for a long time?

Doctors flitted into her mind—in, then out again. Different men. Women. Names and titles all whispered through her mind and back again. She had no idea what or who they were. … Even worse, she had no idea why they were walking in an endless stream through her bedroom. She tried to focus, to force the tidbits into a coherent pattern, and pain slammed into her brain, bringing her to a shuddering stop. She bent over, gasping.

The pain, extreme, … yet familiar.

That worried her. No one should have to experience pain for so long that it became familiar. Was that why the stream of doctors? Had she been in several accidents? Was she suicidal? Born with a physical ailment that needed multiple surgeries?

A vehicle approached, the headlight beams flashing on her sleeve, before zipping past.

A sob escaped, as the red tail lights disappeared into the distance. They hadn't even slowed down. Still, the headlights had shown her something.

A driveway, … just ahead. The one she'd been looking for. At least part of her thought so …

She hobbled forward, desperate for someone to be home, and yet she was terrified at the same time.

What if the wrong man lived here?

And every man could be the wrong man. She couldn't remember who she was running from … or to.

A face zipped through her mind, only to fade too quickly for her to understand who or what that meant.

She kept walking.

Feeling the first few drops of rain, she wanted to cry.

When the thunder rumbled in the distance, the tears rolled down her cheeks in earnest. Could this night get any worse?

Every step to that driveway was one step closer to her goal. She felt a sense of inevitability to it.

She couldn't take her eyes off the reflector on a post marking the start of the driveway. This was the right place.

That phrase stopped her. Right place?

Had she been looking for it?

Or now that she was injured—possibly dying—was she expecting a specific someone to help her?

Surely not. She studied her surroundings, trying to peer through the sheets of rain now beating down on her head. Nothing looked familiar.

She felt so terribly alone at that moment.

Why was she heading to the driveway? For help of course, right?

No, not right, but she didn't understand the mixed messages. Everything was jumbled in her head.

She had to keep in mind that she'd been hurt and couldn't decipher her thoughts or count on the assumptions she was making.

Yet something about this place seemed to call her. At the driveway, she slowly walked up the dirt road. It wasn't even paved. Why?

Was she so far out in the country? She couldn't see other lights to confirm dwellings were close by. Then again, she couldn't see lights on the dark shadow she'd taken to be a building.

Shit.

Her mind revolted, but her feet kept moving, the incline long and slow. Eventually she reached the large trees that surrounded the house.

It was a house. That alone made her feel better. Or maybe just her feet, as they came to a stop.

She swayed in place. The rain had eased. The moon peeked through the prison of clouds to stare out at the world below.

She realized she had to be more injured than she thought, now witnessing the increasing blood flow from wounds on her body.

She focused on her surroundings, her breathing. Nothing was normal about this place. The plants were huge, the leaves oversize. A wind ... or something ... whispered between the plants, but, at the same time, she sensed someone waiting, ... as if she'd been expected.

But that was beyond foolish.

Right?

She shuddered.

And slowly, as if compelled, she turned to face the front door. The intricate faces carved in the wood.

She shouldn't be here. She should be running as far and as fast in the opposite direction as she could go.

Instead, her feet stepped closer to that door.

She took a deep breath, her struggle to stay upright waning. She wouldn't make it back down this driveway. She might not even make it to the entrance. But she managed one more step.

A light flashed on overhead, covering her in a soft white, as she stood in the center of the glow.

She closed her eyes.

And waited for whatever fate was about to hit her with.

NO. NOT THERE. Don't go there. You don't understand. That's not what I wanted. Not what I intended.

Why did you go there?

You were supposed to keep driving.

Away to safety.

This man will hurt you.

You must hurt him before then.

Attack, then run away.

All men are killers.

All men are bad.

All men will hurt you.

Run, child, run.

Oh, it's his house. Wow. Okay, that was smart. I already tried to kill this one once. Maybe you can succeed, where I failed.

AS DAYS WENT, this had been one of the worst—and wasn't over yet. Stefan had been working with several patients at the hospital. All newly admitted, desperately in need of help. *His* kind of help. And Trevor's help. Then Dr. Trevor Johnson had been the one who'd called Stefan in.

One of the patients—a subdued slight man—had attacked without warning and had caught both Stefan and Trevor off guard. The patient hadn't shown any violent behavior up until then. Possibly a multiple personality disorder. Yet it had erupted from one second to the next and had sideswiped both men. Stefan knew to back off and to rebalance before attempting more work, but the trigger had startled other patients, and it took everything Stefan had to control the situation.

Plus, he and Trevor had had to go to the children's ward to see several patients. He'd gotten his center of balance back before arriving there. The energy of that ward demanded that Stefan be in the right place mentally, before he could enter.

He'd found one little girl more distant, colder than ever. So sad. They'd been making such great progress with Anita. Something was wrong inside. He was sure it was a possession issue. Maddy had been making progress—but not enough— and the child was fading before their eyes. Yet Anita had had a violent outburst today as well. Completely out of the blue, she'd lashed out at Stefan with her plastic knife and fork. It had been a mere scratch, but still … Depressed at the continuous lack of progress and afraid they were in danger of losing Anita, Stefan had come home in a rare mood.

Not wanting to taint Celina with his negativity and frustration, he'd gone directly to his art studio. But his beloved Celina always understood his moods and needs and brought her harp to play quietly beside him.

Hours later, his tensions and frustrations eased as he worked. He studied the painting in front of him and shook his head. "This one is garbage."

Celina gently reached out to him. "If it eased your demons, it's never a waste."

He laughed. "True enough." He threw down the paintbrush, wondering what insight this mess was to give him with the requisite multiple headaches. He saw some headscarved old woman but, over that, were slashes of red and black. He narrowed his gaze, his mind twisting and turning on the possibilities. Mayb—

A cry for help reached him on the ethers. The same person who'd called the last time. He'd been sending responses but hadn't received an answer yet.

An insight, one sitting outside the reach of his consciousness, finally broke into his brain, just as someone pounded on Stefan's front door. Someone believing he was hurting her? ... Who was it?

Abruptly he was dragged from one reality to another.

And this one was so much worse.

HANNAH STOOD AT the front door of the stranger's house. Some*thing* pushed her to stay. Some*one* else told her to run. She wavered on her feet. Then the door opened.

Slowly, carefully.

"Hannah?"

If he knew her name, she knew her worst fears had come

true. She feared to look at him. She closed her eyes. Her feet, the betrayers, hadn't understood and had led her to the worst place possible.

She opened her eyes and stared at the beautiful man in front of her.

"No," she whispered. "It's not possible."

"What's not possible?" asked the man standing in front of her, his voice so soft and caring that she wanted to cry. "What's wrong?"

She shook her head, as he gently grabbed her arm and tugged her closer.

"You're dead," she stated, her voice choking up. "I know you are. You have to be," she cried out, as the last of her strength drained from her toes. It was over. Whatever fight she'd been involved in, whatever struggle she'd been working toward? She'd lost. She didn't even know why.

"Why do I have to be dead?" he asked, leading her through the front door and beyond.

She stared at him, trying to sort through the muddle in her head, but couldn't. Only one thing was clear. "You have to be because I stabbed you."

And she collapsed into his arms.

The man she knew deep inside—with as much certainty as she had ever felt in her life—she'd tried to kill once already. A man she would try to kill again, if she had the chance.

But she didn't. And wouldn't. She couldn't.

He'd won after all.

CHAPTER 2

HANNAH OPENED HER eyes and winced. So much damn white. If she had a choice, she'd never see that color on a wall again. Surely she'd spent her whole life in rooms like this one. White ceilings, white walls, white curtains. Was it supposed to be healing or some such nonsense? Because she was sure the constant purity was making her a little sick. Maybe she'd go to hell for her thoughts, but a lot could be said for living a little and splashing all that whiteness with wild colors.

She rolled over for the tenth time, wishing her legs and ribs would stop aching. Somehow she'd hurt herself again and enough to end up in a hospital. Now, if only she could stop the hospital from contacting her family. But she was pretty sure her father already had everyone on full alert for when she showed up at the next medical facility. Not *if* she showed up but *when*. He was nothing if not thorough.

That she had no idea what had happened would be even more ammunition for him to push her back on drugs and, if not to save herself, then to save her fellow man.

Before she did something serious.

She stared down at her hands and had to wonder if it wasn't already too late. She'd been bleeding heavily earlier, yet there didn't appear to be a scratch on her arms or hands. She didn't get it. But neither would she ask. If she wasn't connected to so many tubes, she'd get up and trek to the bathroom to take a look. As it was, she felt fine, other than her legs and ribs—and if she ignored the pounding behind her eyeballs. She'd spent enough time in the hospital to learn to be closemouthed. They freaked out if you asked questions like, *What happened to me?* or *How did I get here?*

These questions burned at the tip of her tongue, but she had no intention of letting them out. Her episodes were legendary in her family. She'd spent the last ten years dodging her father's caring, cosseting—okay, let's be honest—suffocating version of love. He wanted her locked up in cotton batting, and she wanted to run wild and free.

Every time she'd tried though, she'd ended up in the exact same place. A hospital. Within days she'd be transferred to the private *special* hospital, under Dr. Bronson's watchful eye, and he would offer that tiny lip twitch of a smile that never matched his eyes and would then let her know how happy he was to see her safe and sound and back under his care.

Then they'd go through the same dance again, where he evaluated her actions, her mind-set, and her emotional stability, and she'd lie through her teeth. After weeks of this routine, unable to find anything wrong with her, Bronson would be forced to release her into her father's care. There she'd stay, until her father and his ugly henchmen let their guard down, and she found a way to escape.

Again.

She knew, one of these days, that her father would refuse to give her an opening to sneak out, but she couldn't stop herself from trying.

She needed her freedom. Even if she flew and crashed—like she did every damn time—it was still better than being locked up in a cage and never tasting the fresh air of experience.

She'd even started her own business on the sly. Without Tasha, her manager, Hannah would have gone under a long time ago. This was her third episode since Tasha had started to work for her. Hannah wished she had a way to keep Tasha in the loop, but Hannah knew of no such thing. Not unless she could anticipate when the blackouts would happen. Based on Hannah's previous episodes, Tasha would contact Hannah shortly.

In reality, Hannah needed to call her store manager, not the other way around.

Except where was her phone? She glanced around but couldn't see it. Which meant Hannah would need to get yet another one. What was that? Her third already this year? Then again, with her faulty memory, who knew? It could have been a half dozen. Brooding, Hannah stared at the damn white sheets and wondered. *What kind of excuse could she make up this time?*

THE TWO MEN stood in the grayscale world of Stefan's reality. "You have no idea who she is?" Dr. Trevor Johnson asked, a knot of quiet humor lifting the corner of his mouth. "Wow, he who knows everything is stumped."

"*Blocked* would be the correct term here," Stefan Kronos stated blandly. "If you're going to insult me, then do so correctly."

Trevor laughed. "Good enough." He studied the bloody prints on the doorway to Stefan's house. "Have you showed these prints to anyone?"

"I have." Stefan laughed. "A fingerprint specialist."

Trevor frowned. "But to get a match, that would be too easy." The fingerprints were clear and showed the fingers had been drenched in blood and not just a little dab sufficient to leave a partial print. In this case the whole hand stood out in stark relief. He shook his head. "She must have been bleeding at a decent rate."

"Stuff poured off her," Stefan noted cheerfully. "The ambulance drivers were shocked to see she was still alive. Apparently, the amount she lost should have killed her."

"Except you and I know how often the term *should* doesn't apply to people like us." He slid a sideways glance at his friend. "She's like us, I presume?"

Stefan shrugged his elegant shoulders.

Trevor had never seen his friend in any other state except perfectly dressed. Trevor had no idea how Stefan did that. Trevor couldn't manage that one day a month, never mind looking well-dressedevery day. Yet Stefan continuously turned up looking like a cover model.

"I believe she's one of us," Stefan replied in a noncommittal voice. He turned away from his doorway. "I don't know how anyone but someone like us could get past my energy shields. In reality or in grayscale." He turned to stare at Trevor. "That's really got me confused."

"How long after a person walks by can you see their energy?"

"Sometimes minutes only but usually for a couple hours. In the case of a powerful psychic—or someone who has experienced great rage or trauma—longer, sometimes much longer."

"So she didn't experience those, *or* she has such weak energy that there wasn't much power in her residual energy for some reason."

"Right. She keeps it close. That's why I was hoping you could take a look at her."

"Why me?"

"Because her energy is … off."

Trevor frowned. It wasn't like Stefan to not read energy. "Off in what way?"

"I don't want to tell you that. I'd prefer that you make your own impression."

"Right." He cast one last glance at the disturbing handprint on the wall and asked, "Where is she?"

"They took her to the closest hospital. I was hoping to get her onto Maddy's Floor, but there's no room."

"As usual. Beds don't open up there often."

"They are possible these days, with her new wing in place and with the expansion program they are running. Plus, the hospital stays are shorter than ever."

"Sure, but the waiting list is ten times longer than it was, and, now that more people have heard about it, even more applications are coming in from all over the world."

Stefan nodded. "And the same for our project at the children's hospital. But, like you said, the need is great, and the more people who benefit, the more people who hear about the program and want a place for their loved ones."

"Children are the most devastating cases. Nothing like sick children to break your heart. Especially when a life could have been saved."

"We've hired what amounts to a triage nurse for energy evaluation in terms of each application. He's new to Maddy's Floor, but we've come to trust his evaluations."

"So he decides which applications to accept?" Trevor's eyebrows shot up. "That's heady stuff."

"Not really. He goes through his applications and sorts

them. Priorities and easy ones she can help quickly, so the beds are put to the best use. The center is trying to keep a dozen beds for fast turnovers, but they still end up requiring days before the kids are released. The adults on Maddy's Floor still need twice that in the easier cases. Adults just don't heal as fast."

"That's a lot of responsibility."

"It is. We do checks to ensure nothing jumps out at us, but really we don't have time to go through each of the one thousand applications sitting on his desk on any given day, and we can make mistakes too. Maddy has a special program going on, but it's not as if she can expand it to help everyone. She's doing what she can."

"How about training people to do what she does?"

"We're working on it." Stefan smiled. "England has asked for a sister wing in London."

"Sure, but one can't just duplicate Maddy and her world."

"Exactly. If they get the healers together and can manage to find a coordinator like Maddy to guide the energy and to do what must be done, then maybe it can work."

"Right. Let's go meet your mystery killer."

Both reentered the world of reality seamlessly.

Stefan laughed, as he walked to his kitchen counter and snagged his keys. "Except for one thing. It's not me she killed."

No.

I couldn't be hurt. I had suffered enough. They all had. This had to stop. I had done everything I could to protect my girl. But it had all been for naught. Now her girl was helpless. A pawn. Like all women were pawns in the world of men. They saw women only as possessions. Chess pieces to be moved at will to their pleasure. Her girl's life had been no different. Her girl's life had been one big board, arranged and rearranged.

But not now. Now I moved freely.

And could connect to many people—talented people. More talented than I am. But I was learning. And now I'd found someone I could talk to. More than talk to …

Thank heavens.

Little had gone as planned in my life. Including this. But I'm learning.

The men in her life would have laughed and said, *Didn't it figure?* Couldn't arrange the one thing most important in her world without a man's help.

They were wrong. As a woman, as a child of their whims, I had been nothing if not adaptable. And adapt I had. Now I could operate without them knowing.

Now, if only I could help the one who needed me—before the others took her girl out of their game. Permanently.

CHAPTER 3

H ANNAH OPENED HER eyes, her gaze slow to focus.
When she recognized the brightness in the room, she
bolted upright.

"Damn it," she whispered to the empty space. She'd
planned on sneaking out after the nightly rounds, but before
the security guard, who walked the hallways, came by.
Instead she'd fallen into a deep sleep—and had missed her
window of opportunity.

She groaned and flopped backward.

"There, nice to see you're awake. I've checked in on you
a couple times, but you were fast asleep." The nurse bustled
around and plumped up the pillows helping her to sit up.
"And you missed breakfast …"

Damn it. That meant it was later than Hannah thought.
She gave the woman a sleepy smile. "I slept well, but I'm
hungry."

"Good," the nurse replied.

Hannah read the woman's name tag. Tammy. Yeah, she
looked like a Tammy, pink-cheeked and short curly blond
hair, with a comfortable huggable frame.

"I'll see about rousting you up some food. And how
about a coffee?"

Hannah brightened. "Coffee would be lovely."

Tammy finished her ministrations, checked Hannah's

blood pressure and temperature, then disappeared.

Coffee would be excellent. It would help her to get moving.

Hannah couldn't remember much of last night and wanted to ask Tammy for details but knew better.

She relaxed back, letting her body wake up that little bit more. And then wished she hadn't. Last night things hurt. Today they throbbed. She also had to go to the bathroom, but the thought of doing so scared her.

The nurse returned, holding a real china mug. *Nice.* Hannah brightened. She hated those plastic cups they always seemed to bring.

"Now, let's get you to the bathroom."

Hannah winced. "How did you know I hadn't made it there yet?" she muttered.

Tammy laughed. "Because you were staring at the bathroom, as if trying to figure out how to make it happen without getting onto your feet."

That startled a laugh out of Hannah.

The nurse grinned. "That's better. Now let's get you to the bathroom and back again." She flipped the blankets off Hannah, letting a rush of cooler air in. In spite of herself, she shivered.

"We'll get you back under the covers again in a minute."

Hannah sat up, then slowly slid to the floor. The nurse held up weird little slippers that Hannah hadn't seen before and helped her stand up in them. Hannah took a deep breath, held on to the rail on the side of the bed, and straightened. She schooled her features and took one step.

"There. Not so bad, is it?"

"No, it's not." *It was way worse.* But no way in hell would she tell Tammy that. "I can make it fine on my own."

"If you're sure …"

Hannah smiled reassuringly. "I'm fine." And she walked to the bathroom. When she made it inside and had the door securely closed behind her, she dropped the facade, and a gasp of pain broke free. "Shit that hurts," she whispered to the face in the mirror. The lips on the image moved to match the words coming out of her mouth, but it was hard to recognize the rest of her features. Except her hair. Long auburn ringlets. Yeah, those were hers.

But the rest? … She noted long scratches on the sides of her face, dried blood on her forehead. Her hair had thick dried-on clumps of congealed blood at her temple. She reached her hand up to the back of her head and winced.

Her fingers touched more dried blood that poked her. She stared into the mirror. Had she been hit? Attacked? In a car accident? She leaned closer to see one eye bloody around the iris. She still had all her teeth, thank God. She did a quick search to find the ribs on her side turning colorful hues. She already knew her legs hurt like shit, but why? She had a bandage on one thigh, and her other ankle was wrapped in a simple elastic bandage. All of her ached.

She needed a shower in the worst way. But had she time? Or the energy to do so? She noted both a bathtub and a shower in the bathroom. One of those fancy sit-down showers. She could do that most likely.

"Hannah? Do you need help?"

"No, I'm fine." But she really had to go. She used the toilet, then turned on the water to give herself a moment. Thereafter, using the washcloth soaked in warm water, she gently wiped her face. And saw her hands. As in really saw them.

They were completely encrusted in dried blood that

someone had attempted to wash off, only to leave smears on her skin. She opened the bathroom door and smiled at the anxious nurse on the other side, then continued to clean her hands and arms. "I'm fine. I just need to wash up."

The nurse smiled in sympathy, her shoulders relaxing. "Only your hands and face. We'll try for a shower later. After the doctor has checked your stitches."

Hannah couldn't hold back her start of surprise. She hadn't noticed any stitches. She took a quick glance in the mirror but couldn't immediately understand what they'd stitched back together, unless they were talking about her bandaged leg. That would make sense. Then again, so would her head. Still, the nurse appeared agitated the longer Hannah stayed in the bathroom. Not wanting to upset her further, Hannah let herself be led back to the hospital bed and helped under the covers.

In truth she felt a huge sense of relief when she could lie down and relax. With a wan smile, she told Tammy, "Thank you. That feels much better."

"You need to stay in bed," Tammy scolded gently. "Don't try to do too much. You need to stay off both those legs and rest."

"I will," Hannah promised, then confessed, "I'm really hungry."

"I'll go see what I can find for you." Tammy bustled around her, moving a glass of water closer and straightening the blankets. "Don't forget your coffee on the table."

At the reminder Hannah brightened and tried to shift more upright, so she was leaning against the headboard.

"Wait. I'll raise the bed for you." The nurse stepped to the side, and, using the remote control, she raised the head of Hannah's bed, so she could sit more comfortably.

"Thank you," Hannah murmured, wondering just where she was that had such nice fancy equipment and fancy bathrooms. A general hospital didn't necessarily have the funding for a bed like this. Maybe she was in a private hospital. That was always her father's choice. Still, it was comfortable enough here. Given that her legs were both injured, running away was hardly a good option.

"You also have visitors," Tammy shared, as she bustled around Hannah, tucking the blanket in around her legs and moving closer the little table holding her coffee.

"Visitors?" Hannah asked warily. "I'm not sure I'm up to seeing anyone."

"If you're not, then I'll send them away, but it's the man who helped you last night. He's asked to see you, so he can confirm you are okay."

Ah, then there wasn't much chance of getting out of this. Besides, it was important to make it look to the world like she was completely fine. Just a stupid accident was all.

"Then send them in," she replied quietly, "but do please warn them that I'm really tired, so it needs to be a short visit."

"I can do that." She smiled. "And, while they are here, I'll see about getting you a little food."

"Make that a lot of food, and you're on. I'm starving," she admitted. She truly was. She also couldn't identify what her last meal had been or even when. That bothered her a lot. She took a big sip of coffee and leaned back to wait for her visitors.

She didn't have to wait long.

Two men walked in.

She gave them a faint smile, her gaze assessing. Inside, her stomach sank. She didn't *know* either of them. But in the back of her mind? Something … was familiar about both of them …

"INTERESTING," TREVOR NOTED, as he and Stefan stood at the doorway, watching the two women interact as patient and nurse.

"What is?"

"Her aura. It's nonexistent. Normally I'd see that in a dying person, at least comatose."

"I can see how tiny and tight against her body it is. That's why I thought she was severely hurt last night," Stefan admitted. "Yet she's looking damn lively to me."

"She is." Trevor contemplated the woman in the bed before him. He gave a slight snort in understanding. "She's doing it on purpose. She's closely tucking in all the energy to hide something."

"Why? And how? That's a huge drain on a person," Stefan stated. "But you're right. Look. A corner flared off just now."

"*Hmm*, I saw it. I wish I knew what the nurse just said to her for that to have happened." He watched as the patient leaned back in bed, and the nurse walked toward them. As she approached, Trevor asked, "What did she say?"

"She was perturbed at the idea of visitors," the nurse replied. "However, she did say yes, but only for a short while. And she emphasized *short*, so you can't ask too much or be here too long. I will be back in ten minutes," she warned, as she walked past them. "I'll be bringing her breakfast with me." And she walked away.

With a one-raised-eyebrow look at Stefan, Trevor walked into the hospital room. "Good morning," he greeted

Hannah. "I'm Dr. Trevor Johnson, and this is Stefan Kronos. Thank you for seeing us."

She gave them a veiled look and pulled her aura in closer.

Very interesting. She considered them a threat.

"Interesting flight response," Stefan muttered, as he approached the bed. In a normal tone, he said, "I'm glad to see you looking as healthy as you are this morning. You had me scared last night."

"I'm sorry," she murmured, her gaze shuttered. "I wasn't in very good shape. Thank you for helping me out."

"No, you weren't in good shape," Stefan agreed, with a smile. "I'm glad I was able to help."

Her gaze narrowed, and Trevor almost gasped as he watched an energy probe, light blue to almost pure white, slide out from under the bedding to check out the powerful energy in the room, now that they'd arrived. The probe shifted silently with great stealth, as it checked out Stefan's energy.

Interestingly enough, his friend let the probe do its thing.

Then the probe turned on Trevor. Its movement was more hesitant. As if he were a stranger she was unsure of. Sure she'd met Stefan last night but hardly long enough to be sure of him. Then again, Trevor was a complete unknown. He also had to decide quickly if he would allow the probe to retrieve the information it wanted to access.

It went against the grain to give blind access, so he let it in slightly. It didn't appear to want to do more than a cursory glance, before she withdrew it. Hannah sat up a little straighter, when she'd pulled it back. As if the threat assessment had come back as negative.

"Interesting trick," he told her and wondered what it was about this woman that had him going about things all wrong. Normally he would never have mentioned the probe issue to anyone.

She frowned, confusion clouding her gaze. "What trick?"

He waited and studied her. Was she for real? But he read no awareness, no guilt in her. Nothing at all in her gaze. Was it possible she had no idea?

"He meant getting to me and my house. I'm generally very reticent to meet new people," Stefan explained smoothly. "Pardon our intrusion, but I needed to know you were okay. I honestly thought you were dying last night, but apparently, although you lost a lot of blood, you aren't badly hurt."

"I don't remember much of last night, so I can only imagine how horrific I must have looked." She gave a mock shudder. "I really appreciate the help." This part she added with warm gratitude that came across as completely genuine.

The men responded in kind.

"I'm just glad it all turned out well," Stefan shared. "And that you will be fine. The police arrived not long afterward, asking questions," he added. "But there wasn't much I could say, as I didn't see your vehicle, and I live too far out for you to have come from a bus or other mode of transportation."

At the word *police*, her fingers clenched the sheet and squeezed, until her knuckles turned white. So the police bothered her. Why? Trevor studied the energy around her head, as she listened to Stefan.

The energy was still snug, still white, and still locked down. The only flares they'd seen were when they'd watched her interact with the nurse. But, with him and Stefan, she wasn't letting herself relax even a little.

That air of wariness only intensified as Stefan continued to speak with her.

This woman was trying to get through this visit, but it was painful for her. Unnerving. As if she were afraid of them, of what they might ask of her. Something she didn't want to share.

Then he got it.

"You don't remember anything about last night, do you?"

His comment out of the blue cut through her conversation with Stefan.

She gasped, her shoulders hunching in. This woman wasn't just guarded—she was terrified. And he felt his protective instincts rising to the surface. He didn't know what was going on, but this waif triggered feelings in him that he didn't recognize.

He couldn't walk away. Not from this level of fear.

And maybe she should be scared. Not only could that memory loss show signs of more serious injuries, something else could be involved as well. He caught sight of the turmoil inside her gaze, right before she lowered her lashes, and he realized her energy never once shifted with the shock of his question.

Had she been through so many shocks that nothing fazed her energy, or did she keep herself so locked down, so protected, that even when the shocks *could* affect her aura, she wouldn't let them do so? Or did she have so little energy running through her body to allow it to be affected? It was all needed to keep her alive.

The nurse came bustling in just then, with a tray of food.

Watching Hannah, Trevor caught the relief in her gaze

at the nurse's arrival, as if knowing the interview was almost over.

"Now look at this, Hannah. I managed to find you some breakfast. It might not be to your liking, as I didn't have much choice, but at least I found lots." She placed the tray on the small table and moved it over to Hannah. "I hope you like muffins. Nothing hot was left, but I found some cheese and a scone and a couple muffins."

"This is lovely, thank you," Hannah replied, with a delighted smile. "I'm happy to have anything." Her gaze locked on the food in front of her. "The men are leaving. Could you escort them out, please?"

She glanced up at Stefan, and, in a much warmer voice, she added, "Thanks again for coming to my rescue last night."

"You're welcome," Stefan called back. Already moving to the door, he snagged Trevor's arm as he went, dragging him out to the hallway. "Hope you feel better soon."

Out in the hallway the two men stood and watched, as Hannah waited until the nurse walked past the men, before Hannah lifted the lid on the food tray. There was no change in her expression, as she studied the selection of food in front of her. Then she dove in and ate like she hadn't had a decent meal in weeks.

"Look at that," Stefan muttered. "I'd have fed her last night, had I known."

"How could you have? It's like she keeps everything hidden inside. I doubt she'd have told you that she was hungry, even if she weren't injured." They watched her go for the second muffin and polish it off in six bites. By the time she turned to the scone, she'd slowed enough to actually butter that one.

As she relaxed back and ate at a slower pace, Trevor shifted, ready to walk away, but struggling to separate from her. Talk about a weird day already. Then it got a whole lot weirder.

He froze.

He reached out and grabbed Stefan. "Look."

"I see it."

They stared, hoping to see if the same phenomena happened to repeat itself.

Their patience was rewarded. As she finished the last bite and relaxed back, closing her eyes, a shadow drifted across her face.

A dark shadow.

"What the hell is that?" Trevor asked.

"It's not a *what*. It's a *who* ..."

HE'D WATCHED HER grow from a wild teenager, trying to stretch her wings, to a beautiful woman. But, like all women, she was weak. Pliable. Malleable. He needed malleable. That's how he made his world fun. He could manipulate most women and children, young animals. Boys were a different animal. But he could do wonders with them too. It took practice. The world of today didn't understand that. The kids were into instant gratification or nothing. As in life had to be the way they wanted it and now.

No one wanted to put in the work required to get where they wanted to be.

Today's world was all about short relationships, finding better jobs, building a bigger house.

It wasn't about learning long-term skills or developing budding talent. No, even the best musicians of today were still those of yesteryear, forever working on their craft. They weren't has-beens, as the young kids of today assumed.

They were lifelong artists, doing what they could do to stay in the game, as it shifted and changed around them. Everyone now crushed on that fleeting overnight fame of the internet. As if they could go viral once, then they could keep their grasp on the top spot in that world of power and influence.

When, in truth, they never had a spot in the first place.

The fickle audience who put them into the spotlight had already moved on. Without substance, there was nothing. And, without hard work, there was no substance. So nothing sustained their position. The hard truth was that, even with talent and hard work, nothing could keep them up there forever.

He, on the other hand, had put in decades of time and effort. He'd had some piddling success to make him cocky early on, his original talent showing up by accident, giving him the enthusiasm to move forward. The simple success had made him giddy, and he'd gone after bigger and better tricks. He'd been young. Arrogant. With the inherent problems of inexperience. He'd also had the hormonal issues of a developing teenager to contend with. It wasn't until later that he'd finally managed to gain some measure of control.

Now he was after more yet again.

Hannah was naught but a pawn. A practice piece of long ago. But she presented wonderful research of the long-term benefits of his work. As such, he found himself toying with her. A love a long time ago kept him tied to her—in many ways. But the impact of his research twisted with his emotions, the lure of who she was drew him back constantly.

She was special in so many ways. But she was also draining his energy. She had so much power and was gaining more. It took so much more for him to shut her down. And it was getting worse.

What had been easy back then was nothing to the effort he was forced to exert now. He couldn't release her nor kill her. But he knew she'd be the end of him if he did neither. In fact, he should have done the latter a long time ago. She was dangerous to him.

Yet flirting with danger presented its own appeal.

CHAPTER 4

HANNAH MANAGED TO hold at bay the questions barking inside her head while eating, but, as soon as her immediate hunger abated, they returned. Why had they come to see her? Sure, Stefan wanted to confirm that she was okay, and that made sense. She'd have done the same. She should probably have apologized for the mess she had left; she must have left a blood trail to his house. But somehow he didn't seem to need one to find her here in the hospital, and she hadn't thought to give it any further concern. The other man, yeah, she had no idea what to make of him. That whole dark hair and even darker gaze that seemed to see right through her? Well, he scared the shit out of her. And yet appealed to some inner sense. Making her even more nuts. The first man was reassuring and oozed caring.

The second man had been disturbed by something. She just didn't know what.

And she didn't want to know. He reminded her of all the doctors who'd checked her out and who had passed judgment on her over and over again. They had a zillion medical terms they'd used on her over the years. All of them meant the same thing. She was … *delicate*. Needed constant supervision, as she couldn't be trusted to be on her own. Made bad decisions. Couldn't properly assess threats. In fact, the last doctor had made it very clear. She was a danger to both herself and society, and, for everyone's sake, she needed to take her medicine and to live in this nice *home*, where she'd be safe for the rest of her life.

Like hell.

Pushing away her small table, where only crumbs remained of her breakfast, she considered her options. She had to shower before leaving, or she'd attract attention with the crusted blood in her hair. And that had to be avoided at all costs. Her leg had started to throb, even while resting on the bed. Should she stay until she healed? How long would that take? Longer than it would take for her father to hear about her being admitted and wanting to move her to his pet hospital. Something she couldn't let happen.

She tried to calculate how quickly her father would find out.

When she heard heavy footsteps marching toward her, she knew time had already run out. Damn her for sleeping late this morning.

She slid down under the covers and pretended to be asleep. As the footsteps neared, she watched as her father and his two assistants, dare she call them henchmen, entered the bedroom. His usual blustery style came to a halt, once he realized she was sleeping.

It was hard to see his expression clearly through her lashes, but he appeared to be uncertain of his next step. That didn't last long.

"Will, stand guard," he ordered. "I'll speak with the staff." He spun on his heels and left with George, the lesser of the two evils, and leaving Will, her old nemesis, in charge.

She had no idea what this man was, other than her father's lackey, but he seemed to like his job too much. Now that he was alone with her, her heart started pounding. She never could trust Will. She knew that, if he thought he could get away with it, he'd torment her in her sleep or poke her awake so she'd see his horrific face when she first woke up.

He wasn't ugly. He had the kind of features that made women fawn all over him. His connection to her father added to that attraction of the masses. Then there was the subtle air of power around him. What most didn't notice was the cloudiness to the man himself. Instead of a clean, fresh look, there was that edge of violence, a darkness inside that he cultivated—and did not fight against.

Fear was a tool he wielded well.

In her case, too well. He terrified her. The time her father had mentioned marrying her off to Will, so she'd have a strong man to look after her, was the only time she'd pleaded with her father to *not* do something. That she'd commit suicide before she'd become Will's wife.

Her father had listened for once.

At least then.

She was older now. More aware of how the world worked. Understood men better.

And was even more terrified.

How would she get out of this nightmare now?

BACK IN THE front lobby, Trevor walked to the entranceway with Stefan. "I'm going to go to the office, see if I can get some work done."

Stefan nodded. "I need to see Maddy."

Trevor grinned. "Just in case she has a free moment in her day to check out Hannah?"

"To talk to her about Anita. That little girl needs some of Dr. Maddy's magic." With a sheepish shrug, he added,

"*And* for Hannah. I feel responsible."

"You're not. You know that, right?" Trevor hated to see Stefan add anything else to his broad shoulders. That man already took care of half the world. "She might not be one of yours."

Stefan chuckled. "She already is. You know that."

"I was hoping you'd take a break from every stray who came your way."

"Can't. If the strays come to me, it's for a good reason—as you well know. So why don't you try to figure out what's going on in Hannah's world that brought her to my doorstep?"

"She's hiding." The words flew out of Trevor's mouth, without thought. She fascinated him, but he didn't know why. Sure, he had a thing for lost waifs, but it was more than that. A hell of a lot more than that.

"From what?"

Trevor's interest was distracted, as a large limousine pulled up to the front of the hospital, and two men dressed in dark suits stepped out from the back. A third man exited, sporting silver hair and wearing a jet-black suit. They walked toward the front door of the hospital.

"Do you know these men?" Trevor asked.

Stefan turned casually, his gaze sweeping the new arrivals, before moving on to the far side of the room, and shook his head. "No, I don't. Should I?"

"The auras say guards. The silver-haired man's aura has a familial connection to Hannah," Trevor revealed in a low voice, stepping out of the way as the three men strode past.

"You sure?" Stefan's gaze sharpened with interest, as the elderly gentleman strode down the hallway, as if he owned the hospital. "Interesting."

"Very. You sure you want to get involved?" Trevor asked again. "It could get ugly. This guy won't take any interference lightly."

"No, he won't," Stefan agreed, his tone wry. "Doesn't matter. Hannah came to me for help. So I have to help."

Trevor understood. He'd just hoped his friend would lighten his load. But that wouldn't happen. And honestly, the more Trevor saw of this scenario, the more it intrigued him. Something fascinating was happening here. "Do you really think she killed someone?"

"I wouldn't be surprised," Stefan stated softly. "The question is why, and did the other person deserve it?" Then he turned on his heel and walked toward the entrance, calling back, "Keep me in the loop."

"Will do." Trevor waited until Stefan was out of sight. Then, unable to stop himself, Trevor turned and headed in the direction the men had gone. Hannah was in trouble. How much and how deep remained to be seen. Only Stefan was right. She'd gone to him for help, and, in turn, Stefan had come to Trevor. It was against the medical code to not do what he could do. And the repercussions of not helping could be brutal.

Mother Nature was temperamental at any time, but ignoring something like this? Yeah, then she was a vindictive bitch.

NO. DAMN IT. He studied the vision in front of him. *Her.* As always, she was at his mercy. Yet she'd been alone all this time. Now to see her no longer alone ... and so fast ... and all under his radar?

Not more than a wisp of her energy had been evident.

But enough for him to recognize her.

Unbelievable. How had she done that? She couldn't have escaped him on her own. He knew that. It wasn't possible. He'd pretty well shot her ability to do anything on her own by now. What use was a pawn if it was allowed to toddle off on its own?

And *toddle* was a good word for her. She was a child. A gifted child, sure, but those gifts would die, shriveled up inside her. She had no idea of her power.

Keeping her alone and isolated helped to control her. He paused to consider her again. More energy surrounded her right now. Foreign energy. Powerful energy.

The sense of something else was involved. An old enemy. *Was it possible?* He shook his head. Couldn't be him. He was no longer enemy material. That man in his past had been a menace, but he was not as strong as he could be. He had diversified his abilities over the years. Became a do-gooder. Instead of staying focused on the goal, he'd let his energy split off—weaken. *Well, I haven't made that mistake. Sure I had a few sideways journeys and a few setbacks, but they were minor when compared to the rest of my progress.*

He'd made it this far. Like hell they were going after Hannah. She was his.

And always had been.

CHAPTER 5

"**I** KNOW YOU'RE not sleeping. You might fool your father, but never will you fool me," Will stated in a flat tone of voice. "You're a child in this world. And, every time I see you, I keep thinking that one day you'll grow up, but here you are. Twenty-five years old and you're still acting like a two-year-old."

She swallowed hard. Damn it. He was good at that. Cutting her down, demoralizing her, making her feel like that two-year-old he seemed to think she was. Not fair. But he had that power over her. Something she'd hoped to escape. To grow stronger. So, one of these times, she could fight him off.

Or stay hidden long enough for him to turn his attention to someone else. She'd been the mouse to his feline brand of torment for a long time now. She didn't know why he bothered. Couldn't he find someone else to play with, before moving in for the kill? At that, she froze.

Was he moving in for the kill on her?

Was this the last straw, and her father was fed up? Going to do something on a more permanent basis? Lock her up in a home? A fancy hospital? Sign her off to Will in marriage? Then she'd really be in trouble. The thought made her gag, then choke. She sat up on the bed, gasping, as the horror of such a life clutched at her.

That sent her into a paroxysm of coughing. Finally the frantic gasping for air eased, and she leaned back, wiping the tears from the corner of her eyes. She reached for the leftover juice and drank it down, hoping to clear her throat.

Then she opened her gaze, as if first catching sight of Will. With her hand to her aching chest from the bout of coughing, she gasped as if in surprise. "Will?"

"Yes." He walked closer. "Are you sick? Or injured? That was a bad cough."

She groaned and leaned back. "No idea. I feel like shit."

"Should have come home then, shouldn't you?"

Here we go again. "If I wanted to go home, I would have," she replied, letting her head roll to the side. "I'm so damn tired."

"You'll get plenty of rest where you're going," Will stated sharply. "We can't let you run all over the countryside, having your little episodes, can we?"

"Where is it you think I should go?" she asked bitterly. "A *nice* padded room?"

"You don't deserve *nice* anymore," he replied pointedly. "We tried that, and look what happened. You still ran."

"I don't want to be a prisoner."

"Too bad. Until you're healthy, you're not well enough to be on your own. Because, so far, when you are on your own, you can't take care of yourself. Then there is your inability to pick up the phone and ask for help," he added. "Your father was in a right state this morning, when he got the news."

"Ah, sorry about that. I suppose it must have pulled him out of one of those so important meetings too, right?" she snapped, then groaned. Now she did sound like a petulant child, looking for her father's time and affection, when that couldn't be further from the truth. She'd grown up wanting that, even more so after her mother's death. Apparently her mother had handed down the delicate genes to Hannah.

Too bad her father had never had a son. That's what he really wanted.

In fact, he treated Will and George as if they *were* his sons. If she weren't around, she had no doubt they'd inherit everything. Except her father had Wanda, his arm decoration. One of a dozen this last decade, although she'd been the only one to last for years. But she was barely a few years older than Hannah, and that was just gross.

As it were, if any of these people could prove Hannah was mentally incompetent, they'd likely get all of her dad's estate anyway. Not that she wanted anything from her father. She just wanted her freedom. Unfortunately that took money.

She had some of her own, but she had no idea how long that would last. She'd never done a full day's work in her life, until she had bought her business. That had been a rude awakening. Hell, she'd never finished college because of her father's restrictions. After all, she wasn't strong enough to actually take an exam, and the stress would probably blow a gasket in her brain.

Still, she'd bought the florist shop and had hired Tasha to manage it. So Hannah had done something right. The store had yet to turn a profit, but that didn't mean it wouldn't. She considered what she'd done so far a success. Something that would amuse her father and Wanda to no end, if they knew. Good thing they hadn't a clue. Otherwise her father would order Hannah to sell the shop immediately.

Bitterly, she pleated the hospital sheet and stared at the man in front of her. "Where is Father now?"

"He's with the administrators, making arrangements."

"Arrangements?" she asked coolly. "What arrangements? I like it here."

"Well, too bad," her father retorted from the doorway. "You won't be staying. You'll be transported to Rossmoor Hospital this afternoon."

"I am not going back there."

"Yes, you are," he snapped in that *I'll not listen to any arguments out of you, and you have no idea what you're talking about voice.* "And this time you won't be checking yourself out anytime soon."

She shook her head, desperate to find a way out of this. And fast. "I'm an adult, Father. That's not your decision to make."

"Of course it is. You're not capable of looking after yourself," he argued. "I should have locked you up last time and thrown away the keys. You will travel there this afternoon, go through a full assessment, then be back in the same room you were in nine months ago." He glared at her. "And you will stay there this time. Do you understand?"

She glared at him mutely.

"Hannah?" he barked. "Do you understand?"

"Excuse me," Dr. Trevor Johnson interrupted, from the back of the room, startling them all. His voice was hard and uncompromising, but his gaze on Hannah was gentle, caring.

Hannah stared at him in hope. Any interruption right now was a godsend. Even if this man couldn't help her. After all, why would he do anything? She'd barely been civil to him. Still, he'd bought her time. She'd take it.

And that look in his eye. She didn't know what she'd done to deserve it, but she wished she did, so she would make sure to not do that again. It's like he … cared. And that scared her.

"I'm not sure what is going on here, but Hannah shouldn't be upset," Trevor stated in a calm voice. "You will have to leave."

So he was here in a medical role? Really? Surely not.

Hannah's father rose up to his full height and turned on Trevor. She had no idea how or why Trevor was back here, but she needed this distraction—anything to get rid of her father, so she could get out of this room.

"Do you know who I am?" her father asked coolly in his *I'll cut you into ribbons and feed you to the dog* tone of voice.

"No, and I don't particularly care. That you have lost control and are shouting at a level that is upsetting to other patients several rooms down is not only unacceptable but shows that you might need help yourself," Trevor snapped, his gaze locked on her father, as if he knew a python struck with a speed that most of its victims underestimated.

"He's my father," Hannah muttered out loud. Inside she wanted to bounce up on the bed and cheer. Someone had actually stood up to her father.

And she would, as soon as she got over the shock.

Of course Trevor would pay for this show of spirit. If not right now, in a few days Will would visit him and would take care of the job himself. No one crossed her father. Not and lived to tell about it.

He fed on fear.

She should know. She'd been spoon-fed that shit since birth. But only after Will's arrival in her life had she been fed a steady diet of it.

TREVOR KNEW BETTER than to take his gaze off this man.

He had no idea where the asshole came from or what his point was in hauling Hannah out of this hospital, but Trevor would be damn sure to check out what and how and why. If Hannah didn't want to be admitted to the sanatorium, then someone had to be an advocate on her behalf. Trevor was a lawyer *and* a psychologist. The combination gave him many tools to deal with power-hungry assholes, like this one in front of him.

Unfortunately the world was full of them. The psychologist in him gave him insights that helped him to deal with the patients' legal issues in the courts. He often represented patients in this hospital.

The administrators might not know about what was going on, but they would within minutes of him getting these men out of here.

"Who the hell are you?" asked one of the two men standing guard. And, yeah, there was no other word for it. He stepped between Trevor and Hannah's father and shoved his face into Trevor's.

Trevor never took his gaze off the father. Instead he lowered his own tones to just above glacial and snapped, "I'm Hannah's lawyer."

Silence.

Trevor would have laughed, if he could.

Hannah's father's shock was complete. As if no one had ever bucked him or his plans. Well, it was damn time. The guard interestingly backed off slightly and glanced at his boss, as if saying, *You'd better handle this.*

"I will have my team of lawyers contact you," Hannah's father stated. "My daughter is leaving here now. Today."

Trevor reached into his breast pocket and pulled out a card. "Here's my contact information."

The card was snatched from his hand, and the men stormed out. Trevor released his breath and turned toward Hannah. She had the blankets pulled up to her chin, a wide-eyed look on her face.

"Thank you," she whispered. "It was an honor to see someone stand up—no matter how uselessly—to my father."

He studied her. "Uselessly?"

"No one blocks him," she replied bitterly. "I'll be loaded up and hauled out of here this afternoon, and there won't be a damn thing you or I can do about it."

"Have you so little faith in the law?" he asked curiously, walking toward her.

"I have a great deal of knowledge of my father and the men who work for him." She nodded toward the open doorway. "The one who spoke to you is someone who will attack you in an alleyway late at night."

Trevor's eyebrows shot up. "Interesting. I don't suppose you have any proof of such activities, do you?"

She shook her head. "No. I don't. I have nothing to my name legally to prove who I am at the moment either, but that doesn't mean I don't know who I am."

He sat down on the side of her bed. "You went to Stefan for help. But this is slightly out of his bailiwick. So he came to me."

She studied him. "He thought I needed a lawyer?"

"Not quite." He grinned. "I'm also a psychologist. And an energy worker."

She blinked but didn't say anything to that last bit, making him wonder if she understood what that meant. "And it seems to me that, at the moment, Stefan was right, in that I'm likely to be someone who *can* help you."

"What would you want in exchange?" she asked hesitantly.

"Well, Stefan owed you a dollar and gave it to me instead on your behalf," he lied blithely. "So, in fact, you have me on retainer to represent you in your legal issues. As for payment beyond that? Well, if you're as broke as you appear to be, then this will need to be a pro bono case."

"And why would you do this?" Her gaze narrowed in consideration. "You don't know me."

"And, therefore, I can't help you? If you understood my skill sets, you'd realize I'm just a sucker for helping people."

"Do you collect stray dogs too?"

He laughed, thinking about the menagerie he had at home. "In fact, I do. But I'm an equal opportunity savior. I am ruled by three cats and two birds, as well as four dogs."

She gasped, then laughed.

He grinned at the sound. It was a little rusty but held such joy that he wanted to hear it again.

"I wouldn't have known being a lawyer meant that you wanted to help people," she explained slowly, when she could. A smile appeared on her face as she continued, but a note of caution was in her words too, as if she were afraid of insulting him. "My father's lawyers come in the category of barracudas."

"See? That's the thing about the legal profession. There is room for barracudas and saviors. Often we're pitted against each other."

"And you like a challenge," she noted in wry tones.

"I do. And I'm a sucker for waifs. Particularly for ones who thought they killed a friend of mine and left bloody fingerprints all over his doorway."

And for the second time in the last few minutes, silence reigned.

CHAPTER 6

HANNAH DIDN'T KNOW what to say, so remained silent.

After a long moment he picked up the conversation. "Your father is planning on putting you into a sanatorium, is that correct?"

"If that is a cushy private hospital that I'm not allowed to leave, then that would be correct."

"Why?"

This was where it got a little tricky. "He thinks I'm mentally unfit to live my own life," she stated quietly, sadly.

"And are you?"

"No," she snapped. "I'm fine. I did without him for most of the last year, and I can do without him for the next many years too."

"Then why commit you?"

She felt the intensity of Trevor's gaze, that indomitable will of his, saying he needed information from her and that he'd get it one way or another. But maybe not through violence. At least she hoped so.

"He controls my money ..." She started to explain, then stopped.

"How old are you?"

"Twenty-five," she replied, but her voice slowed with uncertainty.

He turned to look at her. "You *are* twenty-five or *will be* twenty-five soon?"

She blinked. "I am ..." She frowned and spoke no more.

He studied her, and she felt that same intensity. Then he told her something that surprised her. "Today is Friday, May seventeen, if that helps."

It did. A lot. In one way. In another, not at all. Like what happened to the last few days? Where the hell had she been in the meantime? And why?

"My birthday is Monday," she noted quietly. "My trust fund is supposed to come to me at that time. Unless, as my father says, 'I'm not competent to handle the responsibility.'"

"And is your father short on money?"

She raised her eyebrows, then shook her head wildly. "No, not at all. He doesn't need my money. He's probably a billionaire by now."

"So getting his hands on your trust fund has nothing to do with his wanting to lock you up?"

"No, he's been looking after it all this time anyway." She glared out the window. "I'd like to think he wants to lock me up because he thinks that's the best thing for me, but ..."

"But?"

She winced. "It's hard to believe anymore."

"I understand." What it did sound like was more about a powerful man bending another to his will. But to what purpose? Trevor had no idea. Surely there was more to this than anything so simple. Why lock her up? To get her out of his way? Maybe to force her to do something and releasing her would be the reward?

"He really thinks you're a danger to others?" He eyed her carefully. "Somewhere in all this is the truth. Everyone has secrets. I get it. But some are more dangerous than others."

She nodded but wouldn't look at him.

"Why does he think you are dangerous?" When she still refused to raise her gaze to him, he pushed deeper. "Have you hurt anyone else in the past?"

She sighed. "A little."

"A little," he repeated, with a note of humor. "How little and who?"

She shrugged. "I'm actually not sure who. Someone who worked for my father apparently. A maid."

"Apparently?" Now he sounded fed up. "The truth," he snapped. "Now."

"I don't know it. It was a long time ago." She lifted her gaze. "Apparently the maid was clearing my room, and I went off my rocker and attacked her. Supposedly I stabbed her."

"Supposedly?"

She nodded but stared at him defiantly.

"Were the police ever brought in?"

She shook her head. "No, Father handled it all."

"And you can't remember anything about it."

"According to the maid and everyone who was there at the time, I was in some kind of altered state," she reported in cool tones. "They spoke to me, but I didn't respond. It's as if I were sleepwalking. When I came out of that state, I knew nothing about what had happened."

"INTERESTING." *VERY INTERESTING.* Sleepwalking was a possibility, if she'd actually been sleeping. "But I presume you weren't sleeping, as the maid was cleaning your room."

"No, I was doing homework. Came off my chair and attacked her without warning." She stared out the window moodily. "I still don't understand what happened."

"And has it ever happened again?" He hoped not, as one incident could be written off as an anomaly, but if it had happened again? Not so much.

"I don't know if I ever attacked anyone, but I have had episodes, where I black out and don't remember anything. Anyone." She stared at him. "Do you know what that's like? To not know what I might have done and with whom? To not remember anything?"

He shook his head immediately. "No, I don't. It's never happened to me."

"Right. It's not something that happens to anyone else," she snapped bitterly. "I'm just the lucky one."

"How long do the episodes last?"

Her breathing hitched. And he knew he'd hit a nerve again. More was hidden here. If only he could get her to tell him. He waited patiently, then added, "Are we talking minutes, hours?" At her look, he asked in a low voice, "Days?"

She waited.

"Shit. Weeks?"

She nodded.

"And no warning?" How the hell did she function like that? Maybe her father had a reason to be worried.

She shook her head again. "I never have a warning, until I open my eyes and find myself somewhere I don't recognize. People who have seen me during my episodes say I act completely normally, so I don't know if I'm blacking out or just losing memories. It's not like the specialists can tell, and believe me. I've spoken to my share of those."

"That's a possibility though. Memory lapses could explain some of what is going on as to why you appear normal during the lost time frame."

"I like that one better than the other options," she admitted. "But, as I don't know what I was doing during these times, I don't know if I am hurting anyone."

She leaned forward, her gaze pleading for him to understand. "I wouldn't want to hurt *anyone*. If the only option to save the rest of the world is to keep me locked up and away, then fine, but why does it have to be in one of those places?" she wailed.

"In theory, you are supposed to get the help you need at these places." Only he had firsthand experience that they didn't always get that. In many cases, they received no help at all. But modern medicine knew very little about the working brain or the psyche. And when it came to energy workers? They knew nothing at all.

And people did end up locked up, so they couldn't hurt anyone—including the energy workers themselves. So maybe her father was doing this out of his brand of love, after all. Trevor had seen parents do many things in the name of love—including kill their children.

"We need to figure out why the blackouts occur and hopefully track them backward to see what you may have done during them." He paused, studying her. "When was the last one?"

She winced.

And he knew. In fact, he'd brought it up earlier, and it had been brushed off. "You woke up on the highway outside of Stefan's house, didn't you?"

Her breath gushed out. "Yeah, but I didn't know who he was, until I saw him at the hospital."

"You were injured though, so that's to be expected," he pointed out.

"Or did I kill someone? I told Stefan that I'd tried to kill him."

"Ah, so you do remember that part." He laughed. "Good."

She frowned at him. "That's hardly something to laugh at."

"Sure it is. Stefan has a lot of weird stuff happen in his life. That doesn't mean all of it was good or bad, but you walking to his door saying you'd killed him? That was unique."

"Not exactly a great greeting." But, in spite of it, she grinned.

"But not the worst either."

A commotion outside the doorway had him straighten. "It's almost showtime."

"Meaning?"

"Meaning, you are in deep trouble, and there are very few ways to get you out of it."

"I'm not going home with my father," she stated flat-out, her gaze darting around the room as if looking for a place to hide.

"He controls your fortune, and you've let him. Unless you appoint someone else to take control and can do so legally, then he'll get what he wants fairly easily. I can block him, try to take him through the courts, but that all takes time."

"What options do I have in the short-term?"

He frowned. "I have one solution, but it's drastic."

Her father's voice sounded in the hallway, along with several other men.

"I'm desperate," she replied quietly, her voice a squeaking sound. "What is the solution?"

It was his turn to feel panicked. He took a deep breath and said, "Marry me."

CHAPTER 7

A S PROPOSALS WENT, this one sucked. But her mind quickly grasped how the husband received priority over a father. And it would stop her father from trying to marry her off to his lackeys, so he could continue to control her.

But marriage?

To a stranger?

And a lawyer?

A savior lawyer not a barracuda apparently but still, … she had only his word on that.

"For how long?"

He raised his eyebrows. "Until we can get to the bottom of this mess in your life. If you want your freedom, you only have to ask for it. But, as long as you are unmarried, and everything goes to your father, who already controls your estate, medical issues, et cetera. …"

"I got it. I got it," she whispered, her hands trembling. The reality was, she was in a bad spot. "It takes time to set this up. We don't have that time."

He had his phone out and was making phone calls even as she spoke. "Your father will fight this, so if he's coming here, you need to stall him. I don't care how but don't mention me or the marriage and definitely don't be too resistant."

She snorted. "If I'm not resistant, he'll know something

is up."

He patted her knee. "I'll be back in a few minutes." He strode to the doorway.

Damn it. Her savior was leaving her … "Wait," she cried out. "Do you have to leave?"

He frowned, glanced down at his phone, and appeared to consider something. "Maybe not, but it would be faster."

"Okay," she agreed in a small voice. "Hurry back, or I might not be here when you return."

"Don't say that." He pointed at her and ordered, "Be here." And he left.

She leaned back and wondered at her options. What could she do to stave off her father? Pretend to be asleep? Pretend to be more badly hurt, so she wasn't capable of traveling? Hurt herself for real?

And then what? Be too injured to participate in her own wedding? At that she almost broke into hysterical laughter. *Marriage.* Dear God, was she really going to marry a stranger? Why? Surely there was another option? There had to be. She didn't know this man at all. What if he was a liar? A cheat? He could be a serial killer, for all she knew. Stefan, the man who'd brought her to the hospital, he knew Trevor. Would he vouch for him? Of course he would, as he already had. He'd asked Trevor to help her in the first place. And that *was* giving her his recommendation.

The nurse walked in just then, a big smile on her face. "Don't you look better?" She held out a small paper bag. "This is the little bit you had in your pockets when you arrived here."

Curious, Hannah opened the bag and saw essentially nothing inside. She pulled out a handful of loose change, a few bills, a crumpled receipt that was bloody and hard to read, and a crumpled photo. She took a quick look but tucked it away so fast that she didn't get a chance to identify who was in it. A man and a woman but that was all. Not wanting the nurse to see, she leaned back and laid the bag beside her.

"Everything okay?"

"I'm feeling a little better. I don't suppose there's more food is there?"

"Lunch will be here soon. At least you're awake this time."

She smiled. "I am but very tired. I want to sleep but don't want to miss out on lunch," she fudged. "I figure I'll be out like a light as soon as I've eaten."

"That would be best. You're moving today, so any sleep you get early will help."

"Moving?"

"Being transferred," she noted, with a bright smile. "Don't you worry about it. Your father is taking care of it all. Such a caring father. Very take charge too," she noted in admiring tones.

"Very," Hannah replied softly.

Carts rolling down the hallway spoke of more arrivals. Hopefully with lunch. She wasn't sure she could eat, but, not knowing where she would end up or what was coming in her world, she'd do her best to get it all down. Besides, she was always hungry. Once she saw the food, it would disappear in a heartbeat.

If this fake marriage thing didn't work out, she might have to make a run for it. And that would be damn-near impossible with an injured leg and a swollen ankle. Adding constant hunger to the scenario would just make it worse.

"When is the doctor coming?" she asked. "I haven't spoken to him yet."

"He's been in surgery all morning. He does his rounds at this time normally. As long as he doesn't encounter problems in the OR, he'll be here soon. One must be patient."

Hannah nodded. "True, but it would be nice to speak with him at least once and thank him, since I'm supposedly being transferred."

"No supposedly about it," Will declared from the doorway. "Your father will make that happen."

She cast him a sideways look. "You can stand outside while I eat, thank you," she snapped. "I'd hate to have my meal turn sour in my stomach by having you here."

The nurse's shocked gasp made Will laugh. "Don't worry about her. She's always cranky when she's hungry."

"No. I'm not," Hannah countered, her temper spiking again. "But you're right on one thing, I am hungry."

The nurse patted her hand. "I'll see about your lunch. Don't you worry. I can see you're worried about that transfer. Don't be. Sometimes we have to trust in those who care about us."

And she walked out of the room, smiling at Will—like all the women who smiled at Will. What was it about him that made women of all ages make fools of themselves?

Will's genial smile darkened as he turned it on Hannah. She'd pay for her resistance. Whatever. She'd been paying since forever already. What did his brand of payback mean now? Especially if she were to be locked away again. A gilded cage was still a cage.

She closed her eyes and tried to block it all out.

Inside her heart pounded. And her palms turned moist. Marriage *was* a way out. If Trevor was for real.

And if they could make this happen in time. But was it

just another cage by another name?

If her father caught wind of the plans and managed to stop them, she knew the penalty would be severe. Her father not only hated to be thwarted, he refused to be. Often he paid a great deal of money to smash his opponent in various ways. Worse, he didn't give a damn what it cost. It was more of a chess game to him. Notches he could mark on the chalkboard in his mind. He didn't give a damn about what was right or wrong in the game, as long as his side won.

He'd win in this issue too, if her husband-to-be wasn't faster, smarter, meaner.

She didn't think he was.

Worse? She wasn't sure she could trust Trevor.

God, she had to be nuts to be thinking about this. Surely she had another choice. But, as she stared at her injured legs, she realized she needed help as never before. She couldn't run away again. Not on her own.

Likely her father would find her store and run her into the ground there. The only reason he hadn't done so already was he hadn't looked in that direction yet. Besides, he wouldn't believe she had the business sense to buy and to run a florist shop in the first place. She might not have at the beginning, but she had learned. She'd also hired the previous owners to teach her the ropes. They wanted to retire to go traveling, having crossed the sixty-year-old line, but didn't really want to retire to the point of being bored. That arrangement had worked for both sides.

Many of the customers had stayed with the shop because of the older couple still appearing at the shop and seeing them help out Hannah, all of which had given her reputation a boost. Then hiring her manager, Hannah had done fairly well for herself.

But she didn't want her new husband to have any of it. Shit. She didn't understand any of this mess. She figured she should have some kind of document in place between her and Trevor, but he was a lawyer. He could document her to death, and she could still miss out on having the right ones to protect herself.

Then again, he wasn't exactly getting a bargain with her either. In fact, she'd be setting him up. Shit. She couldn't do it. Will would go after Trevor. Maybe even kill him.

How could she accept his offer of help if she was signing his death warrant?

She couldn't. There'd be no wedding.

And that meant she couldn't escape her future.

She'd be a prisoner for life.

OUTWARDLY CALM, TREVOR strode down the hallway, but inside he was keyed up. He'd been involved in too many cases not to know how delicate this situation was. The guard stood outside the door, his attention on his phone, but Trevor wouldn't make the mistake of thinking he wasn't aware of every step he took toward Hannah's room.

That the guard was still there was a good sign. It meant Mr. Goodman, Hannah's father, hadn't managed to get her out of the hospital yet. Trevor had been busy throwing up as many legal roadblocks as he could find. When he found out Mr. Goodman likely *was* a billionaire, and Hannah his only daughter, this marriage thing would have serious repercussions for Hannah. She could be disinherited and likely cut off from her father forever, given everything Trevor had managed to learn about the man in the last hour. Goodman hated to lose. And, if Trevor pulled this off, Goodman would lose his daughter to Trevor.

If the man loved Hannah, then he'd work with Trevor to see that she got the best help available.

Stefan figured that help was Maddy. Trevor wouldn't argue that. If Stefan could get them an hour of Dr. Maddy's time, it could tell them so much. If it didn't, then maybe Trevor was needed more than he thought.

Trevor reached the door to Hannah's room, and the guard straightened and threw an arm out across the doorway to stop Trevor.

Trevor shot him a disgusted look and shoved the guard's arm out of the way. And damn if there wasn't an electrical shock as he connected. Shit. Trevor shot him a dirty look and caught the guard's smug grin.

He was a man of energy power.

Did Hannah know? Did she even know what that meant?

He wanted to ask but figured this wasn't the time. Besides, Hannah was eating, like seriously eating.

Again.

Like she hadn't eaten in weeks. Yet he'd watched her polish off scones and muffins for breakfast. Now she was plowing into a bowl of soup and a sandwich. He stopped and waited for her to see him. He didn't want to startle her, and, if he had a chance, he wanted to see if that same dark shadow showed up again on her face.

He'd been dealing with Stefan too long to not know something psychic was going on here. But was it to her benefit or to her detriment?

Her aura was still thin. Strong but such a narrow band that he couldn't read it.

She was skinny and ate thousands of calories right now.

Was this an unnaturally high metabolism or was something else going on?

"You can come in, you know," she offered, without raising her head. "I don't bite."

"I wonder if that sandwich would agree with you," he murmured, approaching the bed. "It looks like you're starving."

She nodded. "I'm always starving. Started when I was a teen, and it just keeps getting worse. Of course I've been tested for everything, but apparently no one knows what's wrong." She lifted the sandwich and took a big bite. Then eyed him. In a low voice she told him, "I changed my mind about marrying you."

He raised his eyebrows. Oh, interesting and dare he say? Almost a relief. "Of course you have." He sat down on the visitor's chair. "And why is that?"

She nodded to the guard standing at the doorway and lowered her voice to a whisper, "He'll likely kill you. Then I'll just be a widow and still at my father's mercy. Only now, a very angry father."

Trevor blinked at the reality she'd laid out so calmly. "Really?"

She shrugged. "Given the circumstances, it's all too likely," she stated candidly. "Of course no one will know. I'll be widowed today, and tomorrow he'll bring up the issue that my husband's unfortunate demise added to my 'delicate' sensibilities and sped up my mental decline.'"

He sat back, as the reality of the situation hit him. It could be presented just like that. No matter how many legal issues came up, her father could make a case for such a series of events.

"I guess I need to add a few pieces of paper to the stack

we need to sign then," he commented calmly.

She frowned at him and took another bite. "What kind of papers?"

"Well, I have the marriage license but figured that, to protect your assets, we needed to sign a prenuptial agreement, so I can't legally take your money. And now you'll sign one that allows my law firm to defend you in the chance of my death or injury that stops me from being able to protect you from your family."

"Can you do that?" she asked in a harsh whisper. She straightened, then glanced at her guard and hunched down again to ask, "Is that possible?"

Trevor nodded. "All kinds of things are possible. The bottom line is, you need to trust me to do this right. We can always add or change paperwork later to tie up any loopholes and to lock down trust funds to keep you and your money safe, but we have to stop Mr. Goodman right now. Or he can have you declared mentally incompetent, and that is seriously difficult to reverse."

She stared at him, the bite of sandwich sticking in her throat, as she thought of those options. He was sticking his neck out to help at a huge cost, and she was grateful as all hell. But something was in that gaze, something special. She wanted to believe him, to believe *in* him.

"I don't think I could live with the guilt if something happened to you because you were trying to help me," she whispered.

"I'm doing this with my eyes open," he declared. Only instincts prodded him forward. In fact, his actions stunned him, but he was quickly becoming okay with them.

"But why? Why would you do this for me?" Her gaze was intense, as she studied his face. "It's crazy."

"It's not crazy. Legal issues have to be put in place to protect you. And, if you don't want to stay married, then we can process an annulment as well. Although I suggest we don't do so too quickly."

She blinked. "And if you meet someone?"

"*Else*, you mean? Other than you, who will be my wife?" he asked, with a wicked grin. "Not likely. But, if I do, then, if she's right for me, she'll understand. If she doesn't, she wasn't, and I'm in no different a situation than before. However, at no time will I be looking, and, as your husband, I will be standing at your side, not dating other women."

She took another bite of sandwich and chewed it slowly.

"What about you?" he asked. "Do you have someone in your life?"

She shook her head. "Not for years. I didn't want to drag anyone into the craziness that my world had become."

"Good. Unless there's someone you can't remember. Other than that, we're both single. Unemotionally attached and adults. Then"—he glanced at his watch—"all I need to know now is …"

Realizing it was the first and could possibly be the last time he'd ever ask this question, he eased onto the bed, reached for her hand, and, in a low careful tone, asked, "Will you be my wife?"

Tears shimmered in her gaze.

He didn't know if that was because this was not the proposal every young woman dreamed of or because of the reason behind this legal maneuvering, but he hoped it wasn't because he was the opposite of the type of man she'd like to have asking her this question.

Even given the circumstances, there was a solemnity to the moment that he'd rarely experienced.

She took a deep breath and nodded.

"I need to hear the words," he said gently.

"If you are prepared for the consequences, then I will marry you and become your wife."

CHAPTER 8

"WHAT DO WE do about the guards and my father?" she murmured in a low voice. "It'll get ugly."

"No, it won't. Trust me. Remember?" He got off the bed, as an orderly walked in. The newcomer smiled at Trevor, then at Hannah, and stated, "Time for a set of X-rays on those ribs. The doc's not happy with the ones we took last night."

"Oh." She glanced up at Trevor in surprise but was reassured by his wink, so she let herself be helped into a wheelchair, a pink blanket around her knees, a chart placed in her hands, before being wheeled from the room.

The orderly said to the guard, "We'll have her back in about twenty minutes." He took her down the hallway. She turned to look behind her, but her bodyguard continued to stare at her, a thunderous frown on his face. He pulled out his phone, as they turned the corner.

Of Trevor, there was no sign.

She was wheeled for another couple minutes, around several corners and into an elevator, then downstairs and down another hallway. A door opened, and she was wheeled into … a small chapel. She gasped at the beautiful candles and the large bouquets of flowers. Stefan walked forward, a stunning woman at his side. She held a gentle bouquet of lilies.

"I'm Celina. Stefan has told me so much about you. I'm so sorry for all this trouble."

"I'm sorry too," Hannah replied in a low voice. "I didn't mean to cause such a fuss."

Celina smiled, and, damn, it was as if the heavy air of the solemn occasion suddenly lit up. "Everything happens for a reason. But no one should be alone at a time like this." She handed the bouquet to Hannah and said, "If you are okay with it, Stefan and I will stand as your witnesses."

Witnesses. Good Lord, she hadn't thought about any of that. "Of course," she agreed warmly. "And thank you so much for offering. And for the flowers," she added hurriedly.

Stefan grabbed the back of the wheelchair and slowly wheeled her toward Trevor, who somehow appeared at the altar. "Our pleasure. And, if you decide that this marriage stands, then we can redo this whole ceremony at my house at a later date."

He meant, as in making this a real marriage. *Oh, Lord.* She couldn't think of that right now. This was too big, and, at the same time, she knew secrecy was paramount. If her father burst in …

With Celina walking at their side, the trio approached the front, where Trevor stood, looking resplendent in his suit. She was still in her hospital gown, and … her hand reached up … and touched the dried blood in her hair.

"Don't worry about it," Celina noted. "You look beautiful."

There was such sincerity in her voice that, even though it wasn't true, it was a balm to Hannah's soul.

At the end of the aisle, Stefan arranged her wheelchair, so she was parked beside Trevor. He reached down and picked up her hand.

Outside, she heard footsteps running down the hallway—not just one set, but several. She frowned, but the minister in front of them was speaking. She glanced up at Trevor. He kept his gaze on the minister but squeezed her hand in reassurance.

The footsteps were followed by shouting. "Where is it? Damn it. The room has to be here somewhere."

And she realized they were likely looking for this chapel. She shuddered and gripped Trevor's hand tightly.

But he held her firm, and together they made it through the ceremony.

"I now pronounce you husband and wife," the minister stated. "You may kiss the bride."

Damn. She'd actually done it. She grinned. She'd thwarted her father.

"Glad to see you're smiling," Trevor murmured, just before he kissed her gently. Realizing what he'd done for her, she threw her arms around his neck and kissed him enthusiastically.

Everyone laughed.

When Trevor straightened again, the minister motioned at them to sign the paperwork, so it would be legal and binding.

In a firm hand she signed the papers, then several others Trevor handed her. She didn't even read them, but inside she knew she could trust him. She had no reason to, but she had no time. Her father was storming down the hallway, ready to destroy the building if they didn't produce his daughter now.

"Let's get you back to your room," Trevor murmured.

"That would be good." She thanked the minister. As she turned to thank Stefan and Celina, she found them, holding the door open for Trevor to wheel her out.

"Not too many brides get married in the hospital," she muttered low enough so only Trevor heard her.

"You're wrong. For many reasons hundreds of weddings are performed in hospitals every year."

She thought about that and realized how many scenarios were likely a whole lot more serious and devastating than hers. "Thank you."

He laughed. "Don't thank me yet. We have some rough patches to get through first."

"Maybe, but for the first time, I don't feel quite so alone."

"While I'm here, you won't be."

Out in the hallway he took her to a large elevator. "This is a different way than I was brought down."

"We took you the back way to ensure no one saw you. Your father and his men have been tearing apart the place, looking for you."

"And why is it they didn't find me?" she asked curiously. She couldn't imagine something as simple as getting lost having stopped her father from doing what he wanted to do.

"He couldn't find the chapel."

"But why not? It's on the signs."

He chuckled. "Well, it was there, but apparently they couldn't see what was right in front of their eyes."

He exchanged a knowing look with Stefan that she really wanted to ask about, but he was already wheeling her into the room.

Her very full room.

"There she is," her father cried out. "What did you do with her?"

Stefan and Trevor stiffened, their glares locked on her

father. Trevor was the first to speak. "Just what are you implying?"

"I'm not implying anything," her father roared. "I'm accusing you of kidnapping my daughter."

"Kidnapping," Hannah gasped. "What are you talking about?"

Her father glared at Trevor, then turned his temper on her. "You weren't here when you were supposed to be. We were told you were in the chapel but couldn't find it either. Then, when one of my men found the chapel, you weren't there," he shouted.

She stared at him. Had she ever seen him lose control like this? No. She wondered just what the hell he'd do when he found out the truth.

She wouldn't have long to wait.

"Sorry if you had trouble finding the room. It's a popular place, and, being on the main floor, I was sure there'd be no trouble finding it," Trevor stated helpfully. "I'd have sent someone to show you the way, if I thought you'd get lost."

Her father's face turned red, and it appeared he was ready to have a stroke.

"Daddy, calm down," Hannah cried out. "You look like you'll have a heart attack or something. For heaven's sake, I got married. That's all."

Not even a spider dared take a step.

And her father went from beet red to a pure icy white. In a very soft, very scary voice, he asked, "You what?"

Well, she was in the soup now. And she'd damn-well better make this look good. "I got married. We wanted a simple ceremony first and thought that we could do a bigger celebration later for the families." She beamed up at him. "That's why I was hoping you'd make it to the chapel. We were so short on time that we couldn't wait for you. But you'll be there for the second one and can give me away then."

"And the urgency?" Will asked in a deadly voice.

"You and Daddy of course," she replied smoothly. "Do you really think I'm going to be locked away in an asylum for the rest of my life at your whim?"

"You were going to marry Will," her father roared. "It was all planned out."

"Did you also plan to ask my permission regarding that deal?" She gasped in shock. "Or was I going to be railroaded into that as well?"

Her father straightened his back. "Make no mistake," he snapped, "you will regret your decision here today." And he strode out.

Will stopped in front of Hannah. "Nice try. It won't last." He bent down and whispered, "And you will be mine but will no longer hold a position of respect, bitch."

He turned and walked out behind her father.

TREVOR STUDIED THE man Will, as he walked out the door. That he'd threatened Hannah was a given. Unfortunately what he'd uttered to her had been in too low a tone for Trevor to hear.

Hannah's already pale face had disappeared under a wave of fear. Trevor's heart ached for her. She'd lived like this for a long time. Considering her domineering father and her terrifying blackouts, she was doing remarkably well. Somewhere along the line she'd learned some serious coping skills.

Trevor could see the aura resonating around Will, but a hard shell protected it. Usually seen in a man who liked to control his surroundings, letting in only the people he wanted. A man who had been hurt early on, and now that he was bigger, stronger, and no longer a victim, he'd dish it out—and as often as he could. Someone with secrets. Someone who operated on the dark side of the light spectrum. The negative side. In the extreme? *Evil.*

In the not so extreme was the person who lashed out, causing a bigger slide to the dark side, then immediately regretted the action and tried to make up for it and ended up in the middle of dark and light. Those people had the opportunity to go either way and could learn to deal with their anger issues and to become happily adjusted.

Whereas Will was firmly on the side of darkness and gloried in it. His dark aura glowed, full of life. Shimmered in joy. He liked where and what he was right now, and, given enough time there, he'd never return to the light. Those were the serial killers who gloried in their work and lived long productive years enjoying their hobby, often never getting caught.

The wafflers in the middle might kill in passion, but, unless something shifted, they wouldn't do it again. If, however, they got away with it, then that lure was often too intoxicating to resist, and they'd repeat the behavior and take a firm step onto the dark side.

Trevor had seen many like that. Unfortunately enough of those who sat on the dark side wallowed there quite happily. Even after getting caught, the men were usually content, as if they had enough memories to see them through their prison years.

Will was an unknown. He liked to terrorize people. Hannah was evidence of that. But, at the same time, Trevor had to wonder if Will hadn't done so much more. Hannah seemed to think Trevor's own life was in danger from her father's guards as of this moment. Yet Trevor wasn't without defenses. And he had a team to call on, if anything went wrong.

He squeezed Hannah's shoulder reassuringly and turned to Stefan. "Did you get everything set up?"

"I did." Stefan glanced at his watch. "You're expected anytime now."

"Right. We just can't be followed." He reached out for the handles on Hannah's wheelchair.

Stefan nodded. "Maddy has one bed opening up this afternoon. You can rest there overnight, then move out."

"Are you sure it's okay with Kali?"

"It is. She's in Guatemala, working the earthquake zone, and Grant is picking her up and taking her for a two-week holiday. Besides, you'll be at their rental property in town here."

"A working holiday?" Trevor had met Kali several times. She and her dogs were dedicated SARs workers. One of her dogs she'd raised from a pup, and another she'd adopted after a coworker had died. Both animals had saved countless lives. Yet it extracted a heavy toll, and rest and recuperation were necessary on a regular basis.

At Stefan's nod, Trevor grinned. "Understandable. The dogs are family."

The dogs and Kali's husband, Grant, were part of Stefan's extended family, and that they'd offered their rental house as a refuge, while Trevor got the paperwork locked down in the courts, was invaluable. Still, Trevor had pets too. If he wasn't there, then he had to get someone else to look after them. But he had friends who would help out, without question. He added that task to his list.

"Kali?" Hannah asked. "Who is that?"

"Another friend," Trevor answered. He pushed her wheelchair to the side of the bed. "The doctor will be here shortly. I have clothing for you that I will retrieve from the car. When the doc's done, and you're ready, we'll be leaving the hospital."

"Right, to stay overnight with Maddy."

Her tone was dry. She was not fighting his plans, but she wasn't sure exactly what they entailed. He couldn't blame her. She had no idea who these people were, but she'd placed her trust in him. And had no idea how lucky she was for having done so.

She'd find out. And have her eyes opened at the same time.

Don't push her, Stefan spoke in Trevor's head. *A lot is going on inside her head that she needs to deal with. It must happen in its own time.*

I remember, Trevor insisted. *Still, she doesn't understand the trouble she's in yet.*

On some level she already does, Stefan confirmed, *but a lot of blocks are in there. Releasing too many, too fast, will cause her brain damage.*

Right. Slow and steady.

You took on a lot, Stefan noted. *Are you sure you're okay with this?*

Trevor shot him a hooded gaze. *It's a little too late for second thoughts. She's hurt and in deep trouble. We're in a unique position to help. How can any of us not help?*

On that note, the doctor walked in, and the men stepped out.

CHAPTER 9

THE DOCTOR STOOD in front of her bed, checking his tablet. While he did his thing, Hannah's thoughts returned to Stefan and Trevor. What had she missed? There'd been something in the air, like a static buzzing going on around her head. She studied the almost empty room. Now that they'd left, the buzzing had stopped. So damn weird. Then nothing was normal about her world anymore. She was married, for God's sake. And to a stranger. How the hell had she gone from waking up on the highway, lost and alone and injured, to being married the next day? Talk about not being able to assess threats.

If she believed in fate, she would have declared that fate had taken a hand in her future. She'd woken up lost and alone and injured many times before, and fate had never stepped in to help. What had changed this time?

A part of her worried that she'd end up locked in a prison cell of some madman's basement. Except then she encountered this sense of well-being whenever she was with Trevor. And that made her question her own mental state even more.

After seeing specialist after specialist throughout her life, she wondered at the cosmic joke that had her now married to a psychologist. Or was he a psychiatrist? Was there a difference?

Not right now. He was her husband. Her life was entwined with his—for truly better or for worse.

The doctor smiled at her. "I'm a little late today. Sorry about that. Let's take a look."

She murmured a polite response, while he poked and prodded her head. It had been fine a little while ago, but was back to booming. Not because of him, more likely because of Will. That the man had left didn't mean he was gone. He'd been a threat held over her since forever.

She could only hope *her* lawyer had put things into place that would give them an edge.

Then again her father's lawyers were hardly honorable players.

And, if there was something slightly less honorable her father's lawyers could do to nail down the job, they'd do it.

"Your head will be sore for a while. Be sure to fill the prescription I gave your husband. No need to suffer while your body heals. And go see your doctor in a week or so to take out the stitches." He moved around to face her and flashed his little light into her eyes. The bloody one closed immediately. "Don't leave it too long or the stitches will grow over. The eye is healing but slowly and will be sensitive to light for a while. Minimize the computer work and generally just listen to your body. It will always tell you when you're doing too much."

Then he had her lie down, so he could check her ribs and collarbone. That latter surprised her. She hadn't even realized that part of her body had been injured, until he checked it. Then shards of pain had her gasping.

"That'll take a little longer than the head wound. No heavy lifting. Bed rest is what you need right now."

She stared up at him mutely. No way in hell she could

run off on her own with these injuries. What would she have done without Trevor's help?

He removed the bandage on her leg and muttered to himself. "This is not looking very good. I do wish you were staying here longer."

"We're heading to Maddy's Floor," Trevor stated from the doorway.

The doctor looked up in pleased surprise. "Really? In that case …" He carefully rebandaged the leg for traveling. "I expect she'll be as right as rain tomorrow. Lucky woman."

He patted her on her shoulder, made a few notes on his tablet, and headed to the doorway. "Take care of yourself. As you married this guy, and we work together, I'm sure I'll see you around."

And, with that, he slapped Trevor on the shoulder and walked out.

Trevor plunked a plastic bag on her bed. As she opened it and pulled out the jeans, T-shirts, and other clothes, she looked mystified.

"These aren't mine." She held up the last item, a warm cardigan in rusty brown colors. "But they are beautiful."

"They are yours." Trevor grinned at her look of surprise. "Celina shopped for you. A wedding gift from her and Stefan. I'm hoping everything fits."

"Wow, that's so nice of them. She has great taste." She looked at the pile, then down at her hospital gown. "I guess the clothes I came with are not salvageable?"

"They are already in the garbage," Trevor assured her. "Never to be worn again."

She shooed him away. "We might be married, but I'll be getting dressed on my own."

"Except for one thing," he noted gently. "You're injured.”

She frowned and assessed her injuries mentally. “I’ll try first. If I need help, then I’ll call you.”

HE HAD NO plans to leave. But she was nervous of him, and this wasn’t the time to push it.

“Fine. However, I’ll stay here, just in case.” He pivoted, turned his back on her and waited. He heard the bedding being thrown back and the tiny *smack*, as she slid off the bed and her feet hit the floor. The clothing rustled.

He waited. And waited. Then frowned. He couldn’t hear much. “How do they fit?”

“Take a look.”

He turned.

She held out her arms. “Well?”

Except for the sheen to her forehead from the effort of getting dressed on her own, she looked fantastic. And then there was the dried blood in her hair.

“The clothes look great,” he admitted. She was slight and relatively average in height, yet the clothes were a perfect fit and made her look special. Then he’d known they would. He’d given Celina the sizes. She’d been an injured waif to him so far, but, in those clothes, she was all woman.

He grinned, as her bare toes peeked out from under the edge of the jeans.

“Sorry, a pair of something is in there, but they didn’t look like shoes to me. More a slipper.”

He walked to the bags and, sure enough, found what he was looking for in the second bag tucked inside the bigger one. He stared at them doubtfully. “I don’t know what they are meant to be either, but you can’t walk in them outside.”

She laughed and snatched one out of his hand, and using his arm for support, she slipped it on. Stretching her leg forward, she admired the ballet flat on her foot. Then put on the second one. "They are perfect," she cried out happily.

"They offer less protection than socks," he argued. "At least socks cover your foot."

"They are how they are meant to be." She reached up to brush her hair back and winced. "Right. Didn't get a shower, so still very grungy despite a prettier exterior."

"I don't know if that will be allowed right away on Maddy's Floor," he noted. "But let's get you away from here and find out." He motioned to the wheelchair that already held her bag of personal belongings. "Hop in."

"I can walk," she protested.

"You might be able to, but the more you can stay off those legs, the better and the faster you will heal." Into the face of his logic, she took a seat, and he wheeled her out into the hallway. There he stopped and assessed the people, the level of danger.

"Problems?" she asked in a hushed whisper.

"No." At least not at the moment. He turned left and took her down to the parking level below.

THEY COULD RUN, but they couldn't hide. Not from him. Not like this. If he could figure out where she went on those times she did manage to get away from him, he'd have total control. As it was, she had some way to escape him, and it pissed him off every damn time.

It went toward why he kept her around. She was a challenge. As he poured more into her, learning who and why, what made her tick, investing in her system, tying her to him, she developed—bigger and stronger—as she found ways to defeat him. That he loved. Most games, once you beat them, they were done. Boring as hell afterward. But not in her case. She just got stronger, more devious. And it challenged him to do the same.

Adding to the fun was she had no idea.

He crept into her dreams and turned them to nightmares. He woke her up in a cold sweat over nothing. He made her panic from the voices in her head, and he laughed.

For all that, she was so malleable; yet she had this one part of her that she held inviolate. And he hated it. He wanted into that part of her. It was the mechanism that continued to defy him. He wanted to know how she was evading him. He had to know. It was the only trick she was doing on her own that he had no idea about. The scientist doing research inside of him needed to know. The man inside demanded to know.

The owner of all control over her was *desperate* to know.

He couldn't help the feeling that there was more to this than he knew, and he suspected there always had been. He hated to be made a fool. And she'd done so time and time again.

How? What? Why?

He needed to understand her tricks.

So he could put a stop to them permanently.

It was time. But not until he knew how she'd been evading his strongest efforts—up until now. Then he'd kill her. And find someone else to play with.

STEFAN STARED AT the phone in his hand. It had been ringing all morning. He'd just gotten off a call with Trevor, letting him know they were on the move, when Dr. Maddy's partner called. "Drew, could you repeat that, please?"

"I said we received an anonymous tip that Trevor was involved in a murder, had a hand in killing a teacher eight years ago."

"Was the case ever solved?"

"It was never closed. It ended up in cold cases. Hence, the file landed on my desk."

"Interesting timing." Stefan shook his head at the ploys of men. Mr. Goodman required having an eye kept on him. How much trouble was he planning to cause Trevor over this marriage to Hannah? Stefan suspected it was just the beginning.

Drew hesitated. "You're sure about Trevor? That he's a good guy?" He cleared his throat. "I've met him but don't *know* him."

Without hesitation, Stefan said, "Yes. He's never killed anyone. Also … something very important is there." Stefan watched as the energy in front of him shifted and changed. "It leads down a convoluted path, but, I think, at the end, there is evidence of wrongdoing—but not at Trevor's hands."

"Great. I like a good puzzle. If the teacher was murdered, then justice will prevail."

Drew hung up, leaving Stefan to deal with the painful yet faded image of a teacher's badly burned body in the trailer, from the blast that had dropped the main science room and the auxiliary trailer at the school.

CHAPTER 10

HANNAH UNDERSTOOD TAKING precautions, but Trevor was being paranoid. Maybe he'd just realized how serious her father was and that Trevor couldn't take *enough* security measures.

At the parking lot, he led her to a small silver car and assisted her into the front seat. She waited for him to make his way around to the driver's side and get in.

His gaze never stopped searching the area.

When he got inside, she asked, "You're expecting an ambush, aren't you?"

"I'm expecting anything and everything," he noted, then added, "especially the unusual."

"My father metes out punishment that is pretty mainstream. Knifings, beatings, a gunshot or two, but mostly he likes to crush people by taking away their homes, businesses, and savings accounts—you know? Their livelihoods. In a perfect world he'd like to see those who defy him injured and homeless."

He turned to look at her. "Your dad sounds like a piece of work."

"He is," she agreed coolly. "I've been fighting with him since forever. But I believe he loves me—in his strange way. Will, on the other hand? I'm not sure he knows what that word means."

Her self-confidence had taken a huge beating at Will's hand. Yet she didn't think he'd be waiting outside on the street for them. Unless it was to follow them. No, he would be more subtle. He'd assign someone else to follow them, but he'd come *personally* in the middle of the night to terrorize her. Maximum pain. That was something Will would enjoy.

"You're really scared of Will, aren't you?"

"Yes," she admitted. "With good reason."

"Has Will ever physically hurt you?"

She frowned, thinking about it. "No, it was always an implied threat. Something hanging over me that I'd better behave or else." She hated that man with a passion.

"There must have been something that made you believe in his brand of fear originally."

There was. But telling it would hurt. She stared out the window. "When he first arrived, he was determined to establish order. One night my dog escaped. I was grounded by my father and not allowed out, but I went out after my dog. Will killed my dog as a punishment," she whispered. "I got the message."

Trevor's breath gushed out. "I'm so sorry. That had to be tough."

"It was," she whispered, tears trying to form in the corners of her eyes. "It was a long time ago."

"Maybe, but that's not a memory you forget."

She glanced around, looking for anything else to talk about. The pain of losing Tidbit was just too much to bear, even now. And then she watched as they whipped down the city streets in an area she didn't recognize. "I didn't even realize we were out of the hospital lot and on the main roads," she exclaimed.

"No." He grinned. "You were thinking of other things."

"You did that on purpose," she accused but with a smile. "I was worried they'd be lying in wait," she admitted, "even though I'd have bet on them not doing something so obvious, but one can never tell."

"I didn't want to take a chance, so came out the service entrance." He turned to look at her. "We're only about ten minutes away from our destination."

She settled back. Before she realized it, Trevor turned into a large parking lot. She leaned forward to study the huge building adjacent to the lot. "What is this place?"

"It's a multipurpose building, that's for sure," he replied, with a laugh. "It's a long-term care home with a hospital attached, and this is where Dr. Maddy operates from." He turned off the engine and pointed to the top of the building. "Maddy's Floor is at the top."

"And why are we going to see her?"

He exited the car and came around to her side, where he helped her out. As she stood here and studied the multiple balconies all along the top floor, he locked the doors, pocketed the keys, and, in a surprise move, swung her up into his arms.

She squealed in surprise and clutched at his shoulders. "I can walk."

"No, you can't. Hospital rules. Wheelchairs are available, but they aren't right here in the parking lot, and I never thought to arrange one ahead of time. Besides, you are a lightweight, and it's not far."

By the time he finished speaking, they were already at the front door. Both double doors opened up to … chaos. She had no other word for it. Sure it was a hospital and an old folks' home, but people were going in all directions.

He didn't put her down. Instead he walked straight ahead to a bank of elevators, then on to an elevator farther back. There he set her on her feet and pushed the Call button.

It opened immediately.

With his help, she hobbled in the small space. "What's this one? A private elevator?"

He grinned. "One for VIPs."

She snorted. "So not me."

After moving up several floors, the elevator came to a stop. The door opened then, and it was as if she had stepped into a completely different world. Gone was the hustle and bustle of downstairs. No one raced in front of her or stood speaking in large groups to the side. This was mellow, a sweet ambiance of peace. She loved it.

"Now this is what the downstairs should be."

"Welcome to Maddy's Floor." A nurse, whose name tag read Glenda, smiled at her. "Come this way. Your bed is ready, and Dr. Maddy will see you shortly."

In pleased surprise, Hannah tried to fall in behind Glenda, but Trevor picked her up again and proceeded to carry her down the hallway. She saw no closed doors, just beautiful small sitting rooms with beds and massive windows. Small seating areas for visitors, each with small balconies, dotted the hallway. It was so nonhospital-like that she was shocked. It was like a five-star resort hotel, and she loved everything about it.

Glenda led them into a small room to the right, which was a similar layout to the rest of the other welcoming spaces she'd seen on the floor. Trevor laid her down on the bed.

"Now relax. We're here overnight."

She stared up at him and smiled in pleasure. She motioned to the huge window. "Wow, it is beautiful here."

"It is, and the turnover on some of these rooms is unbelievable," he admitted.

"How sad." She felt his sharp look and returned it with one of her own. "What did I say?" she asked in confusion.

"Why is it sad?"

"Well, it's a nursing home, so obviously a high turnover means the patients died."

Glenda smiled at her but stayed quiet, as she brought over a tall glass of water and set a pitcher of water beside her. All glass. The bedding beneath Hannah was beautiful cotton. She didn't know what to say or think. *What kind of place was this?*

"It's special," Trevor replied, as if reading her mind.

She frowned and nodded but stayed quiet.

Glenda left silently, and Trevor made himself comfortable on a leather recliner beside the bed. Hannah didn't have anything so nice in her own place. She frowned. *Her own place?* That's the first time that thought came to her. But she knew she had a place—somewhere. "I wonder if my plants are all right."

Trevor glanced at her. "I never thought to ask if there was anyone we should have notified about your accident. I figured the hospital and then your father would have taken care of that."

She winced. "I need a phone, so I can make some calls."

He held out his phone. "Use mine for the moment."

She slowly dialed the store to talk to Tasha. It rang and rang. She frowned. "What time is it?"

"Almost four."

She swallowed and dialed again. Still no answer. Perturbed, she handed the phone back. "No one is there," she stated softly.

"Where?"

"At Some Things Are Forever."

"A store?"

"A florist shop. The manager is a friend, and I need to tell her what happened. She'll worry."

"I can swing by later, but she's likely to be closed."

Hannah shook her head. "The shop closes at six."

"Then you can call again in a few moments."

"Unlikely," said the woman with a melodic voice from the doorway. "And I'm not a big fan of cell phones or anything electronic while healing is going on anyway." A tall woman in a bright blue dress and stilettos—making her well over six feet tall—walked in. "Hello, Trevor."

He bounced to his feet and hugged the woman gently. "You are looking gorgeous as always, Dr. Maddy."

"Liar." She laughed. "But the healing is a nice side bene-fit of my profession."

He grinned at the woman as they exchanged a knowing look. Hannah once again had the feeling she'd missed something.

And then the air filled with static again. "Stop it," she said crossly. "You're doing the same thing you did with Stefan. It's really irritating."

Both of them turned to look at her. "What thing?" the woman asked. "How nice that you got to see Stefan. I'm Dr. Maddy, by the way."

Dr. Maddy spoke, adding the last bit almost absent-mindedly, as if it were the most natural thing in the world. And, for her, it seemed to be. But Hannah was used to doctors who were old and gray and wore arrogance as their coat. Dr. Maddy likely wore sunshine as hers.

It was such a unique experience to see this that Hannah almost forgot Dr. Maddy's question, but, as both people still stared at her, she shrugged. "It's like you're communicating in such a way that no one else can hear you. Hell, I wouldn't have heard you either, except for the static in the air."

"Static?" Trevor asked. "Interesting."

"Very." Dr. Maddy smiled at him. "Now go away. I want to spend a few moments with your new wife."

Trevor hesitated, but, although couched in nice terms, it was obvious to Hannah this wasn't a request but an order. "I'll be fine," Hannah told him. "Go."

He nodded and, in a move that seemed to surprise him as much as it surprised her, he leaned over, gave her a hard kiss, and walked to the doorway, whistling.

"You appear to have made him very happy," Dr. Maddy noted gently. "Interesting, considering you two just met."

Relieved the woman knew the details, and Hannah wouldn't be required to playact at this stage, she nodded. "He's a nice man."

"He is, indeed." Dr. Maddy walked closer. "Let's see what we've got here."

She checked Hannah over. Only she never once removed the bandages and only gave the bruising on her ribs and collarbone a cursory look. The head, however, was a different story. "I'm not too happy about the head, but the rest we can fix up pretty easily. I need to do a full diagnostic on your physical body," Dr. Maddy muttered more to herself—and Glenda, who'd appeared as quietly as she had left.

Maddy turned to Glenda. "She had X-rays done at the prior hospital. See if we can get our hands on those, will you?" And Glenda slipped out again.

Dr. Maddy stepped back and frowned at Hannah. "I

want you to lie here quietly and close your eyes. I need to run some scans. You need to lie perfectly still while they are going on, understand?"

Hannah nodded. She wasn't sure what to think about an exam that didn't involve looking at wounds and that went through clothing in rooms that resembled high-end homes.

But she wouldn't argue. This was much easier on her soul.

She closed her eyes and waited. She heard sounds of footsteps, but, following Dr. Maddy's instructions, Hannah lay quietly, with her eyes closed. No hardship really. And in no way did she feel threatened. That might be partly due to the fact she was fully clothed with her shoes on. As if escape were possible and just right around the corner. And knowing that, she didn't feel the need to run. She could just relax.

Then she began to feel the heat.

It started at her toes and ran lightly up her foot and ankles to shine all over her calves and knees. This must be the scan Dr. Maddy had mentioned.

Letting it do its thing, Hannah relaxed again. When the scan reached her leg she sighed, loving the heat on the injury. It felt so much better already. If she'd known heat would make it feel like that, she'd have asked for a warm blanket at the last hospital. The scan carried on but left the injury warm and tingly. Next it moved across her pelvis and slowly worked up her belly. It moved at a fraction of the speed it had before. Then moved up to her ribs. Again the heat intensified.

In response, her ribs pulsed with healing. Lord, she would have come here immediately if she'd known it was an option. The scan continued up her chest, leaving her ribs to ooze with a sense of well-being. The collarbone received the same attention that the ribs and legs had, and, oddly enough, so did her arms. She must have injured them more than she'd realized. The heat pulled right to the end of her fingertips, then slowly moved back up her neck. She smiled as her face was bathed in that same warm glow. The heat rose and stopped right above her eyebrows.

She whimpered in distress. She wanted that heat at the top of her head. She needed it there. That's where the worst of her injuries were. Surely the scan could pick that up. Dr. Maddy would have requested it.

Hannah sensed the scan trying to go higher. Maybe there was an equipment malfunction. She waited in anticipation, but the heat slowly slid down her spine. The sensation was so surprising and unexpected that she arched her back to accommodate the pulsing efforts.

She groaned when it reached her lower back, then zinged all the way back up to the top of her head and … stopped. Right at the base of her neck. Then inched higher to just above her ears. But no farther.

As if it couldn't go into that area.

She was so frustrated that her entire head was being left out of this incredible experience, and yet it was the one part of her that needed it the most.

As the heat started to fade, she cried out, "No, please don't stop."

And it hesitated.

She tried again. "Please scan my head. It feels so good, and my head hurts so much."

The heat came again, this time in a light warm touch over the top of her head and slowly worked downward to her ears. She smiled and tilted her head into the scan. "Thank you," she whispered.

The soothing warmth jerked to a stop, then continued only to stop yet again, as if it weren't working properly. Didn't that figure? She needed it. Like, she *needed* it. She mentally reached out to plead for it to work. And it worked again for a little while, then stopped. Damn it.

She did it again, and, sure enough, it worked again. Well, if it would work that way, then she wanted it to work properly, and she demanded that it scan her full head, like it had done her body.

Feeling stupid but, what the hell, she reached for the scan in her thoughts.

And the heat of the scanner slammed down on her head and covered all the areas that had been missed before.

She laughed and then cried out as the heat turned up to impossible temperatures and the joy became pain. A scream ripped out of her throat, a long horrible sound that echoed through the room, and she collapsed down onto the bed, limp.

She might even have lost consciousness. ... Finally the pain drifted away enough for her to move.

Lying here, trembling, she opened her eyes to see a very worried man standing here, staring down at her.

And marching into the room, holding a hand to her head, a tall elegant woman.

"Hannah, how are you feeling?" the man asked, reaching out for her hand.

She stared at him and swallowed hard, her gaze darting from one to the other.

"Hannah," the woman said. "How do you feel?"

Feeling as if she'd been here a dozen times before, with the strong sense of déjà vu rocking her soul, she replied in a small voice, "I feel fine now, but ..." She took a deep breath and asked, "Where am I? Who are you? And what's wrong with me?"

TALK ABOUT ROCKING his soul. Trevor sat down on her bed, stunned by her words. He studied the look in her eyes, looking for some sign of recognition of him and Dr. Maddy. Nothing.

He turned to face Dr. Maddy. She didn't look worried. Instead she looked fascinated. And that made *him* all the more worried.

"You're Hannah," Dr. Maddy stated calmly. "I'm Dr. Maddy. You're in my clinic. And this man is Trevor. He's your husband."

Hannah blinked at the beginning of Maddy's words, and her eyes widened to shocked orbs as they stared at Trevor. "How can that be?"

"Why can't it be?" he asked. "You obviously don't remember much about today then." And oddly he was hurt by that. Stupid really. Why should he care that she didn't remember the wedding? Hell, it wasn't much to remember. Except the panic and the fear of possibly being caught.

"No, I don't. But … I'm already married." She frowned. "At least I think I am. Right now I can't seem to think straight."

Trevor wasn't sure what to say. He had done his due diligence prior to tying the knot, and he had found no records of her having married anyone else in the US. But that didn't rule out marriages in other countries. Only that he couldn't find any record of any.

He sensed Dr. Maddy's curiosity and her need to ask questions, so he settled back slightly, giving her the opportunity. "Dr. Maddy needs to check you over, but, first, can you tell me the name of your husband?" he asked curiously. He'd never seen a case like this one. Not sure Dr. Maddy had either. He should call Stefan. He'd love this twist.

She played with the edge of her sweater. When she took so long, he wasn't sure she remembered the name. Then finally she raised her gaze, and something inside that direct look unnerved him. "I think his name is Will."

Of all the names … that she'd say that one …revealed much about her mental state. With a nod at Maddy, he stood and walked out to the hallway. He didn't know what to think. But he'd call Stefan and see what his take was.

"She said Will was her husband," Stefan repeated slowly a few moments later. His surprise was easily discernible through the phone. "Did she sound sure of it?"

"No, she didn't. It's like she was grasping for a name that sounded right, and that's what she came up with."

"Fascinating."

Typical of Stefan and Dr. Maddy. Was there anything in the paranormal sensory world that didn't make them sit up and take notice?

"And Dr. Maddy is checking her over now?"

"Yes." Trevor felt a tap on his shoulder. He turned to find Dr. Maddy motioning for him to move farther down the hallway and away from Hannah's bedroom.

"Let's go to my office," she murmured.

She led the way. In her office, Dr. Maddy sat down behind her desk and closed her eyes, as if to marshal her thoughts. Stefan was still on the phone. Trevor laid his phone on Maddy's desk. "Stefan, you're on Speaker, and we're now in Dr. Maddy's office."

"Good, Maddy. How did it go?"

"I'm not really sure," she admitted. "I did a scan from toes to her head and ran into a complete block. Yet it felt like there was an absence of energy from the space above her ears, right around and over the top. Imagine a bowl placed on her head that came down to her ears. Then imagine all that under the bowl as being missing."

"Missing," Trevor exclaimed. "How is that possible?"

"It isn't of course," Stefan stated in a thoughtful voice, "but for some reason it's how it appears at this point. And likely how she has been functioning for a long time."

"Except she was unsure of her surroundings and didn't recognize either of us when she came out of the scan. I don't believe she lost consciousness, although at the end it was pretty heavy. If she had, it was only for seconds."

"But that might have been enough."

"Obviously it was." Dr. Maddy fell silent.

Trevor, not sure what they were implying, asked, "Long enough to do what?"

"We have to determine if she has a multiple personality disorder," Stefan explained. "Which, of course, is not what the traditional world would think it is."

"No, of course not. And not something I suspected either, until Stefan brought it up," Dr. Maddy admitted.

"Why not just memory loss?" Trevor needed it to be memory loss. Multiple personalities was a touchy subject legally, and, given what he'd seen so far, her father might have had full grounds to believe she wasn't capable of handling her own affairs. Trevor was at a loss. As if he'd had a straight path forward, knew what he had to do, and, indeed, already had much of it in place to go forward, only to have the rug pulled out from under him.

"I'm not sure it is yet," Maddy replied in a low voice, her

face pensive.

"What are your thoughts?" Stefan asked her.

"I'm wondering about autosuggestion."

"Is that possible across such a distance?" Stefan asked, then answered himself. "Of course it is. If there is one thing we know to *not* do is to curtail the abilities by time and distance. We need more information."

"I have something I can look into," Trevor noted. "She mentioned she has a friend who works at a florist shop. I'll go speak to her." He glanced at his watch. "I might be able to catch her now before she leaves work for the day."

"I'm on my way to you," Stefan stated. "I need to speak to you before you leave."

"You two do that," Dr. Maddy agreed. "At the moment, Trevor, your presence will disturb her more than reassure her." Dr. Maddy leaned back. "Stefan, her head was cold. As in icy cold. I approached from several different angles and couldn't get in. Nor could I cover it completely. But more than that, she was getting angry that I couldn't get all of her head scanned, as, of course, she felt so much better after the heat hit the wounds with its healing energy. She reached for my energy and tried to pull it down to her head. As in *really* wanting to heal."

"That's a very good sign," Stefan exclaimed in surprise.

"It is," Dr. Maddy began slowly, "but I have to tell you that I let the energy lower a little more, and she reached up and snatched a hold of my healing energy and dragged it down to her head."

She sighed. "That's when the overwhelming pain hit. She was fighting what was going on inside, but the thing is, she was strong enough to fight off my safeguards and to pull me into the event. She is really strong. Naturally, psychically strong. And she was completely unaware of what she was doing."

"*Hmm,*" Stefan replied. "Maybe she was—but maybe she wasn't the one who was doing it."

STEFAN ARRIVED AT the hospital in ten minutes. He wanted to speak to Trevor face-to-face about Drew's call. Stefan found Trevor still sitting beside Hannah.

"Trevor, we need to talk." Stefan walked forward, studying Hannah's sleeping face. The energy drain on her system was one thing, the physical healing another altogether. He motioned to the hallway. "Let's move out, so we don't disturb her."

In the hallway Stefan walked to the small visiting area and the outside patio. They shouldn't be overheard here.

Trevor walked over to Stefan. "What's the matter?"

Stefan explained about Drew's phone call. As he watched the younger man's face whiten in shock, he wondered how much more dirt they would find on everyone involved.

"Wow. I wonder if that will ever die." Trevor rubbed his temples. "I guess I should have seen that coming. Just haven't had time to think straight. Everything has happened so fast." He laughed, although there was an edge to it. "My history is brought up every time I hit a new high-profile case."

"Just as it is now." Stefan didn't need to study his friend's aura to understand the regret and the anger pulsing at the edges.

Trevor nodded, his gaze far off. "I presume Mr. Goodman is trying to rattle my cage. A warning. Have me placed under suspicion."

"He's the most likely suspect, but it's never as clear as we'd like it to be, so don't presume anything," Stefan warned.

"No, I won't. I've been here before." Trevor shook his head. "Many times actually. It gets easier."

Stefan nodded. "Yes, but there's no easy answer as to how to handle those who try to harm you."

"I prefer a gunfight to this endless stream of innuendos and lies. I like a fight where I can see the enemy."

"Yet most fights are done below the surface. When it involves psychics, it involves even more that isn't visible to the eye."

Startled, Trevor asked, "Do you think Goodman is a man of power?"

"Oh, definitely." Stefan snorted. "Most businessmen who make money like he does are men of power. But, like many, I suspect he just thinks he has killer business instincts instead. However, ... maybe it comes from a close associate."

"*Hmm.*" Trevor turned to study the direction of the bedroom where Hannah lay. "We need to leave here soon. I was going to use Kali's house but wonder now if that's too close. As in maybe it's a good time to go visit my brother in Maine," he joked. "But it would be foolish to do that. We need to stay where we can keep an eye on the enemy."

"I think Kali's house is a good plan," Stefan noted comfortably. "Besides, Grant's office is ready to step in and help, if need be."

"Are we heading into FBI jurisdiction at this point?"

"We'll have to wait for more information to come to light first." Stefan felt the headache coming on. It promised to be a doozy. "You should know that I saw a vision while speaking with Drew. It showed me an image of your teacher's body." Stefan paused. This is where it got dicey. "The message in that image clearly told me that your teacher had been murdered."

"What?" Trevor froze in front of him.

In spite of himself, Stefan studied the energy as it flowed out and around Trevor. Confusion. Shock. Disbelief. Anger. And maybe … a bit of knowledge.

Interesting. Trevor hadn't killed his teacher but that didn't mean he wasn't aware of someone who might have. Or had a suspicion that he had stomped down to never see the light of day again. Except secrets always came to the surface. And often at the worst possible times.

"Tell me."

Trevor didn't pretend to misunderstand.

"There were seven of us originally but five by the end. We were all lost and alone and banded together to survive the school. We were in the alternate school, all dropouts. All needing education but shunning it. We were a mess. Most of us were in the foster care system. Most of us needed a good smacking to set us on our rights, but so many of us had already been given them—too hard, too often, and too many. That being the main reason we ended up on that path in the first place."

He reached up and ran a hand through his hair. "My father was abusive. I ran away several times, until the state put me in foster care, and that was almost worse, as I could relax but couldn't rest. I was always looking for the next place to go. Another home to live in that was safer. I went through several. Ended up at this school and finally found a group of friends who were in the same position I was. Either foster care or desperately unhappy at home. It made no difference. We were discontents. Unable to adjust to the circumstances around us." He stopped, his face showing the strain of accessing the memories.

Stefan waited, as Trevor marshaled his thoughts.

"I turned around after Mr. Stingard's death," Trevor stated in a stronger voice. "He was a good man. A great teacher. I really loved his classes. Had planned to go into chemistry, after catching some of his passion."

"His death was never solved?"

"It was assumed accidental but couldn't be proven as such and became one of a thousand cold cases. At the time, we foster kids had discussed it as being murder. But there was no proof. We kicked around the idea and blamed a dozen people, but we never had any evidence. We were just trying to be big shots."

"Suspicions?"

"Oh, many." Trevor sighed. "If it *was* murder, most of us knew it would have been one of us."

Stefan's eyebrows shot up at that. "Now that you know it was murder, who would you say was the most likely to have done it?"

"It could have been any of them." He raised both hands in frustration. "You have to remember that they—we—were all angry, cocky young men." He shook his head. "So many years where we had planned horrible accidents for many people as a way to vent our anger. It was a game to us. It wasn't just us but everyone at the time. *Wish your enemy dead.* It was part of what we did. Did any of them actually kill anyone? Possibly, but I don't think so."

Trevor groaned. "I felt guilty as hell after Mr. Stingard's death." He stressed the last word. "I hadn't had anything to do with it, but we'd been so angry that day. Over what? He'd pulled a surprise quiz on us, and the anger just blew up.

When he died, and the possibility that he'd been murdered came up, I felt so damn guilty because of how we'd talked about he should be shot for giving us the quiz. Of course being shot was the easiest death we all had imagined for him."

"Which, as you now know, absolutely does add to the potential for this to happen," Stefan murmured. He saw it the world over. People didn't realize, didn't want to realize, the power of their thoughts, and how much more power giving voice to those thoughts helped to create them. "Did the police question all of you back then?"

"Yes, and we were all cleared at the time." He walked to the balcony railing to stare at the gardens below. "I straightened up, but I lost track of all the others."

"Exactly. Hence the guilt."

"I switched schools after the accident and became the best student. A new page in my life—and that part I am proud of. But it meant walking away from them too. Until then, I was a waste. A wastrel. I had a lot to make up for."

"And you have. Don't be so hard on yourself."

Trevor shook his head. "If I contributed at all to Mr. Stingard's death, then I have so much more to make up for."

CHAPTER 11

HANNAH STUDIED THE man at her side covertly. Her husband? How could she have forgotten such a person? This person was dark, dangerous. Sexy. Not her normal partner choice. They were … She frowned, unable to access any images of her other boyfriends or husbands. If she had one, who knew? She might have a half dozen.

That comfortable blankness to her mind scared her. Surely she shouldn't be comfortable with that, should she? Wasn't her mind supposed to be full of memories and conversations, images of friends and family? Stuff …

"I have to leave now," her husband said. He leaned over and kissed her forehead. "Stop worrying," he whispered. "It will be fine." And, with that, he left the room.

How could it be fine? She didn't remember him.

Hell, she couldn't remember her name.

Yet some things were there. The word *amnesia* for instance. She knew what it meant. She frowned as she sat up, opened up the blanket, and threw it across her legs. Warmer now, she stared around the cozy beautiful room and wondered where she was.

"How are you feeling now?" asked Dr. Maddy.

Thankfully she'd introduced herself again but more than that this doctor's energy was soft, calm. She was serene inside. Hannah was envious. Her insides were twisted and confused.

"I'm okay," she replied quietly. "As in, I am feeling no physical pain but emotionally ..."

"You're a mess, got it." Dr. Maddy smiled cheerfully. "Can you tell me what you experienced during that scan?"

"I don't know what scan you're talking about," Hannah replied carefully. "So, no."

"Okay, well, in that case, how about I do a quick repeat."

Hannah studied the woman in front of her. She had no reason to refuse. And maybe it would help clarify whatever was going on. She nodded.

"Great." Dr. Maddy pulled up a chair and sat down. "It's important to remember to relax and to keep your eyes closed."

Obediently Hannah lay down again and closed her eyes. She had no idea what kind of scan this was, but she was willing. She took a breath and waited. Then the warm, caring heat started at her toes. "I remember this," she cried out.

"Good. Then relax, as you know this feels good."

It felt better than good. Soothing heat soaked into her bones and made her moan in joy. The warmth ran up her feet and over her ankles, up her legs and across her belly. She wanted to cry out to slow down the movement, that she needed more time, but it was already up to her shoulders and neck. She arched her back in a sinuous movement as the energy climbed up her spine. It never stopped but eased into her scalp and into her skull. Her head hadn't been aching, but, with the advancing heat, it started to pound. She knew the scan would feel better though, so she gritted her teeth. Only the headache got worse, and the heat seemed to sear not comfort.

She twisted uneasily, a whimper escaping. "It hurts," she cried out softly.

"Can you tell me what you are experiencing?"

"Heat and a massive headache."

"Where is the headache?"

Hannah lifted her hand to the back of her head. "It's like a great pressure building at the top of my head. As if the whole top needs to blow off for it to go away."

She gasped as a particularly loud *boom* crashed inside.

Instantly the heat eased back. And the headache eased with it. She sighed happily. "That's much better."

The scan then came to the front of her head and wrapped around her forehead. "That feels wonderful. I—"

A scream tore from her mouth, as sharp pains ripped through her head—and she blacked out.

DR. MADDY STOOD up and approached the bed. She'd gotten the message. "Go anywhere near the head and be attacked. Nice," she muttered.

"Do we know why?" Glenda asked from the doorway, her gaze on the unconscious woman.

"No, not yet. But I'm wondering about several options."

Unfortunately they had a problem of bed space here too. She had to trust it would all work out.

"I wanted to tell you that we have a delay with one of the patients arriving tomorrow. So if we need to keep Hannah another day, that window is there."

"Excellent. I'm afraid we might need it." Dr. Maddy reached out a hand and gently touched Hannah's head. Again the aura so close to the skull was giving the impression that Hannah was close to death, but Maddy could see for herself how strong and vibrant this young woman was.

A very interesting phenomenon. The part that really intrigued Maddy was the complete absence of anything in the brain. It wasn't possible, and, given the pain that Hannah experienced as soon as the scan hit the head, it was more likely that someone had set a blockage.

Why? What could anyone possibly want to block in Hannah's mind? If Dr. Maddy couldn't get inside the defense system easily, then it would be very hard to tell why and what.

Just then Hannah shifted uneasily. Maddy reached out a hand and soothed the energy along her body, adding a complex layer of healing energy to Hannah's thin aura. The healing energy was accepted, absorbed immediately, almost as if it were thirsty. And that shouldn't be. Energy was available to anyone and everyone in all amounts. There was no shortage. There was no permission or access key required.

One had only to ask, and it was there. Even if one didn't ask but reached out, the energy was always offered. Hannah had no shortage, so why was her energy so greedily sucking back on the healing energy Maddy had given? She poured more into the same channel, happy to see Hannah absorb it all. So very interesting. As if feeling guilty for having taken so much, the energy pulled back in on itself.

Maddy immediately flooded it with a happy, healthy energy.

Hannah's body sucked it in, like a starving man at a buffet. Maddy wondered how long this gluttony would continue, so she poured more and more into Hannah. Hannah's system kept accepting.

Slowly Maddy reduced the flow to a level she could keep

in place, while she went about her day. In this way the energy could continue to heal but would leave Maddy free to work on other people.

An important part of her work was determining the energy flow to an individual at any particular time. Normally she could see a bleed where the energy was being drained out via other people's hooks. One of the things she didn't understand was that Hannah had no apparent drains. Her energy was self-contained.

That was unusual. People of all walks of life shared energy and had energy drains in every chakra. Energy they were feeding to other people who bothered them or who needed something from them, so they allowed that person to hook in and to take what they needed. Other drains were because of particularly bad events in the past, and, unable to let go, the person fed the memory to keep it alive—regardless of how horrid. Equally, the energy could be directed to remembering a loved one who'd died, as if the person was unable to fully let go of the deceased.

Whatever the reason, Hannah had no obvious hooks.

And that concerned Maddy almost as much as the complete absence of energy in the top of her head. It meant she had no emotional connection to anything in her life. Or in her past. Trevor had shared that Hannah had lost her mother, had fought with her father, had appeared terrified of her father's right-hand man, and, when he'd mentioned people he should contact, only one friend was brought up.

She studied Hannah's heart chakra. And found it empty too.

Hannah was a shell living in the moment. She had no memories of most of her history. Of any time—or anyone.

In terms of living and lifestyle, Hannah was living completely isolated.

What fascinated Maddy was that, as far as she could see, Hannah was doing this to herself.

TREVOR FOUND THE florist shop easily. And he got there a few minutes before closing time. So in theory, he should have been able to catch the manager and explain what happened to Hannah.

Except for one thing.

The building had been reduced to ashes.

And it appeared to have been done so recently. A take-out Chinese food restaurant was next door. Trevor walked in and introduced himself. "Hi, I was looking for someone who used to work next door, but I had no idea it had burned down."

That set them off. Apparently the police had come inside the restaurant several times to check them out. And the owners were still smarting from the suggestion that they might have had something to do with the fire. They explained how the manager had been a young woman and was lonesome. She'd planned to leave and go back East to her family. The previous owners had been helping the new owner out for the first three months, but that came to an end, and the couple hadn't seen the prior owners since. They hadn't seen the new owner for over a week. The manager, however, had been really capable but didn't want to stay.

"Do you have any contact information for her?" Trevor asked, notepad out and pen in hand.

Only the older couple shook their heads. "Not on her, but the previous owners were Delilah and Wilson Hunter."

The woman smiled. "They live only a few blocks from

here. Used to walk to work in the mornings."

"Thank you, I can find them from that." At least he should be able to. He closed his notepad and waved good-bye. Returning to the florist shop, he walked in front of the burned-out shell, then kept going until he walked around the block and came up the back alleyway. This was where they would have received deliveries and likely had parking for staff. Sure enough there was a small parking lot and one of those tiny, almost micro, cars—burned to a crisp. He was surprised to see it still here. Normally something like this would have been hauled away. Then again, the area wasn't terribly busy and the shell in front of him desolate.

He stood at the back door and wondered at the extent of the fire. He'd have to contact the investigating officer and see what, if anything, he could find out. From his perspective it looked like an accident, possibly insurance fraud. Failing business, absentee owner who didn't care, but needed the money back out, and insurance was the best option. It was hard to sell a nonviable business.

He could barely see a license plate on the small car but jotted down the partial that was still visible. And walked back to his car. There he phoned Drew, Dr. Maddy's partner.

"I hear you're married." The snickers came through loud and clear. "Figured you do it like this. Don't tell anyone and have it over and done with, before anyone could protest."

"Speed was a factor this time," Trevor replied, with a grin. "But, if it manages to stick, we'll invite you and Maddy to come for the real ceremony."

"Better make it stick. Maddy says something's between you two."

"Yeah, puzzles and deceit." He explained what he knew

so far.

"Jesus. So she didn't know you when she woke up, and this scary dude is her husband. This is another hocus-pocus case, isn't it?" Drew stated in disgust. "Why can't it ever be easy?"

Trevor laughed. "Nothing is straightforward about this one. And the store is the only connection I have to someone who can confirm her former life."

"I've got it on screen. Business burned down yesterday." He paused, reading. "No leads, no clues. Definitely arson."

"Who is the owner, and how do I locate the manager?"

"Manager is dead, presumed killed in the fire, … as one very crispy critter was found inside. Autopsy is still pending. Whoa, this is a whole new level of bad. And, yes, the owner is none other than your new wife."

CHAPTER 12

HANNAH OPENED HER eyes and stared up at the ceiling. Pure white and yet the opposite of an institution. Relief flooded her psyche. She wasn't back in the private hospital. Or was she? Some of them had been damn fancy. Then they were gilded cages, so the birds wouldn't mind being imprisoned. Like hell. As she studied her surroundings, she rotated her neck and tried to ease the achiness in her body. Although most of her felt great, her head and neck were burning, as if she had a headache and a fever combined.

"Hi."

She rolled her head to see Glenda bringing fresh water.

"Hi," she croaked. "May I have a glass?"

Glenda reached down and helped her to sit up. Then handed her the glass full of ice-cold water. Hannah drank greedily. When she was full up, she sighed happily and tried to speak again. This time her voice sounded normal. "Thank you."

"You're welcome." She replaced the glass, her gaze intent as she studied Hannah. "How do you feel?"

"Better, except my neck. It's on fire." Hannah stretched out on the bed. "I'm also hungry. Any chance of something to eat?"

"Sure. I'll see what I can find." And she walked out.

A few minutes later Dr. Maddy walked back in. Hannah

smiled. "That's quite a scan. I'm not sure exactly what technology you used because I never saw it, but the effects were great. Except for my neck." She reached up to massage her sore neck.

"What's wrong with your neck?" Dr. Maddy asked. She reached out and gently removed Hannah's hands and replaced them with her own. Hannah moaned softly as soothing coolness washed through the heated area. When Dr. Maddy removed her hands a moment later, the heat was gone, and a wonderful soothing calm replaced it.

"You have magical hands," Hannah noted seriously. "That did the trick, whatever that was."

Dr. Maddy smiled. "Good. I'm glad to hear it." She shifted position and asked, "How are your injuries feeling?"

"Right, I forgot about those." She couldn't reach her leg to check, as she still wore jeans, but it felt fine. "I need to shuck off my jeans and take a closer look." She frowned. "It feels not only fine but like it's fully healed." And that couldn't be.

She hopped off the bed, feeling better than she had in days, and removed her pants, then laid back down. Dr. Maddy removed the bandage, and both bent their heads for a closer look. There were stitches, but the wound had completely healed over.

"I need to remove these stitches," Dr. Maddy told her. "Just a minute while I get the scissors."

Hannah didn't say a word as the woman left. She was too stunned. In her mind she couldn't reconcile the evidence before her eyes. She lifted her shirt and struggled to see the bruising at her ribs, then checked her collarbone. It was hard to see, but the lack of pain was obvious. Whatever Dr. Maddy had done, it had been a miracle. Hannah reached up to her head, expecting the same progress, and cried out at the pain.

"Your head injury is a different problem," Dr. Maddy noted cheerfully, as she walked back into the room. "But first things first." She sat down on the side of the bed, and, before Hannah even understood what had happened, she felt tiny tugs, and the stitches were gone.

"This looks great. The last bit of healing should happen overnight." Dr. Maddy checked the rest of her body, even her arms. She studied the long clean skin where the scratches had been. "Everything looks good but the head."

Hannah desperately wanted her head to be healed as well. "Is there something you can do for that?"

Dr. Maddy wrinkled up her face. "Well, yes and no."

"Damn. I was hoping for another miracle," Hannah admitted. "It's been a hell of a day, with Trevor whisking me away to safety already, so I guess I shouldn't be too greedy and ask for more."

An odd silence came.

Hannah looked up to see a serious look on Dr. Maddy's face. "What's wrong?" When the doctor didn't answer, Hannah bit her lip. "Is the head injury more serious than I know? Is there permanent damage?"

"No, not like you mean." She sighed and sat down on the chair beside Hannah. "I was in here a little while ago and did a second scan."

Hannah felt her searching gaze and wondered what was going on. "And?"

"Do you remember that?"

Hannah frowned. "A second scan?" She shook her head. "No."

Dr. Maddy nodded.

"Maybe I was asleep?" Hannah ventured slowly. "I don't remember a second one."

"How about seeing Trevor and not recognizing him?"

Hannah gasped. "I didn't?"

Dr. Maddy shook her head. "And you thought you were married but to a man named Will."

Her skin burned hot, then shifted to ice, and she felt the tremors start deep inside. "No!" she cried out. "Never him."

"That's what Trevor said."

The tremors shook her whole body, as she realized Dr. Maddy was serious. "Why? Why would I say that? I hate him. He terrifies me. I know I married Trevor today." Her gaze locked on Dr. Maddy's face. "Please tell me that's true. That I married him at the hospital with Stefan and his wife standing beside us. Please tell me that I'm not making that up?"

"It's true. That's what you did today," she confirmed. "So you can understand my confusion when you woke up, not recognizing me or Trevor."

"Oh, God. Why is this happening to me?" She wrapped her arms around her chest. "I've had blackouts since forever. I want them to stop."

"Let's start at the beginning of what you remember in terms of the blackouts. When was the first one, and do you remember anything that might have triggered it back then."

"Triggered it?" She stared at her in surprise.

"Any emotional trauma that might have given you a rea-son to *not* remember what was going on?"

Hannah opened her mouth to answer but was too shocked to formulate words. "Do you really think this was triggered by some kind of trauma in my life?"

"It often happens that way."

How could such a thing happen? "But lots of people live through all kinds of horrific events," Hannah argued. "Why aren't they having blackouts?"

"Good question," Dr. Maddy stated calmly. "And we can't worry about everyone. We can only worry about you."

Hannah reached up to touch her head and the stitches and dried blood mess. "I'd hate to think of something going on inside my head that is so weak that it hits a Reset button every few weeks. And it's not like I'm traumatized over and over again," she shared. "So why am I blacking out so often then?"

"I don't know."

Moodily she shifted her gaze to the doorway and heard sounds of footsteps coming down the hall. She sighed with relief; at least he was okay. "Trevor is back."

Dr. Maddy nodded, her gaze intent on Hannah.

"Now what?" Why was she looking at her so intently?

"How did you know?"

"I don't know." Hannah frowned. "It sounded like his footsteps?" Yet, how many times in the last day had she heard that man's walk? Once? Twice? "That sounds stupid."

"What's stupid?" Trevor walked in, holding a bag in his hand.

She recognized the label. "Beignets?" she cried out in delight. "You stopped in at the Voodoo Deli?"

He laughed. "I did. Glad to see you recognize the place." He walked in and placed the bag on the small side table, then wheeled it closer. He searched her gaze. "Especially considering the state you were in last time I saw you."

Her face fell. "Dr. Maddy told me that I didn't recognize you earlier. I'm sorry about that."

"But you do now?" He grinned hopefully at her.

She let his gaze search hers. "I do."

"What happened that brought your memory back?"

Silence.

Then Dr. Maddy spoke up. "She fell unconscious again, and, when she woke up, she was in her normal mind."

"Interesting," Trevor replied but without any apparent shock.

She studied these two. "Did you ever consider that maybe *this* isn't my normal mind? And that the other state, whatever it was, was the normal one?"

"So you want to live in a world where Will is your husband?" Trevor asked her softly.

"God, no. That was my father's constant threat. I pleaded with him to not force me into that."

"Why would he want you to marry Will? Is Will rich? Famous? From a huge mover-shaker family?"

Each time Hannah shook her head. "No, he's just a lackey of my father's."

"That doesn't make much sense, unless he figured that this man would take good care of you, but if he's someone you feared …"

"Exactly."

"I'D LIKE TO speak to you for a moment too." Trevor waited at the doorway for Dr. Maddy to join him. When she stepped into the hallway, he added in a low tone, "I'd like you to see her eat."

She shot him a curious look, then stepped to the side, where she could talk to him but observe Hannah. "Why?"

"Just wait. Maybe it won't happen, but I'd like your take, without influencing it."

She nodded.

Hannah lifted the silver cover off her plate and smiled at the large clubhouse sandwich in front of her. Glenda had really come through. Hannah picked up one of the three pieces and dug in. She had that piece gone in five bites and had moved through the second, while they watched. When she picked up the third piece and took another huge bite, Dr. Maddy sighed.

"See what I mean?" Trevor asked.

"I do. She's burning through food as her main fuel source, and the fuel is to keep her energy as low as possible." She rubbed her temple. "That strong aura is a self-defense mechanism."

"Why? That's the opposite of what she should be doing."

"Why does any animal try to keep their energy low, their footprint almost nonexistent?"

"To avoid detection," he exclaimed in a low voice. "But she can't store enough food to keep this up, and she's beyond lean."

"She's a healthy weight, but on the light end of that," Dr. Maddy admitted. "Her body won't allow for anything else with this much food, but she's channeling all that energy into keeping her guard up."

"But there are easier ways."

"There are, but I suspect she has no idea what she's doing or why."

"And do we tell her?"

"We'll have to but not yet. We need to learn more first."

"About what?"

"*Will.* He's the only person she's shown any emotion toward so far. Except you." Dr. Maddy turned to look at him. "I'm not sure how she feels about you."

"Grateful, and that's about it," he replied. "She was in a hellish place, and I helped her out."

Dr. Maddy smiled. "She knew you were coming down the hallway. She already recognized you on an etheric level."

"I found out about that florist shop. Can't say I like that either." After he explained, he added, "The car belongs to Hannah."

Maddy's breath gushed out. "Wow. That can't be good. So the police are thinking she did it herself for insurance money?" She studied Trevor. "Is she broke?"

"I'd have to get a court order to get into her financials to find that out."

"Do you?" Dr. Maddy studied him. "You're her husband. Do you still need that?"

He raised his eyebrows. "I forgot."

She laughed. "Well, I suggest you remember."

"I'll speak with her too. With her permission I can have access to any information we might need."

Dr. Maddy nodded. "I'll have the kitchen bring up double dinners for you and her tonight. Likely, she will need a snack before she goes to sleep at this rate." Hannah had finished the sandwich and was working on the small bowl of Jell-O.

"Good. Can I coax a couple coffees out of your fancy machine too?" he asked, with a smile. "I could sure use one."

"I'll send someone in with two lattes for you." And she turned to walk down the hall.

Trevor walked back inside the hospital room.

Hannah was wiping her mouth and gave him a happy smile. "This place rocks."

"You don't know the half of it." He sat down beside her.

"We're getting coffee delivered in a few minutes too."

She beamed. "Thank you."

"Don't thank me. I have some news you won't like."

She frowned. "You couldn't find Tasha?"

"I might have found her," he noted in a soft voice. "A body was found in the same fire that burned your store to the ground."

CHAPTER 13

HANNAH GASPED IN shock, tears filling her eyes. "What? How?"

"The florist shop was burned to the ground, and a body was found inside. They presume it was her, but an autopsy is pending."

Hannah shook her head. "No. She can't be. She was such a beautiful person."

"This happened just yesterday." He took a deep breath and added, "Arson."

The color faded from her face yet again. She'd taken several major hits today, and, at some point, they would be too much. She wanted to curl up in a ball and crawl back into a hole at the same time.

"I'm so sorry."

"Where was I?" she asked bitterly. "When my best friend was dying, where the hell was I?"

"And don't you also mean, where were you when your business was burning to the ground? Or how about when your car was torched in the back parking lot?"

She stared at him as the hits kept on coming. "I can't believe it."

"Well, you need to because the cops are looking at you as being the guilty party."

She stared at him in shock. "But I wasn't even there."

"Good. So where were you?"

Her eyes overflowed, and she started to sob. "I don't know. I have no idea because I don't remember anything about that time. I have no idea even when *this* blackout started. As far as I know I can only remember a week ago—and even that is full of holes."

He stared at her. "Surely you can remember later than that?"

She shook her head. "No, I don't. Images keep moving in and out, but nothing makes sense." She wiped at her wet eyes. "It's like I wake up one day, and I'm in one world. Then I go to sleep and wake up in a different world. I don't know which is right or wrong, but some people are in both."

"Your father and Will?"

"Why them?" she cried out. "Why can't it be people who love me and are nice to me? I had Tasha, and we were really having fun. She knew about my blackouts. I'd had two in the months she'd worked for me, but they were short and not a big deal. Then I just woke up on the highway outside of Stefan's house."

Collapsing back against the pillow, she said in a low voice, "My father is right, isn't he? I *am* a danger to society. I should be locked up."

"No. He's not right. You should not be locked up. But, yes, we do need to fill in the blanks so that we can clear you of murdering your store manager."

At that she slapped her hands over her ears and curled up in a ball. After a moment she murmured in a small voice, "I need to rest for a little while."

"You can have ten minutes," he stated in a hard voice. "That's it. Then it's down to business. Unless you want to be locked up—and this time not in a gilded cage."

She shuddered. How had her life gotten to be so bad? She lay here, trying to let his information roll over her and through her. "My life has always been like this. Dr. Maddy had asked me about the traumas in my life, and, if they lined up with the blackouts, but you walked in then, and I didn't have time to tell her. Not sure that I know all of them anyway."

"Then start at the beginning, and I'll take notes."

She nodded. Closing her eyes, she started on that day so long ago. "My mother died when I was eight. Apparently I killed her."

AS A PLACE to start, that was a doozy.

Trevor's breath gusted out on a heavy sigh, as he stared at her to see if she were serious. Lying as she was, still in a ball, speaking in a monotone, she continued. "I was eight, close to my ninth birthday. We were outside by the lake, and I went into the water. I wanted her to play with me, but she didn't want to come in. I had no friends back then. I wasn't allowed to play with the neighbor kids, and they lived so far away that it wouldn't have worked out anyway most likely. They were as rich and locked up as I was, so they wouldn't have been allowed to come to my house either." She paused for a long moment, and Trevor wondered if he should prod her.

"I pretended I was drowning," she whispered in shame. "It was just a joke. I wanted to have someone play with me ..."

Ah, shit. He knew where this was going, and it wouldn't be a good place.

"She screamed for help and jumped in. There were two

guards, so I don't know how or why, but she drowned, and I survived," she noted in a bitter voice. "Life was never the same again."

"You know you aren't to blame, right?" Her gaze opened and shot him such a sad look, he knew she'd carried the guilt forever. "You were a child."

"I was a stupid, selfish child," she corrected.

"Did your mother know how to swim?"

She nodded. "I have memories of the two of us swimming. For all I know, she might have had one of her fits, but, if she'd had them on dry land, which is when she always had them, then she'd have been fine. But my father told me that the shock of believing I was drowning likely triggered the episode."

"Episodes?" He stared at her. "As in, fits?"

"She was an epileptic and had seizures occasionally. Apparently they were often triggered by stress."

"They can be, but there can also be many other extenuating circumstances. Sometimes even metabolic imbalances cause episodes. Medical science doesn't know everything."

She snorted. "I am a prime example of that."

"Tell me about her."

"She was a lovely person," Hannah remembered tearfully, "but moody. Either she was smiling and happy or she was in one of her melancholy moods. She went from one to the other, often with little warning. At those times she'd go to her room and spend some time alone, until she felt better."

"That made for a lonely childhood."

"It did. But I had everything I could want, so many kids were jealous. We were rich, but I was so unhappy. My father worried I was getting the same issues as my mother, so he kept me protected all the time."

"He would have anyway. He's a rich man. Kidnappings are all too common. He would have kept a close eye on you."

"Whatever the reason, I lived with guards. What I didn't understand was, after that incident, the guards followed me everywhere. They had before but not as close or as constant. I was always in my mother's care before, so the guards were in the background. But, after her death, well, there was nothing left for me at all. I was a virtual prisoner."

Not unexpected in many ways. He'd heard variations of the same complaint from many members of wealthy families. Money was a nice bonus in life, but it was also a huge headache, with side effects many couldn't see or understand.

"And when was your first blackout?"

She looked at him in surprise. "Right after my mother died. I blacked out for several days apparently."

"So what you just relayed to me is what you were *told?*" he asked carefully.

"Yes," she replied bitterly.

"Maybe only by one person," he suggested gently.

She studied him, as if thinking about what he'd just said, but she never commented. Good. "When was the next time?"

"They were fairly frequent but minor for the first year apparently. Every few months, but I don't remember why or if anything preceded them. Knowing I killed my mother was likely enough of a trigger to do that."

"It quite likely was," he agreed. "What was the next incident that you remember?"

"The guard dying." She snorted at the look he shot her. "No, I didn't kill him. There was an attack on the estate. Some kind of attempt on my father's life. The guard had grabbed me and was carrying me from the living room to the panic room."

Trevor raised an eyebrow at that bit but stayed quiet.

"On the way, he was shot. I fell to the ground, and he collapsed on top of me." She frowned. "Another vivid memory, but yet distant and very foggy almost at the same time."

He shook his head. Lord, one personal death was difficult, but two? "Both are traumatizing. Were the blackouts worse after that?"

"Oh, yeah. Much, but still not lasting too long. A few hours, a day, max."

"Was there another major incident after that?" He knew she didn't need big triggers to set off the blackouts. If her way to deal with a difficult life was to black out, well, that might have been all she could do at the time. But it would become a habit. It was an easy way to avoid dealing with stressors but not a good one.

"I don't know," she replied, her voice fatigued. "There were fights at school, arguments with my father. When he fired my guards, I had more to replace them." She shrugged. "I don't know what to say, but it seemed like the blackouts were always an issue, but they were short, and I recovered fast. I didn't have any major triggers before these events though."

"That's good," he noted cheerfully, trying to lighten the mood. "Considering the options. So when did the longer blackouts start?"

She swallowed. "After my father suggested that marrying Will was the perfect answer for me ..."

Yeah, that would do it. "Tell me about Will. When did he first start working for your father?"

"Before I graduated high school. Father fired all the

guards at that time, something he did on a regular basis, especially after my mother's death."

"I would too," he admitted. "Unless they hadn't been responsible, but it's an emotional decision. If you lose someone you love and have people hired to look after them, then you assign guilt, right or wrong."

"You're making a big assumption." Her voice slipped from guilt to cold and detached.

He leaned back. "What was that?"

"That he loved my mother. We lived in a separate house from him, and I think that was why she was so melancholy."

Interesting. He made a note to dig into her mother's background. "If she was unhappily married, that might help explain her moods."

"And she had health problems. I tried to get some information about her from my doctor a few years ago, thinking that genetically I needed to know, but he told me that I had to ask my father for that information."

"That's not typical."

"There is nothing typical about my family. Remember? My father is the ruler of his universe, and we all live in it."

"Anything else I need to know about your family? The blackouts? How long does it take for you to come out of them?"

She sighed. "Didn't you say coffee was coming?"

As a delay tactic, it worked. "I did. Let me see if that's coming." He got up and walked out of the room.

In the hallway he watched Maddy's assistant walking toward them with two large coffees. "I'm sorry. Things got a little busy."

"No apologies needed," he told her, from the doorway. "I'm sorry for causing you extra work." He took the tray from her and walked back inside. Hannah had rolled into a small ball and appeared to be sleeping.

"Hannah?" he said quietly. "The coffee is here."

"I don't like coffee," she replied in a low flat voice. "You always say I'm too young to drink it."

He froze, then silently moved forward to place the tray on the small table.

He never took his gaze off her. Taking a step closer, he whispered, "Who are you?"

"Hannah, of course, silly."

Mentally he sent out a message to Maddy, *Can you come? Something is happening to Hannah.*

He shifted his focus to look at her aura and stifled a gasp. It was expansive and wildly colored. *Maddy, if possible, I need you now.*

DR. MADDY LIFTED her head from the paperwork. She caught his first message, but his second came faster and more urgently. She was up and flying toward Trevor, before he finished talking. She reached the bedroom and paused as she caught sight of Trevor standing at the end of Hannah's bed, his energy so close, his aura almost touching Hannah's. The same Hannah who had kept her energy so tight to her body that she'd appeared to be dying.

Yet now her aura sprawled with the enthusiasm of an innocent child. Only one without boundaries. And that was also unusual. Hannah had gone from one extreme to the other.

Then she heard Hannah's voice.

"Can I go outside today? Please?" Only the voice wasn't happy. Or pleading. It was flat. Monotone. As if knowing the answer ahead of time. That it was a predetermined no.

"Yes, you can go outside today," Trevor agreed quietly, staring at Maddy.

She approached gently. "If you want to go out, we can go."

"Mommy?"

"Are you okay, Hannah?" Maddy continued, trying to coax the child out a little more.

"I am, but you're not. We have to run away. We have to escape …" The child's voice rose in a panic. "We have to go now. Today."

"Why?" Trevor asked. "Why do we have to run away?"

"He's going to hurt you. He already told me that he would. We have to run before he kills you." And the childlike voice rose in a high-pitched scream.

Maddy reached out and sliced the energy link feeding the memory to Hannah's brain.

The sound cut off, and Hannah's face went lax—instantly.

Maddy looked at Trevor. "Are you okay?"

"I'm fine." He stared down at his fingers, not surprised to find them shaking. "Or I will be if something calms down." He smiled at Maddy. "Between Hannah's problems and my old memories, I'm not short of problems."

"Old memories can be difficult." She nodded at Hannah. "Her memories are all over the place right now, and opening up those blocks are allowing access she didn't have before. But it's also removing the controls that were in place. More instances of fallout like this one are likely."

"That's too bad," Trevor replied pensively. "She's been through a lot lately."

"So have you," Dr. Maddy noted in a soft voice. "Drew

explained to me about the anonymous tip about your teacher's death."

"And Stefan says he had a vision that showed him that my old teacher was murdered. Not by my hand but quite possibly by that of an old friend."

She pulled up a chair and covered his hand with her own. "I'm sorry. That's difficult."

He squeezed her fingers. "It is, but it is also a relief in a way because I had always wondered …"

"Some things can only stay hidden for so long. There is much that is wrong in this world." She smiled. "But all things are shown in time. There is much right in this problem. The truth must be revealed." She nodded toward Hannah. "We need to run some tests. It will take a little while to get the results. The brain scan should prove interesting."

"Are you really expecting to see anything?"

She laughed. "Maybe not. But at least that in itself tells me something."

"I've been trying to work. I have a business to run, papers to file, a wife who doesn't know me, so I am trying to access her life's history to unravel the mystery of who she is."

"She is a conundrum," Maddy admitted. "There is one other thing I feel that you need to know."

He winced. "Whenever anyone says something like that to me, I sense bad news."

"I have been trying to see where the energy might be draining away from her system." She dropped her gaze to their hands. "In the process I sensed a connection to you long ago."

"Meaning? I really don't like the sound of that." He studied her features. "Her life would have been so different from mine, I can't see how they would have intersected."

She nodded. "And yet your energy is in her system."

He shook his head. "I don't think I've ever met her before."

"Well, you have, and it made an impression. Don't try to push the memory but give it permission to come to the surface. And the next time you are looking at her—maybe in grayscale even—see where your energy is in her aura."

"That aura of hers is something else," he admitted. "I can't read any of it." He motioned to where the riotous color had been. "That it suddenly was so wild and carefree is just another puzzle."

"It's a coping mechanism, and one that works very well for her."

"But is it healthy?"

"It's not *unhealthy*. There is much to unravel here. It will take time." Though she winced at that part.

Trevor rushed into speech. "I have another place to take her. A safe place."

"Good. I'm adding a few anchors, so I can continue to help her after you leave." She stood. "You can stay here for the rest of today and tonight. The next patient's arrival has been delayed, giving us a slightly longer window." She smiled and patted his shoulder. "Remember that everything happens for a reason."

He frowned. "Meaning, she came into my life for a reason?"

"Absolutely. But all this trauma and trouble has a reason too."

"Somehow it's harder to see that." He smiled. "But I know rationally that it always goes hand in hand."

"It does, and, for whatever reason," she added, as she

walked to the door, "your lives are entwined, and they have been for a long time."

As parting words, they packed a punch.

He sat down heavily, his mind a blank. How could that be? He had no memories of Hannah. She lived an affluent life. He had been one of the disgusting poor to her. At least to her family. Now he had a murder in his history. Likely at one of his friends' hands.

No way had he met Hannah before.

Not only met because that wasn't enough for Dr. Maddy to have said what she'd said. It had to have been a strong-enough meeting in their history that she'd retained the memory and the energy from it.

Yet he had no memory of such a thing. Was it not a strong-enough event for him? Or had he pushed back the memory because he didn't want to keep it?

CHAPTER 14

I T WAS EARLY morning when Hannah opened her eyes. Had she been here for hours or days? Gazing down at her body, still partially dressed, she realized it had been just since last night. Even now it was early. As in very early. But she felt better. Much better.

She yawned and rolled over. Trevor snoozed in the recliner beside her.

That bag of beignets still sat on the small table. She'd missed her coffee last night, and she'd missed having the treat. Somehow she didn't remember when she fell asleep. Now that she saw the beignets, she wanted one.

Trying to sit up, she winced at the pain in her head. Everything else felt fine. Her head? Not so much. She slipped off the bed and made her way to the bathroom. All she'd done so far since meeting Trevor was be in hospitals. Then again it was likely just since yesterday. So the first twenty-four hours of marriage hadn't changed her life yet.

In the bathroom she studied the shower, realized it was early enough for no one to say yes or no, and she made a fast decision. She slipped off the rest of her clothes and turned on the hot water. She stepped under the stream and tilted her face up, so the warm water poured over her head. It felt so damn good.

She slowly eased her head fully under the water, expecting to have the pain in her head intensify; instead it was soothing. Using her fingers, she gently washed away the dried blood on her scalp. Several small bottles were on the shelf beside her. One was shampoo. She quickly unscrewed the cap and poured a small bit into the palm of her hand and worked it into a lather on her shoulder-length hair. When that was as clean as she could manage, without touching the stitches, she took the bar of soap and sponged down the rest of her. Lord, that felt wonderful.

When she was done, she turned off the water and grabbed the towel. Instead of feeling shaky or fatigued, as she'd expected, her body surged with an inner strength.

What the heck had Dr. Maddy done to her?

Hopefully she'd see her this morning, and she could ask. At this rate of healing, she could walk out of here today. She glanced at her thigh and the healed wound and shook her head in disbelief. There was a fine pink line running across her skin, but that was all. Over time that would fade away too.

The bruises on the rest of her body had faded away to nothing as well. She dressed in the clothes she had worn earlier, but her pants were back in the bedroom area.

Opening the door quietly, she walked over, found her pants folded on a side chair and put them on. Now she felt normal. She quickly braided her hair and looked around for an elastic tie to secure the ends. Nothing was close by. She frowned, then left her hair braided but the ends loose. That wouldn't last, but maybe she'd find something to use. She made the bed and stretched out on top. She closed her eyes and relaxed. After a few moments she opened them again and glanced around.

She gave Trevor one last look and walked out into the

quiet hallway. There had to be a nurses' station somewhere. Fresh coffee to go with the beignets would be lovely.

The place still slept. She wandered from one end to the other, loving the peaceful ambiance. It was a special place. One of the small sitting areas had a balcony. She opened the doors and walked outside. Huge gardens would blaze with color when the flowers woke up to the early morning sun.

She studied the sky and frowned. She thought it was morning. But the sky wasn't as bright as it could be. She'd have guessed it was just before six in the morning. Instead the world looked to be much darker than normal. It was a gray world. And felt … odd. But almost … normal.

She tensed, confused, as if something had happened. She looked behind her but everything appeared fine and well lit inside—as well lit as could be expected, considering it was soft ambient light.

Everything had a gray silvery look to it. The garden called to her, but she wasn't sure how to get down there. She walked back inside to the hallway and remembered the elevators she'd taken with Trevor. She made her way toward them. She didn't meet anyone on the way. She glanced in at Trevor as she passed her room, but he slept on. The poor man had been on a roller coaster ride since meeting her.

She stepped into the elevator and let it carry her down. She wondered at this need to go outside. Surely she'd be better off waiting in bed for the others to wake up. At least she'd woken up as herself. That helped a lot. She must have freaked out Trevor pretty well when she hadn't recognized him. That she'd consider Will to be her husband was scary. He was a hell of an enemy to have—as a husband, he'd be a living nightmare.

But then again apparently, if life got too difficult to live, she switched channels. What the hell was that all about? It made her feel incredibly weird. Dr. Maddy had told Hannah that it was a coping skill, and she wasn't to blame. Hannah didn't know how to feel about that. She'd spent a lifetime being blamed for every wrong in her life, and instead these people here seemed to feel she wasn't to blame for any of it. Who was right? She wished her mother had lived. She missed her so much. It was one of the reasons she rarely spoke about her.

It hurt too much.

The elevators opened to a silent main floor. Odd. That meant she'd completely mistaken the time. But she was here already, and the gardens beckoned. She carried on through the hallway toward the patio area in the backyard. She did see one nurse standing beside a patient in one room. There must be a skeleton staff at this hour.

Craving the first waft of fresh air, she stepped outside and took a deep breath. Only the air had a flat *waitingness* to it. There must be a storm ready to break. Odd. Still, she walked off the patio onto the grass. She stared down at her feet. She'd come out barefoot and hadn't noticed. She shook her head. She'd thought she was wide awake but apparently not so much.

The grass felt odd under her feet. Cool but almost sharp. Freshly cut, so sticky. She twisted around feeling free, healthy, for the first time in a long time. Her body felt loose and relaxed, yet everything had a flatness, and she missed the vibrancy she was looking for. Feeling foolish but needing to try, she spun around a few times, only it didn't feel the same. She turned and walked to the far end of the garden. Farther away, another woman walked alone.

Hannah wanted to say hi, but the woman didn't look

like she wanted company. Hannah understood. She'd spent a lot of time in the same mood. Still, she gravitated closer. The woman might change her mind if she saw her.

They were only a few yards apart when the woman looked up. Her gaze widened in horror.

"No," she cried out in such pain that Hannah stopped in her tracks. "You can't be here."

"*Uhm.*" Hannah looked around. Surely this woman had someone to look after her?

There appeared to be several men farther behind the woman, but none close enough to help her. No one else was around. Unless they were in the woods at the side. She studied the long line of trees and wondered why they looked darker. More imposing than when she'd first arrived.

Surely the light should be getting better, brighter.

"Why shouldn't I be here?" Hannah asked quietly. The woman looked terrified, and the same feeling was quickly transferring to Hannah. She took several steps backward. "I don't understand. It's beautiful out here."

"No, it's not. It's not what you think. You need to run. Dear God, please, Hannah, run …"

Hannah froze when the woman called her name. "You know who I am?"

"Of course I do. Run. Please. Don't talk to me, or they will find you." She spun Hannah around, gave her a push, and screamed, "Run!"

TREVOR WOKE TO a heavy sensation on his chest. He shifted, but it wouldn't ease. Struggling for air, he bolted upright, and, hands to his chest, he raced to the small balcony off Hannah's room in search of fresh air.

What the hell?

He gulped and gulped, but nothing eased the constriction. If he didn't know better, he would think he was having a heart attack, but there was no pain, nothing but the awful inability to catch his breath. The early morning air was dark, dank. Dare he say, *fetid?* That made no sense. Huge flower gardens were behind Maddy's Floor. Then he understood.

He wasn't in the physical world; he had crossed into the gray space between.

Although a regular graywalker, he hadn't been here in several weeks.

He closed his eyes, his fingers gripping the rail hard. He needed the reminder, when he was here, that the physical world existed, but he wasn't in it. He was, but it was a different dimension that no one but those unfortunate—or fortunate, depending on their experience—understand. He knew several who did. They rarely spoke about the experience together, but, when one had a problem, they all came to offer advice.

It was the weirdest thing in that the only person Trevor knew who could access the same gray space as he could was Stefan. The others would be in their own version, as if there were multiple levels or dimensions of a personalized grayscale for each of them.

He opened his eyes, hoping to be in the physical world, but he was still in the half-lit space. That meant he *needed* to be here. He worked through the possible reasons, sensing when his chest eased or constricted the closer he came to the right subject.

When he considered Hannah, his chest squeezed in pain. He grunted and tried to focus on his breathing. He turned slowly to see how she slept and found her stretched out on the tip of the bed fully dressed, her hair wet, as if she'd showered and then lay again on the bed and fallen asleep.

Only she wasn't in her body.

Damn it. He should have heard her. Normally he was a light sleeper, even for astral walkers. How did she get past him? And where had she gone? He went to step back into the room, and his ribs crushed in deeper again. He groaned and hunched over. As he swiveled toward the railing, the pressure immediately eased. He straightened, trying to regain his breath. And his gaze caught sight of Hannah out in the grassy lawn below. She had her arms open, and he heard her call out.

"Why?" She shook her head, adding in a plaintive scared voice, "Please tell me."

He searched the grayness, looking to see who she spoke to.

But he saw no one.

Then he heard a hair-raising scream. Hannah froze, and he stepped forward on the little balcony, only to slam to a stop—as if hitting a solid blank wall. He watched in disbelief as part of her body, energy, soul—call it what it was, and Stefan would likely call it an ethereal body—shattered.

Literally her head *shattered* outward into a zillion little pieces. In slow motion all the pieces floated to the ground. Scattered on the grass.

His throat seized in panic.

What the hell?

He wanted to race down to the lawn. He wanted to run to her aid. But he couldn't move. His feet had fused to the balcony floor. He wasn't allowed to go. Although he understood why he couldn't, he also railed at it. He was in the grayscale. The half world. So was she. But he wasn't in the same grayscale.

He was *viewing* from a privileged position as a guest in *her* grayscale world.

He watched in disbelief, as the impossible happened. The tiny particles of her head slowly pulled back together again, and like a slow-playing movie, now playing in reverse, the pieces reformed her head into the same shape as before.

He gasped, then groaned. Jesus.

Talk about a headache.

Once again, she turned, her face emotionless, and she walked back toward the hospital and disappeared from his sight.

As she disappeared, the mechanism holding him in place released.

He bolted from their balcony back into her bedroom and into the hallway. When he walked in grayscale, the experience exhausted him. She somehow had to be better adapted to do what she'd just done. And what toll did it take on her?

The elevator was empty, waiting to be called. He took the stairs two steps at a time. When he burst through the doors on the main floor, he checked the elevator but it still stood on Maddy's Floor, waiting for a call to bring it down to the main floor. Not wasting another moment, he ran to the back patio. And came to a shuddering stop.

Hannah sat, still as a mouse, seated at the farthest table, but her head. *Jesus.* It moved and shifted, like the pieces were alive.

He screamed, *Stefan!*

STEFAN BOLTED AWAKE, feet already on the floor, racing across his bedroom, before he understood who'd called.

It's Hannah. I don't know if you can see this, but it can't be fucking possible.

Stefan dropped to the floor in a cross-legged position and jumped free of his body. He locked on Hannah's and Trevor's positions and willed himself there. He opened his eyes to see himself on the back patio, standing beside an empty table.

But no sign of Trevor or Hannah.

Trevor, where are you? he snapped. They had to be here somewhere. His tracker could be off a little but not like this.

Grayscale came the terrified whisper.

Shit, that place was tough for anyone, but, if Trevor was in there, it was for a reason, and it was never a good one. It always meant someone was in need of assistance. Stefan shifted realities, wondering at the ease that he could do so. There was a large door in front of him. He knocked lightly.

"Come in," Trevor said. "And fast."

Stefan walked into Trevor's landscape and froze. "What the hell?" Stefan whispered in fascination.

"Yeah, like what the hell?"

Hannah sat frozen, in grayscale, but the rest couldn't be possible. To start with, her head—not her face, but the rest of her head—appeared to be moving, shifting, as tiny pieces sought to find their proper place.

"Tell me what happened, right now," Stefan demanded in a low tone, not wanting anything to disturb the process in front of him.

"I woke up, feeling like I was having a heart attack, raced out to the balcony, and saw her talking with someone but couldn't see to whom. Then, as if she were frozen in place, her head exploded. I was afraid someone took a shotgun to her head. Next thing I knew, the pieces of her essence flew around, as if putting Humpty Dumpty back together again—literally. By the time I got here, it was as if some fine-tuning had taken place."

They stared as the pieces slowed their movements, and Hannah did a full-body wiggle, whereby everything settled into place. As if to accent the new state, Hannah gave a big sigh, and her body relaxed.

"It's done, whatever that was," Trevor noted.

"It was a full realignment," Stefan stated in an awed voice.

"If that's special, I'm sorry Maddy didn't see it," Trevor added.

"I did. I just don't quite believe it," Dr. Maddy replied in a soft voice from inside Stefan's aura.

Trevor considered this to always be special to have her visit in this way. Grayscale was weird in that you didn't actually see what you thought you saw, and all movement acted differently. He hadn't heard her arrive, but he'd sensed her.

"Maddy? You can walk in grayscale?" Trevor asked in surprise.

"Technically I'm not. I'm using Stefan to port in and out. I can't walk in here or do anything but observe. Still, what I just saw ..."

"Amazing, isn't it?" Stefan asked, his vocal tone so damn close to Maddy's now that Trevor wasn't sure if she was her own grayscale entity here or if she was using Stefan's ethereal image to communicate. Things got especially confusing when two powerful energy workers came together.

Stefan glanced at Trevor. As a graywalker in his own

world, Trevor had just experienced a view into someone else's world but with an inability to help. As they watched, Hannah slowly got up from her chair and reappeared long moments later, as she made her way back to her bed.

In her room and looking as normal as anyone could after what she'd been through in greyscale, she relaxed into her body and slept. The pieces of her head slowly sank into position—but were they in the right positions?

Trevor, his voice barely audible, asked, "Can we do anything for her?"

"That depends," Stefan replied. "Maddy, your take?"

"What reality repositioned those pieces in her head?"

NOW THAT WAS more like it. She was splintering once again. A weird and wonderful process he'd seen time and time again. He'd done his best to bring it to fruition, but instead it happened without any push from him.

Although, when it did, it always triggered alarms. Sometimes he managed to get there in time to see it. But he wished he knew what caused it, so he could make it happen. But, so far, he'd failed at every attempt. Was it fear on her part? He'd tried to scare her into doing this but with no success. He wanted it to happen when he called, when he was close enough to see it in person, not this window into her world that only let him see from a distance. He was accessing that window through the blocks in her head. Not a direct link that might have allowed him to do more.

That bothered him. He'd love to be able to cause something like that at his will. Imagine being in a business meeting, or how about an international summit, and have all the world leaders disintegrate in front of him. He'd rule the world, if he could. He could do something so very similar now, but he had to be too close, have a history with the victim to make it last.

He was getting stronger, so much so, but not to the extent of controlling on a global basis. But he entertained the thought fondly. He had money enough for his needs at this point but could always use more. And then there was the power issue—no one ever had enough of that.

Still, he couldn't spend all his day on his games. He needed information. Now. This man, this Trevor, was pissing in his backyard. No one did that. Who would have thought the past could return like that? Hannah married? And to this man?

But he refused to let it upset him. This was a challenge. And those kept him on his toes and put a smile on his face.

It couldn't be allowed to continue of course, but, in the short-term, hey, it kept boredom away.

He couldn't wait until the information came in. Just what had his old friend been up to?

CHAPTER 15

HANNAH WOKE AND was moving in the same instant that her mind regained consciousness. Already dressed, but not recognizing anything around her, she responded to the instinct that screamed at her to *run*.

Someone was yelling at her to escape.

To run.

The instinct was too strong to ignore, and she picked up her feet and ran. Out the door, down the hall, and through the exit. The stairs ahead of her had no bearing on her actions. She didn't slow. Instead she used the railing to help her to run, and the faster she ran, the more her heart pounded and the more her hands slipped with sweat on the railing. Someone, or several someones, were after her. She didn't know why. Or who.

But they'd been after her before. She knew they had.

If only she could remember who *they* were.

She bolted out of the exit and dashed into the backyard. She ignored all the curious onlookers, seated at the small patio tables to enjoy the early morning sunshine.

Sunshine? Why sunshine? She was supposed to be in the dark? At night? Running from a faceless stalker. Right?

She froze.

Images, voices, sensations rippled through her. She was so damned confused. And scared.

What was happening to her?

"Do you need help, dearie?" asked a little old lady beside her, only her eyes were like onyx, dark and compelling. "So many little girls need help." She reached out a hand, as if to reassure Hannah that she'd be fine. Her hand went to rest on Hannah's arm, but Hannah stepped back, so the woman couldn't touch her. There was something, ... well, creepy about her.

Hannah backed away farther. "Who are you?" she cried out in confusion. "And where am I?"

They were attracting attention from several other people, sitting and relaxing.

"I'm the same as you. You'll be fine. Just relax." The old lady gave her a genial smile. "And remember. It's a good thing you are here. It's a dangerous world out there. Some of them need our help, especially the little ones."

Hannah backed away a few more steps. She didn't know anything about the world out there, but she was desperate to leave this one here. She glanced down at her clothing. She didn't even recognize them, and she always wore shoes. Not today apparently. She turned her back on the old lady and started to run.

"Wait, don't go out there ..." the old lady called out, her voice stronger than it should have been for someone her age and size. "Not unless you have someone to watch you, to protect you."

Seriously freaked out, Hannah raced into the trees surrounding the place. As she dove deeper and deeper into the trees, she finally slowed. Surely she was safe here? She stopped to catch her breath, only to note she wasn't struggling to breathe hard. Did nothing make sense anymore?

Then a booming started deep inside her skull, the pain

making her groan, and it built and built. She fell to her knees, her hands to her head, trying to stop the sound from blowing apart her head. That's what it felt like. Something so strong, so powerful, that her head would explode from the pressure, and the sledgehammer inside would finally break free.

Instead of easing, the pain radiated down her back and her side. This wasn't the first time she'd had a headache like this, but she couldn't remember how to deal with it. There was a way. She'd found some trick to ease that pain, but she couldn't remember what it was.

She started to breathe through her open mouth in slow regular breaths, waiting, her body shaking now, as tremors slid down her spine.

In and out. She had to focus on her breathing. Someone important had told her that a long time ago. Who? She racked her brain, trying to think about who, but, like everything right now, the name eluded her.

Forget about everything. Just relax. Breathe slowly. In and then out. Stand quiet, and let the pain slip away.

The voice. … It was familiar, … yet not. It was hers, yet it wasn't. Dear God. She really was crazy.

No. You aren't. But somehow, somewhere, you've been nudged in this direction. We need to help you.

There is no help for me, she whispered. *Listen to me. I'm crazy.*

A different voice joined into the fray. *Of course you're crazy. You've always been crazy.*

Yet another voice jumped in. *No, of course you're not.* There was a light snigger. *You're just delicate.*

She shuddered, as the onslaught continued, until she collapsed onto the ground in a heap. There, but not there.

Conscious, but not conscious. Awake, but not awake.

But aware. So damn aware.

"We have to move her. Take her back to her room? Can anyone help her? Even here?"

Was that Trevor's voice?

"I can help and so can Dr. Maddy, but we must find out what happened. What caused her to bolt the second time? We know panic makes her shatter, but what is the root of the panic in the first place?"

She sensed being picked up and carried back inside. She opened her mouth to speak, but no sound came out.

Then she heard a voice in her head. *Hannah, lie quiet. We need to do something to help you deal with the energies sparking in your system.*

Energies? Sparking? How was that possible? The voices continued. She could hear but not speak. The comprehension was damn slow too. Did they know she was listening?

"Is that what's happening?" Trevor asked, surprise lacing his voice.

Hell, she was surprised too.

Dr. Maddy's calm voice answered, "The barriers that have been in place for a long time are thinning, a few disintegrating. Either she's getting stronger and is ripping them down herself or someone else is releasing their hold. Either way she's getting bombarded by the overwhelming stimulus. Probably listening to voices, commands from yesterday or last week even. Honestly they could be memories from years ago that are sending her running."

Hmm, say what? Surely Hannah hadn't heard what she thought she'd heard? Not possible. It was just more crazy talk in her head. Right?

"So time is bleeding for her?" Trevor asked.

"Not time but I think it has to do with the pieces not going back into the same position, so she's likely responding to a stimulus out of sync. A memory she hasn't tucked away again. Likely recent."

"So knowing that we are trying to escape from her father could have sent her running?"

"Exactly. Quite likely that was the trigger."

"How do we keep her safe?"

"She needs tools. That could be in your realm."

"The shattering is your domain though." Trevor snorted. "What the devil do we do with that?"

Shattering? Tools? What the hell were they talking about? And yet she felt a twinge of something … that made sense inside but not outside. If that didn't prove her crazy, nothing would. How bizarre because she sensed the rightness of the words, but her mind couldn't grasp how.

"It's her coping mechanism. I suggest you walk in her grayscale world and find what her triggers are."

Now that didn't sound good.

"I can't walk in her grayscale. I can only visit."

"Do you know that for sure?" A thread of humor filled Dr. Maddy's voice.

Again Hannah tried to call out. To let them know she was here. But it was as if she were paralyzed and forced to listen.

"No, of course I don't know. I tried that with someone else. Remember?" And bitterness roiled through his tone. "It wasn't good. Poor Anita erupted and attacked Stefan. I know it wasn't the child's fault. I can only think someone from her grayscale world was lashing out."

"Making that an entirely different scenario."

"Was it?" He snorted with disgust. "It feels the same,

and I still screwed up."

"It wasn't a screw-up. I don't understand exactly what happened or why, but the child wasn't hurt by the process. The interference just didn't deliver the right response."

"No, it sure didn't." Now there was pain in his voice. "But I can't take the chance of hurting anyone in that way."

Hannah wanted to reach out and stroke his hand. He'd done so much good. He'd helped out so much, and lately he was always around, just being there for her. She wanted to be there for him. She poured as much strength as she could into her hand … and felt the impression of his hand in hers—a faint contact, as if she were just space and not body.

"*Whoa.*"

The three of them froze.

"What's the matter?"

"Her energy is getting hot. Like seriously hot."

Hannah wanted to laugh. That's not what she wanted, but, as far as getting his attention, it was a start. She closed her eyes and did it again, harder, hotter, faster.

"Jesus."

And she was hustled down the hallway and laid gently back on her bed. That's when she realized she could see— *although her eyes were closed.*

Dr. Maddy's voice whispered through her mind. *Open your eyes and settle your ethereal body back into the physical.*

The instructions were gently offered, but there was no doubt Hannah was meant to do as she was told.

With a gentle sigh, Hannah struggled with the command. It made no sense, and yet it made complete sense. She saw Trevor, staring down at her, with his loving, supportive energy that promised he'd be there forever, if she wished. She wanted him to be. Needed him to be. Because, so far, in her world, there were none who'd stayed. Which meant, in reality, he wouldn't either. It wasn't possible. He didn't know her, so why would he?

Then neither was staring up at him with her eyes closed a possibility.

So she had to trust.

And she needed to take a step forward too.

Toward Trevor. Trust in him. He hadn't hurt her.

Yet.

And she opened her eyes.

DR. MADDY SMILED. "Good, there you are."

Hannah reached out for Trevor's hand. She cast a wary glance at Dr. Maddy. "I'm not sure what that was, but I'd just as soon not go through it again."

Trevor sat down on the bed, his hand clasping Hannah's to his chest.

Dr. Maddy smiled, as she watched Hannah's energy snuggle up against Trevor's. He wouldn't be able to see it, as his focus was on her, not her reaction to him. But, as Trevor's energy was opening and accepting, hugging Hannah's energy, then he already knew. Acceptance happened on the etheric level, way before it reached the physical. "You were awake but in an altered state."

"It felt like that," she stated, with feeling. "I could hear you, but what you were saying didn't make any sense."

"And yet it probably made sense in a natural way." Dr. Maddy watched Hannah's gaze narrow, as she considered those words.

"Maybe, but it also sounded a little too close to the gibberish I've listened to inside my head for so long."

"Well, our conversation wasn't gibberish. It was real, and I'll sit here now and give you a few instructions because you need to learn what you are doing. And, more than that, you need to understand at a cellular level that this is who you are. That you have energy power you are tapping into for a particular reason, even if you don't know it at this time. But it's important for you to realize a couple things.

"One, you are *not* crazy. Two, *you* are in control of your body, including the ethereal body you dissociate from. And, three, you feel like you are being hunted, always need to be running. I don't know how true that last one is, but it's important that you honor the feeling for now and delve into the *why*s and the *who*s. We can help you, but you need to help yourself. You can access all this information, as soon as you give yourself permission," she added, her tone casual, yet certain.

Dr. Maddy stood. She smiled at the newlyweds. "Now I think coffee and those beignets need their moment. I have to get back to work." And she walked out of the room.

But inside Maddy was smiling. Trevor and Hannah had no idea yet, but they were meant to be. They had a connection in the past, although Maddy hadn't delved in to see what or when. That was for them to figure out. Hopefully sooner, rather than later.

TREVOR KNEW WHEN Maddy and Stefan left the room. Then psychics were like that. Hannah's gaze had locked on his face, like a drowning person who'd glimpsed sight of a life raft. "Hey, don't panic. It will make sense. Eventually."

She gasped out a choked laugh. "The stupid thing is it almost does make sense, but it's so far out there. My mother used to talk about stuff like that—but only when no one was around to hear."

"Your mother?" Oh, now that was interesting. And explained much. "She did energy work?"

Hannah frowned. "She didn't work at all. My father wouldn't have allowed it."

He grinned. "Was she psychic? Read auras? Knew things before they happened?"

She stared at him in shock. "I don't think so. I never heard her mention it."

"So what did she talk about?" He studied her frown, seeing the worry collect between her eyebrows.

"Things about keeping my power in close, hiding what I could do from others. Presenting one face to the world and a different one inside."

He stared. "Wow. Okay, that's good."

"Is it?" She scrunched up her face. "How does any of that relate to what just happened?"

"Well, some of this might seem a little off, but, when we have an out-of-body experience, our return trip can be a bit rough and can leave us feeling paralyzed for a few moments. In your case your ethereal body was shocked into paralysis, and we had to direct you back to your physical body."

"Nothing you're saying makes any sense." She shuddered. "What does make sense is just too unbelievable. I have no idea what sent me running in the first place, but this weird paralysis came after the creepy woman terrified me."

"What woman was that?"

She sighed. "I saw her—both of them—when I went for a walk."

"Explain."

"I woke up, and, Trevor, you were sleeping. I was restless, hoped to find somewhere to get a coffee, … some fresh air, but the air was …" She frowned. "Stagnant. Old. I didn't get it. Everything was *flat*." She shrugged. "I met a woman, who appeared to know me. But she was terrified for me. She told me to run, and I panicked." She stared off in the distance. "I must have blacked out," she noted softly, "because, when I woke up, I was back in my bed, but then running in a panic again. The first woman's terrified cry sent me racing outside again. That's when I saw the second woman, sitting on the patio. I stopped, and she talked to me. Something about being the same as I was and something else about little girls needed to be safe …" Hannah dropped her gaze.

Trevor got it but knew she had no idea she'd been walking in the dimension between life and death. Or that she'd returned to her body only to flee yet again. Interesting though that a person from that space told her to escape. "Did you recognize the older woman?"

She shook her head. "No. But her head had a scarf wrapped around it, and she had a shawl around her shoulders." She snorted. "She told me that she was exactly like me."

"But you didn't recognize her? She didn't seem familiar at all?"

"No way. The younger woman I saw the first time I ran out there almost looked familiar, but I can't place her."

"Sounds like you had quite the adventures there," Trevor noted, his voice calm and gentle.

"I don't understand any of this." She yawned. "What was that about coffee?"

"How about a nap, and I'll chase down coffee."

She latched on to his arm. "I'll nap but please don't leave

me alone."

"I promise." He patted her hand. "Just rest. The coffee will be here soon. I'll wake you then."

She searched his gaze for a long moment then nodded. "Not sure why I'm so sleepy."

"Healing takes effort. So does walking in grayscale. A quick nap will do you some good."

"And then what?"

"Coffee and beignets, followed by a trip to the grocery store, and then on to a friend's house."

"Are we going into hiding?"

"That's one way to think of it." In fact, the more he thought of it, it seemed like that's what they needed to do and fast. "You nap, and I'll make the arrangements."

She closed her eyes.

He got busy on the phone. By the time Glenda walked in with the long-awaited coffee, he was ready for it. As he glanced over at Hannah, she was awake and ready too.

CHAPTER 16

HANNAH BUCKLED HER seat belt. They were back in the same small car they'd driven on the way to Dr. Maddy's Floor, minus the bandages and her wounds. Although her head still ached, it wasn't so bad as it had been. The bleeding had stopped, and the wound had healed enough for Dr. Maddy to remove the stitches. So long as Hannah didn't get another head injury, Dr. Maddy expected it would heal fully by morning. Hannah had had enough injuries to last forever, so she was good to go. To return to Maddy's Floor would likely mean she was injured, so that was out—although the woman herself would make for the most caring friend, and Hannah could use a few of those. She still couldn't believe Tasha was dead. How could that be? It was too horrible to believe.

She leaned her head back and closed her eyes.

"I think all you do is sleep."

"Really?" She sighed. "You could be right. I was just thinking about Tasha and wondering if there was any update."

"Outside of the police treating this as arson, … nothing new. They're working on it."

"I feel so bad. I should have been there for her," she murmured in a low guilt-ridden voice.

"There wasn't anything you could have done," he stated

firmly. "If you'd been there, chances are you'd have died with her."

"Maybe I could have saved her," she replied softly. She would never know if she could have helped or not.

"How long had you known her?"

"Not long. Just while she worked for me. But we hit it off immediately." She gave a short soft laugh. "She was a good worker, fun and friendly. She loved people."

"Do you have a photo of her? A description?" he asked.

"She was a few years older than me." She shrugged. "Brunette, slim, always smiling. She wasn't looking for a career job. I think, if she didn't work for me, she would have gone back East, where her family lived."

She looked around. "If my phone was still around, there would be photos of her. I remember taking a few when we were photographing the flower arrangements. She was dynamite at those." A melancholy silence filled the car. Thinly, she asked, "How long a trip do we have?"

"About twenty more minutes. But I thought we'd stop at a market on the way and pick up some fresh groceries."

"As long as you're cooking," she teased, with a spirited smile. "My cooking sucks."

He gave a great shout of laughter. "Well, I am cooking, so we're safe."

"Good. Sounds like I made the best deal out of this marriage. A lawyer and psychologist and a cook." She giggled. "I'm nobody compared to that."

"That isn't true." He grinned. "You are you, and there is no reason for you to be anything other than that."

"Seems like that was never quite good enough for anyone else."

"Not true." He reached over and covered her hand with

his. "Your life has been a roller coaster ride so far. It's time to live a little."

"Sounds good to me." She was looking forward to whatever came next.

The market was around the corner. He pulled in and parked. They walked the aisles, picking out fresh fruit and vegetables. "Pick anything you want to eat," she told him. "It all looks good."

"Any allergies?"

She shook her head.

"Anything you won't eat?"

"Nope. I love food. All of it."

He laughed and filled the basket. "That makes it easy."

Before long they had their purchases and were making their way back to his car. "Now we have just a few moments to get to the house."

Only the few minutes turned to twenty minutes and, when they still hadn't arrived, she turned to ask him and caught him looking in the mirror. She twisted to look behind them. "What's the matter?"

"I was afraid we were being followed."

She gasped. "Have you lost them?"

"I think so." However, he kept looking behind him. "Do you know anyone who drives a black Mercedes sedan with smoked windows?"

She sighed. "My father has a fleet of them."

"Right. Well, let's make sure we don't let them know where we'll be for our honeymoon." With that, he whipped into a large covered parking lot, pulled into an empty spot, and parked. He pulled out his phone. "Hey, Jeremy, can I borrow your car for a few days?"

Hannah didn't hear the rest of the conversation, her

mind still locked on his word *honeymoon*—something she had never thought to have. Yet now that the subject had risen, her mind was warming to the thought, her body as well. Her husband was one sexy man, but they were now exiting the car, taking the groceries, and moving to, … holy crap, a hot red Mustang.

She grinned. "Can I drive?"

TREVOR COULDN'T BELIEVE he let her drive Jeremy's car. But she drove the mean machine like she owned it. By the time they got to Kali's house, unloaded the groceries, had a simple meal, Hannah was tired again. By then, Trevor felt the need for a good night's sleep himself, discovering only one bedroom was in this house. Talk about a reality check and a reminder they were newlyweds.

Hannah had immediately laughed. "It's fine. This is a huge king bed. I won't even know you're here." And she was true to her words. She washed up and crawled into bed, with a sleepy, "Good night."

Trevor wanted to join her in the huge bed, but he also needed a few minutes alone. It was the first he'd had recently after the continuous shocks that had shifted his world. He sat down in one of the only two chairs in the living room and stared at his hands. He had to regain his center of balance.

The talk with Stefan earlier—two days ago maybe—had thrown him off. He'd not had a chance to ponder the implications of Mr. Stingard's murder. He had been a great teacher. An accident was so much easier to accept, but Trevor didn't doubt Stefan. Plus, Trevor hadn't had a moment to consider the ramification or Dr. Maddy's assurances that he and Hannah had a history of sorts.

Both thoughts were unsettling.

The memories assaulting him from his childhood and his teens were bad enough. He hadn't done anything wrong, at least not majorly wrong back then, but every time he revisited those years of his life, he felt like he had. The girls he'd taunted, the boys he'd laughed at. All in an effort to make himself feel bigger, more powerful, and less a victim himself.

He was ashamed of all he'd done.

He had hurt other people. He'd intended to at the time because he was coming from that same hurting place in his life. A place he'd finally escaped after Mr. Stingard's death. His teacher had been a passionate chemist but an alcoholic. The students all knew. They'd all laughed behind his back. Trevor included. But Mr. Stingard had managed to share his interest in chemistry and had caught up many students in its wonders.

Trevor remembered that last day. Mr. Stingard had given them a pop quiz. No one had been ready. Everyone had been pissed. They'd muttered dire threats the whole time. As they'd left the class, the threats had gotten deeper and darker. But Trevor still hadn't thought anything of it. The kids groused about everything back then. Sure, many kids were in danger of failing, but chemistry wasn't the only subject causing them trouble.

All anyone wanted was to get through high school and to get out.

To them, Mr. Stingard represented a block to that goal. The threats had rumbled throughout the school. Why they were directed at that teacher alone, Trevor didn't know. Many teachers had given quizzes that day, as if they'd had a meeting and had agreed to ruin the kids' day. But, for some reason, it seemed that Mr. Stingard held the key spot for their hatred. The anger was directed at him. Trevor heard about the fire later that same day. At first he'd been shocked, then had laughed, like everyone else. He'd only found out the next morning that his teacher had perished in the blaze.

It had bothered him for a long time. The cops too, as they'd spoken to the kids—especially Trevor's group—at length, but eventually the furor died down. Trevor had been relieved. Plenty of rumors flew around. He'd been so afraid that one of his group had done something. There'd been an uneasy silence for a long time, then the tensions eased, and eventually the temperaments of his group returned to normal. But not for Trevor. It had been the turning point. Now he pondered those *friends* from so long ago.

They'd all had nicknames back then, and those were what he remembered. Sticks and his girlfriend Stones, Rags, and Streets. Those four names popped up instinctively. They'd chosen names that spoke of their lack of place in life. Trevor's nickname had been just as bad. Boots. Jesus, he'd actually been called Boots. Worse, he'd chosen that name.

Then boots had ruled his life—as in, they kicked the shit out of him. The group had been bigger, but, months before the fire, several members had broken off. He tried to send his mind back, but his memories struggled to fill in the blanks. Those two had chosen names from a popular TV show. *Starsky and Hutch.* Could they have been responsible? Not likely. Although both were sneaky and arrogant. Trevor had lost track of them all, after he had moved on.

He didn't consider any of the group as his friends now. They were all loners, who'd been flung together due to circumstances. With the change of circumstances, they were no longer together. In fact, they were no longer friends from that moment on. Trevor hadn't seen any of that old group in years.

It was part of his history. And that's where he wanted it—and them—to stay.

CHAPTER 17

HANNAH STUDIED TREVOR'S face. "Are you okay?" She poured them coffee, walked back to the toaster, and brought over the golden-colored bread, placing both slices on the table.

He snagged up one piece and buttered it. "I'm fine."

"You don't look fine." In fact, he looked disturbed, discomforted. Almost ashamed.

"I'm fine," he repeated shortly.

"No, you aren't, but you don't want to talk about it." She nodded. "Got it. Rule number one as a new wife. Don't push for answers that the husband doesn't want to give."

At that, he laughed. Then he stood and said, "Sorry, I don't want to be so distant." He reached for her and hugged her close. "Good morning, Mrs. Johnson. I'm just pondering some news I got yesterday that I'm not sure how to react to."

"Bad news?"

"It's never good news, is it?" He took up his same seat at the kitchen table. "A death of a beloved professor, when I was in high school, has been determined to be murder. Someone in their wish to cause me—you—difficulties has sent a tip to the police, suggesting that I was involved and to take a closer look at me as a suspect."

"That would be my father." She reached out for his hand. "I'm so sorry. He's good at that. I warned you that he thought nothing of crushing his opponents."

"That's all right." He squeezed her hand gently, then went back to buttering the toast. "Let him crush away. I didn't kill the teacher, and I was cleared of that a long time ago."

"Good, but you know the rumor causes as much damage as the truth."

"Let's not worry about me. How are you? You need to know that everything in your head will be fine."

She snorted. "How can it ever be that way? My head is a mess."

"Dr. Maddy is waiting on the test results." He smiled reassuringly at her. "Hopefully we'll find out more soon."

"Are we staying here for long?" she asked. "My father will find us anyway, so we might as well go to your place."

"I'm not so much trying to hide as to stay out of sight, until the legal paperwork is filed. Besides, Monday is your birthday. We need to do something special." He flashed a smile at her, then frowned. "I would like your permission to go through your financials and to ensure you are free and clear."

"As far as I know, I have none," she answered honestly. "There is some money in my bank account, and a set amount arrives every month."

"So a trust."

She nodded. "But it's from my mother."

"May I look into it?"

She studied this man who seemed to have no other interest in her but to help and wondered if he was safe to trust. And laughed. She'd trusted him with everything, including her life so far. Was money any different? "On one condition …"

He raised an eyebrow. "What's that?"

"You explain to me what you find. I have a trust from which I get an allowance every month that has been sufficient for my needs, but that's it. I don't know if I have more, can get more …"

"Is there any chance your father is using your money or needs it for some other reason than saving it for you?"

She shrugged, looked out the window, images of her home surfacing. "I don't know anything for sure, but some of my memories are returning—like my home."

"Great," he said. "Where did you used to live?"

"My mother's old home on one of Father's estates." She studied him. "I presume that, at least for a little while, we'll give the impression of being happily married and, therefore, will live together."

"I have a house a couple blocks away from Maddy actually." He grinned. "It's not close to the luxury you're used to."

"Luxury is lonely," she replied.

He nodded. "It can be, but it's not that way for everyone."

"Tell me about your house," she asked curiously. "Are you really into mowing lawns?"

"I've got no problem mowing lawns, walking a dog, fixing a leak under the kitchen sink." He waved his hand. "I'm just a regular guy."

"No." She shook her head. "You are anything but a regular guy. Regular guys don't step up and be heroes for strangers." She picked up her coffee and took a sip. "And you certainly did that for me."

"That's where you're wrong," he stated in a serious tone. "The circumstances make the regular guys step up. Only when shit hits the fan is the need to be a hero there."

That made a sad kind of sense. "Let's hope you're not called to do this on a regular basis."

"Amen to that."

"What's on tap today?"

"You'll stay here and rest." He stood and refilled his coffee cup. "I'll work from here for the morning."

She nodded. "Good." She rose and picked up her coffee cup. "I'll do the dishes."

"I can help."

"No." She waved him off. "It's the least I can do.

She waited until he headed into the living room, her mood reflective, as she finished wiping the table. She'd woken up with her mind on overload, consumed with the stuff Dr. Maddy had spoken about. Hannah wanted to do some research, but she had no cell phone or laptop to use. She didn't know what to do.

"Problems?" Trevor stood in the doorway, his gaze narrowed.

She realized she was staring out the window, lost. With a reassuring smile, she shrugged. "I'm missing my laptop, and I wanted to research some of this energy stuff."

"We'll pick up my spare, when we go to the office."

"Oh, good. As long as it's not a bother."

He laughed and walked into the kitchen, pulling her into a warm hug. "Never."

She rested against his chest, her arms looped around his waist. "You're a nice man."

"No, I'm not." His laugh rumbled up against her ear, making her grin.

"Yes, you are." She tilted her head back to look up at him. "You're really a teddy bear inside."

"*Shh.* Don't tell my enemies that." He grinned and dropped a kiss on her nose. "And you, wife, are a distraction when I need to work."

"I think I like that," she replied seriously. But she dropped her arms and stepped back. "Can I help?"

He frowned, refilled the empty coffee cup sitting on the counter. "Sure. It's your life I'm looking into. Let's see if you can cut the work in half." He walked to the doorway and stopped, turned back and held out a hand. "Coming?"

"Absolutely."

IN THE LIVING room, he pulled the second chair closer and sat down. The coffee table held his laptop open. "Okay, let's start with your bank account. Do you know what bank and what accounts you have?"

She frowned. "I should, shouldn't I?"

"It would help," he noted cheerfully, "but I can get all kinds of information without it." He started to click through the laptop and quickly brought up the file he'd started on her. He had gathered a lot so far. But a lot was missing.

His laptop beeped, heralding a new email. From one of his assistants. "Oh, good. Here's the list of financials you currently hold." He opened up the file, and his eyebrows shot up at the six-page document. "I guess this would be tough to memorize."

"Does that mean I have money and that it's not all my father's?"

Trevor laughed. "I'll say. But most appears to be locked up. You have an investment portfolio with one firm. You have property ..." His voice fell off. He shook his head. "Honey, you are *very* rich. We need to set up an appointment with your financial advisor and see how this is all supposed to work."

"Does that mean I can get a new laptop?" She leaned forward to look at the pages up on the screen, but it didn't make any sense. "More than that, I feel kind of helpless without a phone," she admitted.

"Understood." He clicked on the bank accounts and came to the log-in information. He glanced over at her. "Any chance you know your password?"

The answer flowed easily from her lips, surprising them both.

He quickly typed in the password and brought up her accounts. And whistled. "Okay, so you can have pretty much anything you want. But, to start with, you need new bank cards." He started a list of things they had to do. After he finally slowed down, he looked at her and asked, "How are you feeling?" He tapped the list. "This could take hours. No, it *will* take hours. But we need to get a start on it."

"Actually I feel really good. The head still aches a little, but that's all."

"Maddy did a lot of work on you, so we have to let the healing continue." He added, "She also mentioned that there could be other side effects, as she started to open up the blockages in your system."

Hannah nodded. "Are we supposed to see her again today?"

"No. Only if we have problems." He clicked through several pages of a Google search and sucked in his breath. Then came an odd silence.

She motioned to the screen. "What are those?"

"Old images of you and your family." He enlarged the page and twisted the screen slightly, so she could see the pictures. "Anything there that's unusual? Familiar?"

"How would I know?" she asked. "The whole thing is bizarre. But …" She leaned forward. "Who is that?"

"Isn't that you?"

Hannah pulled back. "Maybe, but, if so, it's seriously old."

"Did you have any other family?"

"I have no idea. I thought there was mention of a few aunts and uncles, maybe a cousin or two, but, beyond that, I have no idea."

"So we'll do some checking on that as well."

He clicked several other links, and, sure enough, her father had his own page on Wikipedia. "Not that this is a definitive resource, but according to this …"

"I had a brother and a sister?"

As shocks went, this one was a doozy. He studied her face carefully. "You didn't know?"

She shook her head. "No, I didn't know. Does it say what happened to them?"

"Only that they died close to thirty years ago."

Her face paled.

"That's a shock?"

"A big one." She got up and paced the room restlessly. "I wonder why I didn't know. My mother never mentioned them to me. Why was it kept from me?"

"Probably because your father figured you were too delicate."

"He must have hated me. Both my siblings die, and he's left with the weak one. I know he wanted sons and to have lost the one he had?" She shook her head. "It helps to understand him better."

"Does it?"

"Sure. He was cold and emotionless to me and always afraid that something would happen. Apparently with good cause. He'd already lost two children. Since I was deemed weak, he must have thought I had one foot in the grave already."

Trevor wasn't so sure about that, but any excuse that helped her live with this would work for him. "It also says your mother was his second wife."

"Really?" She stared at him. "I feel like I have no idea who I am in all this."

"The children he lost were with his first wife. And …" He read farther. "His first wife was killed in a car accident that claimed the lives of the kids too."

"Oh, my God." She remained speechless at that point. "He lost all three at once."

Trevor found himself feeling pity for the man for the first time. Maybe Hannah was right, and, after losing his first family, he was afraid he'd lose his second daughter too. Like he had lost his second wife. That always brought up questions. Lose one wife, sad but possible, but to lose two? … Now if a third sibling disappeared, … that bore looking into further.

He made another note on his list. Then quickly sent his assistant an email to find out more details on the deaths. He didn't want to suspect Hannah's father of killing his two wives, but Trevor had seen too many shitty men do the same to ignore the possibility. Trevor wondered at how insular Hannah's life had been that even Wikipedia knew more about her family than she did.

"I'm not sure what happened to me," she whispered, her hand going to her head. "Bring that article back up, please."

He clicked to let her see the page and the article on her

father.

"Are there links to my mother?"

"Yes." He clicked it, and they both watched the single page load on her mother's life. And it was mostly blank. Her date of birth and her position as Goodman's second wife, from the date of their nuptials to her death.

Starkly black-and-white information. The article missed out on the human interest side of the story. According to them, she'd lived, had married, and had died. Nothing else was important.

As Hannah crashed back into his couch and wiped her eyes, Trevor could understand the melancholy in her voice. She knew her mother so much better than anyone else. "Remember to hold your memories close," he murmured. With a quick glance at her, he clicked on the link of the first wife. And stared.

She was the spitting image of Hannah.

Like, what the hell?

CHAPTER 18

"**W**HO IS THAT?" Hannah leaned forward, staring at the image on the screen. "That's not me, but it's close enough it could be."

"It's your father's *first* wife."

She stared at him, a choked sound coming from her mouth. "What?"

"Yeah, hang on."

She tried to read the page, but the laptop was facing Trevor, so she couldn't see all of it. She gave up and leaned back against the couch and waited for him to read the rest. For all the shocks, this one was the most confusing. That she hadn't known about her father's earlier family made sense in a way. He never spoke much to her about anything, and he talked to her even less after her mother died. But, with her mother's death, her father had lost his second wife. Bad luck? Or by design?

Scary thought but there was a seed of suspicion. Had her father, who'd been unhappy anyway, rid himself of one or both of his wives? Surely not. He was ruthless, but he could have divorced either of them easily. And he had enough money to set up everyone in style and never miss it, not giving a shit.

Beside her, Trevor gave a deep breath and relaxed. "Well ..."

"What?"

"Your mother and his first wife"—he looked over at Hannah—"were sisters. The younger sister was the first wife, and the older sister was your mother."

How the hell did that work? She stared at him. "I guess that happens …"

"It does." He nodded. "Likely more often than we think. Friends of mine have done the same. Only the older brother died, and the younger brother married his brother's widow."

"I can see that." In fact, she had no problem with it. It was just, in her case, there was an icky feeling to it. Or maybe it was that knowledge how now her grandparents had lost both daughters. While her father was the common denominator. "Does it bother you?" she asked Trevor.

"I'm pondering a man who has lost two wives and whether a third wife would go the same route." He lifted his gaze from the screen. "He never remarried though, did he?"

"No. Years ago he did say he never would, but maybe he's changed that attitude after years with Wanda. She's clearly angling for a ring." Her gaze instinctively returned to the picture of her father's first wife on the screen. "I look a lot like her."

"You do." He studied the image. "There were only two sisters. So you have no other aunts or uncles."

"I remember seeing my grandparents at the funeral," she shared, her brows pulling together. "But not afterward."

"Can you imagine going to both of your daughters' funerals?" He closed the laptop and turned to her. "It would have destroyed them."

"Can you find out if they are still alive? I'd like to contact them." She snorted. "What kind of a person am I who didn't do so anytime in the last decade?"

"I think they passed on soon after your mother," he noted, frowning. He shifted and picked up his laptop. "I thought I remembered something about that."

"Why would you?" she asked in surprise. "Did you know them?"

"It was a B&E that went bad. The media picked up the story because of your father's connection."

As she sat here, contemplating how much of her history was missing, she remembered Dr. Maddy's comment about blocks in her energy. "Were these blocks placed in my energy to help me? So I wouldn't remember this stuff?"

"They could have been put there anytime. And unfortunately, once the first one is put in place, and your system adjusts, it's easier for other blocks to be built as well. Dr. Maddy puts in anchors for those patients she needs to work with long-term. They aren't blocks but are a type of marker that help her to see and to work on someone's system. However, once the body adjusts to those, then she has to do that much more work the next time."

He studied the perplexed look on her face. "For example, if someone were trying to protect you from the trauma of seeing your mother drown, they might very well have put in a block to help you, until you could grow enough to get past it. But then, if there was a second trauma, they might be tempted to put in another block again. And then, seeing as that worked so well, they might …"

"Do it again and again," she finished for him. She reached up and massaged her temple. "I want the blocks removed. Dissolved. Zapped. Or whatever form the removal might need to take. I want them *gone*."

"That can happen, although it might be easier to do one at a time. With each removal comes a flood of information, all those related memories being held back. Not only will that overload your senses and likely knock you out, but also some information in there could be very distressing."

"Like reliving my mother's death?"

He reached out and cupped her cheek. "Yes. Exactly that."

"But other people don't have these blocks, do they?"

He made a face. "Like these? Not likely. Different ones for other reasons, yes. They do. The blocks are intended to help people."

"But not always. Or not long after they served their purpose. So, what if my mother put in place the first block, then, after her death, there was no one to remove it?"

"That's possible but ..." He reached out to brush back a strand of her hair. "Remember. Some of the blocks are newer."

"But, if she did place some, and then she passed on, no one else has been available to remove them until now."

"True, in that scenario, no one would know the blocks were there, unless you saw someone like Stefan or Dr. Maddy. Or another practicing energy worker."

"Stefan does this too?" She frowned. "So actually many people know about this and work with it?"

"I belong to a group of specialists, all who can do this work, but not so many that it's a common ability among the general population."

"Good," she snapped. "I want these blocks out. If that means Dr. Maddy, then fine. Let's ask her."

Trevor picked up his phone, all the while studying Hannah's face. When someone answered at the other end, he spoke. "Maddy, Hannah wants the blockages removed. I figured we should start with one but not sure which block. I don't want her to be too overwhelmed all at once."

The more Hannah considered the blocks in her head, the angrier she got. She reached over and tugged on Trevor's arm. "I want them all out. *Now.*"

He grabbed her hand and stared in her eyes, as he talked to Maddy. "Did you hear her?"

Hannah frowned militantly at him.

He rolled his eyes. "Okay. Pull one now, then I'll call you back, after I see how she's doing."

"What do you mean, 'pull one now'?" she asked, when he disconnected the call. "We need to go see her, and she can remove …" Her head snapped backward, and, like a tiny explosion, fireworks filled her mind, and she actually saw stars.

She collapsed onto the couch in shock. She knew her mouth moved, as she tried to call out to Trevor, but no sound came. Just a gurgle of noise, as images of high school showed up and conversations whipped around her. Fights with her father. Fights with Will. She'd wanted to date. That wasn't allowed. She'd had trouble at school. That wasn't allowed. And it went on and on and on. When the tears started, she didn't know why, but they didn't stop.

In the recesses of her mind, she felt Trevor hauling her limp body into his arms, his warm soothing voice trying to comfort her.

"Just ride the wave, sweetheart. It will be over soon."

Only it wasn't. It seemed to go on forever. She stared up at him mutely, unable to voice the images and the memories replaying like a film on high speed as it rolled through her brain. Not rolled out gently, like a soft ribbon, but like a train that had been held back way too long to stop, now that the engine had finally gotten started. Friends and teachers, her father, his guards. The house she'd lived in. The school she'd attended. All of it as if she stood right there. Right beside them at that moment in time. Even though it was years ago. How could that be? How could anyone have all this stored in their head and not know? That made no sense.

No one could handle all this—surely. If the colors weren't so bright and the sounds weren't so loud, it would be easier. But this was the largest damn television in the world, and she had her face pressed up to the screen. Her body started to tremble.

"Shit. Honey, easy. You're going to crash. You need to just open up your mind and let it all in. Let everything wash in one side of your head and out the other side. Don't try to watch it. Don't try to listen. Definitely don't try to understand. The images come in disjointed. They'll leave the same way. Just let the waves wash through your mind. It's the only way to get through this."

He stroked her cheek, brushed her temple with his lips, and rocked her.

Hannah's trembling got worse.

TREVOR SHOULD HAVE warned Hannah.

What's happening? Maddy asked in his head.

She's crashing. She's in my arms and trembling so badly that she'll nod out on me.

Maddy suggested, *Feed energy into her system to help her stabilize. We couldn't know what this block was originally intended to do, but I only removed a small one from the middle. Figured that would be one of the easiest for her to deal with. I suspect the one from so long ago deals with her mother's death, and that one will be tough.*

And the others?

Not sure, but I am wondering how much the blockages have to do with Hannah's blackouts.

Meaning, she has a blackout when the blockages are put there?

Possibly. Or the blockages allow someone to use a keyword to bring on the blackouts.

That was a chilling thought. *Why would anyone …*

No way to know, Maddy replied, followed with a heavy sigh. *But you know as well as I do that some people out there do things for the damnedest reasons.*

And often for no reason at all.

Trevor glanced down at Hannah. Her gaze was locked on him, huge wells of pain. But he didn't think she saw him. He held her close. *Damn it, Maddy. She's an innocent in all this. She's hurting.*

And she'll hurt a lot more if we can't help her. If someone is using the blockages for their own purposes, then we have to find that person.

Hannah started to cry, not the tears of wrenching grief but the sound of deep agonizing pain.

It'll only get worse, Dr. Maddy warned.

What can I do?

There was silence at first. *I'm not sure there's anything you can do,* she admitted.

No, that's not good enough, Trevor snapped passionately. *I wish I could take her away from all this.*

Then do. Find her a safe haven until this is all over.

Where? How?

If you mean to take her away while her body adjusts, then take her to her grayscale. Or better yet, take her to yours.

He glanced around the living room. *I never thought of*

that.

It will take her out of her physical body for the moment. She will still be overwhelmed, but it will be more distant. Give the memories time to settle, then bring her back.

Trevor closed his eyes for a moment, prepping himself. Then he opened his eyes and gazed down at the woman in his arms. "Hannah, can you hear me?"

"Yes," she cried out. "Make this stop. I can't handle it."

"You can handle so much more than you know, sweetheart. But I can help …"

She stared up at him hopefully, her skin pale wan. "Please help."

"You have to trust me …"

"I trust you," she replied softly. "Just please help."

He smiled down at her. "Okay then." He shifted her position in his arms and reached a hand down, laid it on her chest above her breasts. "Come with me."

"Anywhere," she whispered, and, as if already feeling the pull of his hand, she closed her eyes and went limp.

He closed his eyes and willed himself to his grayscale.

The place he always came to when he couldn't handle the reality of the physical world.

But this was the first time he'd brought someone with him.

CHAPTER 19

"OPEN YOUR EYES, Hannah."

Trevor's voice. She smiled and snuggled close. The pain was gone. The noise was gone. The visual overload—gone. She gave a deep sigh of relief. "Thank you, thank you, *thank you.*" She hugged him close. "That feels so much better."

"You might not thank me in a moment," he noted humorously. "You need to open your eyes."

She opened them lazily and saw that firm square chin above her. She didn't think, she just blew him a kiss. And laughed. Then laughed again. She'd never done that before. Never felt so free.

She opened her eyes fully and gazed around. She was still in his arms, where she wanted to be. And he'd done what he promised he would. He'd taken it all away.

Only he'd taken her into a world of no color.

As she looked around, she caught her breath. "Where are we?"

"In grayscale," he stated calmly. "I took you to my grayscale world in this dimension."

She studied the pearl-gray look to the air and the odd almost metallic look to their surroundings. They stood outside a house but not the same house they'd been in. A big rolling lawn and a glass-and-cedar house stood behind them.

Nice. "It looks familiar. Like I've been here."

"You've been to a similar place but not this one."

She threw him an odd look. "Meaning, I couldn't have come here because it's yours?"

He gave a half laugh. "You're learning fast. Some people can travel from one gray world to another. Not everyone. Most of us are confined to our own grayscale world."

"Not that this is making any sense, but how could I come to yours then?"

"I brought you, but I think you may be able to travel from one to the other, like Stefan can."

"Sounds like Stefan can do a lot of things," she muttered. With Trevor's help, she stood up and turned to look around. "Whose house is that?"

"It's my house," he admitted. "The house I grew up in. I bought it from my parents a few years ago, when they wanted to downsize."

"Nice," she said, studying the cedar-and-glass look. "A family home."

"Exactly."

"And this gray light, this silvery air?" She shot him a sideways look. "And, yes, I did notice that we went from the living room of the house we were staying at to here in the blink of an eye and haven't asked about that yet …"

He grinned. "Ask away. This is the dimension between life and death. I see people here from both sides."

"What?" She slowly turned to stare up at him, her eyes so wide with surprise they almost hurt. "Are you serious?"

"He is very serious."

At the new voice, Hannah turned to see Stefan, walking toward them. She gave him a brilliant smile. "Hi."

"Hi, back. You are looking better," he noted quietly,

that gaze of his assessing.

"I presume you heard us," Trevor asked, with humor. "Got to love the world of psychics."

"You're psychics?" Hannah asked dubiously. "Really?"

Stefan laughed. "No, we are *all* psychics."

She snorted. "No way."

"You are walking in the space between realities. How can you not be a psychic?" Stefan countered.

"I'm here because Trevor brought me," she argued. "I'd have never gotten here otherwise."

"You walked in your own grayscale world several times in the last couple days," Stefan told her. "Both Trevor and I could see in. Although Trevor couldn't move in your space, whereas you appear to be able to walk in his. Interesting."

She frowned and considered his words. She hadn't been joking when she had said this place looked familiar. "I was at Maddy's Floor, when I saw some gray world, like this."

"Yes, that's where we saw you walking the grayscale world," Trevor confirmed, with a smile. "It appeared as if you were speaking to someone, but I never saw who that person was."

She was startled to think that he'd seen her there. "Wow, that's when I saw the young woman who was terrified that I was there and who told me to run."

"Right, you woke up the next time, still running into a different grayscale world, with the creepy older woman."

She nodded. "So was that *my* grayscale?"

"No," Stefan replied, an intent look on his face as he watched her. "You were walking in someone *else's* grayscale world. The question is, whose? Because if you can answer that, I think we'll start to unravel this puzzle."

IT WAS A lot to take in, but, for someone who didn't understand energy work, had never heard of grayscale or alternate dimensions, it was beyond confusing to Hannah. But Trevor had to give Hannah credit. She stood calmly in front of them and laughed. "You're both nuts."

He and Stefan shook their heads.

"Then I'm nuts," she snapped, starting to pace back and forth. "None of this makes any sense."

Trevor reached out and picked up her hand. He tugged her closer and said, "Now touch me."

She frowned. "We're already touching."

He shook his head. "No, it's my grayscale, and I'm touching you. But you're the visitor in my grayscale world, so see what happens when you reach out and deliberately touch me."

She frowned and reached up to pat his cheek. And her hand went right through his jaw. Her face paled, and her mouth opened to scream.

Stefan reached out and touched her. His hand went through her arm, but there was an electric flash.

She jumped back, her hand going to her heart in shock.

Stefan nodded. "See? It's not my grayscale world either," he noted calmly.

To prove his point, Trevor held up his hand and reached out to touch Stefan. And he could grasp the solid shoulder of his friend.

She tapped her chest several times, as if that would help her to adjust to the evidence before her eyes.

Trevor felt sorry for her. She was very talented, if what he'd seen her do already was anything to go by. She just had to believe it, and that would take time. That level of psychic power carried its own challenges.

"Wow. As a demonstration that is very impressive. Okay, so if I'm here in Trevor's grayscale, what purpose is there to this place?"

"Depends," Stefan answered. "I often travel to different grayscale worlds. I come here to talk to people who have died and who haven't moved on, for one reason or another. Or to people whose bodies no longer work, but their spirit is alive and well. This is the only world they can access, but often it's lonely here for them," he admitted.

"So, when I was in this world before, you're saying it was that young woman's grayscale world?" At their nods, she frowned. "I saw several men there as well, but they were in the background, farther away. I couldn't see them clearly."

"Likely part of her grayscale history. People she'd spoken to before from her life or those she met in her grayscale."

"That almost makes sense," she muttered. "But, when I was there the second time, I saw a creepy old lady, who tried to warn me that she was the same as I was and that the world was a dangerous place, so I should stay where she was. Many people were around her too."

Stefan shrugged. "When you can trip into and out of other people's grayscale, then you have to learn which is your own and which isn't. And, when you're shifting from one world to the other, without realizing what you're doing? … Well, … no wonder you're confused. But it will help you to understand who the people are to you when you trip into one that isn't yours." He gave her a slow smile. "And that's only if you have a connection. Maybe you are one of the few who needs no connection. And maybe these people are actually contacting you. They might recognize your abilities, even if you don't."

"Wait. So are you saying that the creepy old woman

could have been in a different grayscale as well?"

"Most likely she was," Stefan stated. "Did she try to touch you?"

"You know what? I think she did, but …" Hannah lifted her shoulders. "I think I backed away before she could make contact."

"And that touch would have shown you more, presumably." Stefan studied her. "Did you know her?" At Hannah's headshake, he asked, "Did she look familiar at all?"

"No. At least I didn't think so. Honestly she seemed so creepy that I just wanted to get away from her. I wasn't sure what to think or what I was seeing."

"Right." Trevor added, "It would be interesting to know your connection to these people."

"Does there need to be a connection?" Hannah asked.

"Not always," Stefan confirmed. "When I walk the grayscale worlds, it's like seeing a subdivision, with all the backyards connected. I can move from one to the other and never hit the same one twice."

"So you walk through other people's worlds too?"

"I do." He nodded. "Along with a fair number of other parlor tricks."

She laughed. "Is there any value to being able to do this?" She waved her arm wide. "I can't imagine any benefit to walking in a world only half lit and empty."

"I do a lot of rescue work," Stefan reminded her, "so this is where I often come to find those who need help."

"Rescue work?" she asked cautiously.

Trevor laughed. "Stefan helps the dead cross into the light. Those people who are caught between death and what comes afterward."

"Jesus." She glanced around. "Are the people I meet in

this gray world all dead?"

"No. Right now you're in my grayscale, and I'm not dead."

She let out her pent-up breath. "It's a lot to get my head wrapped around."

"It is. But another reason to master this world is for the reason we came here," Trevor added. "You were being inundated by the memories flooding your psyche, after Maddy removed one of your blocks."

Hannah gave a mock shudder. "I remember. So, when life gets to be a bit much, you escape to your grayscale?"

"As you do too," Stefan said, a smile in his voice but his gaze intent.

"No, I've never—other than, of course, those two times at Maddy's Floor. … Wait." She froze. "The night I came to your place, … the world looked something like that. Gray silvery tones to it but it was at nighttime, and I was injured, so I put it down to that. Was I … in grayscale?"

He nodded. "Yes, and that's the state you arrived in at my doorstep. You'd been calling out for help earlier, only you didn't hear me responding. I managed to direct you to my place. You collapsed, and I tracked you back to the highway, where your body was. It looked like you had been walking and just fell down, when you couldn't continue."

Her gaze couldn't have gotten any wider. She gasped. "Other people couldn't see me, could they?"

Stefan shook his head. "Not unless they were like us."

"That makes so much sense. Several vehicles passed by, but not one stopped to help me," she murmured. "I didn't understand why not."

"They couldn't see you," Trevor noted. "It seemed real, didn't it?"

"I'd have sworn it was real," she cried out. She spun slightly to look at Stefan. "So I didn't leave a bloody mess on your doorframe, fingerprints? I felt bad that I'd left such a mess."

"Sure you did but only on the etheric level." He laughed at the look on her face. "There are investigators who work on energy signatures as well."

"Who knew?" She frowned. "Unbelievable."

"That's the problem. It's a complete other world," Trevor stated. "As a psychologist I work with people who spend more time over here than is good for them. I come to visit them here," he stated flatly. "I try to get them to come home."

CHAPTER 20

HANNAH STUDIED TREVOR'S face, hearing the flat tone to his voice. "The work you do is hard but so very important."

"I can only help so many people," he admitted. "And there is such a real need for more like me."

"So are you really a lawyer as well?" When he nodded, she asked, "Why?"

"Because I finished law school before I realized I was a grayscale walker. Once I saw how many people were here and in need of help, I went back to school to learn more. The school couldn't teach me any of what I needed to know on this level, but it gave me the piece of paper required to access the people who needed my help."

"And the lawyer stuff?"

He laughed. "It paid for my schooling. Plus, considering the problem of patients' rights and the need to protect patients' assets until they returned to reality, it's been a very handy combination."

"I can imagine." And she could. "But how did you get two degrees, that both need far more than four years at college, and begin your practice of both too, when you are only eight years out of high school?"

Trevor gave a shrug.

But Stefan told the tale that Trevor was too humble to

profess. "He's amazingly brilliant. That would shock his former high school."

Hannah frowned, staring at Trevor and Stefan.

Stefan added, "He doubled up on courses and earned those degrees much faster than the norm."

"Wow." Hannah was focused on Trevor for a long moment, then turned to his companion. "Stefan, do you have any crazy degrees like he has?"

"None. I never did go to a conventional school," he answered, with a wry grin. "My skills in this field are a little more advanced, and I'm fairly specialized."

"It's none of my business, but, last I looked, there wasn't much demand for psychics. So how do you support yourself? Or are you like me, have family wealth?"

"Nope. There isn't any hereditary money. I'm an artist."

"He's not *any* artist," Trevor added. "His canvases hang in private galleries all across the world. He also paints his psychic visions."

She shuddered. "I can't imagine."

"No one can. That's why I paint them. Sometimes it's the only way I can see clearly. And speaking of seeing clearly, are you ready to go back to your body? It looks like your memories are fully aligned again."

"Back to my body?" she asked cautiously, wondering that she could even listen to him and not have this freak her out. "How do you mean?"

"This way." Trevor reached out and grasped her arm gently. His hand was warm against her skin. "We'll go home now."

She gave a gurgle of laughter and said, "Well, I'm game."

"Open your eyes."

She frowned. "They are open."

His grin widened. "Close your eyes, then open them again."

Obediently she shut her eyes and opened them again. "See?" she argued.

"See what?" he asked gently.

She twisted her head to look around. And saw they were back in the living room of the house they were staying at. She was in Trevor's arms on the couch. The same place she'd been when the pain had hit. Pain? She gasped and slowly reached up her hand to touch her head. The pain was gone. There was a sense of peace on the outside but a sense of disquiet inside.

She didn't know what to think. Her memories were calm. In fact, they were there, but she had no wish to access any. It was like they were old and better stuffed away. She could probably drag one out and look at it now. There was no barrier except that of time, saying, *It was over and done with.* She let out her breath, only now realizing she'd been holding it in. "Okay, this is beyond ..." Her words failed her.

"Science fiction? Fantasy?" Trevor teased.

"I have no idea what or how, but my head feels so much better. I'm tired, in a different way than physical," she noted. "It's a peaceful tired, like that good feeling you get after a workout. Yet, at the same time, I didn't do anything."

"Not on a physical level you didn't, but, on the etheric energy level, you did a lot. It could take a bit of time to assimilate."

"I hope not." She smiled, then shifted, so she could reach up and kiss Trevor's cheek. "Thank you for removing the blocks. I feel much better knowing I'm whole again. It felt foreign to think of those things in there."

"In that case, I have bad news. Dr. Maddy removed only one block. And a small one at that. Others are still there."

"Oh, Lord." Her skin went from hot to icy. She stared up at him in shock. Others? Crap. "I have to go through that again?"

"You saw how hard it was for you to get through this adjustment. Pulling all the blocks at once might have sent you into a coma," he explained seriously. "We couldn't risk it."

She leaned against his shoulder, hating the idea of what was still ahead of her. But being in grayscale hadn't been too bad. If they could repeat that trip, she'd be okay with it. "Maybe we could leave a little bit earlier for your grayscale world next time, so I'm not so overwhelmed." She tilted her head back. "It will get easier, right?"

A muscle in his jaw twitched. "Not necessarily," he told her. "The other blocks are bigger. Possibly more important, holding back some very painful memories and responses. So, no, I doubt they will be any easier."

"Ouch." She sighed. "So when can I get rid of the others?"

"Just a minute and I'll ask Dr. Maddy."

When he didn't make any move to grab his cell phone and call, she figured he had changed his mind or meant to do so later. Then she heard that annoying buzz.

Now he spoke. "She recommends no more today, but, if you want to try again in the morning, she can pull another one."

Hannah lay here and thought about everything he'd said and didn't say. Then she added in a very low voice, "You just talked to her, didn't you? Without using a phone?" His laughter rumbled up his chest and past her ear. It was such a joyous sound. So fun and free.

"Absolutely I did. Like you noticed before, when you complained of the buzz. Stefan can do the same thing. We often speak that way. It saves time and effort, and cell phones are not always convenient. Nor do we always want people to hear what we are saying."

"I don't think I've ever met anyone quite like you."

"Oh, I bet you have," he said, with a warm smile, dropping a kiss on her nose. "I suspect your mother was very talented too."

"Too?"

"*Too*. As in, you are as well." He reached up and placed a finger over her lips. "You are talented. You couldn't walk in grayscale if you didn't have these abilities. You've clearly been surrounded by energy people, if they have placed these blocks in your mind all these years."

She felt the intensity of his gaze right to her toes.

"Someone likely started out helping you deal with trauma, then it changed. Either they didn't know what they were doing and kept adding in more to help or someone else came along and did the same thing but for a different reason."

Her mind kept turning the issue over and over again. "I guess I can see the initial one. I was incredibly traumatized after my mother's death."

"And that might not have been the first time," he cautioned her. "Maybe something happened earlier, and that led another to repeat the process after your mother's death."

"To think of one person having access to that part of my psyche is one thing, but to imagine that there could possibly be more than one digging around in my head? I can't see it."

"That's the point," Trevor noted drily. "You can't *see* it. You can't *feel* it. But you need to understand that you somehow allowed it to happen. In a way, you were okay with this happening. If you weren't, you'd have fought it. Now the first time was likely to help you, and you'd have been okay with that. The second time could have been the same, and, by the time more were placed in there, you probably couldn't tell one block from the other."

Hannah frowned. "So I might have known but wouldn't really have understood, as by then it was common, comfortable?" She shook her head. "The things we do to people in the name of what's good for them."

"And it likely was good for you initially," he clarified. "It's just *no longer* good for you, and the process of removing them can get painful."

"No *can* about it." She stroked a finger along his jaw. "You helped me get through this time, so can't you help me on the others?"

"Hopefully, but I don't know what might be released each time, and the blocks could fall when I'm not here."

She pursed her lips. "Another reason to do this right here and now, so that you *are* here, and so I can find out whatever information someone has been keeping from me. Maybe it's what I need to know about my father—to get him to back off. Hell," she added in disgust, "maybe he's the one putting in the blocks." She studied Trevor's square jawline. He was a protector and a damn good one. "Can't Dr. Maddy find out who did this?"

"She feels it was more than one person. One female and one male and there could be more. Beyond that, you have to realize you are both male and female energy yourself. We all are," he stated simply. "Our energies blend with those of the people we live with. If we care about them, we incorporate their energy into our systems. If we don't like them, we don't let their energies become quite as close. Over time it's almost impossible to see who did this. Until you go in and look. And to do that, you would have to open up messy and very difficult memories."

She winced. "As more and more blocks are removed, does it get easier?"

"It gets easier to remove them, yes, but the memories being held behind them are likely more painful."

"Right. That makes sense." She pursed her lips. "Are these something I can remove?"

"Absolutely. As soon as you became aware that they were there, they became something you could deal with on your own. You just need to be ready."

"Sounds horrible."

"No. The stronger and the older that you get, the more the pain of whatever is behind the walls will be easier to bear. The blockages, at least originally, were never intended to be there forever. Only until you got old enough to deal with the trauma."

"So likely the blockages were installed by someone who cared about me."

"Exactly. And yet you were thinking that the first one was there to help you deal with your mother's death. And, in that case, who would have put it inside you, with her gone?"

"I don't know," she exclaimed. "I had a nanny when younger, but I was always with my mother. And the guards."

"The nanny might have done it. If she'd been with you for a long time, she'd have loved and cared for you."

"True enough, but, at the same time, I don't remember her after my mother's death." She frowned, trying to dredge up an image of her old nanny. "I can't even see her face, remember her voice, except when I see a photo."

"Those memories could be behind the blockages."

"Those feel warm and cozy. Like I want them back."

"Of course you can have them back. When you remove the blockages, you'll have access. The memories haven't disappeared. They are there for you, whenever you are ready."

"And if I said I'm ready now?"

He studied her face. "We can try another one, but you're already tired. Your energy's frayed."

She nodded but couldn't leave it alone. "Do we have any idea how many blocks there are?"

"I'm not exactly sure. Three bigger ones and a couple smaller ones for sure."

"Then let's zap the smaller ones."

Silence. "How about *you* zap the smaller ones?" he suggested slowly.

She blinked. She got to her feet and walked to the window, then turned to face him. "That's the thing, isn't it? If I'm ready, then I should do it myself."

"Not necessarily. We all need help sometimes."

Although she nodded, she felt like she'd opened up a can of worms that she wasn't ready for. And yet she'd brought it on herself. She just hadn't realized this would be something *she'd* have to do. She couldn't rely on everyone else all the time. Given the strangeness of her circumstances, she should only call for help when she really needed it.

"Okay. Let me try." She turned to face him. "How do I do this?"

TREVOR WAS REALLY proud of Hannah. He wished she wasn't going down this pathway, but success and a little bit of freedom made everyone want more of both. In her case she'd been caged mentally for a long time. He couldn't stand the thought of such a thing himself, so he could just imagine how she felt right now.

"It's a fairly easy process, but, as you've never done it before, I can't tell you which method will work the best for you." He stood and motioned to the couch. "All I can say is that you need to lie down and to visualize the blocks and to find a way to mentally zap them out. If you'd played video games anytime over the years, I'd say do a mental seek-and-destroy process. As you haven't ..."

"So ..." She walked slowly toward the couch and sat down. "What you're saying is, finding them is likely to be the bigger problem. Destroying them, not so much."

"Exactly." He smiled and walked over, so he stood in front of her. "You can mentally zap away a block, and it will disintegrate under your own positive energy."

"And finding them?"

"Yeah, you have to look for something that feels normal but isn't actually yours. That's more difficult."

"Nice. *Not.*" She sat back and closed her eyes. But thoughts just kept tracking through her mind. She opened her eyes and stared at him. "I can't even see into my memories. So how am I supposed to find anything in there, when it's not accessible?"

He sat down and reached over to grasp her hand. "That's the thing. You have to *think* yourself there. You can't sit in this space and try to access the thoughts because the effort to do that comes to you as more thoughts. You have to think your way into your memory banks. Visualize that space in your head, and see what kind of image you get." He laughed. "And, if you don't mind, I'll follow along and see what you see." She shot him a look of disbelief, then shrugged, "Why not? Maybe you can help."

CHAPTER 21

OBEDIENTLY SHE CLOSED her eyes, laid down, and thought in her head, *Show me my memory banks.*

Instantly she was in a room full of filing cabinets. She had no idea her imagination was so literal. But lined up in front of her were wall-to-wall filing cabinets. Walking to the wall of file drawers, she read the years on the front of them. But how to know which had the blocks? She wandered the room, throwing out the command, *Show me where the blocks are. What years are they in?* The drawers didn't move.

She stood, her hands on her hips in frustration. Damn it. There had to be an easier way to do this. "I know you're here somewhere, Trevor. Can you help? Can anyone help?"

Silence.

Then she got a shock, as a tired voice answered, "Someone *is* here. You are asking as if you need permission to see into your own world. You don't need that. As long as you act like you don't own that space, then you don't. But it is *your* space."

"Stefan?" She felt Trevor's laughter, but, as she spun around, she couldn't see him. Yet she knew he was here. In the background. Like Stefan.

"Yes." This time the tired voice was ringed with humor. "You called. Even though apparently you didn't know you called. Could you tone down that ringer of yours, please?

Some of us are trying to sleep."

She gasped. "I woke you."

Trevor's laughter rolled free. "Yes, you did, sweetheart. Sorry, Stefan. She's trying to find the blocks in her mind and is learning this on her own."

"Right," Stefan noted, his voice all business. "Then stop making it linear. There is nothing linear about time. If you want to see a block, demand it show you its location, regardless of the time of your life it was placed in. And do start small, please. I haven't slept all night. No rescue mission for me if I don't have to, okay?"

"Okay," she said in a small voice.

And his presence winked out. She wasn't sure where he'd come from in the first place, but apparently he was there all the time.

"He *is* there all the time," Trevor confirmed, "but we try to avoid calling on him, if we don't need to."

She took a deep breath. "Right. Do this on my own, and, if we have a panic, he's there, if need be."

"Exactly."

Armed with the knowledge that she wasn't alone—and with Trevor in the background—she tried again. Stefan had told her that she didn't need to know what year the block had been in. "Remove the years and just show me the blocks. Arrange them from largest to smallest."

First came a stillness to the air, then a sudden *whoosh*, and her visualization completely changed. Now large concrete-like walls stood in front of her. Of various sizes. But all were menacing.

"They can look however you want them to look," Trevor murmured. "If these scare you, turn them into purple balls of lint."

She gasped. "Purple fluff balls?" She laughed. "Really? I can do that?"

"You can do anything you want to in here."

Instantly the huge menacing walls that looked insurmountable shifted into purple cotton candy. She laughed again. "Oh, my gosh, this is so much fun. I had no idea."

"It takes energy to do what you're doing," he reminded her. "Since you're not used to this, I suggest you get on with zapping the smaller ones, as fast as you can, before you become so fatigued that this all disappears."

"Right." She turned to study the smallest. "They don't look bad."

"They aren't."

She zapped the first one, and it kind of slowly sagged in front of her but still existed. "I want something more permanent than that. Don't I?"

"Yes. I'd agree."

Cotton candy was just sugar, so she visualized water pouring over the first flattened mess, and, sure enough, it dissolved in front of her. "Yay," she cried out, dancing around. "One gone."

"How do you feel?"

"Exuberant. Happy. Free."

"Then how about another one?"

He was serious. His tone of voice wasn't lighthearted or teasing. He wanted her to do what she could and get out. There wasn't urgency in his voice, but a forcefulness to keep her on track. He knew so much more about this than she did. She got down to work and found that every one after the first one was harder. But she persisted, until she had the four smallest blocks done. Another half dozen remained, and they were all bigger. She'd have to take them one at a time—

and not likely today. But maybe she could do one more.

She turned to the first of them and took a deep breath. It had grown in the time she'd been destroying the others. "It's bigger now."

"It is."

"Why?"

"Either it has its own self-preservation instinct or someone else is feeding it."

She gasped. "Feeding it?"

"Someone put this in here. That means, someone has access to it. And that means, if they feel the block is in danger, then they will pour more energy into the block to keep it there."

"So you're saying someone is consciously keeping this here?" She didn't like the sound of that.

"Not only keeping it but preserving it. Feeding it. Quite possibly on a daily basis."

IT WAS A lot to take in. It was also an experience for Trevor to see Hannah exploring her new world, like a child. When she'd flipped the imposing blocks visual into cotton candy, he'd wanted to dance and cheer with her. He was in her space with her permission, but, outside of communicating with her, he was limited as to what he could do to help her. He used the same technique with his patients. It allowed him to see their progress and their difficulties, without him affecting them. That was important. This was all about them regaining their power. About learning what they'd given up and what they could grab back and control again.

So many mental disturbances were, at their root, just a power issue. Once people let go of their power, often in childhood, they were unable to regain it. Or what they regained, they felt apologetic for, instead of realizing it was their right. They needed to honor their integrity as a person. Sacrificing something like that did no one any good. It was damn important to remember that.

"Is this right?" Hannah asked him.

"Looks good to me." He watched, as she approached the first of the bigger blocks, buoyed by her success so far. He knew these would be different animals altogether. He studied the six and could easily see two creators were behind them. Some blocks were older.

She was working on a newer block.

He chewed on his lip, while he considered the problem of doing that. "Hannah, try the block that is two over."

"Why?" she asked, as she turned the bigger block into an ice cream cone and proceeded to apply a welding torch to it.

He wanted to laugh, but, inside, his instincts warned him that this one was dangerous—that it would cause more problems at the moment than they needed.

"It's working."

"Well, you're melting the ice cream, but I'm not sure it's disappearing." That was a concern. With his instincts prodding him to pull her out of there, he had to stop and to wait … and watch as she tried to dissolve away the first of the bigger blocks.

The melted ice cream pooled at her feet.

"Hannah move back," he snapped. "Don't let the ice cream touch your feet."

She jumped back. "Why not?"

But the ice cream seemed to have locked on to her whereabouts and was following her. She raced farther back, but the faster she ran, the faster the ice cream followed.

"What's happening?" she cried out.

"It's your visual," he responded, trying for a calm voice but knowing she needed to change this visual now. "Turn it back into a stone block."

"Why?" she asked, retreating farther, trying to torch the melted ice cream. But it seemed to continue to run underneath its crusty surface.

Then he understood. "The person who placed this block has noticed your attempts to remove it."

She spun to stare at him in shock. "They can do that?"

"He already has." While she'd been looking at him, the ice cream puddle slithered even closer. "Hannah, look out!"

Too late.

Trevor helplessly watched, as the ice cream touched her foot and instantly shot up through her body.

Her curdling scream terrified him.

In a move he hadn't thought possible in this dimension—hell, in any dimension—she shattered into small pieces in front of him.

Again.

SHE COULDN'T HAVE done that. Please say she hadn't found the block and tried to take it out. 'Cause that would never happen. Not as long as he lived. Jesus. He sat at his desk and held out his hands. They were trembling in shock. Then came the headache, pounding in the back of his head. That had been damn close.

He hadn't prepared for this day.

It hadn't occurred to him that it was even possible. So why prepare? It was a waste of energy. Energy he couldn't lose.

She'd shown no signs of personal power since she'd been a child. No signs of even being aware there was more in her life than the simple world she lived in. Of course she lived poorly in that world as well. She wasn't whole. But that damn splintering bullshit was something else again.

For the longest time he'd thought he'd been responsible for it, but he'd come to wonder if it wasn't a defense mechanism instead.

And that she could do that subconsciously, when he didn't want her to, and he wasn't capable of stopping her or inciting it? … Well, that just made him mad.

But this? … Today? … Not possible.

But it had happened. She'd actually tried to dismantle a block. She couldn't do it of course. She wasn't strong enough. But she was spreading her wings. Accessing her power. Testing him.

He laughed in sudden joy. Oh my. He hadn't seen *that* coming. It was late for her. Most people developed way earlier. Then he might have had a hand in hindering that. He could crush her puny efforts like a bug beneath his feet or he could let the little chrysalis be born and allow the butterfly to learn what the air really smelled and felt like.

Then he could crush her like the bug she was.

At that, he broke into a huge booming laugh.

This was exactly what he needed. Life had been so damn boring for so long.

Finally something to make it exciting.

Who would have thought it would be the little nuisance he'd kept at his side all these years?

CHAPTER 22

HANNAH OPENED HER eyes. She'd had the most horrible nightmares ever. Lord. Even now it felt like her world was on the verge of collapsing. And she couldn't do anything about it. As if she'd put something into motion, and there was no going back, even though she needed a Reverse gear. And, as if understanding this moment would come, that Reverse gear had been removed in preparation.

Dear God, what had she done?

She lay on a bed. In a strange room. It looked like her old bedroom. She frowned. How long had she been here? Surely she hadn't gone home for a visit, had she? She and her father were hardly on speaking terms. Then again, it was just the two of them. At least she thought so.

Her mother's face loomed big and beautiful in her mind. Hannah smiled, even as tears came. "Mom," she whispered. "I'm so sorry."

"Don't be," said a man, with a strong voice. "She's in a happier place now."

Hannah frowned. "Trevor, why are you in my bed-room?"

"You're not there. You're visiting all the memories you released through the blocks being destroyed."

She let his words drift through her subconscious. *Blocks. Destroyed. Visiting her memories.* They made sense, and yet, at the same time, they made no sense. Who could possibly make sense of any of this?

"Open your eyes."

"They are open."

"Now open your physical eyes."

She froze and slowly, ever-so-slowly, opened her real eyes. And found him staring down at her. Instantly memories flooded into her world. "Oh, my God. What happened at the end?"

"I tried to stop you, but it seems like the person who put the newer blocks in your system is still alive, still cognizant, and so very aware of you."

"He tried to stop me from wiping out the blocks?"

"Yes."

With Trevor's help, she sat up, then made it to her feet, where she slowly walked around the living room. Her legs cramped and ached. She shook them out several times to loosen the tension in the muscles. "I feel like I've done several massive hard sprints," she admitted.

"That's due to the shifting energy. You were looking into some of the memories you regained." He paused, then asked, "Did you see anything interesting?"

She shook her head. "No, I didn't. I just saw my childhood bedroom. As if frozen in time. It was the exact same little girl's room I remember from a long time ago."

"And yet surely it changed through your teenage years? Becoming something else?"

She nodded. "It was painted mint green and lavender when I was fourteen."

"But this image was from earlier?"

"Around eight."

"Interesting."

His tone was low and flat. She looked at him sharply. "What do you mean by that?"

"Were you alone in the room?" he asked, his gaze searching. "What was the mood? The overall atmosphere?"

"Flat. Empty. Still. Like I was in there but not. Kind of like when we were in grayscale."

"But you were alone?"

She nodded. "I was. At least I think I was. I was staring at the bed but not on it."

"Okay." He appeared to be happy with that answer.

She wasn't. "What were you afraid of?"

"I'm afraid that something happened to you there, and you've been blocking it all this time."

She shook her head. "I doubt it. I was protected every minute of the day."

"Right. This nanny of yours. Do you remember her name?"

"Susie." The name popped out of her mind. "No idea what the last name was."

"I'll see if I can find her. It might be helpful to talk to her."

"She's dead."

He froze. "Another dead woman in your father's world?"

"She died of an overdose. At least that's what I was told."

He pulled out his notebook and a pen and jotted down something. "Okay. You liked her though?"

"Yes, I did. She was friendly. Young. Playful."

"Good. At least you had wonderful memories with her."

"I did. She was with the guard who'd been on duty, when my mother drowned." Only the last bit came out slowly, as if she wasn't as sure. "Or maybe she was there earlier, then was brought back again. Or that's what I was told. I don't know. I'm definitely confused on that timeline. That big block is starting to mess me up."

"Honey, that block has been there for a hell of a long time. It's not *starting* to do anything. You are regaining your power. You are shifting things now, and that's what's 'messing' you up."

"So this is a good thing?" she asked, cautiously taking her cue from the humor in his voice.

"It's very good." He grinned. "Something did surprise me. Over the last couple days that I've known you, you are always hungry. Yet this morning, you ate normally, and so far you don't appear to be screaming for more food yet."

"Food? Ha, I'm so damn hungry," she cried out. "I didn't see you buy much," she confessed, "and I didn't want to eat it all up. But if there is any chance of having food like ten minutes ago …"

He laughed and stood.

"I'd be so damn grateful," she added, with an exaggerated moan.

"Then let's leave the energy work for the moment and top you back up." He held out a hand and waited for her, as she jumped up to grab it.

"And go shopping for more?" she asked earnestly. "We really didn't buy much. Now that we know I have money, I can buy the next load."

"I've got money of my own, and I can afford to feed my wife just fine," he scolded her gently. At the entrance to the kitchen, he swung her around and pulled her into his arms. With his free hand he nudged her chin up, and, with a smile, he bent his head.

And kissed her.

HE HADN'T MEANT the kiss to be anything other than a fun *Hey, it's great to see your progress and congratulations* type of kiss. But even though he'd dropped a couple on her forehead, and maybe one or two on her lips, he hadn't really kissed her before. Not like the kind of kiss he'd been planning to give her down the road, once life calmed and if the attraction building between them continued. He never wanted her to be wary of him or to be wishing he'd disappear in the wilds. Which, given the circumstances in how they'd met, was always a possibility. He was a nice guy now, but he carried a lot of guilt over his earlier days.

So he might be someone she'd like—eventually when she got to know him.

Only, … when she threw her arms around him and kissed him back enthusiastically, all his good intentions went out the window. And he kissed her like he really wanted to. Not like she was hurting and needing comfort, but like the passionate woman in his arms who seemed to want so much more.

But did she? Or was she responding to the stimulus of the moment, her success so far? Their proximity? And, of course, the fact that he'd saved her from an ugly end. And so much more.

Then he couldn't think at all, as she deepened the kiss.

All he wanted was to take her upstairs and show her what a bed for two was really made for.

She shivered in his arms.

And that's where he had to pull back. Damn it. She'd been through a lot recently. He wanted her, but he wanted her to be whole and not to say he'd taken advantage of her.

A light sigh escaped her lips as he eased back. She reached up, brushed his lips with her own, then stepped back and smiled at him. "Nice to see you're a great kisser."

He swallowed his surprise but couldn't stop the wave of red climbing up his neck. "I'm glad you think so." He smirked. "You're not so bad yourself."

And that was a different issue altogether. Had she had boyfriends? If so, how come they hadn't been mentioned yet? Nor shown up in any research. Yet she had said that her father and Will had done their best to stop her from seeing anyone.

"Yeah, well, my guards made sure I didn't get much experience," she noted gaily, as she walked into the kitchen. "But I did manage to sneak in a few relationships. Although the guys were more likely in it for the thrill."

He could imagine. But kept his mouth shut regarding that. "What about after you grew up?" he asked quietly. "You've been living on one of your father's estates for a long time. So free, but not free."

"I have, and I've had several boyfriends, but they tended to not last longer than a few months. Usually Will or Father got wind of it and put a stop to it. I actually asked one to marry me, so I could get the hell away. He lived in Norway, and, at the time, I thought naively that would be far enough away." This time her laugh was bitter. "But it wasn't. My father scared the poor guy and paid for his flight out of the country and back to his homeland. It didn't matter he was working for an engineering company here in the States. He left in a heartbeat."

She didn't say it but he could see her mentally adding, *and left me behind.*

"Not too many can stand up to that kind of threat, and your father is a master at intimidation."

"Isn't he though?" She stood in the kitchen and glanced

around. "See? I know that good stuff comes out of this room. That there is a room like it in every house, but I really don't know how to get my hands on the finished product."

He snickered and set about collecting the fixings for big sandwiches. "What did you live on while you were alone?"

"I had a housekeeper."

He rolled his eyes at that.

"At least in the beginning. Then, when it was just me, I did a lot of takeout. I tried to make several egg dishes, but it was *hard*." At a choking sound, she turned and studied his face suspiciously. "Are you laughing at me?"

"Hell no. Cooking eggs is *hard?*" He managed to imitate the long-drawn-out way she'd spoken the word. Then he cracked up laughing.

She glared at him, then glanced at the fixings on the table, and stated, "I can manage a sandwich though."

"Go for it."

She sat down and enthusiastically made up four. He hoped he was getting two of them, but, from the intent look on her face, he figured she was thinking to have three of them herself.

While she worked, he brought out the fruit he'd bought and washed a selection to create a quick fruit platter. He carried it over to the table.

"Oh, pretty."

"Not so much. But edible." He reached over and popped a bite of watermelon in his mouth.

A few minutes later they were munching through the sandwiches. She'd cut them into quarters and placed them on a larger plate to share.

After a few moments, she sat back and smiled up at him. "Starting to feel better already."

"Good." He smiled and reached for a second piece, but

his internal alarm system twinged. He narrowed his gaze and looked inward. "Someone is hunting you ..."

"That's okay," she said, shaking her head. "That's my father and Will. They are always hunting me." She grinned. "Why do you think I keep my energy so tight to my body? That's my mother's doing. She knew I needed to do that to stop others from always being able to track me." She waved her hand toward the window. "Apparently those outside can't find me as easily when I do that."

He stared at her in surprise. "So you keep your energy close to stop your father from finding you?"

"Well, it slows him down but doesn't stop him completely." She picked up her third piece of sandwich and stared at it happily. "Honestly, between you and me, I think Will is the most dangerous."

"What about the other security guard? Isn't he as dangerous?"

"George is, but I don't get the same sense of menace from him as I do from Will. Then again, Will cultivates that image. Loves to project that dark, deadly image. Wants others to see him as the alpha in any situation."

"Except around your father."

"Well, he takes on the alpha protector persona, whereas I see him more like a grizzly bear on a rope. My father uses him like a tool, and Will likes to believe he thinks independently. George is always there but in the background. Not bothered about fighting the other two for position. Will can't do Father's job, and Father isn't interested in taking on Will's role. One is the aging patriarch and the other the upstart. But their codependent relationship works for them."

Trevor didn't quite know what to say, but, as an assessment, it was fairly accurate. And it showed she had a greater insight into those closest to her than he'd expected.

CHAPTER 23

HANNAH LOVED FOOD. That's just all there was to it. But she'd enjoy this moment more if Will wasn't on the hunt. She felt her energy snugging in even tighter, as Will reached out mentally for her. Damn that man. Why couldn't he find someone else to torment?

"I've never told anyone before—about how I hold in my energy. It seems so minor." She shrugged. "You guys are seriously talented."

"What you are doing is not easy or simple to do," Trevor noted. "Your aura actually appears as if you are in a coma or dying within the next hour."

She blinked. "Say what?"

"You heard me." He grinned. "Stefan and Dr. Maddy were amazed when they saw you for the first time. It's one of the reasons Stefan reacted so fast to get you help when you arrived, bleeding and hurt at his door."

"Sure, but he'd have seen I was fine in other ways."

"He reacted to your low-energy reading and poured his into your system to try to save you."

She had to consider that. "Would I have felt his energy surge?"

"I don't know. Did you?"

"At the time I didn't feel much but shock," she replied candidly. "That he was someone I was supposed to have attacked. And that made no sense to me. I'm very noncon-frontational."

"You've never mentioned it before." Trevor sat back and stared at her. "Stefan told me what you said though."

"What's to say?" she asked quietly. "I don't know any more than you. It's yet another mystery I can't explain."

He nodded and continued to eat.

She studied his bent head. "What are you thinking?"

"I don't know what to think," he replied. "It's disturbing to think you had thoughts of killing my friend in your head, but I do understand that they might not have been your thoughts."

At that, she stared down at the last bite of her sandwich in her hand, the mouthful she had just swallowed churning her insides. "Can people do that? Put thoughts in your head?"

"Yes, absolutely. Not easily and not often. But it happens."

"So, what then? I walked past someone, who thought he'd killed Stefan, and, on a whim, he dumps that knowledge on me?" Her voice held a note of incredibility.

"That's one possibility." He picked up a strawberry and popped it into his mouth. When it was gone, he added, "It's also possible that someone could have deliberately planted that idea and sent you to Stefan's house as a warning." He took a deep breath. "Or you walked into someone's gray space, and they saw you, could communicate with you. Someone who wants Stefan dead."

"Are there people like that?" she asked in a hushed whisper.

He snorted. "Stefan helped put dozens of serial killers behind bars and has been attacked by dozens of assholes in the last year alone. So you seeing him and thinking you'd killed him already has implications on many levels."

"Oh boy." She stared at him, mouth open.

"As you can see, whatever is going on in your head is of great interest to us all."

"So—" And a shard of agony split through her head. She cried out and dropped her sandwich, both hands reaching up to clasp her head. "Make it stop …"

"Make what stop?" Trevor raced to her side, clasped his hands over hers, and instantly the pain eased.

She shuddered, as he continued to work. Whatever he was doing was easing the pressure.

"What was that all about?" he asked, when the tension in her shoulders and neck eased, and she slumped in place.

"It's Will. He's hunting me."

"We knew that already. Is this headache part of some further detection mechanism?"

"Yes."

"Interesting. Crippling you with pain makes you more vulnerable to whatever Will is up to." He sat back down and studied her face. "I'd like to know how he is tracking you. Do you know?"

"No, I'm sure you'll say it had something more to do with the energy blocks in my system or that he was tracking me on a different dimension or something."

"That's definitely what he is doing. How interesting that your mother understood."

"And yet, like you said, this system of blocks cripples me more than it helps me."

"And, like *you* said, she died when you were little and likely thought she had lots of time to teach you more."

"What did you do that made the pain ease so quickly?"

Hannah asked, rotating her neck. "Does it stop Will from finding me?"

"I removed the building pressure of energy in your head. It's probably caused by conflict between the need to remove these issues and the need to keep everything in place to protect you," he replied rotely. "And, no, it doesn't stop Will. I can put an energy security alarm around the house, but the large amount of energy it generates alone will possibly attract him to our location, letting him know exactly where you are."

"That would be bad," she said in a very low voice. "I don't know what his problem is—if he's just joyfully doing my father's bidding or what—but he'll never let up."

"Well, he will but not on his own. We'll have to step in and let him know that he's got to stop, or we'll stop him ourselves."

"Is that possible?"

He sighed. "Very possible. Often the only ending we see in this world. The asshole dies, or his energy abilities become so burned out that he is institutionalized for the rest of his life. It's not an easy scenario for anyone."

"No. But I wouldn't mind either of those. I don't know whether my father is involved or not, but if he is ..." She shook her head. "It's hard to imagine doing that to anyone you love. He must have loved his first family. But the second? ... I don't know."

"Give him a chance to explain. He might not have known how to deal with his own emotions after such a huge loss. That's not easy."

"Unless it's a loss he wanted, so he'd be free again." She fell silent. "I don't know what to believe."

"Hopefully we'll get more information soon, some that

will help us to figure this out." He walked to the sink and filled it with hot soapy water. "Stay positive."

She laughed. "Hard not to with you around."

"Always happy to help."

"We need to go to the bank now, don't we?"

He nodded. "Lots of errands." He came and joined her at the table again.

She watched that glance of his land on her, doing a quick assessment, then, as if satisfied, he added, "I might even pick up coffee and snacks while we're out to keep you fortified."

"Be still my beating heart. I thought the way to a man's heart was through his stomach, not a woman's. Aren't you supposed to buy diamonds for me instead?"

"Ha, you were likely raised on those, and I'm not in the diamonds-with-coffee category." He grinned, and, as if he couldn't help himself, he snagged her up in his still-wet arms and said, "Besides, a double-Dutch chocolate and walnut coffee cake will probably have the same effect."

Her eyes widened in wonder. "There is such a thing?"

"Indeed, and, as soon as we get the kitchen cleaned up and a few errands run, I'll take you there."

That did it. She spun into action, and they were out of the house in ten minutes.

TREVOR WOULD HAVE laughed, but she was so damn serious that he wanted to cry instead. He was right in that she'd had everything she needed in life but not the little things, like enjoying a coffee and a baked treat out with friends. He was pretty damn sure she had never experienced something so simple before. He walked her into the Second

Home Bakery and Coffee Shop, only a few blocks from his house, and stopped to take a big inhale of the wonderful aroma. They roasted their own coffee here, and it was delicious. Not tasting burned, like so many places that tried to do the same thing.

"Oh, wow." Her voice held a certain reverence.

He followed her gaze to the large glass display counter, with dozens of fresh baked goods. "See? Isn't this a great place?" He led her to a small table and chairs set off in the corner. "I'll go order."

She stared at the goodies and nodded.

"What would you like to eat?" he asked.

"All of it," she replied in a hopeful voice. "No, that would be too much. How about what you suggested earlier. And a latte, please."

He made his way to the order counter and stood in line. Ever since that first twinge to say they were being hunted, he'd been on his guard. It was wearying. Normally he'd hole up at home or at work, until the danger eased. Except, instead of easing, the sensation was getting worse. He had his guards up, but to know that someone was tracking them just added to the tension.

They'd survived getting new bank cards and ordering new credit cards for her. They'd also set up a PO box address.

It still wouldn't take long for anyone to track it all down, but he hoped it would take a day or two. He had meetings set up with her financial advisors for Monday, her birthday, and had managed to schedule a couple days off at the beginning of the week, so he could get this all locked down.

She was holding up, happy even. There'd been no new attacks, but even he could see her energy tight around her frame. Constantly aware. Constantly in defensive mode. Likely from sensing Will getting closer. It blew him away she could do such a thing and have no idea what that meant in terms of energy work. She was really special.

What would they have to do to stop her father from destroying her life again?

Stefan stepped into his mind. *You'll have to stop him. The father legally. And the minions? Likely the hard way.*

Are you picking up this presence?

Yeah, definitely something the hell is going on. Grayscale has shifted, Stefan noted. *The energy fields all over are tweaked. We need to stop this asshole, before he creates permanent damage.*

But who is it?

I don't know. I thought it was Will, but unfortunately I keep getting a female vibe, and that's not blending with the other information.

Stefan paused and asked in a low voice, *Did you get any information on the dead wives?*

Not yet. You think they are key?

Yes, Stefan said softly. *They are key, or at least they are one key …*

CHAPTER 24

TREVOR FASCINATED HANNAH. She'd had ample time to study him today, with all their errands and business stops. They'd arrived at his office, where she'd remained close to him, while he introduced everyone. She loved watching him. He was confident and strong, always in control. Always helping out.

From her experience, it was this last trait that made him so unique. She found herself wanting to know more. Wanting to know everything there was to know.

His office was an experience in itself. She'd been in legal offices before. Ornate dark, somber atmospheres, as if heavy, weighty issues would happen in those places and those places only. Yet this office was bright, cheerful, and airy. Lots of windows. It was on the first floor of a building on a small side street near the hospital. He had three assistants, and yet he was the only lawyer.

As they crossed the front office to head toward the back, where his bigger office was, she asked him about it.

He laughed. "As soon as I can find people who do anything even similar to what I do, I'd be delighted to have them come on board. In the meantime"—he waved at the two men and one woman who were busily working—"these people are my lifeline."

"Any paralegals among them?" she asked curiously.

His gaze assessed her. "Yes, actually Charlie here is help-ing me draft documents, while all do research as needed. I gather you've been around lawyers a lot of your life."

"Not much choice. They came and went through my father's home office on a daily basis." Too damn often, as far as she was concerned. They were all the same stuffed-shirt, ostentatious, unsmiling personas.

She nodded to Charlie, who happened to look up at that moment. She smiled at him. "Do you really understand all that Trevor does?"

The young man grinned. "I'm not sure anyone under-stands that but him."

Trevor led her to his office and motioned at a chair for her. "I'll try to be as fast as I can be."

"Not an issue," she replied easily. "If you have that spare laptop, I'll pass the time easily."

"I can do that." He got up and walked to the doorway to speak to Charlie, turned to her again. "He'll bring a spare we have for the office in a moment."

"Nice to have spares."

Charlie brought her one and asked, "Do you need a mouse?"

She shook her head. "No thanks."

She turned it on, and, once it loaded, she went to her email. As expected, it was full. She sighed and started to delete the bulk of them. Once she'd deleted those, she returned to the ones that required responses. An old school friend was asking for money for a charity fund. An old teacher contacted her about a friend of hers who was trying to raise money. She sensed a theme here.

She ignored those and moved to the others. There was a request from her financial advisor to confirm the request for information that Trevor had submitted and a confirmation of Monday's meeting as well. That was a given.

By the time she'd made it to the bottom of the heap, she was done mentally too. Nothing in there about her florist business. The lack of her business. Nothing. So what happened to it now?

And yet ... she could barely remember it.

And she should.

She glanced over at Trevor, who had been on and off the phone since they'd arrived.

She checked out her social media sites, unsurprised to see nothing was going on in her world, which was, after all, infinitely small. She groaned and went to Tasha's page, only to find there wasn't one. She frowned. Hadn't it ever existed? Her world was a mess of assumptions but lacking in facts.

She couldn't even trust her memories.

Although she had more memories there now than before. It wasn't the time or place to work on the remaining blocks, but she had to wonder at what information could be so important as to place blocks in a child's mind to begin with. Sure, trauma was one thing, but that block should have disappeared or been removed over time. Time was a warm cozy blanket that eased the load for many things. But maybe not a personal loss like that.

If she thought about it, losing her mother still felt like it had happened only yesterday. And she could only imagine if she'd lost a child or a husband instead.

The losses would be so personal.

And devastating. Her mother had lost her sister and her sister's children. But Hannah's grandparents? They'd lost two daughters and two grandchildren. Hannah was the only one left. That had to have been terrible for them.

She also had no idea how much contact she'd had with them, after her mother's passing. Had she had any? Or had she been sequestered away, and they'd essentially lost her too?

All painful questions.

And she needed answers.

"Okay, I think I can leave." Trevor's voice was distracted. "I'll bring work home with me. Maybe I'll ask my neighbor to look after my animals just in case."

She stood. "May I use this laptop?"

"You can. Or we can buy you one on the way home."

"I'm not up for that."

"Good. Neither am I." He smiled at her. "Yet we might need to do more shopping on the way home, if your appetite doesn't ease back."

"It's not bad right now, but I think the energy work boosted it."

"It does do that. In your case, we have a lot more to do."

"So we are stopping on the way home?" she asked with spirit. Then she paused. "Could we drive past my store too, please?"

"We can do that."

She sensed the intensity of his gaze, as she walked out of the room, but knew the other employees had been studying her furtively as well. Hell, by the time they left the office, she knew they'd be discussing her and the new situation of having the boss's wife around. Couldn't really blame them. Their boss got married unexpectedly to someone they didn't know, and, of course, they would have questions.

Everyone had questions. Everyone talked. All the time.

HE PARKED OUTSIDE the Chinese food restaurant beside the burned-out shell of her store and motioned toward it. "Shall we do takeout?"

"Yes, please." But her voice was faint. Sad. She stared at the remains of her business and looked about to cry. He hated to cause her more pain, but she was disassociated from so much that he had worried if she'd cared about the business in the first place. The whole rich-kid syndrome. But she did care.

"I want to get out." But she sat immobile.

"Then let's go." He turned off the engine and hopped out, coming around to her side to open the passenger door. She stared at him. Then took a deep breath and accepted his help to get out.

"It's like a grave," she admitted. "It's so shocking to see it like this."

"How was business?" he asked curiously.

"Not great. But I loved being here. It wasn't making a profit, yet it could have—with time."

She spoke as if from memory. Trevor thought that a good sign, as he glanced around the neighborhood, run-down and tired looking. He could imagine the store being in the same condition.

Immediately her hand went to her forehead. As if in pain. He'd noticed it a couple times before but hadn't understood. Now he wondered if her thoughts, her questions, related to areas that had been blocked or maybe the areas where she'd blacked out. "Do you remember the last time you were here?"

She shook her head. "No, I don't. That's part of the problem. I can't remember anything."

"Do you have the company books anywhere?"

She motioned to the store. "In there. On the laptop that had been in there as well."

"What about cloud storage?"

She frowned. Then her gaze cleared. "Yes, we used an online storage system to keep the information for income taxes."

"Good. We'll take a look at that when we get home." He studied the building remains. "What made you buy it?"

"I was looking for something …"

"Was it a good price?"

"It was cheap," she admitted. "It's the only reason I could buy it in the first place."

"Right." And probably a complete and total rip-off in the first place. But he stayed quiet. "Did you have fun here?"

Her face lit up. "I did. It's the first time I had anything of my own that my father didn't have his fingers in. I loved being around the flowers."

That made the most sense of all. "Did someone help you with the transition?"

"The previous owners. This would make them cry now," she murmured, motioning to the shell in front of her. "They'd wanted out for a long time. They were tired and getting older, and they needed to close it down but had lots of loyal customers they didn't want to disappoint."

"So you bought it. Did you buy it so they could have that extra boost for their retirement, then give them the job of training you, so they also had some purpose in their life?" he asked, intuitively knowing she hadn't been rooked as much as she'd deliberately helped them out.

Her sideways glance in his direction confirmed his suspicions.

"You are really a sweetheart, aren't you?" he told her.

"You mean, *bad business person?*"

He grinned and tucked her fingers into the crook of his arm. "Let's order a bunch of Chinese, and, while we wait, we'll walk around to the alley, so you can see all the damage."

And that's what they did.

As they stood in the back of her store and stared at what remained, she shook her head. "I wasn't here, so my car was torched."

"That's the part I don't get. If you weren't here, where were you? And if you weren't in your car—which, since it's parked here, I assume you weren't—what car were you in that took you to Stefan's house?"

"I have no idea," she whispered, staring at the remains of her vehicle. "Any chance I own two cars?"

"I'll check the DMV."

"Good, at least you know where to look. I haven't a clue."

He wrapped an arm around her shoulders. "Do you need to see any more?"

"No," she replied in a soft voice. "I don't. It would be nice to see Tasha again though."

"Sorry, Hannah. Remember? We still haven't confirmed whose body was found here in the fire." With his arm around her shoulders, they walked back to the Chinese restaurant. He went inside to pick up the order, while she waited outside.

The owner nodded. "Order ready."

"Good. Thank You." He took out his credit card to pay. "I brought Hannah over to look at what's left of the flower shop." He nodded outside to where Hannah stood, looking over the blocks around them. He figured she'd want nothing to do it the place again.

"Hannah?" The owners' faces scrunched up. "Who is Hannah?"

Trevor, his Spidey sense tingling, explained, "She was the young owner of the store next door, wasn't she?"

The little Asian woman stood at his side, and she burst into a spate of Mandarin. Then she stopped, and she and her husband both turned to look at Hannah, then back at Trevor.

As if synced together, they both shook their heads and replied, "No. Miasha owner." They pointed to Hannah outside. "Her Miasha."

And his stomach heaved.

It took him a long moment to regain control, but, when he could, he nodded, paid for the food, and left.

He glanced at Hannah, as she stood pensively leaning against the car.

What were the chances that her blackouts were at the core of this? Still, his training brought up many other possibilities. The institutions were filled with examples. He just never thought to be married to one. And not for the first time did he wonder why the hell had he gotten involved in this mess. *Stefan? Got a moment?*

He heard a faint response. *Sure,* Stefan replied. *Don't mind me. I'm just here working with Anita.*

Any change? Trevor asked, hoping for good news. The little girl was such a sweetheart. *Did Dr. Maddy get a chance to stop by?*

She has but not long enough to learn anything new. Although she did mention some foreign energy here as well. Female and older. Then we already knew the older part. We're looking into her family history at the moment. His voice faded slightly, the fatigue hitting him. Trevor didn't know how Stefan could keep helping so many people. Then Trevor was in the same boat himself.

What did you call about?

Trevor filled him in. Before he was done, Stefan was barking questions.

She could be just using a pseudonym to hide from her father, Trevor suggested.

Anything is possible. Particularly if her father was controlling, overbearing. But Stefan's voice was doubtful. *It will eventually make sense, but we need more pieces of information first.*

I'll go lock down a few more bits of paperwork and see if there has been an ID on the body found in the florist shop.

Good. Stefan paused. *How is she?*

Better. She's learning more. Coping better. She keeps her energy in to avoid detection. So her mother must have thought the enemy was an aura reader. Or someone who could track by signature.

Essentially she's been in hiding all her life, Stefan noted. *That's so sad, yet proves the strength and ability of the human spirit to survive.*

CHAPTER 25

T REVOR MADE IT to the car and placed the two bags of Chinese food in the back seat, then walked around and unlocked the passenger side for her. She stared at the flower shop with such sadness on her face that, if nothing else, it made him feel better for seeing the grief. Whatever the hell was going on, he had to trust she'd been doing whatever for a damn good reason.

Considering her father's domineering presence and that someone was hunting her, … survival was the best reason of all. Second to the freedom to do something on her own for once.

Back at the house, they ate quickly and moved to the living room. There she went into her business records to see what she had to do for income taxes and to shut down the business due to fire.

Trevor kept his head down, as he looked for the information he needed. An email from Drew came in. No positive ID on the victim in the fire yet. Except there was one major point. The victim had been male.

The business was registered to Hannah M. Goodman. The *M* made him realize he likely had the clue he needed, and that was huge to unravel this. Seeing she was buried in her own research, he asked in a calm and casual way, "What's your middle name, Hannah?"

"Miasha," she replied distractedly.

Bingo.

He settled back and studied her. She was lively as she did her research. She had her fingers on the screen, and her face twisted and fell, as she looked for and found the information she sought. "This is so confusing. I have to contact someone to make the last business day the day of the fire." She groaned and settled back on the couch. She turned to look at him, a frown on her face. "You know how frustrating this is?"

"It'll get even more frustrating," he noted and turned to look at her directly. "The owners of the Chinese food restaurant didn't know you by the name Hannah."

She scrunched up her face. "They didn't?"

"No. They knew you as Miasha."

She stared, but confusion ruled. And he understood that. He didn't get where or why she'd pretend to be someone else, but apparently she chose her alter ego when she wasn't Hannah. The clinician in him was fascinated. The man in him was worried, and, as a new husband quickly becoming more interested in her than he likely should be at this point, he was suddenly wary as hell. *What was going on?*

"Why would I use my middle name?" she asked in bewilderment.

"No idea but I presume so people didn't know who you really were." He paused, then added, "There has been another development."

She raised an eyebrow.

"The body found in your shop was a man."

HER EYES LIT up. "Really?"

He nodded. "So Tasha is presumably alive and well, and, if we can track her down, you should get more answers."

"Thank heavens for that," she whispered. "I'm so glad she wasn't killed because of me. I couldn't have lived with that. Not again. I think she's likely gone back East to her family. The question is, did I know about it?" she asked wryly.

Trevor stretched out a hand and grasped hers in his much larger, more capable one. How did one scale this information and get a handle on it?

Then she gasped. "If that's not Tasha, who burned in the fire?"

"We need to figure that out," he noted quietly. "And I'm wondering if the Miasha issue might have to do with your splintering."

"What's splintering?" She watched, as he stared around the room. At anything but her. "Am I blacking out and becoming Miasha during those times?" Her voice rose in horror. "Do I have a split personality or multiple personality disorder?"

"I doubt it. But you have those blocks that affect your memories, that close you off from memories. The splintering issue appears to be the trigger for the blackouts, and the blackouts appear to be the trigger for so much going wrong."

It made no sense. Then it didn't matter right now, as pain slammed into her brain. "It feels like my head is about to explode." She clasped her hands over her ears and bent over, gasping for breath. "Oh, dear God, he's here."

Trevor reached for her, to cancel out the pain.

However, the pain intensified. She fell to her knees on the floor, groaning loudly. "It's Will. He's here. He's found me again," she cried out in a panic, overridden with pain.

"Oh God, I have to leave. I have to run."

"Run where?" Trevor grabbed her hands. "You aren't alone anymore. Remember that."

"No, I have to leave." Her voice was young, terrified.

"You can't," he told her. "There's nowhere to go."

TREVOR STOOD AND saw a vehicle similar to the one who'd followed them yesterday parked outside. She appeared to be correct. Only he saw no sign of anyone approaching. The bastard, would he try to break in? Trevor felt the same frisson of energy stirring on the ethers that he'd felt earlier, but in a much milder way, like a snake tasting the air, while it poised to strike. "Let me check the doors. We don't want him sneaking in the back."

He turned to grab Hannah, to keep her close to his side, when she said, "He won't. Have to stay safe. Have to stop him."

"We will. Don't panic. It will be fine," he stated in a low voice. He couldn't sense Will around the house but surely he wouldn't march up to the front door, would he?

A hard knock pounded on the door.

He would.

In surprise Trevor stepped toward the door, but Hannah cried out, "No. Don't."

He reached out for her ... and watched her shatter. As in completely come apart.

He caught his breath as the energy burst outward. Like an explosion, the force went well beyond the small room. Energy blasted out from where she stood—in huge colorful waves.

Stefan?

I'm here, he replied in Trevor's mind. *Jesus. Look what's happening to her energy.*

The explosive waves rolled ever outward, out of the room, out of the house, and out to the vehicle parked outside. Trevor shifted to the window, so he could see what was happening.

And to find Will at the door.

Trevor was in time to observe the waves crash over Will, not just once but in continuous rolls, as Hannah's splintering set up these mini–shock waves.

Will bent over, his hands clutching his head, and he staggered back down the steps.

As Trevor watched, Will slowly straightened and looked around, confused, as if not having any idea why he was here or even where *here* was. Moving carefully, as if woozy or drunk, he got into his car and slowly drove away.

Trevor turned to see Hannah desperately pulling herself back together. He caught his breath, as he studied the woman who had done something so amazing, yet struggled to regain herself. "Can I help?" he asked quietly.

No response came.

Not that he'd expected one. How could there be? He saw her face, but she was so damn fractured. … If anyone else came in right now, they'd think he'd shot her with a shotgun. Only there was no blood. Just broken pieces. Moving on their own.

He took a deep breath and watched.

It's fascinating, Maddy murmured. *I've never seen anything like it.*

Is there anything we can do to help Hannah? Trevor asked.

I can't see how, Maddy replied. *We're likely to mess her up more if we step in. We don't know how she's doing this.*

Fascinating, Stefan repeated.

As the three watched the process near completion, Trevor caught sight of something dark, ominous. *See that?*

Yeah, it's a block, Maddy confirmed.

But it's in the way, Stefan noted. *Causing her problems. She is struggling to fit it in the right place and can't get it.*

Of course there's no right place because the block doesn't belong, Maddy replied.

Trevor took a deep breath and asked, *Can we remove it?* His fingers itched to reach out and to just pluck the damn thing from Hannah's head.

I don't think you'd get anywhere close, Maddy suggested. *The weapon she has is unbelievable.*

Stefan added, *It's damn-near impossible to fight it too.*

CHAPTER 26

HANNAH DID A full-body wiggle and slowly straightened, stretching her arms overhead. At the same time she opened her eyes.

Trevor studied her intently.

"What's the matter? Do I have my shirt on backward or something?"

He snorted. "Or something."

She slowly lowered her arms. She hadn't ever seen him in this mood. Then they'd only been married for a few days. "So tell me what's wrong."

"What do you remember about the last few minutes?"

She cast her mind back. "Not much. Headache that seemed to build and build, then maybe a knock on the door?" Puzzled, she turned to look at the door. "I'm not sure about that. Was someone there?"

Trevor sat down on the couch, his gaze more detached, as if she'd done something that twigged his shrink side.

"Damn it. What did I do? And do you hate me for it?" Her lips trembled at the thought of losing him. She hadn't planned to do whatever she'd done. Her laptop was open, and there'd been some talk about her middle name. Eagerly she asked, "We were discussing my middle name, right?"

His gaze narrowed, and he nodded slowly. "What about your middle name?"

She sat down beside him. It was obviously important, whatever it was. "It's the same name as my mother's. I was named after her. She loved flowers. Buying the shop made me feel closer to her. As if she'd approve."

She felt his start of surprise and then his frustration, as he pinched the bridge of his nose. "Anything else?" he asked.

She shook her head. "No, the headache, then the door." Her voice softened. "I'm sorry. that's all I remember." He opened his arms, and, with a cry, she fell into them. "I don't know what happened. Obviously I had a blackout or something."

"Or something." He held her close. "Give me a minute. Then I'll explain. Or at least I'll tell you what happened. The explaining part? I'm not sure I'll ever be able to do that."

He started off in a slow, calm, and controlled voice.

She let him talk without interruption, as he explained the last few minutes of her life. She had a lot of questions, until he got to this part.

"… and then your head blew into a zillion different directions."

He had to be joking. She slowly pulled out of his embrace and stared at him. He nodded. She shook her head. He nodded again. With effort she reached up and touched her head.

"In grayscale. Your head blew to pieces in grayscale." He shook his head and snatched her back into his arms, as if that were the only way he could reassure himself that she was okay and added, "It's not the first time we saw this happen."

"But only in grayscale?" she asked cautiously. This was too far-fetched for anyone to believe.

"I couldn't tell," he stated honestly. "I was so shocked. I presume so. No blood was anywhere, and it happened so fast …"

She didn't know what to say. "I feel okay right now."

"You do?" He half laughed, a broken sound that rumbled out of his chest, his hands rubbing up and down her back. "We watched you pull yourself together." He took a deep breath, making her realize how hard this was on him. "One piece at a time …"

"It's just too bizarre. I'm not saying I don't believe you …"

"Hell, *I* don't believe me. But I wasn't alone. Both Stefan and Maddy could see it happen after the explosion."

"But why would I do such a thing?" she cried out in disbelief. "That's an insane concept."

"Maybe, but it had a very interesting result." He stared into her eyes and said, "And could be the reason behind it. Right before you shattered, you had a horrible pain in your head. You said that Will had found you, that it was him knocking. For me not to answer the front door. You hit him with your shattered grayscale body in a shock wave that stunned him senseless. He didn't know where he was or why he was here. He stood confused on the step and held his head, as if it hurt. Then he walked to his car and left." Trevor laughed. "It was almost divine justice."

She reared back and stared at him. "A shock wave." She hopped to her feet and, full of restless energy, paced the room. "Did you talk to him?"

"No. Not sure anyone could at that point. He kept looking around, back at the house, but I swear he was as confused as all hell. He had no idea why he was there. I'll make a further guess …"

She turned to look at him.

"I think he'll never remember why he came to the house

in the first place."

She flopped back down on the big couch and shook her head. "It's unbelievable."

"It actually makes sense."

"Why is that?" She reached up to rub her temples. She'd always been plagued by headaches, but, since meeting Trevor, they had been continuous. Then look at the craziness in her life. She could hardly blame the headaches on his arrival.

"Because I think these shattering moments are where the blackouts originate from."

Her jaw dropped.

He nodded. "We watched the pieces of your head, your memories, your energy, small blocks, all trying to fit back together like a 3-D puzzle, and, at times, the pieces themselves looked confused. As if they didn't know where they belonged. And in the middle of it all was one large black block. The pieces couldn't get back together again properly but that, and potentially other blocks, were taking up their places. It was a game of musical chairs. When the pieces struggled to realign, I believe is when you blacked out and woke up, with pieces of your memory missing. They weren't missing, they were reassigned to a new position."

She released her breath. "Damn."

"That big one was taking up space that the other pieces looked to belong to." He laughed. "The block was so damn clear, it was as if I could reach out and pluck it from the center, while all the rebuilding went on."

"You know how crazy that sounds, right?"

His grin widened. "I do. You know how freaking fantastic it is that you can do that, right?"

"Not really. So I get scared, panic, blow off my own

head, and, while trying to pull myself together, I end up blacking out and losing complete chunks of my memories?" She snorted. "That is *not* cool."

"You have a built-in defense system. One that has protected you for decades. And likely has continued to confound the people who have done this to you." His voice slowed, as he added, "You know that it's also possible that's why the blocks haven't been removed yet."

"Why?"

"While we were watching you rebuild, I told Dr. Maddy that I was tempted to reach out and grab the black chunk that was causing you so much stress. And she suggested that the chances were good I wouldn't be able to. That you had more defenses than anyone she'd seen to date, and likely I'd get seriously zapped if I tried. We also had no idea what would happen to you, if you were interrupted in the rebuilding process."

She didn't have a clue what to say to all that. Maybe it was a good thing, as Trevor continued to talk.

"I've never seen anything like it. It's a hell of a weapon."

"How sad that I needed it in the first place." She didn't know how she felt about any of this. "How sad that the eight-year-old child had to do something like this to survive."

"No, she shouldn't have, but she learned to do it and quite possibly saved her own life in the process."

"But she lost her sanity. Many times." Hannah felt the tension twisting inside her mind. That never-ending stream of questions and confusion. She didn't know if they were the result of the incident—and that's all she would call it at this point—or because of the discussion afterward.

"It doesn't matter because your circumstances required

you to cope. You survived. This is a huge win for you, sweetheart. I'm pretty sure you could use this method anytime you thought you were under attack. With Will, you've likely done this several times. It might make him angrier, or it might make him more peaceful toward you, but, the bottom line is, he's not here now because you managed to send him away. In a nonthreatening manner."

At that, she laughed. "Oh my God, how can you say that?"

"Well, it's not as if you picked up a gun and shot him. Neither did you attack him directly, although I think you probably could if need be," he noted. "You could have been so much more aggressive, but you weren't." He smiled. "If Will had this ability, he'd wield it with more cruelty."

"Am I wielding this? Or is this happening to me because of the circumstances? Maybe even the blocks are causing it?"

"Not from what I saw," he noted cheerfully. "How many blocks did you find?"

"Six left," she replied. "But let's not lock on that number. That's just what showed up when I did that visualization. For all I know those blocks were in my imagination too."

He shook his head. "It's hard to come to grips with, isn't it?"

"I'll say." She waved her hand. "First off I'm full of these blocks, and now you tell me that I go to pieces—literally—to get away from Will."

"That's a good way to describe it. You use this system to stop him from finding you," he stated in admiration.

"Outside of being hungry, I don't feel too bad. Maybe I should give it a try to remove another one of those blocks?"

But he stared at her quizzically. "Hungry?"

She shrugged.

"The energy work is what's making you so hungry." He smiled. "Makes sense. So what do you want to eat? Then we'll try another block-removing session. I doubt Will would be back anytime soon. Makes a perfect opportunity for this instead."

She preceded him into the kitchen, and her gaze fell on the muffins they'd brought home from the coffee shop. "How about a snack now, then an early dinner?"

"It won't be an early dinner at this rate. It's already after five." He brought out a pot and filled it with water. "I'll get the pasta started. You have a muffin and coffee, and then, in a half hour or so, we can eat."

"Sounds good." She went to pour a coffee and realized the pot was empty. She knew how to do it, but it seemed like the first time. All her movements were stiffer, more unyielding. She caught him studying her, as she worked. "I'm fine, you know."

"Good." He turned his back to her and worked on something at the stove. When he pulled out some bacon, butter, and cream, she knew she would love it. In fact, she wished the meal was ready now. She walked back to the table, pulled out a muffin from the container, and took a big bite. "Oh, Lord, these are so good."

He laughed. "They could taste like sawdust, and you'd say that right now. Hungry people rarely concern themselves with how food tastes, when they finally get to put it in their mouths."

"That may be," she agreed spiritedly. "But, as this is divine, I'm glad I don't have to be happy with sawdust." She sat down at the kitchen table and watched him work. "If your friends rent this place out, why is it furnished?"

"They rent it to people who live out of town temporarily. Almost like a hotel but with a homier feeling."

"It would be easier if they had long-term renters."

"They do rent long-term to several large companies who have offices here but need to fly their people in and out for meetings and special projects. It's warmer, less formal. Easier on the people who are away from their families. Besides, it's cheaper."

"But the people who are here have to cook for themselves, clean up behind themselves, and so on. It would be easier in a hotel."

"Easier is not always better."

"True."

The coffeemaker beeped. She got up and poured two cups and watched the pasta water pot start to simmer. Wonderful smells started to fill the kitchen. "It smells delicious."

"Hopefully." He picked up his coffee and turned that electric focus on her.

She felt the intensity of his gaze and smiled. "I'm still fine."

He studied her for a moment longer, then nodded. "Good. Then you can set the table." He shot her smug look and turned back to stir his pots.

She watched as he dumped pasta into the boiling water, then stirred the food in the frying pan. "Will you teach me?"

He twisted to look at her, a question in his eyes. "Teach you what?"

"To cook. I don't remember tons about the last few months, except a sense of despair over food. As if everything I tried to make didn't turn out."

"Sure, I can do that."

IT WAS A simple enough request from someone who had little-enough training in the basics in life, but, at the same time, Trevor's heart had taken a hit. It sounded like Hannah wanted to learn, so she could be independent after this was over. Whatever *this* was. And that was something Hannah likely didn't want to think about. That she wanted to learn to cook was a good thing. Being independent was a great thing. And it didn't have to kill their relationship. He had no idea what he had with her right now. It just got deeper and deeper and more confusing every day. Still, she fascinated him. No doubt they had something potent simmering. What it would grow into was anyone's guess.

He was jumping the gun. No point in worrying about something that wasn't happening at this point.

Hannah jumped up and joined him at the stove, and, like a child let into a forbidden world, she peppered him with questions.

"What did you put in the water? When did you know it was ready for the pasta? What's in the cream sauce?"

He gave a shout of laughter at her enthusiasm and proceeded to answer her questions.

Her questions carried on until dinner was served.

With plates served, she sat down and inhaled the aroma. "Oh my, that smells so awesome."

"Now taste it and prepare to dive into joy."

She picked up her fork and took a small bite. He was happy to see her savor it. He wondered, with her extreme appetite, that she'd be able to do that. Still, he watched her face as she got her first taste—and her closed-eyed reverence as the flavors hit her taste buds. "Oh, that's delicious."

Grinning, he turned to his own meal. He would need the fortification for the evening ahead.

CHAPTER 27

F OR SOME REASON Hannah was nervous about tackling these blocks, now that she knew more. Had a better understanding of what could go wrong. What *had* gone wrong? She really needed a couple blocks to just dissolve lightly and easily under her command to get her confidence level up. So far, that hadn't happened, but that didn't mean tonight wouldn't be the night. She sat cross-legged on the floor, leaning back against the living room chair.

"Okay. Ready?" Trevor asked.

She nodded, took a deep breath, and slipped into the same place as she'd been before. Whatever that would be called. Immediately she ordered up the same blocks. The final six appeared; the first one was even bigger, darker, and more terrifying. She'd fed it with her fear. That much understanding was terrifying. How could such things be happening to people without their knowledge?

She closed her eyes and turned the blocks to Jell-O. Large quivering, jiggling balls of sugary gelatin. She figured that childish image would remove her fear. When she opened her eyes, she laughed and reduced their size down to nothing. It was fascinating to see her imagination happen in real time. At the same time she wondered, *Why Jell-O?* Of course she'd chosen a food item. One she hated.

"Don't lose your concentration," Trevor warned. "Time

to get rid of the Jell-O."

Right. She'd seen the blocks in the Jell-O form in her head but hadn't gone so far as to figure out how to destroy them. She could hardly burn them or wash them down the sink. Instead she managed to turn one of the Jell-O blocks into a dog, and it turned and inhaled two of the Jell-O blocks. She grinned. That was easy. But he didn't seem interested in the other Jell-O blocks.

"Now you have to get rid of the dog."

She refocused and turned the dog back into a Jell-O block, only slightly larger. She frowned at his size. "Did I get rid of those two blocks the dog ate or did I just combine three blocks into one?"

"It's slightly bigger, but it's only one now. You have it and the other three. So four left to deal with."

She visualized the ocean and turned the big block into rain and let it drop into the ocean, absorbed by a force bigger than itself.

"That was good," he declared in admiration. "Nice one."

She sensed the surprise in his voice, but she was happy. "So three now."

"Exactly." He added a note of caution. "You've done really well getting rid of three so far. How do you feel?"

"Fine. Invigorated. Happy."

"Tired?"

"No, not really," she replied. "I've only been working for a few minutes."

"Actually a whole hour has gone by."

She froze and spun around, looking for a clock. He held up his watch for her to see.

"Really? How? It seems like no time has passed at all."

"It's easy to get caught up in the work and to lose track."

She shook her head. "I could have sworn that wasn't very long."

"If you're going to try to do the next one ..."

Right. They weren't running out of time, but her energy levels were a concern. She was doing fine but could crash. The three blocks left were bigger. Badder. Nastier looking than the others. Okay. She quickly turned the first one into water, only it became a thick dark molasses-like substance that she couldn't in good conscience put into the ocean. "Do these visuals actually have an effect on the real world?"

"What do you think?"

"I think it does." She frowned. "I wanted to dump this into the ocean but don't want to hurt the ocean."

"Then run it through a filter."

"That might work." She stopped to think, then quickly built a large filter to purify the dirty liquid, and poured the clean water into the ocean, hoping it was a healthy system for the environment. Only it wasn't easy or very successful. It took a ton of effort.

After what felt like ten minutes of hard work, she ended up breathing heavily. "What am I doing wrong?"

"It's working, isn't it?"

"It is, but it's hard."

"So make it easier. But remember your low energy could be contributing to that heavy-effort sensation."

Right. She grabbed up the bits of strength she had left and forced the molasses through the filter. She knew she was doing it the hard way but couldn't seem to find the energy to change it. She just wanted this done. It would still leave two blocks, but, compared to what she'd started with, that was nothing.

She'd call this a success, if she could just finish this one.

And, just like that, the job was done. She collapsed back on the floor. She held up her hand, hating that her fingers trembled and that her back and face were moist with sweat. "That was …" And she stopped, at a loss for words.

"Exhausting? Tiring? Invigorating? Or terrifying?"

She groaned. "All of the above."

He smiled and reached over to take her hand in his. He squeezed it reassuringly. "You did it. That's what counts."

"I did four of them. But the last two will be brutal."

"You did do four, so that's huge. And, while you sleep overnight, your memories will reset."

"Good. I hope they do it while I'm in a deep sleep," she noted in a faint voice. "I don't want to be woken by nightmares, as the hidden memories filter back in."

"No, but you aren't *wanting* to see, so you must put up a slim barrier at the same time."

"Of course. That makes so much sense. I tear down blocks and put up barriers instead." She shook her head, dispirited.

"Except, since they are your barriers, they are easy to remove. The blocks are old and other people's work." He hesitated.

She heard him holding back. "What?"

"Just wondering if you had a sense of anyone behind this work?"

"No, I was too busy arguing with Jell-O and molasses."

"Yeah, I love that. Of all the things you could possibly turn the blocks into, you chose food."

She twisted slightly to look at him. "Is that a problem?"

"No, but it tells me that you'll likely need a snack again."

"Oh, good Lord." Her stomach growled. "How come

you're never hungry?"

"You're burning through so much more energy to keep your aura snugged up tight." He grinned and patted her thigh. "Add in the other work of blasting these blocks …"

"I need more energy. More energy means more food."

"Well, you can pull more energy from other sources, but your system, particularly this last while as you felt under attack, has chosen food as its direct source."

"And why this last while?"

"That is something you need to ask yourself. I wondered if a block tried to be placed and couldn't be, but in the process may have triggered your appetite." He shrugged. "Or if it was something else."

"My growing appetite started when I hit adulthood. Always that pressure to eat was in the back of my mind, but it wasn't as active. But after I turned eighteen, something shifted."

He caught his breath back. "That's been what, seven years? That's a long time. What changed?"

"It was as if, the more I focused on self-protection, the more I ate. It wasn't so bad in the beginning, but, after that initial year, I felt like I was always fighting off some invisible foe." She stared moodily at the small living room and the big glass doors leading out to the backyard. "Sometimes I felt fine, safe, normal. Then, at others, the sense of foreboding was horrific." She shrugged. "I thought I was going crazy. After spending enough months in psychiatric hospitals, I believed I truly had gone crazy for a long time. I was also on medication for many months in there." She dropped her head back. "Seriously set me back."

"That's in the past, not right now. You haven't been on medication for months, and you are getting the help you need. More than that, you are learning to do what you need to do—for yourself. That's huge."

It was huge. It gave her confidence and security to know she was getting the right training. Something she couldn't get anywhere else.

TREVOR WONDERED IF he would have done half as well as Hannah had, given that she'd been through so much already. A lot of mysteries were in her history, but they'd get to the end of it all soon enough. He had filed the necessary legal paperwork, and Monday they'd have a clearer picture of where she stood financially and how the trust money was set up. Then she had decisions to make regarding her trust. And she needed to see how her will had been established—if she even had one. There was so much to do, but, if they could hunker down and stay safe, they'd make it. He studied her and saw the fatigue, the lines on her face, her drooping shoulders. It wasn't much past nine yet, but she was done.

"Bedtime for you," he said, getting to his feet. "Energy work is exhausting."

He helped her to stand, then walked around the house, locking up and turning off the lights. He grabbed his laptop and motioned to the stairs. She still stood in the middle of the living room, where he'd left her. He wrapped an arm around her shoulders. "Let's go."

"You don't have to go to bed just because I'm beat."

"No," he agreed cheerfully. "I don't. But I could use the extra hours myself. I'll do a little work before sleeping though, but I can do that upstairs."

Together they climbed the stairs. In the bedroom, she headed to the bathroom and came back out a few minutes later. "We need to go shopping tomorrow."

"We can. What do you need?"

"Something to sleep in," she replied. "I was so tired last night that it didn't matter, and I'm in no better shape now, but sleeping in the T-shirt that I've worn all day is not something I'd choose to do every evening."

He'd been sorting out the files he'd brought up with him. At her words he glanced over at her and frowned. "Not to mention you only have the one outfit." He shook his head. "Why didn't we grab clothes today?"

"It wasn't on the top of the list. It still isn't, but, considering the list is likely to be very long for a long time, let's move it closer to the top."

"I have several clean T-shirts, if you'd like to wear one of those. They'd be loose and comfy."

She glanced down at hers and sighed. "Not to mention mine is dirty."

"Right. Sorry, I never even thought of it."

She shrugged. "It's not that big a deal."

It was a simple matter to reach for one of his clean T-shirts and to hand it over. She accepted it gratefully, and he realized that it *did* matter. And he was an idiot for not thinking of it sooner. Mentally he added it to the top of the list. "Tomorrow is Sunday, but the mall is open after eleven. I suggest we see what we can find."

"And go out for lunch while we're at it." She tossed him a big grin, as she walked to the bathroom, already stripping off her dirty T-shirt. He swallowed hard when he saw the long line of her back, the gentle curve of her ribs, and the dip of her tiny waistline.

She disappeared into the small bathroom to get changed. Leaving him with just enough to fire up his imagination.

Damn it. She was beautiful, and he was alone with her, soon to be sharing the same king-size bed—and, to make matters worse, she was his wife. His mind, already happy to move in that direction, had no intention of hitting the brakes.

Hannah was back out almost instantly, her hand over her mouth, trying to cover a yawn, and he saw the heavy dark shadows under her eyes.

That cooled his ardor.

"Into bed with you." He flipped back the covers.

She tumbled into bed beside him, and he flipped the covers back over her. She rolled once to face him, punched the pillow under her head to fluff it, and closed her eyes.

He watched her, seeing the layers of awareness drift off her back and her aura, seeing the tension ease as her body succumbed to the need for rest. In her case, the healing, the effort of keeping that aura snugged up tight, and the work she'd done tonight had taken its toll. Well, he couldn't imagine how she'd been going this long. It was only nine-thirty, and he wasn't tired. Maybe that was a good thing. He was way behind on his work.

To that end he turned to his laptop and the files he'd brought upstairs. Files he would have explained to her if she'd asked, but, given she hadn't, he didn't feel guilty poring over them. They were files on her father, Will, Hannah herself, and, yes, Mr. Stingard, Trevor's old science teacher. Drew had sent him a lot of information on the old case. As it was originally considered an accident, the information wasn't hard to get hold of. The question was, did the file he'd received hold anything that Trevor didn't already know?

He read it through first. The fire had started in his teacher's chemistry room. Had quickly consumed the room, as any number of flammable materials were stored there. By the time the fire department had arrived, it had been too late to do anything but execute damage control for the other building. Thankfully the "building" had been a trailer on the back of the schoolyard, while the school underwent renovations. It also meant the fire burned hotter, faster at the trailer, than if it had been in a standard wood-and-stone structure. No one had realized that Mr. Stingard had been in the trailer, until the fire had cooled and his body had been found.

That had sent shock waves around their small community. Stingard had been well-liked, and his penchant for booze tolerated, as long as he didn't drink at school and did his job. But the kids knew that he kept a bottle in a locked drawer of his desk and that the occasional sips had turned to full-on shots between classes.

His attempts at hiding it had been a joke. Kids always saw what other teachers didn't see. Trevor knew one male teacher was having an affair with a female student, while his wife was home pregnant with their third child. The girl involved had thought it was great fun. Likely it had been, until the wife found out.

The girl involved had dropped out. The teacher had been fired. But Trevor didn't think the teacher had faced charges, and Trevor wasn't sure why. He sat back and tried to remember the name of the teacher. But it eluded him. In a way he felt sorry for the man. He'd disappeared afterward, whereas the girl had laughed and talked about it like a conquest. As if she'd gone after him on purpose.

And she likely had. She'd been that kind of girl. She'd also had a boyfriend at the time, who hadn't been as impressed. But she'd just laughed it off and told him to deal with it.

But the teacher ... and his wife? ... Interesting that Trevor couldn't remember their names. Surely it wasn't important. But it bugged him. The names just sat in the back of his mind, taunting him, refusing to come forward.

He returned to the file information, but, although the police had done their due diligence, nothing had come of it, and, as the case had gone cold, they'd deemed Stingard's death an accident.

Trevor had always wondered if it hadn't been suicide—at least when he wasn't looking at his fellow students and wondering if one of them had killed their chemistry teacher.

CHAPTER 28

HANNAH ROLLED OVER, then rolled over again, hating the sense of unease lying just beneath the surface. She'd slept heavily, but only for a few minutes, while Trevor worked beside her.

Damn he was sexy. In that half-light, the shadows highlighted his lean features, his square jaw, and his total focus on his laptop.

Was he as unaware of her as she was aware of him? Lord, that would be seriously sad. She'd been attracted to him since their first meeting, but, being a mess, she would hardly take him over that step into an intimate relationship. With her memories all screwed up, she couldn't trust the nudges in her head. The only one she couldn't ignore was the one that kept reminding her that she'd met him before. But who knew where?

Trevor was special. A knight in shining armor. Look at the way he'd stepped in to help her. Not just at the beginning, when he gave her the protection of his name, but even now. She had gotten bank cards but hadn't thought to take cash out. So far he'd paid for everything.

He obviously wasn't broke, but she didn't want to be beholden to him any more than she was already. Maybe she could gift him a chunk of her trust fund as thanks for saving her.

Somehow she figured he'd be horribly insulted if she did. Her eyes drifted closed.

Still, she couldn't have him go to all this expense for a stranger.

She opened her eyes again. The room was dark, but he still worked on the laptop, his brows furrowed in concentration.

"You should be sleeping," he murmured, without looking at her.

"I was," she replied in a sleepy voice. "Memories are rolling through my head. I did use the name Miasha to hide from my father. Silly because I had to use my legal name to buy the shop in the first place." She sighed. "I feel like such a failure at times."

"Maybe. But it was an understandable attempt on your part. Besides, the flower shop made you feel happy, so who cares about him." He frowned at her. "Go back to sleep. You haven't had anywhere near enough rest." He sounded so concerned.

She wanted to laugh. He was so damn good-looking. Somehow she'd fallen into a marriage with someone she would have never considered as available to her. Her boyfriends had been on the bad side. Because those guys were the only ones who were only a little terrified of her father. She'd dated one badass from the bad school a long time ago. It hadn't lasted obviously, but, as a trip on the wild side, it had been crazy and disheartening.

She'd walked away after six weeks. Some things should be experienced in small doses, and this guy had no intention of sticking to one girl. So, when she caught him with another girl—his previous girlfriend, as she'd found out later—she'd walked. He'd yelled behind her, *Good riddance, but you'll be back. They all came back.*

Well, his ego had been healthy, that was for sure. Hers had taken a beating back then, but it wasn't as if she had anyone to bemoan her situation to. She knew her father would do something seriously bad to the kid who'd taken his daughter's virginity in the bed of his pickup truck on a starry night. She smiled. Theirs had had a shitty ending, but she remembered some very good things about the relationship. Never knock a guy who's got a lot of sexual experience and is quite happy to take his time—at least in the beginning.

She'd loved her time with him. But it was stolen. She knew it. He knew it. Regardless of how he felt about it at the end.

No way she'd even recognize him now. He'd been headed down an ugly path in life. He'd hung out with a rough crowd. She'd spent some time with them all, got to know several, had really liked one, but she wasn't the type to pull a double-cross out of the air or to cheat on her partner, so she'd regretfully kept her hands off.

When her eyes drifted closed again, and she gently dozed in that history in her mind, she wondered if these thoughts were only now coming to the surface because she'd disposed of a mess of blocks. Had they been in the deep dark recesses of her mind for a reason? She let the memories drift in closer, reveling in the sense of completion she felt. She wasn't done by any means, but she could now remember the boyfriend, his group. That stage of short-lived rebellion …

She opened her eyes and caught sight of Trevor's profile.

And sucked in her breath.

"Boots?"

Trevor froze. That gaze swung her way, and, like a laser, it locked on her. "What did you say?" he asked in a shocked tone of voice.

"Boots? Were you called Boots way back when?"

He took a deep breath, then gave an abrupt nod. "I was. How did you know that?"

Frowning, she struggled to sit up in the bed, then turned to face him.

"Can you read minds now?" he asked, only half joking, but his tone hard.

Damn. She shook her head, wondering why she hadn't kept her mouth shut. The name had just blurted out.

"Pick up images, do psychometry? Telepathy?"

"I don't even know what those are," she whispered. "It was a name from my past."

He reared back. "Sweetheart, we lived in very different worlds back then. And that name is definitely part of my history but not a good part. How do you know it?"

At that, she remembered the boyfriend's name. "Remember Sticks?"

His eyebrows shot up toward his hairline. "Not too many people know either of those names."

She winced. "Right. I can't say that stage of my life was happy either."

He closed his laptop and turned to face her. "Tell me."

"Not sure I should actually. Kind of wishing I'd kept my mouth shut, if the truth be told," she muttered. "I guess the blocks were good for something."

"Ah." He nodded in understanding. "The blocks you removed are allowing memories to slide back into your consciousness." He laughed. "I have lots of memories that I'm glad are nothing but distant bits and pieces."

"Right, and presumably I will have that same benefit with time, but right now it seems like the memories are in

Technicolor and right here in my face." She winced. "And I'm wishing they weren't."

"So where do you know those two names from?" he asked, his gaze intent, as he studied her face.

"I dated Sticks for a few weeks," she admitted.

"You what?" Trevor reared back to stare at her. "How the hell …"

"Yeah, see? I have a rebellious streak. My father and Will refused to let me date any of the nice guys I met, so I dressed up and went to find some bad guys, who might have the guts to face down my father." She shrugged. "It was stupid. Dangerous as hell and, yeah, it didn't last long."

"You and Sticks?" He shook his head. "No way I'd have ever guessed it."

"Right, until the blocks were removed, I didn't recognize you." She was also a little miffed he didn't recognize her, but she kept that to herself.

"Lord, if you'd been my daughter, hanging around that group? … I'd have given you a good spanking and locked you up until you were thirty."

She laughed. "Yeah, my father pretty much threatened the same thing, when he found out I was going out with a college boy, not long after Sticks and I broke up."

"How old were you?"

"Seventeen."

"Sticks liked them all ages." He stared at her in bemusement. "I still can't get my head wrapped around the idea."

"Neither can I." She paused. "But I remember you. I really liked you. Liked the way you were inside."

"Well, there wasn't much to like on the outside." He snorted. "I hated my life and was ready to do anything to make it better."

"Why do you think I was slumming?" she asked, with a grin. "But I went straight to a college boy afterward."

"So you had to dip into the ghetto for a taste, and, after that, you ran straight upscale."

"Hey, I might not have made the best decision at the time, but it was pretty damn easy to see the writing on the wall and to recognize I was out of my element."

"I'm still trying to figure out when you were there. If you knew me …"

"Sticks had gone back to his old girlfriend. I found them together, so I walked," she shared candidly. "I don't think he was faithful at any point in the six weeks I went out with him, but what do I know."

"Six weeks?" He snorted. "For Sticks that was a long time, except for his one on-again, off-again girl—but he had a diet of side dishes. No wonder I don't remember you."

"Well, I wasn't a redhead then, like I am now. I was a blonde. Wore a beat-up and scratched-to-shit leather jacket from my father's gardener. A ton of makeup to hide my face. And heels. I always wore heels back then."

His gaze widened. "Oh no. You weren't Candy, were you?"

She laughed. "Oh God, even that name sounds so bad."

"And you were bad," he cried out. "You drank with him, attended our stupid parties down at the railroads …" He grabbed her chin and turned it toward him. "Holy crap, it is you …"

She grinned. "Yeah, but you'll never see me look like that again."

"Good," he replied in all seriousness. "You never be-longed there. Even then. We used to wonder what the *rich bitch* was running away from. You were there for a few weeks then gone."

"And now you know why." She paused. "I guess I didn't really fit in, did I?"

"No, honey. You were way too nice." He smiled at the memory. "You had manners. Expected to be treated well, and maybe, because of that, we did. We joked about you all the time. But it was more about how Sticks was moving up in life. Hell, I had the hots for you back then, but you were Sticks's girl, and I didn't poach. I figured that, when it was over, I'd see if you were interested, but, when it was over, you checked out, and I never saw you again. And I looked," he admitted.

"And now I'm your wife," she said, with a fat grin.

He looked startled at the reminder, then laughed. "Oh my God. You *are*. That's so funny. Sticks was pissed when you left. He was supposed to be the one who did the ditching, … and yet he hadn't been too kind about you leaving." Trevor paused, then added thoughtfully, "I think he might have known you were pretending to be someone else. He often joked that you were his ticket out of the ditches. When you disappeared like that …"

"He'd been pissed." She grinned. "I acted like a lady then too. I lifted my nose in the air, gave his girlfriend a snooty look, and walked. All the way back home and back to my life, I ditched the biker tough-girl look. After seeing his girlfriend, I knew I'd been just playing and put on the clean-cut lady look and danced into the closest college."

"You were a player?"

"I was a player. It's the only way I could defy my father. That meant I did it as often and in the most wrong direction as possible." She shook her head. "I look back and wonder at the things I did to defy him."

"Why do parents make life so tough that we feel that's our only option?"

She nodded. "You do understand." Her grin lit up the room. "By the way—I had a huge crush on you back then too. Figured I had to break with Sticks first, but, when I saw him with his previous girlfriend, I figured you'd be the same, so I walked away from you too."

TREVOR STRUGGLED TO reconcile the girl he'd known briefly back then with the woman sitting in front of him now. He'd been attracted to her years ago, and apparently that hadn't changed. He'd known she hadn't belonged with them when he'd met her. She'd tried hard, but that innocence to her had been out of place. With it was a desperation that overlaid her actions. They'd been desperate back then too, but that was to survive, to be someone. In her case it was like a caged bird, desperate to live a little. She'd had such a clean-cut look. The manners she'd used. She was every inch a lady and had no idea.

All of this matched what Dr. Maddy had said. That they knew each other from before.

"Do you remember what else was happening around that time?" he asked curiously. His gaze caught sight of the files on the bed. He'd been reading about the murder of his old teacher, when Hannah's memories returned. It was a hell of a connection. Coincidence? Only there was no such thing.

What year had Hannah been there? Sticks had broken up with his girlfriend several times but usually only during a fight, and, by the time the fight was over, the breakup was too. But this time his girlfriend had broken it off with him because she was seeing someone else. "When had that been?"

"It was in the summer, heading into my last year of high school. Another reason the college boys were off-limits. They were too old for me."

She smiled a sideways smile that let him know quite clearly she'd known what that meant and had likely been all over it. Especially if it pissed off her father. Not for the first time he wondered about staying single and not having kids. He'd die if his daughter went down the same path that Hannah had taken. He shuddered at the thought. "And for good reason."

"Sure, but I wasn't about conforming then. I was all about escaping."

That he could understand. "What year did you graduate?"

She told him, and he checked the file. "Do you remember when you broke it off with Sticks?"

"The middle of August. Father was coming home from Europe, and school was starting in a couple of weeks."

Of course. It would have to be the same time. No other way this could be going down. For the first time he realized that her blocks and his friends, the murder of his science teacher, might just all be connected. As completely off-the-wall as that sounded, he struggled to fit the timing together. He explained his confusion to her.

"Wait, so my father is suggesting that you might have killed this teacher—or at least knew more than you are saying—and that all happened the same summer I was with Sticks?"

He nodded.

"No, it can't be. It was during the summer holidays. No teachers. No school."

"Our school ran twelve months of the year. It wasn't a normal school. It was for those who had burned their chances at any other school. They called it an alternative school, but it was for dropouts and kids who wouldn't conform. So, when you were with Sticks, we would have been in school. We did have two weeks off, but that was at the end of August. Then we started again in September, the same as everyone else."

"He should have been studying for exams then?" she asked cautiously.

"No, we never really had exams. That was part of the normal system that didn't work for us." He smiled at her confusion. "We did a lot of reports, projects, and hands-on experiments. We had four breaks in a year."

"So, if I'd have stuck around, I could have seen you guys more? That's part of the reason the relationship wasn't working. We only met in the evening. I had the days to fill, and I thought you and the group were off doing stuff without me all that time. I tried so hard to get involved in your daily lives, but Sticks wouldn't let me."

"He couldn't. We were in school. He was also on the edge of getting suspended, and that would have been his last strike, and he'd have been out."

"Why didn't he—you—tell me?" she asked in amazement. "If I'd known school was the reason, it would have been a lot easier on me."

"We were ashamed," he noted calmly. "That school wasn't anything to be proud of." He shrugged. "I didn't stay after fall session. I finally woke up and changed my life."

"And Sticks? The others?"

"I don't know," he admitted. "When I walked, I walked all the way forward and never looked back. I heard from a couple of them over the years, but we never hung out again. I finally understood the world didn't owe me anything. That, if I wanted the future I envisioned, I had to make it happen—no one else."

"That's a tough lesson."

"It's brutal. But I learned."

She nodded. "Until you met me—and my father brought it all back."

CHAPTER 29

"**I** GUESS WHAT they say is true—you can never escape your past," Hannah noted in a pensive voice.

"You may not be able to escape it, but you should be able to live with it." Trevor tapped the folder. "I didn't kill my teacher, but part of me always wondered if one of my group did."

"You mean, Sticks?"

"He's just one suspect. There were seven of us originally, then down to five by the time you showed up. Me and Sticks and three others. But remember. That whole school was full of misfits."

"I remember Streets and Rags."

"And Stones was the last one," he noted. "I lost track of them all."

"I'm glad you got out," Hannah said. "You guys looked like you were going straight downhill."

"Heavens, you and I have come back full circle." He grinned at her. "Here we are together after all."

She laughed. "That's the best part. From me slumming to you now up on my level …"

"Whoa, there is no way your father will think I'm on your level. To him, I'm a nobody. An upstart who dared to defy him …"

"Good," she agreed, with spirit. "How do you think I

ended up in Sticks's arms in the first place?"

"I just wish you'd ended up in my arms instead …" he muttered. "That's where I wanted you to be. I wasn't impressed that you were with him."

She smiled, a part of her heart and mind that had been determined to stay apart started to melt. "And that's where I wanted to be. But you were part of that world, and I wasn't staying there."

"And you did something I always wanted to do—you managed to leave."

"Sorry." That was a sobering thought. It must have been hard for them to see her pop in and out, like she was on a day-trip jaunt, when they were stuck in that world. "That was a tough childhood for you. At least you got out eventually."

He shrugged and placed the laptop and file folders on the floor beside him. "See? The good thing about that is, it's over. I survived and grew out of that stage and made something of myself, in spite of it all."

"And where does that leave us now?" she asked curiously.

He caught his breath.

She didn't have to be psychic to feel the air crackle and the atmosphere suddenly heat up. Damn, he was hot. And she wanted him. … Like now …

"Wherever we choose to be."

Her lips quirked, as he sidestepped the issue. "Scared?" She slid closer, shoving back the bedding and coming up onto her knees. "I promise to be gentle."

His gaze widened in shock, and a half-laugh, half-snort escaped. "Really? Are you sure about this? Like maybe wait until you have a better idea of who you are and what you want at this stage of your life?"

Her grin widened. "I am married and living with my husband, while I heal from the traumas I've recently experienced. Both physically and mentally. I'm sure psychically is another level of damage."

"You are, and *recovering* is the important word here." But his gaze was hot and his voice strangled.

She had to consider his note of caution. "I am better and getting better every day."

"But not fully healed." He took a deep breath, as if trying to interject some control into the situation. "And not fully aware yet of the choices in your life and the events that brought you here to me."

"Ha, I tried to get to you a long time ago." She stared around the room and wondered if he was right. She wanted him sexually, but how much of that was a good thing? Did she want him because he'd saved her? No, because she'd wanted him a long time ago. ... So what was the right step to take now?

With a heavy sigh and shooting him a disgruntled look, she spoke up. "You know what? Being too reasonable and too sensible isn't good for the soul."

It was his turn to smirk, but there was a calming of the heat in his eyes; regret was there too. Did she want to push it? Or was that taking advantage of the situation? And maybe she should let things happen in their own time.

Damn it.

She flopped back onto the bed, her head hitting the pillow with more force than necessary, and groaned. "Fine then. Don't make love to your wife," she snapped in a laughing tone. "See if she cares."

"Is my wife protected?" he asked in a strained tone. "Because I sure as hell didn't think to bring condoms with me."

She froze. Then rolled over to look at him. "I have no idea."

"Exactly," he noted ruefully. "And I'd love to make love to my wife, but, at the moment, my wife isn't exactly sure who she is."

Hannah laughed. "Details, details."

He grinned and reached over to turn out the light. He snuggled under the covers beside her.

After a moment she said, "You'd better add it to the list."

A thick silence filled the air. "Add what?"

"The doctor's visit so I can find out what I need to do."

And just in case he would be obtuse, she added, "So that you can make love to your wife."

He snorted. "What if I said that my wife can make love to me anytime?"

"I'd be riding in less than five minutes."

"Fuck." But his voice was strained, guttural.

"Exactly." She smirked and, happy now, murmured, "Sweet dreams."

And closed her eyes.

TREVOR MIGHT NEVER sleep again. His mind had conjured up the image of Hannah naked, head thrown back, riding him hard. And hard was now the reality. Damn it. The need ripping through him was so strong, it was all he could do to lie here still. She had to know the shape he was in. The damn bed vibrated with his shaking.

She on the other hand appeared to have no problems. He heard her deep gentle breaths, as she lay on the bed beside him. He wanted to wrap her up in his arms and hold her tight. Tonight he'd have to be satisfied with lying at her side. He didn't trust himself to do more than that. To distract his body, he started running through the information he'd learned today and how it could impact their situation.

He still couldn't believe Hannah was Candy. Yet it all made a stupid kind of sense. As he and his friends had been playing at being a big tough gang to make themselves feel more powerful in this world, so had she. At least she'd survived the process. He shuddered at her going straight to the college after other men. *I will never have a daughter.*

And speaking of daughters, he hadn't managed to track down very much information about her extended family. The grandparents had been killed in the B&E, but there was no evidence they had any close extended family either. There appeared to be only her father. And worse, Trevor couldn't find family on her father's side. If she lost her father, she'd be all alone. Then she'd probably say she was all alone now.

Unable to sleep, Trevor sat up quietly, brought his laptop out again, and turned it on.

He wanted to reread the statements of those he'd gone to school with. See if something had been overlooked.

His phone buzzed with an incoming text. From his assistant. The office had been broken into.

God damn it.

He'd half expected Hannah's father to make a dick move like that but had hoped he wouldn't. Of course the police found out it was a junkie looking for a score that could never be traced back to Mr. Goodman. Trevor slid out of bed and walked to the far side of the room. He phoned his assistant. "How bad is it?"

"Both front windows were shattered."

Trevor frowned. "Why the big windows?"

"A stupid prank? Kids?" Leo guessed. "Who knows?"

"Anything taken?"

"We all had our laptops with us. Your wife even has the spare, so those are all accounted for. It looks like they tried to snag the printer because it's unplugged and shifted from its normal spot and either decided it was chump change or too big to deal with."

Trevor nodded. "We got the big one just a few months ago."

"The filing cabinets are under lock and key and in the back room. It doesn't look like they even went in there. Of course it's a storage closet, so they might not have thought it worthwhile. Your desk was upended."

"Well," Trevor exclaimed, "sounds like they were either searching for something or just wanted to mess up the place."

"That's my take. The police are here now, and I'll stay while they do their thing. They've found several sets of fingerprints, so they'll run comparison prints from us, so they can cancel out our prints."

"Okay, keep me posted. I'll come down if I'm needed."

"Not to worry. Get some sleep. I don't know what was behind this, but it looks like someone is trying to hurt you. If someone was looking for something in particular, then I'd be very careful—because they didn't get it."

<h1>CHAPTER 30</h1>

THE NEXT MORNING Hannah rummaged in the kitchen to make coffee. She could do that much. Breakfast seemed a little beyond her. She'd woken up bright and cheerful, had a shower, and immediately felt tired and worn out. It made no sense. She'd have stayed dirty if she thought that would be the end result.

Bread was on the counter. She popped a piece into the toaster and turned to stare out the window, while she waited. It would be a glorious day. Unfortunately they'd be inside for most of it. Still that didn't mean they couldn't take time to enjoy it. Parks were at the mall. Also a large greenway that boasted paths on either side crisscrossed throughout the city as well. She'd love to take a long walk.

If it was safe, she'd also love to go to her house and get a few things. She'd rather do that than go shopping for clothes. She had lots at home. But home was actually one of her father's estates. Had her father changed the locks? Or could she go in and get her belongings?

"Thoughts?" Trevor's sleepy voice sounded behind her. "Coffee smells good."

"Just thinking we should go to my house and collect my stuff. And I was hoping for an update on Tasha."

"I honestly haven't had too much time to look for her. Sorry. After the documents are legally filed on Monday, and we're in the clear, then, yes, we can do both of those."

"Ouch. Sorry, I forgot that part."

"Not an issue. A lot has happened in a short time. Hard to remember everything. As long as she wasn't in the store at the time of the fire, which apparently she wasn't, then we'll contact Tasha as soon as we can." He came up behind Hannah and wrapped his arms around her, tugging her back against his chest. "Did you sleep well?"

She snuggled in close. "I did. You?"

"Not as good as it could have been."

She sensed a hesitation. Twisting in his arms, she stared up at him and saw the heavy shadow on his chin, the drained look to his features.

He reached up and rubbed his face. "Sorry, I haven't shaved. My shaver isn't recharging here. When we're out shopping, I'll pick up another one."

She rubbed the soft hair on his cheek and grinned. "It looks good on you."

"I'm not keeping it. It's scratchy and hot."

"Reminds me of a walk on the wild side." She reached up and kissed him.

He gave a shout of laughter. "In that case, it's definitely coming off. Back then we could only grow super-fine and splotchy beards. But we tried hard, and the sparse hair growth added to the whole scruffy look."

She grinned. "Well, whatever it was, it worked for you guys."

"Only to the girls who were looking for the same thing." He leered at her, causing her to giggle.

"Oh my, don't you look fine." She batted her eyes, and he laughed, hugging her close.

"You are very cheeky this morning." He released her and

stepped around to pour coffee from the pot for them both. "I'm glad to see it."

"I am feeling better. You, however, look to have more weighing you down."

"Yeah, I do." He held out a cup for her. "The office was broken into last night. My assistant called from the scene, while the police were there."

"Oh, my God," she cried out. "Was he working there? Did he get hurt?"

Trevor shook his head. "No, he was at home at the time. There is a bunch of damage that insurance will cover, but we don't know if this was a random attack or if they were looking for something or if it was a warning."

She sucked in her breath. "Likely a warning. From my father."

He nodded. "That's my first impression, but we can't count on that yet."

"Do you need to go there this morning?"

Again he nodded. "Yes. We'll stop by on our way to the mall."

"Right." She stared out the window. "What a pain."

"The mall or the office?"

She laughed. "Both really. I have a ton of clothes at home, so don't need to buy new ones, and you certainly didn't need this extra headache."

"Your clothes might not still be there."

"I thought of that," she agreed in a pensive voice. "In the scheme of things, I don't care about much there, but there are a few things of my mother's."

"Like what?"

"Her diary, for one." She sighed. "I never did open it. I loved her so much, and the guilt just crippled me."

"Maybe we will swing by then. See if we can find that."

She glanced over at him. "What value would it have?" She frowned at him, not sure she wanted anyone prying into her mother's personal thoughts. It felt wrong. Intrusive. And it was the last thing she had of her mother, Sharing that felt like a betrayal.

"We need to confirm how she died. And if she had any worries, fears, ideas of her impending death."

Hell. Hannah would have to read the diary. And share it with him. "I wouldn't want her diary to become public knowledge, and neither would I want to lose it."

"Understood. Let's cross that bridge when we come to it. If there is evidence of her own demise, you might want to consider that justice has a price. And sometimes lack of privacy is part of it."

TREVOR DIDN'T WANT Hannah worrying about her mother's diary. He'd seen enough cases where someone held privacy at a higher value over truth. That couldn't happen in this case. Hannah needed to be safe. And he needed to stop being harassed. If her mother's diary held any nuggets of truth, then Trevor needed to hear them. And as soon as possible. And that brought up a possible reason for the break-in.

Could it be someone was looking to see what Trevor was up to? Cases he was working on, evidence he'd collected? And possibly stop him from getting further on these cases? Not that a break-in would do that. A fire might though. He frowned, thinking about it. He had an offsite storage locker but only for old files.

"We can leave right now, if you'd like." Hannah leaned

against the counter in front of him, munching on a piece of toast. "It's obvious we need to go as soon as possible."

He glanced down at his coffee and wondered, but that inner prodding wouldn't stop. "Let's go." He threw back the rest of his drink and rinsed the cup under the tap.

Within five minutes they were on the road. He glanced at his watch. It wasn't nine yet. On a Sunday morning. The roads were empty, and the sun was shining bright. He felt foolish. But he hadn't done this job for so long to ignore his instincts. He pulled up beside his ground-floor office and stared at the large plastic sheets over the windows. His office was in a general office building. He had a small sign, but generally he didn't have much in the way of walk-in traffic. It wasn't the nature of his business. Outside, he checked the ground around the broken windows and quickly realized that was likely how the intruders had broken in. He unlocked the front door, wondering what the point of locking it now was but …

He stepped back to hold the door open for Hannah, who stared at the broken glass on the ground. "It was Will," she stated softly. "I can feel he was here."

Trevor froze. "You can feel him?"

"Sure. I'm the one who shatters when he gets too close. Remember?" she noted, her voice droll.

He did remember but had no idea she'd recognize Will's signature after the fact. Interesting. "Can you feel whether someone else was with him, or was he alone?"

She closed her eyes and stood still. He watched her tight aura open up slightly, and a wisp of energy slid out and away from her body. Like any hunted animal, it took stock of the situation, then dashed back under cover into safety.

"I'm only feeling Will's energy," she replied. "But I

don't know whether that's because I can't, in theory, recognize other people's energy or Will was, in fact, alone." She turned to give him a lopsided grin. "So no help there."

"It's a help already. If this was done by Will, then either he was acting alone or this was done on your father's orders." He glanced at her. "Would Will do something like this on his own?"

"Oh, absolutely. He has a lot of free rein these days."

"Because your father lets him have it, can't control his pet, or because he doesn't care what Will does?" He studied her, curious to see her reaction to his comment.

"I don't know," she admitted. "All three are possible. I haven't spoken to my father—outside of the lovely hospital visit—in months. I'm not sure what his mental state is these days. At the hospital though, he was as bullish, arrogant, and controlling as ever."

He had been, but that could have been bluster. Something to consider. "You are his only child."

"Maybe," she noted cheerfully. "At least I'm the only legal one. Given my mother has been gone over seventeen years, I wouldn't be at all surprised to hear he'd fathered a half-dozen other kids with his ex-mistresses."

"Do you have any names of these so-called mistresses?" he asked, when she finally walked into his destroyed office.

"No, and I don't remember them. Wanda has been his main squeeze for years."

Goodman might not have wanted any more legal heirs either. They did have a tendency to want inheritances early. Not that that was the case with Hannah. More likely her father had changed his will, so she'd never be able to inherit, given his opinion of her mental state. Handling his vast business dealings would be well over her head. A trust was sensible. Trevor doubted Mr. Goodman would have cut off Hannah entirely because, in Goodman's mind, she couldn't live an independent life, and she was still his responsibility. Even if only for show.

Trevor would like to think that Goodman loved his daughter.

But in Trevor's business, all too often the relationship between family members was about anything but love.

CHAPTER 31

THE OFFICE LOOKED terrible. Hannah stood in the open doorway and wanted to cry. It had been such a nice office. But not only had the intruder—Will, and this was definitely Will's handiwork from the get-go—broken in, but he'd destroyed damn-near everything he could get his hands on. The associates' desks had been stomped, and, from what she saw, one had been severely broken. The other two had been metal, and he'd tossed those around. The drawers had been pulled out and dumped. Still, for all the two-year-old temper tantrum effect, the place wouldn't take too much to set to rights. At least she hoped. Office supplies, like staplers and pens and scissors, were all over the floor. Pads of paper had been ripped and thrown. Loose sheets on the floor.

The printer was beside the door. That made no sense. Had he thought to make this look like a robbery? Because, if so, he had failed. Big-time. And Will didn't fail at much.

Or maybe it was an afterthought. Hell, maybe he just liked the printer. She studied the machine. Then motioned at it. "The printer doesn't have a memory card, does it? Because Will could take the memory card and could retrieve the information that had been printed."

"Nope. No memory. We don't have a big expensive network here, partly for that reason. We buy new printers almost yearly." Trevor studied the square-looking one on the floor. "This is a printer-scanner-copier model but bigger than the last one." He shrugged. "Easy to replace, just irritating. All this has done is set me, us, back one day to clean up."

"You're sure nothing was here for him to find? Not your home address, your bank accounts, your friends' names and places …" She spun to look at him. "Would he have gotten Kali's address from here?"

"He might have," Trevor noted slowly. "I had wondered how he'd found us there." He frowned. "But the break-in here happened after he had shown up at Kali's place."

Hannah snorted. "Or he came here first and got what he needed, then—after I changed his mind by shattering mine—he came back here. Probably to look for whatever it was he'd come for the first time. Then he destroyed the office in a fit of temper because either he couldn't remember what that was or couldn't find it again."

Trevor stared at her. She could see him slotting the information into the correct boxes, and he grinned. "You know what? That's very possible."

"The question is, did he get what he wanted the second time?"

Trevor looked around. "This is a temper tantrum. So my guess is no."

"The issue is, are we safe at Kali's house?"

"I'm not sure any house is safe." And that bothered him.

She saw his face twisting in a frown.

"I'll call a security company that has done a lot of work for me in the past." He pulled out his phone and walked away.

Hannah turned her attention to the mess in front of her. She knew psychically that Will had been here—but could she find any physical proof? She'd love to see him in jail for a year or two, although her father would most likely get Will off. Particularly if he'd done this on her father's orders.

She wandered through the mess and studied the area. She had no idea what kind of proof she'd be looking for. Just because she recognized his energy didn't mean it would stand up in court. The place was such a mess that she couldn't see anything that might have been new or different. She studied one corner. A crushed disposable coffee cup was close to where the window had been broken. Would that have been Will's cup? She didn't recognize the company logo on the side. If it wasn't from a coffee house around here or one that Trevor's staff regularly visited, then it could be Will's. He was a steady caffeine addict.

Trevor walked up behind her. "What did you find?"

She pointed to the coffee cup on top of the broken glass but still under pads of paper. "Do you think that was from one of the police, your staff, or from Will?"

"Interesting." Trevor crouched to take a look. "Believe it or not, my staff aren't coffee drinkers. They are green tea addicts. The cops know better than to add to a crime scene, but neither should they have missed this."

"It's partially hidden, and I wouldn't have noticed, except I accidentally kicked these pads of paper."

He nodded, got up, and went into his office, then came back out with tweezers and plastic bag. He carefully bagged the cup. "I'll let the police decide if this is valuable or not."

"Good. I'm all for anything that will nail Will's ass to the jail cell wall."

"So feisty," he murmured. That grin of his flashed. "I like it."

"Ha. You like it as long as it's not turned on you," she replied. She wandered the rest of the room, looking for something that was out of place.

"Can you see his energy or just feel it?"

She spun. "One can see energy?"

He laughed. "Absolutely. I can see your aura. Or rather, the little bit of your aura that you let us see."

She blinked. "So you're thinking I might be able to see Will's energy?" She motioned with her hand. "As I look around, I don't see anything different. I see the destroyed office."

"Well, you are in tune to Will's energy to such an extent that it would be very possible. What brought you to the cup?"

She opened her mouth to say nothing, then slowly paused. Had it been nothing, or had she been following something? "I feel like I followed something, but I'm not exactly sure what that was."

"It would be Will's energy." He studied her, hands on his hips. "Willing to try something?"

"Sure," she said cautiously. "Like an experiment, you mean?"

"Yes." He walked toward her. "Close your eyes and reach out for Will's energy. You know when he's close, so see if you can sense him here."

"I already know he isn't here now, but I know he *was* here," she stressed. "So not sure what else I could pick up."

"Can you see him? In your mind, do you see him walking through here? Touching things. Breaking windows?"

"I can see the energy, like a human shape, but no features, walking through here," she noted excitedly. Then froze. "Wait. What if I'm making this up?"

"Are you?" he asked in a reasonable tone. "Why would you do that? It would take a lot of effort to imagine him here."

She frowned. "But making something up and trusting what I see are two different things."

"So don't think. That's the trick. Open your mind to Will's energy. An energy you know so well that you've escaped his tracking energy many times …"

"Not escaped. He's always found me. I just found a way to hit back."

"Exactly," he noted softly. "And now you have another chance to hit him in a different way. Did he touch anything?"

"Sure he touched it all, but the glowing stuff around his hands is much less than the rest of him."

"That's because he wore gloves. So we don't need to worry about fingerprints."

"I'd expect nothing less," she grumbled. "He's done stuff like this before. I used to call him my father's enforcer." She closed her eyes and tried again.

The snort came from the direction of Trevor, but she didn't open her eyes. "The whole room is glowing," she noted in surprise. "I can see his energy, but there is a glow almost everywhere."

"That could be the energy of the objects in the room, including the floor. Remember everything is energy, so you have to filter out certain things to read his energy more clearly."

She slowly spun in this room. "But my eyes are closed."

"Right," he agreed, with humor. "So tell me. Are you in grayscale or not?"

"Not," she replied in astonishment. "This … This space is full of color. Will's energy is still red but fainter."

"And the other colors?"

"Your assistants, their colors are green and a light blue. Yours is complex, mostly deep forest green." She frowned. "Is that healthy to have a dark color like that?"

"Look in my direction now."

She opened her eyes and looked at him. "I can't see anything."

"Close your eyes and look again." This time humor overlaid his voice.

"It's not nice to tease the newbie," she quipped lightly, but she looked at him in her mind. And found him flowing in a soft mint green. "That's beautiful," she cried out. "So was the dark green because its old energy, and the light-mint green the new energy, or the dark because you were angry and frustrated?"

"Well, in this case, the dark energy was old, *and* I *was* angry and frustrated. So maybe both reasons came into play there."

"And the light-mint-green energy?"

"That's who I am right now. I'm happy," his voice deepened. "Even in the middle of this mess."

She studied the green energy and realized it kept wafting toward her. She glanced down at her own body, her energy snugged up tight, as it always was. His energy was reaching for her, and she wasn't reaching back.

And, for the first time, she realized why she might not have had any relationships that felt right. Her relationships had always seemed to be cold and, of course, had been short-lived. And now she knew why. It wasn't the others. They had likely reached out to her too, but, like now, she'd never reached back. Damn.

"What's the matter?"

She sighed. "Apparently now I know why I suck at relationships." She explained a little of what she saw. As she did so, she watched his energy pull back against his own body. "Don't, please. I have to learn how to do this. I don't want you to feel that you can't reach out for me. I'm just not sure how to reach back."

"First off," he shared, "you have to want to."

"Didn't I make that clear last night?"

"That's on a whole different level. On the physical level, yes, you did. But on this level? No, you didn't."

IT WAS FASCINATING to watch Hannah process new information. She was damn fast at it. Now that she had a grasp on how some of the energy systems worked, she was picking it up quickly. The more she did, the more she found she could do.

"I won't pull back consciously," Trevor shared. "But it is natural to not want to continue to put yourself out there without getting a positive response."

"A horrible thought," she admitted. "I've spent a lifetime keeping my energy in close to my body to avoid detection, and now I find that very same system has kept me from having happy, loving relationships."

"Avoiding detection?"

"My mother's words. Potentially a reason why my mother was also so very unhappy. Maybe she never realized how she was shortchanging herself and my father by keeping her aura close."

He nodded. "Very interesting phrasing she used." It revealed so much about her mother's life. "We need to see her diary."

Hannah took a deep breath. "I hate to say it, but I think

you're right." She turned in a slow movement. "First, we finish here. Then we go to my house." She motioned with her arm and gasped. "I can see energy sliding off my arm with the movement."

"That's normal," he stated. "Think about the energy that remains behind when you pick up an object." At her sharp look, he nodded. "It's the same thing. All movement leaves behind remnants of energy."

She closed her eyes. "Based on that information, I can see a trail of Will's energy as he created his carnage. He left a lot of energy in your personal office." She walked forward to stand in his doorway. "And lost a lot of that energy in what looks like a fit of temper."

"I always lock up my files out of the office, so nothing was here for him to find. We have an onsite storage vault. But I was in the process of doing cloud storage, and then taking everything physical offsite. I deal with some angry families. Particularly where inheritances and trusts come into play," he stated quietly. "I can't ever leave anything to chance."

"Scary thought." She closed her eyes again and surveyed the rest of the rooms but couldn't see anything else helpful. He collected the cup she'd found—just to have Drew confirm the lack of prints—and walked her back out to the car. "My house?"

"Your house."

Her stomach gurgled.

And he laughed. "Your house first, then we'll have brunch."

"Drive fast," she said. "I'm really hungry."

The roads were still empty this early on a Sunday. He followed her instructions to a beautiful house, backing up to one of the many rivers throughout the area. Large wrought-iron gates secured the front of the property.

"Let me out," she said. "I can open it manually."

He paused to let her open the door, then texted Drew to give him their location, in case of trouble.

He got an almost instant response.

Not smart. You shouldn't go in there alone.

No choice. Mother left Hannah a diary. It's important to the case.

CHAPTER 32

ANNAH USED THE manual release to open the gate. The newer security systems had a code you punched in. She'd hoped her father hadn't had enough time to change this one to something like that, or she couldn't get in. Although she had no qualms about climbing the fence. In fact, it might be a lot easier to leave the car parked out here, instead of inside the grounds. She thought her father had control of the gate at his house, and, if he didn't want to let them out, it was quite possible he had the means to stop them from doing so.

Frowning, she held her hand up to Trevor to stop him from driving farther down the driveway, past the gate. He rolled down the window, and she explained the problem. He nodded and shut off the engine.

She really liked that about him. What she said had value. He listened. He didn't knock down her worries or trample over her concerns. Even if he disagreed, he acted in a respectful way. "It's not very far to walk."

"This will be fine," he noted. "We can always hop the gate if need be."

"I lived alone. There won't be anyone here."

"And what about Will? What if he came here next?"

She sent him a look of outrage. "Then we'd better check out if he pulled the same stunt as he did on your office." She stormed ahead, only to have her feet falter. She slowly turned back to face him.

"I think he probably found your office through me. We'd been there the day before. What if he tracked us there? Found it was your place and came back to destroy it."

Trevor immediately tugged her up against him, and, in that firm take-charge voice, he allayed her fears. "My office would be even easier to find than that. I gave your father a card the first day. The address is there. That had nothing to do with you."

She beamed up at him. He smiled and dropped a kiss on her lips. "Now lead the way."

They walked, arms linked, down the winding driveway to the large stone house. It could have been imposing but instead ended up being endearing. The rounded stones gave it more of a cottage look, instead of a mansion, although it appeared to be well over six thousand square feet and three stories high. They passed another small building sitting beside the driveway.

"That's the gatekeeper cottage," she explained. "This was my mother's house at one time. The housekeeper back then lived there with her husband. He looked after the gardens."

"Convenient."

"They were a lovely couple," she said warmly. "I really missed them afterward."

"After what?"

"After my mother's death. I was moved to my father's other estate and only came back here after leaving college."

"And that's the first time you mentioned attending college."

"Ha, that's because I didn't finish. I was placed in a private hospital again. So, of course, I wasn't competent enough to continue my studies."

"He let you live here? Alone?" Trevor's voice sounded doubtful. "That doesn't sound like him."

"Well, I had a housekeeper, who was a dragon lady, and some guards—luckily not Will or George, for they remained with my father. So I was a virtual prisoner. Later, I fired the housekeeper and told the guards to go back to my father's estate, as they were no longer welcome here. That's how I lived this last year."

"Fascinating."

"I was still under Father's surveillance though," she muttered. "I wouldn't be surprised if he has the house bugged."

At that, Trevor sent her a sharp glance, but she ignored it. "I couldn't get rid of the guards fully. But they did move to the cottage. That at least gave me some privacy and independence."

"Until you blacked out?"

She nodded. "Exactly."

They climbed the steps to the long lazy front porch. She reached up above the doorway and pulled down a hidden key, then unlocked the door.

She pushed it open and stepped in, walking around the door. He watched as she turned off the alarm system. The inside of the house was beautiful and spacious but comfortable.

"Will your father know you are here?"

"I believe so. But it depends on whether he's traveling or sitting at home and plotting our demise," she noted lightly. "We'll find out soon enough."

She walked into the kitchen and stopped to turn around. "It all looks the same." She turned and motioned to the side. "The stairs are this way." She led the way upstairs to her bedroom. There she cried out in joy, as she saw the open closet. "Clothes. Yes!"

"So he hasn't touched anything?"

She rummaged into the closet, pulling out several different items. "Not that I can see." She walked back for another load and this time brought out a small carry-on bag. She packed it with several changes of clothes and added in her nightwear and underclothes. Finally she straightened and looked around. "I should grab a second pair of shoes and a warm sweater."

"And your mom's diary," Trevor whispered.

"Right." She walked to her night table and from the bottom drawer pulled out a small box and placed it on the bed. She stared at it, memories flooding her mind. "She gave this to me herself."

"When?"

"A week before she died."

"What's in it?"

Hannah looked over at him. "I have no idea. I've never opened it. I couldn't before. Then, well, … I forgot all about it."

CRAZY. TREVOR LOOKED at the keepsake box, and that Pandora's Box tale came to mind. That Hannah's mother gave it to her daughter just before her own death said a lot. Whether she was in fear of her life or had psychic abilities that foreshadowed her death, it was a little unnerving to see this sitting there.

"And the diary?"

She frowned and pulled the drawer out farther. "It's supposed to be in here." She dug to the very back.

"She gave you the diary and the box at the same time?" he asked to be clear.

She nodded. "Yes, and here it is." She pulled out a small leather-bound book and handed it to him.

"Not very diarylike?" he commented. He'd half expected one of those little teenager books with a tiny clasp and a key with a lock that would keep no one out. Instead this had all the earmarks of a little black book. He opened it to see some writing but not a lot and only on a few pages. He tucked it in his pocket for her to read later. Then he picked up the keepsake box and put it into her bag. "Are you ready?"

She nodded. "I guess."

Trevor picked up her bag, waited for her to grab a sweater and a second pair of shoes, ones that had a whole lot more substance than the tiny ballet slippers she currently wore. "Are you sure you don't want to pack up more, in case your father tries to lock you out of here?"

She shook her head. "There's too much. We also don't have a place to call home yet. So it might as well stay here."

"Good enough. Let's go. Brunch is waiting."

Then a shoe scraped on the floor outside her bedroom door.

Instantly Trevor had Hannah tucked behind him, both of them flattened against the wall.

Silence.

He heard her heavy breathing behind him. He squeezed her hand reassuringly.

And the sound came again. He freed up his hand and waited.

At that moment an old grizzled man peered into the room. He caught sight of them and straightened up, puffing out his shoulders. "Only there won't be any brunch for you," he declared in a mean voice, letting them know he'd been close enough to listen in on their conversation. "Not yet anyway."

The man standing in the open bedroom wasn't anyone Trevor recognized.

And from the shock on Hannah's face, neither was he anyone she recognized either.

"Who are you, and what are you doing in my house?" she snapped, showing Trevor a side of Hannah that he had yet to see. She stepped forward, anger vibrating through her voice. "This is my home, and you're not welcome."

"I doubt it. Besides, I was told to let him know if and when you ever dared to show your face here again," he sneered.

"My belongings are still here," she stated. "Or is he into stealing too?"

"Not to mention that I'd like your ID so I can make sure to spell your name correctly when I submit my report to the police," Trevor stated. "I'm her husband and a lawyer. And she has a right to her privacy. You, however, are in her bedroom, and you entered this house illegally."

"I did not. I had the owner's permission," the guard said in a surly tone. "You aren't going to pull a fast one on me."

"We already did," Hannah snapped, walking past him. "I'll be contacting the police over this. Even my father has to follow the Landlord Act. And that includes giving me thirty days' notice and a reason to evict me—if he has such a thing. Not to mention twenty-four hours warning if he needs to access my house." She waved a hand in dismissal.

She raced past him and exited the room like a regal princess in a pout. "Feel free to tell him I was here."

"I already did. You're supposed to stay here until he arrives," the guard called after her.

"We're going for brunch, so how about he phones me instead?"

Trevor walked quickly to the car, unlocked it, and put her bag in the trunk. She was already in the front seat, waiting for him.

Trevor turned on the engine and backed away from the gates. "What will happen to the guard?"

"My father will fire him."

"Really?"

"Oh, yes. On the spot. If he gets here in five minutes, and we're not here, he'll be fired in the sixth minute. My father is nothing if not consistent."

Trevor pulled the car down the street and turned onto the first main road. "Good thing we're leaving then. I know he's only doing his job, but … I didn't like him."

She laughed. A wonderfully light pealing sound that put a grin on his face. "Besides, we couldn't stay," she added. "You promised me food."

The place Trevor had in mind was only a few blocks away, but, not sure if they'd been followed, he went a convoluted path. By the time they arrived, she'd relaxed, and he had as well. That is, until he drove into the parking lot and saw three black sedans with smoked windows already parked here. Leaving the engine running, he sat and stared at the vehicles beside him. "Can you sense Will close by?"

Hannah, in the process of opening her door, fell back into her seat and stared at him. "What?"

"I see three familiar-looking vehicles parked beside us. A coincidence?"

She took a deep breath and studied the vehicles. "We used to come here on occasion. It's not out of line to consider they might be here."

"Right. Let's find another place."

She reached across and laid her hand on his. "How about we don't? Let's walk in, like the adults we are, and have a meal calmly." Her tone was determined. "I'm not terribly impressed with the idea of a life on the run. He *is* my father. However, you and I are married." Her gaze turned on the restaurant. "Is there any reason *not* to go in?"

"Only to avoid trouble."

"I'm not sure avoiding *them* is helping *us*."

"If you're sure?" He was willing, if she was up to it. He was all about facing life head-on, but he preferred to wear crash helmets on suicide missions.

"I am." She smiled pensively. "You know what? In spite of everything, he is my father, and I have a mixed ball of emotions over that relationship."

Trevor turned off the engine and opened the door. He had no way to know if her father was in here, but, like she said, it was a public place and wouldn't be a bad way to see them again. Trevor was just being overly cautious—the only way to be when dealing with bullies. "Let's go in."

She grinned and hopped out. He was happy to see her spirit. Surely this wasn't the same girl he'd met at the hospital, who barely knew her own name. She'd changed and grown so much. In large part he was sure it was due to the blocks coming down and her own memories filling the holes in her head.

She had adjusted to her new situation and had gained confidence in who she was. That was likely the biggest impetus to this growth. She had come to terms with some of her abilities, maybe not fully confident in them yet, but she no longer looked at them as something to run from. He was proud of her. He opened the restaurant door for her, his senses on high alert—just in case.

She gave him a beaming smile, then reached up and kissed him in full view of the restaurant patrons. He laughed and wrapped an arm around her shoulders.

A waitress walked toward them, a bright smile on her face. Right behind her was Will.

CHAPTER 33

HANNAH SMILED AT the waitress. No way to miss Will's looming scowl barreling down behind the hapless woman. Hannah upped the wattage in her smile and directed it at him. "Hello, Will. Did you get hungry after pulling the B&E at my husband's office?"

Shocked silence filled the restaurant.

Gazes turned to watch.

She heard Trevor suck in a breath.

Hannah wasn't scared, and she'd had quite enough of Will's particular brand of terrorism.

The waitress, as if understanding the explosiveness of the situation, stepped in front of them and said hurriedly, "I have the perfect table for you." She motioned to the left. "Please, if you'd like to come in this direction."

"Sure, I will, thank you." Hannah ignored Will's stone-faced look and deliberately turned her back on him. She knew Trevor would protect her. She also realized she'd snugged her energy tighter against her body—if that were even possible.

Whereas Will's energy waffled in place, bright red and flaring with sparks. He had no idea what to do and was so damn angry. She threw her head back and laughed. Lord, it felt good. All she'd had to do was stand up to the man. He was a bully. A boogeyman in the dark. He preferred to torment his victims when they were more vulnerable, and, in a public face-to-face confrontation, he had no idea what to do.

The waitress, who'd thought she'd avoided a problem, took them past another table—where her father sat, Wanda at his side.

Hannah stopped and glared at him. Trevor's heavy sigh whispered past her. She realized Trevor wished she wouldn't antagonize everyone in the vicinity, but it appeared she had no way to control the impulse. She needed to stand up to these people. Now that the gate had opened, she couldn't seem to stop.

She wasn't trying to cause trouble, but she was damn sure she wouldn't lie down and take it either.

"Hello, Father. I was just at home, getting some clothes. We had an altercation with a new guard, who didn't seem to understand his place."

Anger lit her father's gaze. "I'd say you were the one who didn't understand your place," he replied in a low hard voice.

She raised her eyebrows. "Oh, am I being evicted then?"

There right out in the open, she gave him a slow smile. "It will be odd to live anywhere but at Mom's house, that's for sure. She lived in it, even when she was married to you, didn't she?" She studied her father's gaze intently and watched it flicker. She cast a disparaging glance at Wanda, catching her smirk.

She turned her attention back to her father. "It wasn't your house. It was her house. And I was her heir. So I guess my lawyer"—she reached out a hand and caught Trevor's in hers—"will need to take a look at that as well."

She nodded at her father. "I'd hoped to have lunch with you today, but I can see we're not welcome. Have a good day." She turned to leave, then twisted back, and deliberately hardening her voice, she added, "And call off your henchman. That Will broke into Trevor's office and caused the damage he did is already pretty disgusting and quite low for even you, Father, but to know he's coming after me? … Well, the police are very interested in his whereabouts already. I'll be more than happy to let them know he was here at the restaurant right now and is still in your employment—and thereby acting on your orders." Having delivered that final coup, she turned and walked away.

The entire restaurant had stilled to listen. She knew a dozen cell phone images had flashed and likely a video of the meeting as well. How nice that the new age of social media was everywhere.

She smiled sweetly at the waitress, who led them to a table at the far end of the room. "It's a nice table, thank you."

The waitress bolted.

Trevor took the chair on the opposite side of the table, where he could watch her family. "They are leaving."

"Good. Let *them* run this time."

His lips curled upward. "Feeling cheeky after that, aren't you?"

She grinned. "I am. It feels good to dump the victim mentality—at least for a few minutes."

"Just remember. They aren't schoolboys, and you will pay for this rebellion."

She waved her hand around. "It's a minor blip on my father's radar. He might want to squash me for my short-lived insurgency, but he's seen them before, so will assume I'm going through another stage …"

He laughed. "Well, enjoy it because I highly doubt this

will go unpunished."

She closed her eyes, so she could sense Will better. She lived for the day when she could see his energy as strongly as she could sense it. She saw it now, but it was faint and—in this light—barely visible.

"Will's leaving," Trevor noted quietly. He reached across and covered her hands with his own. "Are you sensing something?"

"Anger. No. Make that rage," she replied quietly, squeezing his hand. The stuffing seemed to go out of her. "I probably shouldn't have done that, should I?"

"No, probably not, but it's done now."

"Right." She twisted her features. "And now what? We wait?"

"No, I've already contacted Drew. I had my phone taping that scenario. Should have some interesting video to look at on the monitor. Maybe someone somewhere gave something away."

"Not likely. They are all professionals."

"What about the man sitting beside your father? George?"

"Oh, the other henchman. He doesn't like to get his hands dirty. Whereas Will thrives on it."

Trevor stared out the window.

"What are you thinking?"

"The men present an interesting wall of dark energy."

"Will, yes, but who else?" she asked.

He laughed. "Do you really think your father isn't a man of energy?"

She stared at Trevor, as she considered his question. "I think we talked before about that, how he was but with a business bent. As in, that's how he's managed to become so successful."

"He's that all right, but I think his skills are so much more. I'm just not sure in what way."

"Maybe when the three of them are together, it just seems like energy power, when in reality it's all about emotions? I remember seeing him years ago and thinking that inside he was a really lonely man." She laughed, humor overlaid with bitterness. "But then he'd do something mean again, and I'd forget about those times."

"I certainly won't excuse his behavior, but you might want to remember there would have been times when life had been very difficult for him."

"Maybe. And maybe they were only difficult while he tried to figure out how to get rid of his families."

"What?" Her father's voice boomed. He stood beside them alone. Hannah could see the rest of his party standing outside by the vehicles. He'd approached quietly, when she and Trevor were deep in conversation, and neither had noticed. Her father collapsed on the chair beside her. "What did you just say?"

"Nothing."

He shook his head slowly. "No. You did say it. I'm just struggling with the concept. You actually think I killed my first wife? My kids? Your mother?" His voice rose in shocked horror at the end.

She didn't know if he was a damn good actor or what, but he gave the appearance of being in pain. She glanced over at Trevor. He sat back and surveyed her father, as if he didn't know what to make of this sudden turn of events but was willing to see it through.

"Did you?"

There. She'd asked. Clear and concise, so as to avoid any

misunderstanding. And she waited.

For the first time in all these years she'd known her father, words appeared to fail him.

"No," he finally managed to get out, his face stark white with shock. "No, I didn't." He rested his face on his hands on the table. "Jesus, how long have you thought that?"

"I don't know. I only just found out about your first family," she admitted, not sorry to be here, having this conversation now. "I'm sorry for them … and you."

A strangled sound escaped his mouth, but he shook his head wildly. "I never did anything to your mother." He held out a hand. "I wouldn't. I couldn't."

"And your first wife and two kids?" She didn't know where she was getting the courage for this, but it was obvious this was the right time to have this discussion. She glanced around at the restaurant. Most of the patrons were focusing on their own lives, but a few still stole glances in her direction.

Her father, however, looked *shattered*. A good word, considering what happened to her all the time. But she felt sorry for him. For misjudging him. For what he'd lost.

"I gather you didn't?" Not that a murderer would confess.

"No, I never did. I loved her. Them," he added in a soft voice. "They were my life."

"And yet …"

"Yet what? They were hit in a head-on collision by a semi on bad winter roads," he revealed, his skin a pale, wan color. "I was at work. And, in one moment, they were gone. As in all gone." He turned to stare at the full restaurant, but she knew he was looking down the long line of his memories. Maybe he had blocked them so he didn't feel the pain. Like someone had done for her. Now she could deal with the remaining blocks. Maybe tonight.

No, she glanced over at her husband, and she had something else planned to do tonight. But they needed to go to a drugstore first.

"I'd have done anything to have died with them," he whispered.

A sheen of moisture clung to his eyes. She closed her eyes, hating the pain she'd brought up. She hadn't planned on it. She hadn't wanted to hurt him. She'd wanted her own nightmare to stop. "I'm sorry," she whispered. "That must have been tough."

"It was the worst day of my life."

She couldn't imagine. To lose everyone all at once. "Then why marry her sister?"

He glanced down at the empty table. "Because she reminded me of my first wife. They looked alike, and I was so damn lonely for what I'd lost."

"But it wasn't the same, was it?" she asked smoothly, remembering her mother's loneliness.

"No, not at all. It was a mistake. I couldn't give her what she needed, and obviously she couldn't give me what I needed." He gave a broken laugh. "I thought I'd healed, was whole going into it, but knew immediately I hadn't healed. I was far from whole. And she knew too. I'm so sorry she was unhappy. I tried hard to make her happy, but it wasn't to be. We'd have divorced if she'd lived. We'd talked about it but hadn't gotten to that point. And, yes, that house was hers. I gave it to her. It returned to me upon her death. However, it was intended as your birthday gift, which is tomorrow. Once I set up the paperwork, so your new husband can't get his hands on it, it will be yours."

"Really?" She gasped. "Thank you," she said warmly. "I really love that place. Why the guard though?"

"Because it was empty and needed looking after." He narrowed his gaze at her. "You never understood that, but assets require care too."

"I do understand." She glanced over at Trevor to see him paying attention but not showing any reaction. She didn't know if he believed her father or not. She did. Yet she had no real reason to do so. But it was hard to fake that kind of loss, and unfortunately she could see him marrying her mother for the reason he stated. He was an indomitable force, and, if he thought he could get his old life back—albeit slightly different—then he'd do whatever he could to make that happen.

She sighed. It was hard to find acceptance and forgiveness for all he'd done, but she knew it would be much easier now.

As if having shoved the heavy memories back into place and ready to move on once again, her father stood. "I'm late for a meeting. We'll talk again tomorrow."

She raised her eyebrows. "What's tomorrow?"

"The meeting with the financial advisors," he stated smoothly, shooting Trevor a shark's grin. "You didn't think you'd be there alone, did you?" He smiled at Hannah. "Besides, it's my only child's twenty-fifth birthday. Surely you won't begrudge me some of your day."

And, once again back in control, he strode off toward the exit.

INTERESTING TURN OF events. Trevor pondered the implications of her father meeting the financial advisors at the same time. As an attorney, Trevor saw an ethical issue involved. He'd requested and had been assured of a private meeting. So much for their assurances. "It just might be time to find yourself a new financial advisor."

"Really? Do you know one?" she mocked. "Not too many people know how to manage big money well. Not that I have big money."

"Of those few, you need to find an honest one but …" He frowned. "I do know someone. He was involved in big business but now handles money for a few select clients. He's very gifted. He handles Stefan's investments too."

"Another friend of Stefan's."

"Absolutely. And another energy worker, although his passion is his wife so …" At her blank expression, he laughed. "Not to worry. I'll set up a meeting later in the week."

"If I don't like him?" she stated, with a certain tartness he was coming to really enjoy.

"Don't use him. Find someone else." He smirked. "But I can guarantee you that he's honest and that his energy work makes it so much easier for him to do well in the slippery industry."

"Then it's hard *not* to choose him."

"But no reason to change, if you are happy with the men we meet tomorrow."

The waitress appeared with two heaping plates of food. "Here is your meal." She placed the food down in front of them.

"Oh, thank you."

And with a quick nod, the waitress left.

Hannah laughed at Trevor. "I didn't even have to order."

"I ordered for both of us, while you were talking with your father." He looked up from his meal. "How are you feeling about that conversation?" She dug into her meal and didn't answer. He waited for her to get through a little of the food to take the edge off her appetite, then asked, "Well?"

"I think I believe him," she replied slowly, still chewing one mouthful of food. She swallowed. "What about you?"

He nodded. "Good. I do too."

"If we both believe him, who do we think is responsible for all that's going on?"

They both answered together.

"Will."

CHAPTER 34

THEY DROVE BACK to the house later that afternoon. All Hannah could think about was having a nap. Surely there was time for that now. "Maybe it was the heavy lunch or the zillion stops we had to make on the way home, but I'm tired," she said, yawning.

"Go lie down." Trevor unloaded the bags from the car. "I'll take care of this."

She yawned again, grabbed the small bag of stuff she'd picked up while shopping and exited the car. "If you don't mind?"

"I don't mind. Go."

At his word, she stumbled upstairs and collapsed on the bed. She didn't know when the fatigue had started to pull on her, but it was bad right now. Hell, it had been bad two stops ago, and trying to make it through the last of the errands had been painful. She'd tried to nap in the car, but that hadn't worked so well. She kicked off her shoes and stretched out. And fell into a heavy sleep.

And found herself being chased by men with wild looks on their faces. And behind them, screaming, was a creepy old woman in long skirts with a headscarf. She was brandishing a stick of some kind. Rationally Hannah knew she was dreaming, but it didn't matter. She was in an all-out panic, and her feet were moving as fast as she could possibly make them. Her heart raced, and her chest squeezed so tightly that she couldn't breathe. A door opened up ahead. She raced inside and turned to slam the door shut. The men behind her continued to roar outside the door.

And the old woman was wailing.

She turned around and looked at the room she was in.

And screamed.

"Hannah!" Trevor's voice slowly penetrated through the panic in her mind. "Wake up."

She stared at him in a panic, recognized him, and slowly, shudders racking her slight frame, calmed down. "What the hell was that?"

"I was going to ask you the same thing." He sat down on the bed beside her. "I was bringing your bag up from the car, when I heard you."

She felt the intensity of his gaze. She rubbed her temples. "In my dreams, I was being chased by wild dogs and an old woman who chased them. Then someone opened a door that offered freedom. I ran inside, closed the door, and turned around—then screamed. But I don't even know what I was screaming at." She shuddered. "I do remember the old woman wailing outside, and, damn it, she looked like the creepy woman from the grayscale world."

He stroked her hair back. "It doesn't matter. A lot has been going on in your life lately. So much so that nightmares are almost a given.'

She lay still, shaking. "I was so damn scared. Fell asleep, then *boom*. That nightmare—it came out of nowhere."

"And instead of thinking about the scary parts of your life, think of all the things in your world this last week that have come out of nowhere and were good things. The new information you've learned, the skills you know about. Also remember that dreams or nightmares can be bits and pieces of other people's worlds that you picked up as you traipsed through their backyards in grayscale."

She nodded, but her lips trembled; she was afraid she was going to cry. "I know that, but …"

She opened her arms, feeling very much like a child who needed the comfort of a hug. She shifted to her side, so he could lie down beside her.

He gathered her up in his arms and held her close. "It's okay. You're safe."

"I am now." She yawned. "But, if all this energy stuff is true, can your nightmares be real?"

"It was that bad?"

"Yes," she whispered. "It was that bad."

"Was Will in that room?"

She shook her head. "I don't think so." She frowned, as she ran her fingers across his chest. "But there was an edge of familiarity to it. As if I should have known who it was. And that, at one point, I did know. But no longer." She tilted her head back. "More blocks?"

"It's possible. You have at least two big ones to deal with."

His hand slowly moved up and down her spine, soothing her tension, while massaging her back muscles to be smoother and more pliant. She sighed. "You're so good at this.'

"At what?" he asked, a look of bemusement in his gaze.

"Making me feel better," she stated, with a grin. "You'll make a great father."

He laughed. "I wonder."

"I don't have to wonder," she replied, laying her head on his chest. "I know."

The warm rumble under her made her feel all squishy inside. He was such a damn good man. She'd lucked out. He was strong, powerful, capable, and caring. Then there was the fact that he was sexy as all hell. Something she hadn't really let herself dwell on up until now. She'd wanted him like she didn't remember ever wanting a man, but, at the same time, she understood all the practical barriers to a sexual relationship. And put credence in none of them.

"We did go to the drugstore."

She heard the breath catch in the back of his throat. She smiled and leaned her head back, so she could see his face. "Good. That'll cover us for now. I got something too."

He slanted a gaze down at her. "And what did you buy?"

She grinned. "Got my birth control prescription refilled."

He swallowed audibly. She smirked at the look on his face. Propping herself up on one arm she asked, "Scared?"

A laugh rumbled free. "Of you? Never ..." And he lowered his head and kissed her. But it was a light testing kind of kiss. Giving her a chance to back out if she wanted to.

That was not the direction she planned to go. In fact, given that it was close to four in the afternoon, she figured a whole evening in bed was what the doctor ordered. She'd been surprised at how easy getting the prescription refilled had been. The pharmacist had made a couple phone calls, and she was good to go. She threw her arms around his neck and kissed him back–hard. She'd take this from zero-to-sixty seconds the first time, then would repeat in slow-mo, loving the old-fashioned way for the second time.

"Easy, we have all evening."

"And night," she whispered against his lips. "If you had planned to work, you'd better think again." She slid her hand down his chest and straight to his belt buckle.

"We're supposed to take this slow," he protested half-heartedly.

"Next time," she promised. "We'll take it slow next time."

Skipping the belt buckle her fingers slid down over the hard bulge below. "Definitely next time," she whispered, as she stroked the long, lean length of him.

"Shit," he murmured. "You are something else." Then he rolled over and crushed her under him.

SO MUCH FOR his plans to take the relationship slow. To not make love to her until she was ready. Hell, *ready* wasn't quite the word he'd use right now. How about *hot? Passionate?* Then there was *sexy as hell.* Gently he cupped those breasts that had been driving him mad all day, felt the soft weight of them. There'd been something about that T-shirt she'd worn and the way the supersnug material curved them so tenderly. It might have had to do with the fact that the size was probably slightly too small. He'd appreciated the view all day. That she was warm and always reaching out to touch him and to cuddle up close had kept the fire stoked. That he'd kept it to that level was a bloody miracle. She'd set the tone last night, and his ardor from her riding comment hadn't cooled yet.

He'd been hoping for something like this but hadn't thought it would happen for several days. Or weeks.

Instead she was kissing him like there was no tomorrow. Her kisses were hungry, her touch greedy.

And he loved every minute of it. But if he didn't dial this back, it would be over in minutes. Her hand was under his shirt and working at the belt buckle. Something he rarely wore. He rolled over slightly and undid the belt and the top button on his jeans. Instantly her fingers dove inside.

He groaned. "Slow down," he whispered.

"Nope. Next time." She pushed him onto his back and straddled him.

He tried to grasp her hands as they undid the buttons on his shirt and splayed the sides open wide. Then she stopped, transfixed. With a smile that made his groin tighten, she lowered her head and dropped kisses on his ribs and down to his belly. His erection swelled in response, and she laughed.

He grinned. "At least you're having fun."

"Oh, I am." She shifted her weight so she was squarely across his hips.

In perfect position. Except for one thing. She was fully dressed. He lifted his hips slightly. "You're wearing too many clothes."

"So are you." She reached down and undid the zipper on his jeans. He sucked in his breath and gasped, "I'll take them off."

She scampered off and proceeded to do the damnedest striptease he'd ever seen.

He sat up and took off his shirt. Then hopped off the bed to drop his jeans. He was stepping out of them when she stepped in front and said, "Let me."

She dropped to her knees, and he began to quake. "If you start that, it will be over before you know it," he warned.

"And that's okay too," she whispered, her hand tugging his boxers to his knees and freeing his erection. She grasped him in her hand and licked him, like he was her favorite ice cream cone. His knees buckled, and he dropped to the bed. He couldn't think, as that eager tongue sent him to the edge of madness and kept him there. He dove his hands into her hair. "Come up, please, sweetheart. Come to the bed. Let me put on a condom."

In response, she took him in her mouth and sucked him hard.

And he lost control, his hips pumped once, then twice.

His body exploded, shuddering in the wake that was Hannah. He lay on the bed staring up at the ceiling and wondered how they'd gone so far off course to the plan he'd had in his head. Soft romantic music and a wonderful dinner, followed by a slow seduction. Not this wild hungry woman who went after what she wanted and—got it.

As he lay here in the aftermath, his boxers tangled around his ankles, she leaned over and kissed the inside of his bent knees. Then his thighs. And damn if his penis didn't start waving at her again.

Groaning, he said, "I'm going to need a moment."

"No, you don't." She slid her tongue up the side of his groin, and spent several minutes lapping at his hip bones.

Fully erect now—and how the hell was that possible so soon? Kicking off his boxers, he reached for her and said, "Hell no, now it's my turn.'

She wiggled in his grasp, but he was determined and gently dragged her to lie beside him. He slid his fingers down through the curls at the apex to her thighs and the wet heat waiting for him. He dropped his forehead to her chest and let his fingers stroke and explore the softness at the heart of her. She shivered in his arms.

He pushed her legs wider apart and slid one finger inside. Christ, she was small. He worked the second finger in. And without warning she cried out and shuddered in his arms.

Shifting upward, he kissed her hard and replaced his fingers with himself. And slowly pressed deep inside. She whimpered once but didn't stop him. When he was finally seated at the heart of her, he rested on his elbows and stroked her hair off her temple. "You okay?"

"Better than okay," she whispered. "I've been wanting this since I met you. But it's been so fast, the days so full, the timing never right."

He kissed her deeply, wondering at his need to hear her say the words that had yet to be brought up between them. How could they? They barely knew each other. But what they knew? … Hell, he was half in love with her already.

She reached up and pulled him down to her again and gave him the sweetest, yet hottest, kiss he'd ever had. "I'm sorry you weren't Sticks."

"So am I." He kissed her eyelids and nose and then her chin. "But maybe it's for the best."

"How's that?" She twisted sinuously beneath him. Now that the urgency had eased off, they could both relax and enjoy. He'd never made love this way before, but there were huge benefits. Like not rolling over and saying good night immediately afterward. This slow second buildup enticed him, teased him. He loved knowing what was coming.

"Because you broke up with him. And likely we'd have broken up then too. We were kids and desperate to find our place in the world."

"And looking everywhere but where we should have been looking," she murmured against his lips, her tongue gently stroking and caressing.

"And given all the hell we were living in back then, we wouldn't have been a good fit."

"Except in one way." She wiggled beneath him. He

threw his head back and clenched his jaw, as he worked to control the need suddenly surging through him. "Witch," he muttered, when he could.

She laughed. "I was just making a point." She wiggled again.

He shuddered and held still. She slid her hands down his back and dug her nails into his hips. And he plunged deep. And again and again, like a dam that broke, he couldn't stop. In a race to the end, he dove, shifted her leg to hook it over his arm and slammed home one more time.

And exploded.

Dimly in the background, as if coming from far away, he heard her cry out, as she hit the cliff and toppled over. His arms shaking, he collapsed beside her and closed his eyes. "Jesus," he gasped, when he could. "I've died and gone to heaven."

She snuggled close. "I can't think of a better way to go."

He tugged her closer. "How did I get so lucky?"

She smirked. "You let Sticks keep me back then. I swear to you. If I hadn't seen him with his girlfriend, him angry as hell and her bawling her eyes out, I might have stuck around long enough to be with you."

"Sticks's girl cry? Her name was Stones by the way. Hell, no way was she crying. She was one hard bitch."

"I don't know why, but she was definitely upset," Hannah murmured, her voice deepening and losing the battle with sleep.

Trevor held Hannah close and let her drift off. She needed it. Hopefully she wouldn't have another nightmare.

CHAPTER 35

THE BUILDING WAS dark. Damn. Why? It wasn't supposed to be, was it? Then again she didn't remember this area, so who knew? Larger buildings loomed to the left, and some kind of parking lot was on the right. But it was empty. The whole area was empty.

She wandered the empty lot, wondering why she was here. She hadn't come alone. Had she?

No, she was meeting someone here.

Too bad she couldn't remember who or why.

And damn it, where were they? She'd been running a little late. She'd apologize, but they had to show up for her to do that. She wrapped her arms around her chest, feeling a chill. It was summer. Cool for this time of year, so she'd deliberately worn a sweater.

She stopped and turned in a slow motion spin. No one. She wandered back down to the side of the building. And lifted her nose to the air. What did she smell?

It wasn't food. But there was an odd odor. She frowned and looked around nervously. She wanted to call out but was afraid to attract someone she didn't want to see. She racked her brain, trying to figure out who it was she had come to see. And why?

Everything was foggy.

But they'd better come soon, or she was going home. She shouldn't be here in the first place. It's not as if her father would miss her. He was at a meeting. Who had meetings in the evening? Likely he was after another young woman. And that was just disgusting.

Still, he was rich, and the women loved him. Too bad they didn't get to really know him. He was all icy indifference inside. And she'd had enough of that. She was all about making sure she didn't end up the same way.

More nervous now, she walked around the small building to the far side. "Hello?" After a moment, in a slightly louder voice, she called out, "Anyone here?"

Still silence.

Until she heard the splash of something liquid. Like a large glass of water being filled right beside her. Only she was alone, and no water was around her.

Hearing footsteps behind her, she spun, her heart slamming in her chest, and peered into the darkness. "Hello?"

Out of nowhere, something slammed into her head, and she collapsed to the ground.

And woke up, crying out.

Hannah lay in the darkness, her limbs shaking so damn much that she couldn't believe Trevor slept beside her, unaware. She snuggled up closer and realized his sleep was deep, maybe too deep. She couldn't help herself from checking that he was still breathing. He was, thank God. She relaxed back against the pillows. Inside though, the weirdness of her nightmare disturbed her. She didn't remember having nightmares like this before. In fact, she rarely had anything *but* a good night's rest.

And she would have, wouldn't she? Except ... those damn blocks. Shit, were these nightmares something she'd had long ago, and once again someone "blocked" them out for her? The nightmares were disturbing to her as an adult, so she couldn't imagine the pain and terror she would have experienced as a child. Once again she realized how much might have been done to help her out. Regardless of their good intentions, it had left her with less than half her memories. And no coping skills to deal with the nightmares now. If she'd adapted to them as a child, then she'd have adjusted easier today, but instead it all piled up on her now.

Lying in the darkness, she had to wonder. Was she capable of handling this nightmare?

Trevor made an odd sound beside her. She reached out, stroked his shoulder. He was such a special man and dare she say it? He was hers. She leaned over and kissed his warm shoulder. She draped her arm over his chest and smiled at the joy of being in his arms.

His body jerked.

She shifted back to study his face. And realized he wasn't sleeping normally. Given all she'd learned lately, she had to question if he was "off" somewhere. She had no evidence of that, but his face was too slack for him to just be asleep. His breathing was too deep. She wondered if he was just having heavy dreams, or did he do energy work at night? Or was he in grayscale? Just the thought gave her the shivers. Listen to her. A week ago she would have been placed under observation for speaking like this.

This was all so new to her. She closed her eyes and pondered that. It wasn't new. Not really. Because of her mother, Hannah had been dealing with this type of work for a long time. She just hadn't known it to be anything different than what everyone else did on a daily basis. The graywalker business was really bizarre though.

She threw back the covers and walked to the bathroom. As she passed the window she caught a glimpse of a strange light. Slipping to the side of the glass, she stared out. And realized something else. She couldn't see her reflection.

She raced to the mirror and studied the face looking back. Silvery gray tones hid her flesh-colored skin, and her eyes—already a deep purple—had turned more violet. "Well," she whispered, "what the hell happened to you?"

Yet she knew that she was in her grayscale world. So that's how people saw her—if they saw her in this world. She had thought she was in the normal physical dimension. And that Trevor was the one walking in other realities.

But, if this was hers, why did Trevor look normal? Her mind instinctively supplied the answer—because that's how she knew he looked.

Oh, Lord.

She walked back out of the bathroom, swallowing hard. She was in her own grayscale for once. The people looked normal, so that was one indicator she could learn to judge by. She clasped her hands together and felt the pressure. So that was a secondary indicator that this was her world. She walked back to the window, and the weird light flashed outside again. Only it looked odder still. And yet familiar. She closed her eyes and tried to control the panic welling up inside. Should she take a look?

She opened her eyes again, only to realize she'd teleported to the spot outside by just thinking about it. She wanted to laugh, but the only sound she heard was hysterical laughter.

Then there was nothing to laugh about when she saw the odd light clearly now.

It was fire.

Burning.

All around her.

TREVOR HEARD HANNAH cry out. Heard her jerk in the bed beside him. He shifted realities to return to his sleeping body, only to realize he was too late. Whatever she'd felt or seen had passed. She lay curled up in his arms, sleeping peacefully, while he'd been wandering through grayscale. Checking up on some patients. Visiting with others. It was a nightly ritual he went through to touch base with those in his world.

He yawned gently. The early morning light hit the room and gave just enough visibility to see shadows, yet enough light to also see through them. Gently he rolled onto his back, his arm coming down to tuck Hannah up against him. And found her skin cold.

Not just chilled but cold.

Holy crap. He rubbed her back and pulled the covers higher to her neck. He rolled her over gently and studied her face. *She* was off traveling. Of course. Like most people, she likely did that every night. Only, instead of being deeply relaxed, waves of tension rolled off her. She could be in her grayscale. Chances were good that was her main traveling system, but she could be many other places too. During sleep, people astral-traveled anywhere. Including, for some, back and forth in time.

He had no idea what *she* could do.

And neither did she.

Should he just wait and try to wake her up?

They'd gone to sleep early, so, of course, they were awake early. But this early? Frowning, he got up and walked over to the window, his mind consumed with the changes in his world. Didn't it figure that everything had crunched together right now? Hannah's return to his life. His marriage. Mr. Stingard's case being reopened. Too much was going on now for this not to have the hand of fate involved. And, when fate went to work, all kinds of shit happened.

He knew. He'd been on the receiving end many times. Maybe this time he'd be on the right end. He worried where Hannah was now. Could he find her? Follow her? He called out to her.

And found himself in grayscale in the middle of a scenario he'd dreamed up too many times—fire.

As an arrogant teen he'd had nightmares of burning alive in a fire for years. Mr. Stingard's death had brought them on. Trevor had hoped to never see that particular nightmare again. In grayscale the immediacy and the panic of the situation was diluted. Thank heavens.

He centered himself, then turned to see where he was and why he was here.

And found Hannah, staring at the flames.

He walked closer, worried about startling her. Did she know where she was? Why she was here?

At her side he studied the location. He was at his old high school. The building on fire was the chemistry trailer that killed his teacher. Jesus. He saw several people milling about, trying to help, but no help was to be had.

The building was past the point of saving, and he knew that the body hidden inside wouldn't be found until the morning.

He slowly turned to study the people around him.

There were a few firefighters, but they were focused on saving the other buildings. A few neighbors had come over to see what was going on. And, ... in the back, ... by the trees, stood two people.

He tried to shift over there, so he could see better, but

the images stayed frozen, locked in time and just out of reach. He squinted, searching for something identifiable. And came up blank, but something was furtive about them. And something familiar.

One turned, and he caught sight of her profile. *Stones.*

Jesus. That meant the other person was most likely Sticks. But Trevor had to be sure.

And yet he had no way to do that.

CHAPTER 36

W HY WAS SHE here?

Hannah didn't know this place. At least she didn't think she knew this place. But it did look … familiar. Was this Sticks's old school? Was that possible? She cast her mind back and found she could pull forward a few of the related memories. Something about his school. Had they gone there one evening? Yes, they'd sat on the front steps, as he'd told her a little about the future he envisioned for himself. She didn't remember the details. But she had assumed that he hadn't been attending school at the time. She wanted to believe in him, but it was a little hard when he'd had such grandiose plans for a kid like him. At the same time, many a man carried on to be someone important.

It had been nice to sit out in the schoolyard—a place so different from her own. Hers had huge hallways, a big old stone building that had seen generations of the rich and famous walk its hallowed halls. She didn't fit in there either. But Sticks's school had been undergoing renovations, and many classes were being housed temporarily in trailers. Old and decrepit-looking trailers, and the comparison to trailer trash had been hard to miss.

Still, they'd shared a few beers, ones she had paid for, but he'd bought. Some buddy of his could score the booze for him. A connection she didn't have, but she had plenty of money. She'd been a little obnoxious about that—she could see that now—but, at the time, it hadn't seemed like she'd been that way. Only kids who'd experienced hard knocks could pull off the act. She'd been playing at it.

She'd been a fool, trying to get back at her father. Lord, he must have hated that. She'd been a hellish child to raise. She was either acting out or in a mental hospital, where doctors were trying to fix what was wrong. And what was wrong was that she'd been fighting him, and he'd been trying to protect her. But her fighting had been about his tight rule over her, and it made her look more irrational. They'd been in a cycle that no one could win. Then, of course, somewhere along the way, these oh-so-lovely blocks had been placed in her head, and Will had started to stalk her.

Lord, no wonder she appeared to be a mess. She had been. But no longer. Clarity was winning—finally.

Now she was a graywalker, traipsing through someone else's memories. How unbelievable was that? Imagine if her father knew? None of his well-meaning medical staff had a clue what being a graywalker was all about. Given that, people like her couldn't get help.

That's why Trevor's assistance was huge. He held a unique position to help people like her. Without him, she'd have been lost forever behind closed doors.

What a horrible future. Add in the drugs given to her healthy body, and there would be no end to the muck going on in her system.

How many people like her were out in the world? Messed up and thinking they were getting help, when in reality they needed to ditch the help and to become one with their souls.

She smiled at that.

"Hey, Stefan," she called out randomly. "Do you like that phrase?"

I do.

The instant answer sent goose bumps down her spine. She gasped. "Is that really you?"

It is. Trevor is standing beside you as well.

She spun around. "I can't see him."

He can see you. He's opened a window into that particular gray world, so he can look in where you are. If you shift your view slightly, you'll see him.

"Shift my view?"

Just mentally say you want to see him.

She did, and, just like that, Trevor was beside her.

With a shout of joy, she threw her arms around him. And grasped *nothing.*

He laughed. *So, this isn't your or my grayscale.*

"Oh, Lord. I thought it was." She squeezed her hands together, but, sure enough, she felt no pressure. "So I switched into someone else's grayscale and didn't know?" She spun around in shock. "When? How?"

With your skills, Trevor noted, *it could be as easy as a blink for you to switch from one to another.*

She shook her head. "The school is behind you. The trailer is burning. That's the one you told me about," she said quietly. "Only it's happening all over again this year, not eight years ago."

No, Hannah. You are in the grayscale world of someone who has access to his memories in a way most of us can't see. He's traveling through them in grayscale.

She froze. "So I'm back in time?"

I don't think it's time travel as much as he's reliving his memories—ones he loves so much so that he spends a lot of time here rejoicing, and that's where you found him.

"What am I supposed to say to that?" she whispered. "That's so bizarre."

Stefan spoke up. *Although this may look like real time, you can't actually walk about the buildings and see the back of them. You can only walk where he walked, as that is part of his memories. Any place that he didn't go, you can't access.*

She blinked. "So the person whose grayscale I'm in is ..."

The man who set the fire, Trevor replied in a low tone. *And very likely the man who killed my teacher.*

She gasped. "I'm in the grayscale of a murderer?"

Yes. And now the question we need answered is, do you know whose grayscale world you are in?

TREVOR WATCHED HANNAH shake her head. *Damn. Too bad. That would help us tremendously.*

"I have no idea. Why would I come here? And at this time frame? I never knew anything about the school fire. I wasn't even with Sticks when it happened. That was after we broke up. There's no way he did it *because* we broke up. He didn't care about me in the least."

We're not saying it's him at all.

She seemed to calm down slightly at that reassurance. "But, if I'm here, you're saying that I'm connected. If I'm connected, that means it has to be through one of your old group, Trevor."

And that leaves us five options.

"Seven, you said."

Right, but the other two had left a long time ago.

She nodded. "Does that mean they are ruled out then? Or are they even more possible suspects, as they might have left for a reason."

I don't remember the details. They were both heavy drug users, so who knows if they are even still alive. His tone of voice changed. *But it's time to come home, sweetheart. Stefan needs his beauty sleep.*

Why would you let me get it now? Stefan teased. *Hannah, before you leave, take a close look around and try to retain this image. Not just with your eyes but also with your ears, your nose.*

"That's it!" she cried out. "I stood here before the fire started. That's when I heard liquid pouring, but I couldn't see where or what, until I recognized the gasoline smell. Someone was pouring gasoline around the trailer."

Do you know who? Trevor asked.

She shook her head. "No idea."

Was it male or female? Can you tell that much?

She closed her eyes, trying to draw that memory back to her. And caught a whiff of perfume. "It was female," she whispered. "At least a woman had been there."

If that was Stones, Sticks wouldn't have been far behind.

We don't know it was either of them, Stefan cautioned.

"Didn't you say another teacher had been fired because of having an affair with a student? Stones had been a hard type and likely had the affair to bring down her teacher, maybe even blackmailing him."

Yes, that was the same girl. Trevor's voice slowed. *She'd broken it off with Sticks, before you came on the scene. Then Stones had the affair with the married teacher. It was short-lived. So she wanted to get back together with Sticks. Or he managed to get her back on his side.*

I suspect the fire was lit to hide their tracks, Stefan stated. *My gut instinct says that's key. We need to locate them both now.*

"How do we do that?" Hannah asked. "It happened almost a decade ago."

Lots of ways. Fingerprints are one, Trevor said. *We were all printed back then. The cops had found a couple gas cans thrown away with prints on them, we heard, but nothing more was mentioned about it. We all assumed they never matched a suspect. But we were kids, and no one was sharing information with us.*

Stefan added, *Considering their prints haven't shown up since, they've managed to keep under the police radar, so we won't have much luck there. And, if that doesn't work, we'll have to try to track that energy backward and find them that way.*

DID HE SEE what he thought he saw?

No, … hell no. She couldn't be here.

Not in his dreams.

Wait. … If she was here, was he dreaming her presence? Not that he had any idea why he'd do such a thing. He wouldn't. No way he would.

This was bullshit. Then he realized she wasn't in his dreams; she'd walked into his memories. Memories he held precious. Memories where he'd snuck in and around, watching the others. … Always watching what everyone did.

And icy fingers walked up his spine.

Jesus. That couldn't be.

She couldn't do that.

There was no way.

And, if she could do that, could others?

No way in hell he wanted anyone walking through his mind—past, present, or future. He'd done some shit that no one could know about. And he planned to do a whole lot more.

CHAPTER 37

TRYING TO FOLLOW Stefan's instructions, Hannah studied the fire burning around her, looking for someone she'd recognize. Looking for a face to take back with her. She might walk in this person's grayscale world again, but that didn't mean she could walk in this particular memory twice, so she had to make this visit count.

Was he a pyromaniac? A person who thrived on fires? Fascinated to see the world burn? If so, then why kill the science teacher? Or had his death been an accident? Maybe no one knew he was in the trailer, marking papers. From what Trevor had said, the teacher had lived alone, and it wasn't unreasonable for him to stay late at school, with his assignments to mark and with his bottle to keep him company.

"Here, hold this," some guy said.

Something was thrust into her hand. Instinctively she reached out to grab it. And found a gas can in her hand.

She searched around for the person who'd given it to her, but she'd only seen the black gloves.

Oh, my God. Was she in her grayscale for real now, or was she still in the other person's grayscale, whose memories she had wandered in from eight years ago? Or was he showing her a picture of something special?

She squeezed the gas can.

And felt the pressure. Oh, shit. Oh, shit.

This was so damn confusing. She stared down at the hand holding the gas can. It was small. Feminine. It wore a ring on the one hand. She looked at the other hand and found a matching ring on that hand too. How could that be? She stared at the fingers. The rings. She felt her throat squeezing shut. Dear God. She knew these hands. They were hers.

She was holding the gas can. In her own grayscale world, she had switched into her own memories.

Had she been here the night of the fire? Been involved? She searched the cavern of her mind. A block had started to crumble. As if its time had come. She was afraid of what she'd find. Please let her not have had a hand in setting this fire.

Please not. Surely not.

She'd never do anything like that.

That didn't mean Sticks wouldn't have tried to involve her. He'd been the one she'd met here that night. He'd called her out of the blue and had said she'd left something behind, and he wanted to see her one more time. She'd come to the school against her best judgment and had hoped to go home quickly. He hadn't shown up.

Until he'd asked her to hold that can.

Now the memories flooded her psyche.

That dark handsome face as he turned, gave her a sardonic grin, and threw a lit match. She cried out, "Now what are you doing?"

A loud *whoosh* whistled through the air, as the gas caught fire, and the trailer had gone up in flames. She screamed and threw up her arm to protect herself. And found the gas can in her hand.

"Oh, my God, you set me up." She threw the gas can at him.

He laughed. "What's the matter, rich bitch? Can't take the heat?"

She cried and backed away. "You wanted to meet me. You told me that I'd left something behind," she screamed at him, panic clawing at her throat.

"You did. You have now left your prints behind."

A bright flash came from the trees, and he howled with laughter, as she turned and ran. As far away as she could go. She ran, stumbled, and ran some more.

Hannah bounced from one wall to another, as she tried to work her way safely back out from her memories. She hit an already damaged wall, the top half had already crumbled and fallen down. The force of her contact was hard enough that she heard a *crack*, as the rest gave away.

She spun around to see it slowly crumble before her.

It hadn't been a wall. It had been one of her blocks. One of the last ones. And she realized that the half-fallen-down one she'd passed before had released this memory. Allowing her to see what had happened, … her part in it. Or rather what had been made to appear as her part in this nightmare. She shook like a leaf, as voices rolled over her and through her and around her.

With the block in place, she'd never known she'd been at the school that night.

"HANNAH? ARE YOU okay?"

Trevor stared down at her in concern, until she finally opened her eyes to stare up at him, features drawn, her gaze shadowed.

"Oh, thank God," he muttered and swung her up into a tight embrace.

She rested in his arms, her body exhausted, her mind strung out on betrayal and pain. "It was Sticks who lit the fire," she whispered. "I don't know if he knew the teacher was inside or not, but he had me hold the gas can, so my prints would be on it."

Trevor froze. *But this isn't in the file. Oh, … dear old dad would have made sure of that. … Or, knowing Sticks and Stones, they've been blackmailing Mr. Goodman for eight years.*

She shuddered. "Dear God. I never knew."

He sagged in place. "I gather the block came down."

"Yeah, it was well on its way to crumbling down, a barely held together wall as it was by the time I got there. It literally gave up the ghost when I accidentally slammed into it. I couldn't, … can't believe what I saw, what I heard …"

"And you were in Sticks's grayscale?" he asked cautiously. "Do you know that for sure?"

She shook her head. "No, I don't. I don't understand yet whose space I was in."

"Did you grasp the can?"

"I did." She shuddered. "And I felt pressure, so I think it was my grayscale …"

"But did you feel the pressure or did you just *see* it in your hand and assume that you were grasping it?"

"I don't know," she whispered. "When I realized that I'd been there, that he'd set me up …"

Trevor nodded. *Sticks had always wanted a wealthy mark to blackmail. Him and his get-rich-quick scenes. Found it in Hannah. Used to call her "Rich bitch …"* Trevor repeated out loud.

"Yeah, that's what he said." Tears welled up in her eyes.

"Now that I know I was there, what he did, it's like finding out I was a whole different person back then. And that he was so much worse," she cried out. "Why did he do that?"

He wouldn't mention his theory yet. Trevor crushed her against his chest. "I'm so sorry. Sticks was like that. He always said he didn't want anything to do with rich white people. That's one of the reasons we were so surprised when he showed up with you. You weren't his type."

"Did he set me up right from the start? Plan this from the beginning?" She stared up at him. "Did he pick me as the gullible one?"

He winced. "Honestly I can't say." Not yet. But he could guess, and, yeah, that would be Sticks all the way. "I'm sorry. He was hurting like the rest of us hurt."

She shook her head violently. "No. He wasn't. He loved that fire. Thrived on it. I wouldn't be surprised, when you do find him, that he's done this many times since." She reached up to grab his shirt. "Trevor, you have to understand. He was *fascinated* by that fire."

"Then we'll take a closer look at other arson cases too," Trevor reassured her.

"But why the teacher?"

Trevor sat back and considered the issue. "I might know why, but I don't want to say anything for sure."

She waited, her gaze quiet.

"Stones had that affair with the married teacher. She lost the baby soon afterward." He leaned his head back, wondering at the dysfunctional people he'd met in that lifetime so long ago. "I think she may have gone after Mr. Stingard as well. Maybe he rebuffed her. Or maybe he suggested they get together, and she rebuffed him. Either way something went wrong. Sticks would have done anything that Stones asked."

Trevor shook his head. "With your confirmation, I have no doubt that Sticks set the fire. But, *if* he unknowingly killed Stingard with the fire, that's not the same thing as premeditated murder."

"No, but we need to get to the bottom of it." She snuggled up against his chest.

As if he heard her mind spinning, he asked, "Now what are you worried about?"

"Do you think he's the one who planted the blocks there?"

"I don't know," Trevor replied slowly. "I never felt any of that kind of energy power coming off him. Was it possible? Sure. But why would he?"

"Maybe to stop me from remembering who was involved in setting the fire."

"That's about the only thing that does make sense," he admitted. "But there has to be so much more."

"Does there? I've always found things to be—at the very core—simple."

He shifted his position and let the pieces float around in his head. "Simple is right. It's always about sex, money, and power."

"And one more," she whispered. "A huge one."

He opened his eyes to turn and look at her. "What's that?"

"Love."

HE'D HAD ENOUGH. When he thought he'd seen Boots's face in his memories, he'd known he'd crossed some kind of bullshit line. Was it his mental state, or had these two gotten together and pulled off some stupid magic that he didn't know about?

That possibility pissed him off.

No one beat him. He might not be the best, but he was the meanest and the most underhanded in the game. What really got him was he didn't know what game Boots was playing. Boots didn't play games like this. At least not with opponents who fought back. Like himself. He wasn't just about the game. He was about playing. Moving the world to do his bidding. Not about getting beaten. Or even challenged. There was a huge difference between a challenge to surmount and being challenged. One was fun. The other was something to be avoided at all costs.

He loved his life.

He had no plans to change it. No fucking way would he let that little rich bitch do it for him.

She was done. Tonight.

He'd make sure of it. That she was married to the weak do-gooder wasn't something she should be proud of. Losers, both of them.

He didn't know what the fuck was going on, but he was putting a stop to it now. Like right now.

Who the hell did she think she was?

Walk into his memories, would they? Not twice.

Only he could do that kind of walking.

CHAPTER 38

L OVE WAS EVERYTHING. Now that they had an idea of
what had happened back then, they just needed to figure
out what was going on today. The past had jumped into the
present. If they didn't solve this—stop this—there wouldn't
be a future. "We need to find out if my prints are on record.
If anyone did anything to hide my involvement."

"You weren't *involved*," he stressed. "You were set up."

"I know that. What if my fingerprints from Stefan's
house match up to that crime?" She couldn't bear to have to
deal with this all over again down the road. "The comparison
is bound to come up."

"Even then you'd be questioned but not charged. Besides ..." He grinned. "The fingerprints at Stefan's are
energy prints."

"So bizarre." Unbelievably so. It showed how much she
still needed to learn. "I hate to think so, but I feel like my
father might have stepped in and stopped the police from
looking at me back then."

"The only way your father would have done that is if the
cops already knew you were there," he noted slowly.

"And why wouldn't Sticks tell them, if he'd gotten away
with leaving no evidence of his own?"

"He might have chosen to have done so in another way.
And waited to see if the cops ferreted out the truth. When it

was deemed an accident …" Trevor stopped and frowned. "Wait."

"Yeah, I'm on the same train of thought. How could this be an accident, if I saw him pour gasoline and light it with a match?" She snorted. "The cops would have figured that out fast enough." She slumped back. "My father made this all go away. He's the only one powerful enough in this group of us to have done that. And this mess just added to his belief that I was unstable and had to be watched all the time."

"Why?" Trevor stared at her. "Your prints were never corroborated."

She closed her eyes and groaned, as her intuition flashed to the surface. "I know. Oh, dear God, I know."

He waited.

She opened her eyes. "I saw a flash in my mind. I didn't get it at the time. I didn't even think about it, but what if someone—Stones or someone else—took pictures of me standing there, holding the can in front of the fire. And used it to blackmail my father?"

"Sticks's ticket to a better life. And Stones's too." Trevor threw his head back and groaned in dismay. "And back then, I always thought he figured he was moving up *into* a rich girl's family, but instead he was looking to score *off* the *rich bitch*. Jesus."

TREVOR WAS SORRY for using that insult again. But it was how Sticks had referred to Hannah—no, Candy—when he was with the gang. Trevor hadn't thought anything of it. They'd all talked up around the gang. It was what they did. Big egos on braggarts.

The information rumbled through his head. "I wonder if

your father is planning on dropping any of these bombshells on us at the meeting tomorrow."

"I wouldn't be surprised," she whispered. "God, I feel like such a fool. I thought I'd pulled one over on my father, and instead I'd been a gullible and naive fool, once again in trouble, that he had to fix."

"*Shh*, take it easy," he whispered against her hair. "Nothing is easy when growing up, and neither of us are proud of who we were back then, but it's what we do with our lives now that matters. We have to do the best we can going forward."

He believed that and worked every day to make it happen.

And he thought she did too.

Her body trembled in his arms, reminding him how much she'd had to adjust to in the last few days.

And how well she'd done.

"Do you think you can go back to sleep again?" he asked, hugging her close, his hands easing up and down her spine. He wasn't tired, but they had a big day tomorrow, and they both needed to be rested up.

She shook her head violently. "No, I don't think so."

"That nightmare really unnerved you, didn't it?"

"Yes. More than that, it's Sticks's betrayal. He wanted me to take the fall. To ruin my life."

"Yeah, that was Sticks."

"Then why were you part of that group?" she cried out. "He was a horrible person."

Trevor was lost for words. How to explain back then that he'd have done anything to fit in? To not be a loser? To have someone like him? His self-esteem had been nonexistent. He'd been suicidal at one point.

"Sorry," she whispered, her hand stroking his chest. "I'm just in shock. It was a horrible awareness, seeing Sticks's true character."

"Likely why you had the block."

Her head burrowed deeper against his chest, but he heard her speaking low.

"Yes, but did he do it?" She frowned. "Or did I?" she asked slowly. "To avoid facing my—his—actions?"

"Sorry, sweetheart. A lot is hitting you at once."

She didn't answer. Then what could she say?

He groaned and tucked her up close. All he could do now was ease her stress and hold her close.

He let his eyes drift closed and relaxed. Surely this would come to a head soon. The meeting tomorrow could bring more out in the open.

As he lay here, he heard something that chilled him to his soul.

The crackle of flames.

Outside. *Jesus.*

"Move!" Trevor bolted from bed and shook her awake. "Now." When she rolled over to look at him, he pulled her up from the bed. "The house is on fire."

She bolted upright, comprehension lighting the depths of her eyes. Smoke billowed into the room. She coughed and scrambled to her feet.

Stefan, Trevor screamed. *We need the fire department here now. And the cops. Someone has lit the house on fire.*

There wasn't any discussion. Stefan appeared and disappeared from his mind, as Trevor jumped into his clothes and dragged Hannah behind him. He raced from the bedroom, Hannah's arm in a tight grip, as he pulled her with him. They raced down the stairs and bolted out the kitchen door.

In the distance the welcome sounds of sirens were already on their way. Trevor loved this telepathic highway. It was beyond fast.

The neighbors called out to him, "Anyone still inside?"

"No, we're the only ones," he called out, as the fire engines raced toward them. The trucks arrived at the house at the same time as the neighbors reached them.

Immediately they were all pushed back out of the danger zone, as the firemen went to work. From where he stood, Trevor saw the smoke coming from the garage area.

Not the front. Thank God. He'd hate for Kali to lose the house because she'd helped him and Hannah. But he couldn't see any flames from here.

Although the amount of smoke made up for it.

The police arrived. They were immediately pushed farther out of the way.

Trevor knew it was a good thing they'd gotten what sleep they could.

There'd be no more shut-eye for them tonight.

Still they were safe. That was the only thing that mattered—and now putting a stop to this shit.

Enough was enough.

CHAPTER 39

HANNAH STOOD UNDER the hot water in the master bathroom in Trevor's house and let it roll down on her face and head. Tired and worn out after the questioning, and with all the smoke in Kali's house, they couldn't remain there. Still, she had a hard day ahead. She had to face her father. After a shitty early morning surprise, that's the last thing she wanted.

And on her birthday. Crap.

She needed this to be over with. She had a life she was looking forward to living. Now that most of her blocks were gone, her mind still reeled at what floated freely in her brain.

It would take time to heal her mind. Even more time was required to make her comfortable with the memories. They were familiar in that they were hers, but, at the same time, they were foreign, as if someone else had lived them. Just as she found a level of comfort with some of it, more flared up. And she was assailed by the pain and the fear all over again.

She didn't want this. She needed to get through it so that the memories slid into the recesses of her mind by her choice, not by someone else's hand.

"Hannah?"

She turned off the water. "I'm here."

"Are you okay?"

Silly question. She understood why he was asking, but it seemed foolish. Of course she wasn't okay. She'd been to hell and back, and still it wasn't over. Now someone was trying to kill her.

Enough! There had to be a way to end this. Bolstered by the thought, and loving the future that waited on the other side of this nightmare and the other side of the shower, she opened the door to give him a game smile. "I'm okay."

He cuddled her close for a long moment and dropped a kiss on her nose. "We'll get through this. Then life starts for us for real."

Now *that* was something she could get behind. He left her to go downstairs.

After her shower, she dressed quickly and headed to the kitchen to find Trevor deep in conversation with a big blond stranger. Imposing and capable looking, when he looked up at her, she found his smile friendly, gentle even. She immediately grinned back. "Hi."

"Hannah, this is Detective McNeil, Dr. Maddy's partner. The man who's been helping me."

"Call me Drew. Nice to meet you." Drew held out a hand to shake.

She shook it and stepped closer to Trevor's side. "I guess the police have to be involved now, don't they?" She leaned against Trevor, not sure if she was that tired or just wanting the security of knowing he was here.

"Arson does that," Drew noted, with a grim smile. "We don't like people wandering around, trying to burn down houses—especially not with people in them."

"Any chance you're coming to the meeting today?" she asked. "Likely a murder will be committed there."

Drew's eyebrows shot up toward his hairline.

Trevor laughed, but it was dark. "Not likely to be *that* bad," he replied. "We're meeting Hannah's financial advisors, and apparently her father has butted into the meeting without our permission."

"Did you ask for a private meeting?" Drew asked curiously. "I'd have thought that meeting would be as confidential as one could get."

"You'd have thought so, but then there is my father," Hannah replied, "and the rules he forces the rest of the world to live by."

"I haven't received confirmation from the company that they are aware of Mr. Goodman's impending presence during the meeting," Trevor noted. "I was clear that such a thing would not be looked upon favorably."

"Might be time to talk to Roman," Drew suggested.

Trevor nodded. "I've mentioned him to Hannah, but she's got a lot on her plate right now. We'll see how the meeting goes."

"I sense a *but* in there." Drew frowned. "Are you seriously expecting trouble?"

"We are today. I don't know about at this meeting. But it's crunch time," Trevor admitted. "Someone tried to burn us alive last night. I suspect a second attempt will be made today."

A strangled sound erupted from Hannah's lips. "That sounds horrible." She stared out the window. "But you're right. It feels like it'll come to a head today."

"What is?" Drew frowned at Trevor. "You need to fill me in a little more."

"It's woo-woo stuff," Trevor noted, with a small grin. "Are you sure you want to know?"

Drew gave a curt nod. "I live with Maddy. What do you

think?"

Trevor laughed. "True enough." He motioned to the kitchen table. "Take a seat. You'll need to be sitting for this one."

In as concise a way as possible, Trevor walked Drew through the events from the fire that killed his old teacher to finding Hannah outside Stefan's door to last night's fire.

Listening, Hannah couldn't believe how twisted and convoluted her life had become. In her heart she knew that one person was at the root of the problem, likely Sticks. But he hadn't acted alone. Had Stones helped? But who was Stones today? Hell, who was Sticks today?

How did they know Hannah? Why go after her now? She hadn't done anything to warrant these attacks, had she?

"COULD WILL BE Sticks?" Drew asked, his glance going from one to the other.

Trevor heard the question. "I actually considered that, but the coloring is different. The way he speaks is different. His facial features—different again."

Drew nodded. "All of which can be changed."

"I don't think so in this case, as Will's also older," Hannah added slowly. "Besides, Will was working for my father back then, … I think." She shook her head. "No, maybe not. But it was around the same time that …" And she stopped.

"What?" Trevor asked. "If it's a memory, let it come into your psyche fully, then consider the information. It's too unstable to believe otherwise."

"No," she whispered. "Will was pissed when George came on board."

"Why would he be pissed?" Drew studied her. "Will

wasn't the only guard then, was he?"

"Something about not deserving the position," Hannah murmured.

"What about George? I've only seen him twice. And I wasn't paying close attention to him either time." Trevor frowned at her. "He couldn't be Sticks, could he?"

She twisted to look up at him. "I'd have recognized him back then, wouldn't I? That was within months, a year at the longest, since I had dated him, I think. It's hard to remember. I didn't think it was important back then. And he doesn't look similar at all. Sticks was close to three, maybe four, years older than me. He had failed a couple grades or been put back or something, I believe." She shook her head. "George looks even older than that."

"How old?" Trevor asked, then a horrible premonition slid into his mind. "Oh, Jesus."

"Trevor?" she asked. "What are you thinking?"

He shook his head. "It couldn't be."

"What?"

He took a deep breath, turned to Drew, and asked, "Have you had a chance to look into Sticks's whereabouts?"

"No. Why?" Drew narrowed his gaze at him.

"Could you check the morgue first?" he asked in a low voice. "Particularly any deaths in a fire?" He cast a sidelong glance at Hannah. "Especially the fire in Hannah's store."

They all stared at him.

"Trevor, what's going on?" Hannah asked, her voice rising.

He winced. "The other two members of our group left early. Remember? They called themselves Starsky and Hutch. One of them was Sticks's stepbrother. It's the reason he walked away. He couldn't get along with Sticks. They fought all the time. His real name was Victor."

Hannah whispered, "Who was his partner? You said two of them left. Both hung tight together."

Trevor stared down the long memory lane. "His first name was Hank, I think. It was a long time ago. I don't think he'd have anything to do with this fire." He shrugged. "But who the hell knows?"

Drew picked up the phone and started making a few calls.

Hannah just sat, lost in thought.

Trevor struggled to consider if either Sticks or his stepbrother, Victor, could have had anything to do with setting the fire at Kali's, when Hannah asked, "Trevor, did Stones ever have an affair with Sticks's stepbrother?"

Trevor's mind flooded instantly with that one night years ago that had forever separated Sticks from his stepbrother, Victor. The fight had been nasty. And violent. And ended up with Sticks getting his face smashed in.

"Oh, yeah." Trevor nodded. "It wasn't an affair. Stones was with Sticks's stepbrother, Victor, first. They were together for a long time. Then she switched to Sticks, only broke up with him and went back to his stepbrother. I don't know what's happened to the three of them, but they were very entangled back then—and looking to score big."

"Shit. Did she break up with Victor to come back to Sticks that night I saw her crying in his arms?"

"Maybe." He lifted his head and stared at her. "Now I have a question for you …"

"What?"

"Was George ever married?"

She let out her breath slowly. "He wasn't married, but he had a partner around for a long time, until she switched partners," she noted caustically. "I gather she liked variety."

CHAPTER 40

THEY STOOD OUTSIDE the ornate building, where the meeting with the financial advisors was due to take place. Hannah knew it would be impossible to prove any of their conjectures. Drew needed time to find proof of the identities of those involved. It would be even more impossible to catch these assholes in the act or to get a confession.

She had an idea but didn't know if it would work.

Stefan was here in spirit; she could feel him. She knew Dr. Maddy was on alert. Kind of like she felt at the moment.

"Ready?" Trevor asked her.

"Hell no," Hannah snapped, with spirit, "but we need to get through this."

Trevor held out his hand and led her to the front door. Drew accompanied them.

"We'll feel pretty stupid if we're wrong," she warned them.

"I'd rather feel stupid than dead," Trevor noted.

She winced. The offices were on the third floor. As she looked at the flashy lobby with loads of gilt and marble, she shuddered. "Please tell me that your friend Roman doesn't have an office like this."

"He doesn't. He has one in his house and one downtown but operates out of his house most of the time. That way he's closest to his studio."

"And his favorite subject to paint?" Drew teased, with a smile.

Trevor chuckled. At the look on Hannah's face, he added, "Roman's wife."

At the humor in his voice, she studied his face. "She must be beautiful."

"She is, and they make a great couple."

The elevator opened to a quiet wealth that made her feel slightly better. "At least this floor doesn't look like a pimp hall," she muttered.

Trevor gave a bark of laughter at that.

They walked through to a large office, where they were greeted by a receptionist, who led them into a private boardroom. After offering refreshments, which they all refused, the receptionist walked out, saying, "They'll be here in a few moments."

"They?" Hannah asked.

"It's not uncommon for partners to show up together for a big client. This way *they* cover their asses, should one make a mistake."

"Right." Knowing she had her own agenda and was hard-pressed to still her nervousness, Hannah walked around the room to work off some of her nervous energy.

Soon the second door opened, and two men walked in. Followed by her father, Wanda, and both henchmen.

Instantly Drew and Trevor stiffened.

Hannah's reaction was the opposite. She was delighted to find her father true to form. She laughed. "What's the matter, Father? Couldn't leave well enough alone?" She sat down with Trevor and grinned at Wanda. "Come to check on the family bank accounts, did you, Wanda?"

"Leave her out of it," her father growled.

Hannah laughed again, but inside she was trying to fit Wanda's face into Hannah's memory of the girl crying in Sticks's arms.

The door behind them opened, and another stranger walked in, with a cheerful greeting to all. "Sorry, I'm late." And proceeded to sit down beside Drew.

It was as if the two sets of parties had lined up on opposite sides of the negotiating table.

Hannah glanced over at Trevor and watched him hide a grin. Okay, so this was a good thing then. Right? She studied Drew's features, but he never lifted his eagle eyes from the henchmen.

Hannah turned to the stranger and, behind Trevor's back, whispered, "Thanks for coming."

The stranger turned his warm twinkling eyes her way and smiled. "You're welcome."

She knew this must be Roman Chandler, the investor suggested by Trevor and Drew. That he'd come to the battlefront on her behalf—likely because one of the two men on her side of the table had called him—meant she liked him already.

"Hannah, who are these people?" her father asked in harsh tones.

Trevor smiled. "Well, I'm her husband, as you know. This is Drew, a friend and a local police detective, who has been working to help us solve some big issues happening right now, and *our* financial advisor, Roman Chandler."

At Roman's name, the two advisors' faces pinched up tight.

Hannah snickered silently. They knew Roman and didn't like him. That was a good enough recommendation for her. "As Roman will be handling my financial affairs going forward, it seemed prudent that he be here to facilitate the process as easily and as quickly as possible," she explained in haughty tones she'd learned at her father's knees.

"But we haven't had a chance to speak to you," the first advisor protested. "Surely we deserve a private word with you, before you make such a major decision."

"That's too bad," she stated coolly. "We deserved and asked for the same respect of a private meeting and didn't get it either." She waved around the room at all the people gathered here.

She felt Trevor suck in his breath. But he stayed quiet. She looked at the first advisor, then the second. "You may proceed with the full description of my portfolio."

The men looked uncomfortably around the crowded room. "It's not normal to have so many people hear the financial details of your estate."

"You know what? You're right." She turned to face the two henchmen, who'd come in with her father. "Victor and Will, neither of you are entitled to hear this. You can both leave."

Her father grumbled impatiently. "As you well know, that's George, not Victor, and Will and they go wherever I go. Don't be tiresome."

She locked her gaze on Victor's face and studied the lethal predator in the back of the room. And crossed into grayscale. *His* grayscale world. Out loud she said, "Hello, Victor. Did you really think you were the only one who could play games like this?"

The room stilled in shock at her words. The financial specialists turned to each other and then slid a look toward her confused father. She ignored them. None of them were energy workers. But one should never turn their back on a predator. And Victor was the most lethal predator in the room.

You fucking bitch, he roared in her mind. *What are you doing in my world?*

Better things than you were doing in mine, she answered, her voice hard, her tone clipped. *Asshole. Did you kill that teacher in the school?* She snorted. *And what about Hank? Did you bury him deep somewhere, where he can't be found?*

There was a stunned silence—inside and outside of her mind. She sensed Trevor's and Stefan's shocked presence in her mind. She'd shocked them all, and maybe that was a good thing. She'd always been too meek. She'd blame that on the blocks and the drugs. That girl was gone now.

Victor was stuttering at the blow.

She went in for blood. *Oh, and let's not forget your stepbrother, Sticks's, passion for fire. Did you kill him because of it? Was that him you left behind in my store? Did you use him as your scapegoat to hide your crimes?* She snorted. *Typical that you'd hide behind your little stepbrother.*

She felt the parts of her mind stir, as if Victor was in there. Like hell she'd tolerate that. She reached around and kicked him out. He jolted back into his chair, the others staring at him in surprise. But their gazes quickly turned to her, as she snapped, "No, you will not go into my memory banks again. Not that you were the one who placed the blocks there, were you?"

"Hannah, stop this. You need help ..." her father tried to say.

She ignored him.

"You don't know anything, you stupid bitch," Victor bit off.

The financial advisor who sat at his side shifted back and

out of the way. He might not understand what was going on, but he knew he was too damn close to whatever it was.

I don't know everything, she admitted, *but I know what I need to know. You fed the blocks in my head to keep them strong all these years. You were just no good at building them in the first place. Stones did that for you, didn't she?*

She heard the shock all around her as Stefan and the others listened in. But the biggest shock waves emanated from Victor.

Good. The rich bitch finally understands what had happened and why. Too bad it took her this long. Too bad she was such a conniving greedy bitch and couldn't leave well enough alone.

Don't speak about her like that, Trevor roared.

In the rest of the room, Hannah knew this conversation must look odd. Half in her mind on the ethers and half out loud, so the rest of the people in the boardroom were only getting tidbits. Just enough to make her look looney.

"What the hell is going on?" her father roared. Then he pointed at his daughter. "She's lost her mind. Surely you don't need more proof than this."

Hannah ignored him and focused on the lethal killer in the room.

Stones never did like to stick to one man, did she? She wasn't happy unless she was playing games. Games she'd played with anyone she fancied. Your stepbrother and my father for a couple of them. Will for another.

She snorted at Victor's look of outrage. After a quick glance at the uncomfortable faces on the far side of the table, she turned her attention back to Victor. *Will's been walking around like a peacock for years. Screwing Stones on the sly, thinking he was pulling one over on both you and my father.*

Will always acted the most dangerous, loved to terrorize people, but you were the dangerous one, Victor. You're the one who walked into people's minds and caused all kinds of havoc. Made them think, believe, and do stuff they didn't want to do. Then, with Stones's help, blocked it out of their memories.

So what if I did? If we did? Victor sneered at Hannah.

But the look in his eyes? Chilling.

You can't prove anything.

She studied him closely for a moment, seeing the tension in his energy, the frustration and anger at her words. *Did Sticks know Mr. Stingard was in the chemistry trailer when he lit the fire?* She thought the answer was yes.

Of course he did. How do you think he ended up in trouble at that age already? He burned his mother alive in their house when he was only eight. But no one blamed him. I knew what he was though. I watched him give you the can, after he lit up the trailer.

And his mother, did she deserve to die like that?

Damn right she did. He glared at her. *That's why I never said anything. That bitch was psycho. She'd burn all of us with her fucking cigarettes. One time she held Sticks's hand on a hot burner as punishment for stealing one of her smokes.*

Hannah felt her stomach churning inside. It made sense though. Some people were born bad, and others turned that way, depending on how they were treated. *Right, so why the chemistry teacher?*

He tried to get Stones into bed. He was drunk one night and propositioned her. After all, he knew about her affair with the other teacher.

But did he really, or was that more of Stones's games? She probably screwed the teacher, then knocked him out with his own bottle, and came to you and your stepbrother with her lies.

There was an odd silence as Victor contemplated her words. He shrugged. *You know what? She just might have. She's that kind of bitch,* he said affectionately.

Well, nice to know that you understand her, Hannah noted in a quiet voice. *And my mother? Do you know what happened to her?*

Well, I didn't touch her, he snapped. *We weren't around back then. For the longest time I figured your father did the job. Then I wondered if she hadn't committed suicide.* He shrugged. *Whatever. Whoever started putting blocks inside your head did us a favor. Once the first one was there, we had no trouble adding more. Of course that was Stones's work. But then the blocks started to fail, and I've been shoving energy to shore them up, but it's no use. They're coming apart at the seams.* His face twisted with malicious humor. *Sounds like you are too.*

But I'm not. I'm healing—on my own. She smiled. *Once I knew the blocks were there, they became foreign bodies to roust out of my head. Once the first few fell, I had no trouble dropping the rest.*

He nodded. "So what now?" he asked out loud. He waved at the group of confused faces staring at them. "Do you really think they can prove any of this?"

"I'm sure, with some time and effort, they will prove you burned down my store and tried to kill us last night in that fire. As for the rest of what you've done ..."

There's no way to get proof, Hannah, Stefan told her in her head. *He has to confess in the physical world, or he will walk.*

Walking free isn't an option, she replied, studying Victor's grayscale world. *Stefan, why is his world so dark?*

No idea, Stefan muttered. *Something is really weird here.*

"Yeah, well, what about the man *you* killed," Victor

asked Hannah in a hard voice to their stunned audience. "That should open up a painful truth."

Her heart slammed against her chest. She froze. "And who did I supposedly kill?"

"What?" her father gasped.

"Sticks. My stepbrother," Victor said, with a smile. "You were covered in his blood, and you took off. I'm sure the cops will be able to match the DNA of the blood you were covered in to the charred body in your shop." His smile deepened, darkened. "Especially when they find out you were lovers long ago. Back when the school fire occurred. And, of course, your prints were all over that gas can. Evidence that didn't surface back then. Nice trick, by the way."

"I don't understand," her father roared. "Someone explain."

Hannah ignored her father. She had to keep her focus on the snake in front of her. "You killed your brother and burned him up in my store?" she asked in horror.

"No, Hannah, *you* killed him." And he laughed and laughed.

Everyone in the room turned to stare at her.

With that, the last of the crumbling heap of the broken wall in Hannah's mind fell. And she watched herself walk out of the store at the end of the business day, about to lock the door, only to find Sticks standing in front of her, a knife in one hand and a gas can in the other.

She hadn't recognized him. And there'd been no time. He'd attacked her. Had he even known it was her? With that memory she remembered the details around Tasha. She had gone back East, and Hannah had known about it. Tasha had wanted to move back home to be with her family. She'd left that same day. At closing time, right before locking up the store, Hannah had been attacked. And lost everything.

"He planned to burn down my store, and I caught him. He pulled a knife. We fought," she whispered, as the memories flooded her psyche. "I fell, and he tripped too. I thought he was dead, and so I got up to see if he was breathing. … He was unconscious, but still breathing. I searched his pockets and …" She fell silent, remembering just what she'd retrieved from him. Was this the time to show them? She'd kept it on her ever since. The only physical evidence she had had from that part of her life, before arriving at Stefan's door. "… found something."

Everyone stared at her.

She shook her head as the memories stopped. "I don't know what happened after that."

Victor added, "I'd been waiting out back, hidden. My stepbrother, who you know as Sticks, wanted you dead. That would leave more money for your father to hand to someone else. Like me. And my stepbrother figured I'd share with him. When he didn't return as fast as he should have, I picked the lock and slipped inside the back door and went to check on him. Sticks was inside, almost dead," he snarled. "By the time I ran outside the front door, you'd stolen my stepbrother's car and had taken off."

"Then you set the fire, with your own stepbrother inside? But not until later that night, right?" She shook her head and frowned. "Did you follow me?" She stared at him. "You did, didn't you? Only you never found me. Otherwise I wouldn't still be alive, would I?"

He stared at her. "You always did have the luck. I found Sticks's car and moved it. But I couldn't find you. I have no idea how I missed you. I checked that stretch of highway."

"No, it wasn't luck. I was being guided." Her memories were still messed up, but … she had to ask. To make sure. *Stefan? I thought you were leading me. But my memories are back now, and it was a woman's voice, showing me the way to your house.*

No, not me, although I knew you were coming. I heard you calling out. You weren't responding to me. As I told you earlier, you were in grayscale, and I backtracked to find your body.

Right. She swallowed several times. *So the voice guiding me toward you? She told me that she had tried to kill you first, but she wanted me to finish the job. I think she's this creepy old lady in grayscale. And she sent me to you.*

I have an open door policy, Stefan explained. *Any energy worker in need of help—like you, Hannah—is attracted to my energy and can find me if they need to.*

So I'd have found you, even without her?

Yes. Hannah, I think the old woman put a suggestive thought in your mind. I think you were guiding yourself to my house because you knew I could help you.

Stefan, no way. She told me where to walk, where to go, how to find your driveway in the dark rainy night.

Stefan laughed. *I think you are giving the old woman too much credit and not giving enough credence to your own skills.*

But, in effect, I brought her to your doorway. She didn't know where you lived, did she?

No, not until you arrived.

Christ, this keeps getting better and better.

It's not an issue. Along with my open door policy is a barrier that only allows loving energy inside. So, even though you led her to my door, she couldn't hurt me.

His warm hug of acknowledgment made her feel cared for and loved. *Do you want to see her? Maybe you'll recognize her and understand why she is after you.*

Hannah knew it was the creepy old woman she'd seen on the patio at Maddy's building, but in grayscale. Somehow Hannah knew now that that woman had a powerful hate on for Stefan. Hannah had a lot to learn about grayscale, and reading others' auras, but if Hannah had her memories now, she could begin to sort out who was who. And that old lady on the patio she'd met was not a nice lady. And she wanted Stefan dead—badly.

Hannah took a deep breath and hopped into the grayscale of the patio and the woman who'd told Hannah that the two of them were the same. *But we aren't.* Hannah called to Stefan, then showed him the woman's face.

Dear God, now I get it! I have to leave. Someone else is in danger, he whispered. And then he disappeared from her mind.

Good, maybe Hannah could help someone else for a change. But she had Victor in front of her to deal with right now, and a roomful of people who thought she'd lost it. She smiled. "It doesn't matter what you say, Victor. Nothing you say matters. Not anymore."

He glared at her. "You can do nothing to me. Now get the fuck out of my life."

TREVOR HAD LISTENED and had tried to take it all in, but a lot of information pertained to his life here too, and it was hard to hear. So much was becoming clearer now. All these people he'd known. For a time had cared about …

Then there was Stefan. Trevor had felt Stefan's start of surprise turn to shock, from Hannah's vision she had shared, before Stefan had raced away. But was he okay? *Stefan, are you okay?*

Yes, but I know what's the matter with Anita now, thanks to Hannah. It's Anita's grandmother possessing the child, trying to protect her granddaughter from men. She thinks I'm hurting Anita or at least is afraid, if I remove her possession, that'll leave little Anita vulnerable to be hurt. She was behind Anita stabbing me earlier that day.

Christ.

I don't know how the old woman knew about Hannah, for I hadn't met Hannah yet. However, with Hannah's skills in graywalking, maybe the two women had crossed paths, and the old woman saw Hannah's great talent. Regardless Grandma had hoped to finish the job on me by possessing Hannah too. Only it must have been a partial possession at best. Hannah spent her entire life being controlled by others—so, in her grayscale world, no one would control her. Besides, Hannah was already inside my safety zone at the house and couldn't have acted, even if she'd understood what she was being guided to do.

Anita? Trevor was confused for a moment. *So we were right about it being a possession issue. Only, in this case, it was the grandmother sitting in grayscale, pulling the little girl's strings?*

Yes, her Russian grandmother. The woman had a horrible life and hated men. All men. She'd been demented at the end. Never making any sense. She'd been on a rampage, trying to separate the women from their men in her family, before she had a heart attack and died in the middle of a huge argument. And Anita had been at the center of the argument.

Trevor nodded. *Hannah had a nightmare, where she was chased by dogs and then an old woman. She ran into a small room to escape the creepy old lady and woke up screaming. At the time, she didn't know who was in the room who scared her so.*

If you ask her now, with her blocks removed, she'll be able to confirm it was the creepy old woman. Yes, Anita's grandmother. She'd been trying to save Anita from me. She wasn't stable at the end and only wanted to keep her granddaughter safe. Stefan laughed. *I can save Anita now. Not sure if I can convince Grandma of my good intentions though.*

And Stefan disappeared.

Although Trevor turned his attention back to Hannah, his mind worried about Anita's grandmother. So many people figured that a person with mental health issues would be fine and healthy again after their body died, but it wasn't always that way. Many times, getting caught in between in the gray world made the situation worse.

Until recently poor Hannah never knew what was her knowledge or someone else's. Not knowing she was a graywalker and what that meant, and with all her blocks, it was amazing she'd survived mentally at all.

Not only survived but had thrived.

He studied the woman who'd come to matter to him so damn much in such a short time period. He hadn't expected her to charge in like she knew what she was doing today, but apparently she *did* know what she was doing.

So had Stefan, when he'd sensed Hannah in trouble nearby and had followed her energy to find her body collapsed near the road.

Switching directions, and looking carefully, Trevor saw the resemblance to the Victor he'd known years ago, but it had been a hard road for Victor, and, without Hannah's confirmation, Trevor would not have seen it.

Victor stared at Hannah, with a deep abiding hatred in his eyes.

She smiled cheekily at him, then turned to her father's

longtime girlfriend and said, "Hello, Stones. Have you killed anyone today?"

And the place went deadly quiet.

Mr. Goodman jumped into the silence. "See what I mean?" he cried out. "She's completely unbalanced. No way she can handle her own affairs."

Hannah laughed. "Actually, Father, you're the dupe. Stones has been sleeping with George, whose real name is Victor, who she's known and slept with since they were teens—even slept with his stepbrother, Sticks, whose body was in my burned-out shell of a store." She motioned to Drew. "He'll confirm it all for you. Stones has been screwing Will on the side for years too. She does like her variety." She turned her hard gaze on the woman who'd caused so much pain. "Don't you, Stones?"

"I don't know what you're talking about." Wanda gasped. "Darling, don't let her talk to me like that …"

"Hannah," her father warned. "Behave yourself."

Hannah turned to Will. "Did they promise me to you, or was that just my father?"

He glanced at her and curled his lip. "I don't want you at all. Ain't enough money in the world to make me take you on."

"Right. Keep saying that and you might believe it." She smirked. "Was Stones supposed to marry my father, kill him off, and share the money with you and the other men she was sleeping with? However, if my father never remarried, then Stones's bid for the money was out of luck. That meant I was the next best thing for you. To get to all that money. But either way, Stones had to keep you on the string too." Hannah leaned forward, staring down Will. "I know you've been screwing her. But you're not special. She sleeps with *everyone.*"

"She does not," Will snapped. "You can't say shit about her."

Hannah gloated. "I don't have to. I saw you two together," she lied easily. "Stones is nothing but a greedy whore. As long as my father was happy, I didn't care. But then I saw what you guys were doing and figured you might not know about the double-cross."

"What double-cross?" Will asked, coming halfway out of his chair. "You didn't see nothing."

"Ah, see? The first thing you latched on to was the double-cross, not about what I had seen. So you're really worried about the double-cross. Think about this. What if my father reconsidered the marriage issue." She smirked again. "Even if they live together, he lavishes her with money. He may die and leave *her* in the money, and *you* out in the cold. Particularly if he manages to wrest away control of my money from me."

She smiled. "Either way, they don't need *you*. You're the new kid on the block. She and Victor have been lovers for years. The term here is *Love*. She loves Victor, but, more than that, Victor loves *her*. Always has. And when she marries my father, Victor will kill Father soon afterward, so Victor and Stones can live happily ever after." She leaned forward. "See, Will? Yet Stones doesn't know about my father's decision to never marry again. So you might come out of this after all with some small bequeath in my father's will for your years of service."

Silence.

She sensed the shock of everyone caught in the middle. She'd pegged Will as the weak link. He was slimy and nasty, but he wasn't hard-core inner strong, like the other two. She pulled out the picture she'd had in her personal effects at the hospital. She held it up for Will to see. "This is Victor's stepbrother, Sticks. The one he just killed a few days ago."

She turned to Victor. "You finished him off at my store, after I ran. Decided it was a perfect opportunity to get rid of a problem. He was getting pretty unstable, wasn't he?"

She turned her gaze to the photo. "See who he's with? Both are nude. Both of them holding onto each other. Yeah, my father's girlfriend. The same one who's been screwing you in the background all these years, Will. See the date here? Only a few weeks before Sticks died. He had it on him when he came to my store. I found it in his pocket." She shrugged. "I didn't even recognize the people until last night."

Hannah leaned back and gave Will a big fat smile. "You've been threatening me all my life, your evil presence always there, haunting me, terrifying me. But you're just a bully, a street thug. You weren't the one I should have been scared of. It was the other two you worked with. Victor here is the one who made me feel threatened all the time. I just didn't know it. And Stones, aka Wanda, was the block builder." She turned her mocking gaze on her dad, who sat shell-shocked beside Stones. "And my poor weak father. He had no idea Wanda was sleeping with every man she could get horizontal with. Or vertical." She held up the image for her father to see clearly. "Sorry, Dad."

His face sagged.

She was sorry to do this in such a public and harsh way, but she had no option. She was fighting to show how sane she was, among all the craziness in this room.

"You stupid bitch," Will snapped at Wanda. "Why the hell would you sleep with Victor? He's scum."

"Because I love that dirty scum," Stones cried out. "He's twice the man you are. And a way better lover." She flicked her hand at Victor. "Are you coming, darling? I do think this show has had its final curtain."

Victor stood up to leave.

Will spluttered. "It's true? All of it? You have been sleeping with him?"

"And me," Mr. Goodman said faintly. "Why?"

"Victor is the love of my life. The rest of you are just for entertainment." She smiled at Victor. "I'm so happy this is over. This game has been tough to keep up all these years." She turned to Hannah. "Who knew you were smart enough to figure this out?"

And she jumped into Hannah's mind, slamming blocks around like they were toy Lego blocks. But Hannah hadn't gone through what she'd been through for nothing. She flicked Stones out of her mind with such force that Stones slammed against the wall in the boardroom in the physical world.

Stones did a slow slide to the floor.

Her father cried out and jumped back. The two financial advisors raced to the other side of the room.

"Let's get one thing straight," Hannah snapped. "My father might be foolish and *woman stupid*, but your days of playing head games with me or my father are over."

And she slammed her own hands into Stones's mind and reached in to pull up the horrible memories that must have started this woman down this nightmare path of destruction.

Instantly Stones curled up in a tiny ball and chanted in an eerie voice, "Hush, little baby, please don't cry. Daddy's got something to make you smile." She repeated it over and over again in a sick parody of her memories.

"What did you do to her?" Victor cried, racing over to her. He crouched down beside Stones.

Hannah replied in a calm voice, "I gave her a dose of her own medicine—in reverse." She glared at him. "I pulled a handful of memories forward to the front of her mind."

"You can't do that. She suffered terribly. Look at her," he roared. "You can't hurt her like this."

"Oh, I can fix it," Hannah stated, her gaze locked on his. Her heart was breaking, but she dared not give in at this point. They were almost there. She didn't want to hurt Stones more than she had to, but, damn it, Hannah needed to make sure she was free too. "But Detective Drew will be the one to tell you what's needed from you first—before I hide the memories again."

"A full confession, a full list of crimes. And everyone involved," Drew ordered in a hard voice. "And that's just a start."

"Anything," Victor cried out. "Just help her."

Instantly Hannah grabbed the memory and shoved it back deep behind the blocks that Stones had built for herself. Inside, Hannah felt sick. She'd had no idea such a thing could happen. And knowing what had happened to Stones as a kid? Well, that was just wrong.

Drew asked, "Is Wanda's father still alive."

Victor shook his head. "She killed him. A long time ago."

"Good," Hannah said. "It's hard to feel sorry for that bastard after what he did to her."

"And yet you did this to her." Victor stared at her in hatred.

Hannah nodded, her expression grim. "And I will do it again if you renege on your part of the deal. And that includes all of Will's crimes as well." She glared back at her tormentor. "Remember, Will. I know all the shit you pulled in my mind."

"He was never really involved, except it made it easier to track you because he was screwing Wanda and following her energy blocks. But he didn't understand what or why. He figured he was just *that* good," Victor said tiredly, his hand stroking Wanda's forehead, brushing the hair off the unconscious woman's face. "She liked to keep multiple strings in play and to tug on them a little—in case she needed them. She had to use men, or she didn't feel in control. Her men never bothered me because I understood."

Victor studied Will and added, "Except for the threats Will made in Goodman's name. The beatings. Accepting and keeping payouts. A job Will liked a little too well."

"What? Did I just hear all this correctly?" Hannah's father asked. He sat frozen in his seat. "How is this possible? I don't understand. I never authorized Will to threaten anyone."

"No, I'm sure you didn't," Drew agreed. "But, for the moment, I think it's safe to say that you have escaped an early demise."

The door behind them opened to admit several cops. Victor and Will were both taken into custody. An ambulance was called for Wanda.

Hannah sat off to the side, hating her part in all this, but, at the same time, knowing it would be traumatic for everything to come out.

Her father? Well, she wondered just what he'd do now. She didn't have long to wait.

He walked over to her and held out his arms. She stood rigidly in place, not sure how to react. He dropped his arms, and his shoulders sagged. "I never wanted to hurt you. I don't even understand what's just happened."

"All you need to know," she stated, "is that I'm not mentally incompetent. I'm fine, and we will survive this."

He studied her for a long moment, as if searching for something. "You were so distraught when we lost your mother. I didn't know what to do." He shrugged. "I got the best doctors in the world to help you, but ..."

She knew there'd be no way to explain about the blocks in her head or her psychic abilities. So she kept quiet. Later she'd remove the blocks in his head and let him find a way to deal with his past too. Maybe they could both be free to move on.

"I do have a question about Hannah's mother's death," Trevor asked quietly from behind her.

Her father looked bewildered. "It was an accident. She had a seizure while in the water and drowned."

Trevor nodded. "Did she die right away?"

"No." Her father shook his head. "She was in a coma for several weeks before she passed on." He raised both palms. "I have tons of money and still couldn't save my family. Either of them."

"So you turned away from me—your only remaining family—to make more money?" Hannah didn't get it.

"No," he argued. "I turned *to* the only thing I knew to do and focused on that. And I buried myself in work."

Maybe she could understand after all. And now she knew where the oldest, biggest block had come from. Her mother's last gift to her before she left the physical plane. Hannah would need time to come to terms with everything that had happened. When she was ready, she'd take that block apart too. Finally she could read her mother's diary and could look at the keepsakes. They were gifts to be treasured. She doubted anything helpful to the case was in there, but maybe it would help her to know her mother better.

If she could find her again in the grayscale worlds—now that Hannah realized her mother had been the young woman who'd panicked and had told her to run—Hannah would love to walk back into her mother's grayscale world and spend some time with her.

It would be fine now, and Hannah wanted to ensure she had a chance to let her mother know. To help her mother to heal and to cross over into the light, where she belonged.

Hannah's father motioned at the financial advisors, huddled in the corner. "I've instructed them to hand over the trust and your mother's inheritance to you. It will take a few weeks to settle the paperwork, but they are good people," he added. "They will look after you."

She shook her head. "They look after *you*, Father. I have someone—several someones now—who will look after me."

Her words seemed to hit him hard. She winced, seeing them from his perspective. "Trevor is a good man. I've been lucky enough to find some good friends too. But ..." She took a deep breath. "They will never replace my father."

A light of hope flowed into his gaze. He slowly opened his arms again.

This time she rushed into them.

CHAPTER 41

"WHY AM I so nervous?" Hannah cried out, smoothing down the stunning white silk wedding dress. "We've been married for months."

Celina laughed. "Because last time was for safety, but this time is for your heart."

Hannah turned to her and grinned. Dr. Maddy stood behind her. Both were dressed in lacy blue bridesmaid dresses and looked gorgeous. Hannah was so damn lucky. "Thank you both. You look wonderful," she said warmly.

"Not as beautiful as you."

A knock came on the door. Her father's voice rang out. "Hannah, are you ready?"

She laughed and opened the door. "I'm ready."

With her two bridesmaids walking ahead of her, she held on to her father's arm as she walked down the aisle to Trevor, who waited with Drew and Stefan at his side.

"Are you sure about this?" her father asked in low tones.

"I've never been so sure of anything." She reached up and kissed him on the cheek, then took the last step to her husband's side.

Trevor reached out for her, tucking her up close.

Together they reaffirmed their vows. When it was over, he bent to kiss her. She threw her arms around his neck.

"You were right," he shared in a caring whisper against

her ear. "The most powerful motivator of all is—"

And, at the same time, they both said, "Love."

This concludes Book 9 of Psychic Visions: Shattered.
Read the first Chapter of Into the Abyss: Psychic Visions,
Book 10

Into the Abyss: Psychic Visions (Book #10)

When she was a child, Tavi's family was taken from her by a serial killer that was never caught. As an adult, she puts on the appearance of normalcy while burying herself in law enforcement as a detective. All her private energy is spent trying to find answers to what happened to her family…and preparing herself for the day she intends to exact revenge from the culprit.

Jericho is just as much of a predator as Tavi is. He's caught the scent of old prey – a serial killer, one he's been a step behind all along. Discovering who the next victim is surprises him. Tavi is clearly a detective who gets her man – every time. The tug-of-war is on. She wants nothing to do with him; all he can think about is her. She doesn't want or need his protection; he can't leave her alone to save his life. Sparks fly between them the first time they meet, the last, and all the times in-between.

Two hunters converge, set to follow their prey into the

abyss if need be – right where he can take out two enemies for the price of one.

He's cleaning up. Turning a new leaf. And wants no one left alive who can stop him…

Find Book 10 here!
To find out more visit Dale Mayer's website.
https://geni.us/dmabyss

Psychic Visions: Into the Abyss
(Book #10)
Chapter 1

T AVIKA BANTRELL OPENED the door to the police station and stopped in the doorway. Her neck cramped at the laughter inside. It always did when she was forced to return here. She belonged on the streets, not at her desk.

She understood the streets. But the computers, databases, and reports sucked the life out of her. As she entered, she slowly rotated her neck. The tension was balled up under her atlas bone and would hang there, until she could pound it out. Such a thing wasn't on her agenda anytime soon.

It was determined to sit like an irritated gnome and to make her life miserable.

And she'd had enough of that today. Yet something stirred in her world. She didn't like it. It brought back memories she had worked so hard to keep hidden. Forced her to burn more energy and roughed up her senses.

"Hey, Tavika. Nice job on that drunk in the tank."

"Yeah, Stoner has a thing for you."

The sniggers started at her left and worked around the office. She did her best to ignore them. It was hard when she knew her shirt was ripped off at the lower right-hand side, showing her abs. Of course she wore a series of scratches and colorful bruises instead. Compliments of the six-foot-tall brute in the tank.

She'd gone out to walk the streets right afterward. Her way of working out the tension. She loved Portland. It was seriously beautiful, but it was just another big city in so many ways.

The homeless problem had hit an all-new high. The geese had returned for the winter and were shitting all over the place. And the heat, late for this time of year, made everyone crabby.

Including her.

"Nice job, Tavika." Mark smacked her lightly on her shoulder, as he walked past. "You know anyone else would have gone home and changed."

She snorted. "Like I'm anyone else."

"True enough." He motioned at her desk in the back of the crowded, noisy room. "Someone to see you."

She locked her gaze on her visitor's face. Her heart stilled, … then raced ahead. She tried for a deep calming breath. "I'm not expecting anyone."

His voice lowered, as he nodded once more to where her desk sat in the corner. "This guy doesn't look like he marches to anyone's orders but his own."

Damn. This was not what she needed.

Giving Mark a curt nod of thanks, she stopped at the coffee station and poured a cup of black sludge. Sour, burned tasting, and hot. It was perfect. Fortified, she headed to her desk, determined to get rid of the visitor as fast as possible. If he was a snitch? Good. He could dump all over her, then hit the skids. She was so done with people today.

His aftershave hit her as she approached. She wanted to wrinkle up her nose in disgust; in fact, she started to, but something about the scent had her closing her eyes in appreciation instead. Her damn feet slowed too. Mentally she jerked hard on her errant body and slammed down her coffee cup atop her desk. She fell into her chair and lifted her scarred boots to rest on the desk, as she eyed him over the top of her steepled fingers.

"You wanted to see me?" she asked, proud her voice was solid. She was solid. No flights of fancy in her world. She was a black-and-white, by-the-book cop.

But right now, ... at this moment, she wanted to jump this man's bones.

She clamped down on her jaw and stared at him suspiciously. She was pretty damn sure it was illegal for anyone to be this pretty.

He studied her, a secretive smile playing at the corner of his mouth. "I do." He lifted that gaze of his and locked it on hers. Shivers started to quake her insides.

Dear God, his eyes. ... They were silver. As in molten mercury. They shifted with the same glimmering light too.

She swallowed and struggled to remain in control. "What can I help you with?"

"It's more what I can help you with."

"Oh, and what's that?" Like she hadn't heard that before.

"I want to report a murder," he murmured, the wisp of humor obvious in his voice. "If it's not too much trouble."

Her boots hit the floor, and she straightened up. All business now.

"Who? Where? When?" She barked out the questions in rapid-fire fashion. This was her domain. Where she excelled. She hated to say it, but she loved a good old-fashioned murder.

"I can't say I have all the information you need," he replied, a note of apology in his voice. "But I can tell you the name of the victim."

"That's a start." She grabbed a pad of paper and pulled it toward her. "What's your name?"

"Jericho. Jericho Sands."

She frowned, but inside she sent a mental high five to Jericho's mother. It was a freakin' perfect name.

"Who has been murdered?"

"Her name is Tavika Bantrell. Detective Tavika Bantrell."

Her hand was already in the process of writing the name before she understood. She threw down her pen and leaned back in her chair, glaring at him. "That's hardly a joke," she snapped. "You're wasting precious police resources here."

"My apologies."

"No, you're not sorry," she snapped in an accusing voice. "That's my name, as you perfectly well know, if you came here asking for me." She threw her arms open wide and added, "As you can see, I'm fine."

Lord, she hated cases like this. Someone needed to escort this guy away from her desk and out of the station, where he could blend into the landscape. Silver eyes or not, she wasn't into looney tunes.

"I meant no disrespect," he said. "It's just that I know this killer, and he knows you. Worse, he's about to make you his next victim."

She slammed her hands down on her desk and glared at him. "And you know this how?"

The silver in his eyes shimmered at her. She swallowed, struggling to not get lost in the potency of that gaze.

"The same way you knew I was here before you entered

the building. The same way I knew when you arrived. The same way I know your body is aching to be mine—because I'm psychic."

Her body shivered. She locked down her hormones and stared at him, trying to hide her deep unease. This was *so* not good. Could he know? How? No one knew. She'd made sure of it. She had worked hard to keep that part of her life hidden, buried so far below the surface that no one would ever know. Particularly the one person hunting her. Who had always been hunting her.

Instinctively she jacked up her shield. Her head boomed. She took a shaky breath. *Don't panic.* She was safe. She'd stay safe.

Then he said it.

He lowered his voice and leaned closer, that mercury-colored gaze holding her captive. "So, my dear Tavi, are you?"

Her safely contained world buckled.

Ripples slid through her aura, shaking the pillars of her soul. This was *so* not good.

And no way in hell would she let him know. She gave a loud snort and sat back, crossing her arms over her chest, and sneered. "The circus came into town two days ago. I suggest you go apply for a job."

He smiled.

That deep intoxicating movement of his lips made her heart thump against her chest. At the same time, she wanted to rip his heart out and toss it across the floor.

"I understand you're afraid …"

She leaned forward and hissed, "I am *not* afraid." She waved her hand around the room. "Do you see this? This is a cop shop. This is where we actually work at catching criminals. This is not where we sit and pay five dollars for palm readings."

At that, he laughed. A full-on belly laugh, completely amused at her response. Damn. His silvery eyes glistened with all things unknown. She'd seen other eyes like that. They could see past the barriers, slide under others' defenses, and rip open your secrets.

Her mother had been like that. She'd never let Tavika have secrets. Or privacy. According to her it was too dangerous. Tavi had no protection against her maternal pushiness. Of course her mother had secrets of her own. Like her first marriage and the son she hated to talk about. Tavika could count on one hand the number of times her half brother was brought up in conversations and never in a good way.

Jericho stood up in a smooth and elegant movement that she hated.

If she even tried to act half as suave, she'd trip over her size-ten boots. Still, she rose too, not to let this irritating man lord over her, if only via sheer physical positioning.

"Only time will tell." With a quick flick of his wrist, he pulled something out of his pocket.

She tensed. She'd been on the streets too long. She'd expected a gun, not the business card he tossed on the desk. She reached down and picked it up and gave a hard laugh. "A private investigator." Deliberately she ramped up the scorn in her voice. "I should have known."

"That's okay. I love you too." With a wink and a sexy smile, he turned and strode from the room.

As the door closed behind him, silence descended. She plunked her ass back down on her chair and glared at those few hapless detectives who were still looking in her direction. "What's the matter? Don't you have any work to do?"

Lawrence, who sat at the desk closest to her, but still a half-dozen feet away, said, "Part of our job is to observe people. And that was one of the most interesting interactions I've seen in a long time." He gave her a toothy white smile that shone bright against his black skin. The color of dark ebony, Lawrence was a good guy. A solid cop.

With a wave of her hand, she dismissed her visitor. "He's definitely looney tunes material."

"Intriguing. I didn't know you went for the crazies." With a half whistle he sauntered off to the coffeepot.

Damn. Had her attraction been that noticeable? Inside, her system was still absorbing the shocks. How had that asshole found her? And what did he really want?

And how would she shake him off her tail?

JERICHO STOOD OUTSIDE the station, staring at the drizzling rain. "Well, that went well."

In fact, it had gone better than he'd expected. He'd done his research before walking in. He knew so much about her and yet understood so little.

He'd only confronted her now because time was short. The killer had moved up his agenda, and her name was rising up the list. She could be a hard-ass all she wanted. Jericho would still keep her safe. He knew full well she was psychic. But that was no guarantee of staying alive if the Ghost wanted her dead. Ghost was the code name for the killer. A prolific sadist who liked torture. As Tavika well knew.

But she was also a survivor. She'd been traumatized by her encounter with the Ghost when she was younger. From what Jericho could see from the energy waves around her system, she was stronger than ever.

And, if he were honest, not only did he want to keep her safe but he also wanted to utilize her abilities to catch this killer once and for all.

All he had to do was get her on his side. Easy, right?

Knowing his phone would ring, he pulled it out and held it to his ear before the chime went off. He smiled like he always did at the ring tone. It was a few stanzas of music from the movie *Halloween*. He walked in the shadows himself. Nothing like a good horror movie to make him laugh.

Reality offered more than movies ever could.

He lived it. He watched other people do the same, and, as far as he was concerned, it was his job to take down the assholes who created it.

"Stefan, I got nowhere. You were right. She won't admit to that side of her personality."

"And yet she's very talented and uses those abilities for her own purposes," Stefan argued, fatigue creeping through his voice.

Jericho understood. Stefan saw too much. Heard too much. Understood even more. The one thing they could always count on were the horrors people inflicted on each other. Like Jericho, Stefan had no choice but to help.

"She shut me down." Jericho laughed. "She wanted me gone and fast."

"She is no ordinary woman."

"She might be no ordinary psychic," Jericho corrected, "but she's a hell of a woman. And I don't think she has any clue."

"I wouldn't push that right now," Stefan warned.

"No worries," Jericho replied comfortably. "Plenty of time to rock her bones later." Stefan's sigh made Jericho laugh out loud. "Okay, I won't push it. At least not right now."

"She's likely to rock your bones and not in a good way. She is tough. Sharp. And has honed her psychic skills like no one else I've seen. She also has a shield …"

"That's killing her," Jericho butted in. "She ramped it up while I was sitting there. The minute I mentioned the word *psychic*, her system went into overdrive. And she got hit with a hell of a headache. I watched her cringe, as the energy slammed into her head."

"The more she denies it, the more she locks that down, the worse the pain will get." Stefan's voice faded slightly.

"You and I both know that's just the beginning of it. If Tavika doesn't take better care of herself, her energy systems will kill her."

He lounged against the outside wall of the police station, completely ignored by the world around him.

"Did you pick up anything more on the Ghost?" Jericho asked, as he turned to study the busy street. He loved that about the city. No one noticed anybody because they were so busy trying to mind their own business as they traveled from point A to point B.

"Not yet. He's in Portland, but I haven't narrowed down the location any better."

Jericho waited a minute to see if Stefan had anything more to add, then asked, "Anything new and ugly appearing now that he's in town?"

There was an odd pause.

"Stefan?" Jericho nudged him.

"Not sure yet. Drew is on it."

Drew was a cold case detective. And engaged to Dr. Maddy, a friend of theirs. Only there was no budgetary money for this case, unless they came up with solid proof the Ghost had resurfaced. Drew had been keeping track of Jericho's progress on the case for years. That the killer had appeared to sleep for the last five had been both a relief and a concern—if he resurfaced.

And he had. Jericho knew it. So did Stefan. Tavika too, regardless of what she'd let anyone else believe.

And no way the Ghost would disappear again. Drew was just as adamant to find him. Drew had eleven cold cases with the Ghost's name attached. Files that, even with Dr. Maddy's and Stefan's help, they hadn't gotten far on.

Jericho shook his head, wondering what it would be like to have Dr. Maddy in his life. But he was too ornery—and apparently contrary as well in his taste for women—because all he could think about now was having one very irritating detective under him. He didn't think she'd go down easy. Surrender was foreign to her. But, when they got there, he knew they'd burn down the house.

He couldn't wait.

HE STOOD AND stared out the front window of the police station. Coming here today hadn't been part of his plan, but life was like that. And sometimes there was a damn good reason for it. Like maybe right now.

His mind was consumed with what he'd just heard. Surely the gossip had been wrong. But the station buzzed with overheard tidbits of Tavika's visitor. Something about the psychic calling Tavika the same. Hell, everyone for miles had heard by now. And that was wrong. There was no way she was. And gossip like that was a career killer. She'd never do anything to jeopardize that.

But, … if she was psychic? That was bad news. He'd saved her once. No way he'd be able to do that again.

Love made one do stupid things, and he was no more immune than anyone else. Still, if she was one of those, he wasn't sure anything could save her this time—and why should he?

If she was one of those, she needed to die—just like the rest of her family.

Find Book 10 here!

To find out more visit Dale Mayer's website.

https://geni.us/dmabyss

Simon Says... Hide: Kate Morgan (Book #1)

Welcome to a new thriller series from *USA Today* Best-Selling Author Dale Mayer. Set in Vancouver, BC, the team of Detective Kate Morgan and Simon St. Laurant, an unwilling psychic, marries all the elements of Dale's work that you've come to love, plus so much more.

Detective Kate Morgan, newly promoted to the Vancouver PD Homicide Department, stands for the victims in her world. She was once a victim herself, just as her mother had been a victim, and then her brother—an unsolved missing child's case—was yet another victim. She can't stand those who take advantage of others, and the worst ones are those who prey on the hopes of desperate people to line their own pockets.

So, when she finds a connection between more than a half-dozen cold cases to a current case, where a child's life hangs in the balance, Kate would make a deal with the devil himself to find the culprit and to save the child.

Simon St. Laurant's grandmother had the Sight and had warned him that, once he used it, he could never walk away. Until now, her caution had made it easy to avoid that first step. But, when nightmares of his own past are triggered, Simon can't stand back and watch child after child be abused. Not without offering his help to those chasing the monsters.

Even if it means dealing with the cranky and critical Detective Kate Morgan …

Find Simon Says… Hide here!
To find out more visit Dale Mayer's website.
https://geni.us/DMSSHideUniversal

Author's Note

Thank you for reading Shattered: Psychic Visions, Book 9! If you enjoyed the book, please take a moment and leave a short review.

Dear reader,

I love to hear from readers, and you can contact me at my website: www.dalemayer.com or at my Facebook author page. To be informed of new releases and special offers, sign up for my newsletter or follow me on BookBub. And if you are interested in joining Dale Mayer's Reader Group, here is the Facebook sign up page.
http://geni.us/DaleMayerFBGroup

Cheers,
Dale Mayer

About the Author

Dale Mayer is a *USA Today* best-selling author, best known for her SEALs military romances, her Psychic Visions series, and her Lovely Lethal Garden cozy series. Her contemporary romances are raw and full of passion and emotion (Broken But … Mending, Hathaway House series). Her thrillers will keep you guessing (Kate Morgan, By Death series), and her romantic comedies will keep you giggling (*It's a Dog's Life*, a stand-alone novella; and the Broken Protocols series, starring Charming Marvin, the cat).

Dale honors the stories that come to her—and some of them are crazy, break all the rules and cross multiple genres!

To go with her fiction, she also writes nonfiction in many different fields, with books available on résumé writing, companion gardening, and the US mortgage system. All her books are available in print and ebook format.

Connect with Dale Mayer Online

Dale's Website – www.dalemayer.com
Twitter – @DaleMayer
Facebook Page – geni.us/DaleMayerFBFanPage
Facebook Group – geni.us/DaleMayerFBGroup
BookBub – geni.us/DaleMayerBookbub
Instagram – geni.us/DaleMayerInstagram
Goodreads – geni.us/DaleMayerGoodreads
Newsletter – geni.us/DaleNews

Also by Dale Mayer

Published Adult Books:

Shadow Recon

Magnus, Book 1

Bullard's Battle

Ryland's Reach, Book 1

Cain's Cross, Book 2

Eton's Escape, Book 3

Garret's Gambit, Book 4

Kano's Keep, Book 5

Fallon's Flaw, Book 6

Quinn's Quest, Book 7

Bullard's Beauty, Book 8

Bullard's Best, Book 9

Bullard's Battle, Books 1–2

Bullard's Battle, Books 3–4

Bullard's Battle, Books 5–6

Bullard's Battle, Books 7–8

Terkel's Team

Damon's Deal, Book 1

Wade's War, Book 2

Gage's Goal, Book 3

Calum's Contact, Book 4

Rick's Road, Book 5

Kate Morgan

Simon Says… Hide, Book 1

Simon Says… Jump, Book 2

Simon Says… Ride, Book 3

Simon Says… Scream, Book 4

Simon Says… Run, Book 5

Hathaway House

Aaron, Book 1

Brock, Book 2

Cole, Book 3

Denton, Book 4

Elliot, Book 5

Finn, Book 6

Gregory, Book 7

Heath, Book 8

Iain, Book 9

Jaden, Book 10

Keith, Book 11

Lance, Book 12

Melissa, Book 13

Nash, Book 14

Owen, Book 15

Percy, Book 16

Quinton, Book 17

Hathaway House, Books 1–3

Hathaway House, Books 4–6

Hathaway House, Books 7–9

The K9 Files

Ethan, Book 1

Pierce, Book 2

Zane, Book 3

Blaze, Book 4

Lucas, Book 5

Parker, Book 6

Carter, Book 7

Weston, Book 8

Greyson, Book 9

Rowan, Book 10

Caleb, Book 11

Kurt, Book 12

Tucker, Book 13

Harley, Book 14

Kyron, Book 15

Jenner, Book 16

The K9 Files, Books 1–2

The K9 Files, Books 3–4

The K9 Files, Books 5–6

The K9 Files, Books 7–8

The K9 Files, Books 9–10

The K9 Files, Books 11–12

Lovely Lethal Gardens

Arsenic in the Azaleas, Book 1

Bones in the Begonias, Book 2

Corpse in the Carnations, Book 3

Daggers in the Dahlias, Book 4

Evidence in the Echinacea, Book 5

Footprints in the Ferns, Book 6

Gun in the Gardenias, Book 7

Handcuffs in the Heather, Book 8

Ice Pick in the Ivy, Book 9

Jewels in the Juniper, Book 10

Killer in the Kiwis, Book 11

Lifeless in the Lilies, Book 12

Murder in the Marigolds, Book 13

Nabbed in the Nasturtiums, Book 14

Offed in the Orchids, Book 15

Poison in the Pansies, Book 16

Quarry in the Quince, Book 17

Revenge in the Roses, Book 18

Lovely Lethal Gardens, Books 1–2

Lovely Lethal Gardens, Books 3–4

Lovely Lethal Gardens, Books 5–6

Lovely Lethal Gardens, Books 7–8

Lovely Lethal Gardens, Books 9–10

Psychic Vision Series

Tuesday's Child

Hide 'n Go Seek

Maddy's Floor

Garden of Sorrow

Knock Knock…

Rare Find

Eyes to the Soul

Now You See Her

Shattered

Into the Abyss

Seeds of Malice

Eye of the Falcon

Itsy-Bitsy Spider

Unmasked

Deep Beneath

From the Ashes

Stroke of Death

Ice Maiden

Snap, Crackle…

What If…

Talking Bones

Psychic Visions Books 1–3

Psychic Visions Books 4–6

Psychic Visions Books 7–9

By Death Series

Touched by Death

Haunted by Death

Chilled by Death

By Death Books 1–3

Broken Protocols – Romantic Comedy Series

Cat's Meow

Cat's Pajamas

Cat's Cradle

Cat's Claus

Broken Protocols 1-4

Broken and... Mending

Skin

Scars

Scales (of Justice)

Broken but... Mending 1-3

Glory

Genesis

Tori

Celeste

Glory Trilogy

Biker Blues

Morgan: Biker Blues, Volume 1

Cash: Biker Blues, Volume 2

SEALs of Honor

Mason: SEALs of Honor, Book 1

Hawk: SEALs of Honor, Book 2

Dane: SEALs of Honor, Book 3

Swede: SEALs of Honor, Book 4

Shadow: SEALs of Honor, Book 5

Cooper: SEALs of Honor, Book 6

Markus: SEALs of Honor, Book 7

Evan: SEALs of Honor, Book 8

Mason's Wish: SEALs of Honor, Book 9

Chase: SEALs of Honor, Book 10

Brett: SEALs of Honor, Book 11

Devlin: SEALs of Honor, Book 12

Easton: SEALs of Honor, Book 13

Ryder: SEALs of Honor, Book 14

Macklin: SEALs of Honor, Book 15

Corey: SEALs of Honor, Book 16

Warrick: SEALs of Honor, Book 17

Tanner: SEALs of Honor, Book 18

Jackson: SEALs of Honor, Book 19

Kanen: SEALs of Honor, Book 20

Nelson: SEALs of Honor, Book 21

Taylor: SEALs of Honor, Book 22

Colton: SEALs of Honor, Book 23

Troy: SEALs of Honor, Book 24

Axel: SEALs of Honor, Book 25

Baylor: SEALs of Honor, Book 26

Hudson: SEALs of Honor, Book 27

Lachlan: SEALs of Honor, Book 28

Paxton: SEALs of Honor, Book 29

SEALs of Honor, Books 1–3

SEALs of Honor, Books 4–6

SEALs of Honor, Books 7–10

SEALs of Honor, Books 11–13

SEALs of Honor, Books 14–16

SEALs of Honor, Books 17–19

SEALs of Honor, Books 20–22

SEALs of Honor, Books 23–25

Heroes for Hire

Levi's Legend: Heroes for Hire, Book 1

Stone's Surrender: Heroes for Hire, Book 2

Merk's Mistake: Heroes for Hire, Book 3

Rhodes's Reward: Heroes for Hire, Book 4

Flynn's Firecracker: Heroes for Hire, Book 5

Logan's Light: Heroes for Hire, Book 6

Harrison's Heart: Heroes for Hire, Book 7

Saul's Sweetheart: Heroes for Hire, Book 8

Dakota's Delight: Heroes for Hire, Book 9

Tyson's Treasure: Heroes for Hire, Book 10

Jace's Jewel: Heroes for Hire, Book 11

Rory's Rose: Heroes for Hire, Book 12

Brandon's Bliss: Heroes for Hire, Book 13

Liam's Lily: Heroes for Hire, Book 14

North's Nikki: Heroes for Hire, Book 15

Anders's Angel: Heroes for Hire, Book 16

Reyes's Raina: Heroes for Hire, Book 17

Dezi's Diamond: Heroes for Hire, Book 18

Vince's Vixen: Heroes for Hire, Book 19

Ice's Icing: Heroes for Hire, Book 20

Johan's Joy: Heroes for Hire, Book 21

Galen's Gemma: Heroes for Hire, Book 22

Zack's Zest: Heroes for Hire, Book 23

Bonaparte's Belle: Heroes for Hire, Book 24

Noah's Nemesis: Heroes for Hire, Book 25

Tomas's Trials: Heroes for Hire, Book 26

Heroes for Hire, Books 1–3

Heroes for Hire, Books 4–6

Heroes for Hire, Books 7–9

Heroes for Hire, Books 10–12

Heroes for Hire, Books 13–15

Heroes for Hire, Books 16–18

Heroes for Hire, Books 19–21

Heroes for Hire, Books 22–24

SEALs of Steel

Badger: SEALs of Steel, Book 1

Erick: SEALs of Steel, Book 2

Cade: SEALs of Steel, Book 3

Talon: SEALs of Steel, Book 4

Laszlo: SEALs of Steel, Book 5

Geir: SEALs of Steel, Book 6

Jager: SEALs of Steel, Book 7

The Final Reveal: SEALs of Steel, Book 8

SEALs of Steel, Books 1–4

SEALs of Steel, Books 5–8

SEALs of Steel, Books 1–8

The Mavericks

Kerrick, Book 1

Griffin, Book 2

Jax, Book 3

Beau, Book 4

Asher, Book 5

Ryker, Book 6

Miles, Book 7

Nico, Book 8

Keane, Book 9

Lennox, Book 10

Gavin, Book 11

Shane, Book 12

Diesel, Book 13

Jerricho, Book 14

Killian, Book 15

Hatch, Book 16

Corbin, Book 17

The Mavericks, Books 1–2

The Mavericks, Books 3–4

The Mavericks, Books 5–6

The Mavericks, Books 7–8

The Mavericks, Books 9–10

The Mavericks, Books 11–12

Collections

Dare to Be You…

Dare to Love…

Dare to be Strong…

RomanceX3

Standalone Novellas

It's a Dog's Life

Riana's Revenge

Second Chances

Published Young Adult Books:

Family Blood Ties Series

Vampire in Denial

Vampire in Distress

Vampire in Design

Vampire in Deceit

Vampire in Defiance

Vampire in Conflict

Vampire in Chaos

Vampire in Crisis

Vampire in Control

Vampire in Charge

Family Blood Ties Set 1–3

Family Blood Ties Set 1–5

Family Blood Ties Set 4–6

Family Blood Ties Set 7–9

Sian's Solution, A Family Blood Ties Series Prequel
    Novelette

Design series

Dangerous Designs

Deadly Designs

Darkest Designs

Design Series Trilogy

Standalone

In Cassie's Corner

Gem Stone (a Gemma Stone Mystery)

Published Non-Fiction Books:

Career Essentials

Career Essentials: The Résumé

Career Essentials: The Cover Letter

Career Essentials: The Interview

Career Essentials: 3 in 1

www.ingramcontent.com/pod-product-compliance
Lightning Source LLC
Chambersburg PA
CBHW072000190726
48293CB00001B/100